UNCOMMON

JUSTICE

JUS

TERRY

TERRY DEVANE

TERRY

TERRY DEVANE

UNCOMMON

JUSTICE

G. P. PUTNAM'S SONS

NEW YORK

G. P. Putnam's Sons
Publishers Since 1838
a member of
Penguin Putnam Inc.
375 Hudson Street
New York, NY 10014

Library of Congress Cataloging-in-Publication Data
Devane, Terry.
    Uncommon justice / Terry Devane.
        p   cm.
    ISBN 0-399-14717-9
        1. Women lawyers—Fiction.   2. Trials (Murder)—Fiction.
3. Homeless persons—Fiction.   4. Boston (Mass.)—Fiction.   I. Title.

    PS3554.E923 U53   2001   00-062675
    813'.6—dc21

Printed in the United States of America

10   9   8   7   6   5   4   3   2   1

This book is printed on acid-free paper. ♾

Book design by Victoria Kuskowski

TO DEBORAH SCHNEIDER,

WITH THANKS FOR FINDING MAIREAD

A GOOD HOME

UNCOMMON

JUSTICE

PROLOGUE

"TOO DAMN COLD THIS December night, not to have your own warm coat around you."

Zoran Draskovic stamped his feet on the bank of the partially frozen river, the soles of his scavenged boots crunching against the crusted snow. Zoran knew he talked to himself—and could count plenty of others that did the same—but he figured his Mission gave him sort of a . . . dispensation.

After all, it wasn't everybody God charged with saving the Charles River—his Great Lady of Boston—from the Blighters.

And they took all forms, Zoran knew that, too. The Corporate Blighters, pouring their industrial shit into the water upstream. The Rich Blighters, driving their boats onto the spawning beds downstream. The College Blighters, smashing their beer bottles against the shoreline rocks. The Great Lady had suffered all this and more, from the Pilgrims to the Punkers. In fact, it was a miracle She'd survived to this point.

The point where Zoran was there to save Her, that is.

Oh, people called him names, sure. Like "fucking hippie," which Zoran had gotten used to decades before, when he'd first grown his hair to the length he'd thereafter kept it. "Stinking bum" was another, but let any loud condo owners try dry-damping the year 'round and see how *they* smelled. Among all the names for him, though, "Old Man River" had become Zoran's favorite, even if he didn't understand why so many of them used that one, him not being even forty—or colored, for that matter.

Of course, Zoran really didn't care what people called him, as long as he could continue his Mission.

Shivering, Zoran stopped for a moment, his nostrils, throat, and lungs burning from the cold air he was huffing. "Good God Almighty, give me Thy strength."

Zoran started moving again, now trudging uphill toward the bridge abutment over Alpha's "cave." What that crazy Mick called his digs, tucked under the stanchions, where he claimed it stayed dry enough to keep his "library of the mind" from rotting.

Imagine that, a crazy Irishman calling himself a Greek name and reading philosophy books?

Zoran shook his head but began to walk more carefully. He stayed mindful of the squeaking noise his feet were now making against the snow, and he began to time his steps to the rumbling sounds of the car traffic passing overhead on an elevated section of Storrow Drive.

Wouldn't do to get this far, then wake the bastard up before getting back what you came for. What was rightfully yours.

Zoran slowed even more, because his eyes had spotted the entrance to Alpha's cave just ahead. The crazy Mick built himself a door from the lumber scraps he got—or stole, more likely—from that construction site downtown. Well, Alpha's patchwork wood might keep out the worst of the wind but not a crusader like Old Man River on a Mission of Righteous Recovery.

Reaching the door, Zoran pushed it open just a bit. Then he registered the snoring sound coming from a mattress mostly in shadow.

Drunk again, the Greek Mick lucky to reach home before he froze to death in a slushy gutter somewhere.

Zoran moved into the cave slowly, still shaking from the cold outside but now more confident in the dim moonlight spilling through the doorway. He could see Alpha's war club—his "shillelagh," the drunken bum called it—just next to the jamb. Briefly, Zoran considered picking the club up by the tapered end and bringing the heavy part down—wham!—on the head of the man sleeping off his bender.

But no, said Zoran, this time completely inside himself. No, you serve to

protect Her, and for all his faults, Alpha isn't a Blighter. At least, you don't think he is.

So Zoran just lifted the shillelagh and silently laid it against the wooden wall outside the door, well beyond the reach of its sleeping owner.

Then the man stirred in his bed, rolling over maybe, because the snoring stopped.

For another moment, Zoran held his own breath, afraid the crazy Mick had awakened and would rear up and come after him. However, when Zoran slowly exhaled, he heard no sound whatever arising from the mattress now.

With nearly numb fingers, Zoran felt around the cave for his big, heavy trench coat—not one of those yuppie rain things with the double-breasted lapels, but a green Soviet one from the *real* trenches of Stalingrad or some such place. Made of wool, and warm as a mother's womb from the time Zoran first found it in the AmVets store over by Brighton. At the cash register, he'd paid two bucks, probably what it cost the Russkies to sew the coat together back in the forties.

But it wasn't even the money, no. No, it was the principle of the matter: That drunken Greek Mick stole your property, and you're entitled to take it back.

So long as he doesn't wake up while you're doing it.

Zoran's fingers skimmed over many book bindings and the occasional pair of underwear, hanging stiff from being scrubbed in cold water and then left to dry in colder air. You had to give a man credit where credit was due, and Alpha tried to keep himself as clean as he could, you don't count the lice and all. Even had a couple of ratty blankets. Which was a good omen, because it meant the Mick didn't have to sleep in the coat to keep himself warm.

Then Zoran's right hand came into contact with coarse, gritty fabric, and tears practically surged from his eyes.

You know the feel of this coat better than your own skin.

Carefully—lovingly—Zoran feathered the coat off a nail that stuck out from one of the bookshelves he'd seen Alpha building during daylight.

Pausing to rub a woolen sleeve over his eyes, Zoran backed slowly out of the cave.

Once he was clear of the doorway, though, he couldn't wait to put the coat on, as much for sentiment as warmth. Zoran reveled in the way his body felt enveloped by the garment.

He began walking down the riverbank, nearly stopping as the vista of his Great Lady struck him once more. She was different most every time Zoran looked at Her, because he was rarely in the same spot with the same lighting at the same time of the year. Tonight, the Charles was covered eighty percent by ice, and powdery snow from an evening flurry swirled on the silver-and-black surface. Zoran could feel more tears come into his eyes, but they were good ones. Tears of love for the Great Lady and for this reunion with his Great Coat.

In fact, Zoran was a good thirty strides away from Alpha's cave before remembering he hadn't closed the door. He glanced back, hoping not to see anybody standing outside it. But hope—as life had taught Zoran more often than not—just wasn't enough.

As soon as the figure straightened up, the Mick's shillelagh appeared in silhouette against the dull gray of the bridge abutment.

And Zoran began to run.

Run till his ears roared.

Run till his heart pounded.

Run till the hem of his trench coat flapped under a boot and caused him to stumble forward.

Zoran hit the rocky ground hard, trying to break his fall but feeling the skin on his palms, jaw, and cheeks shear off in layers. He cried out, his own voice sounding wrong to him.

Not even . . . human.

Zoran tried to rise by doing a push-up on his elbows, but the first blow from the shillelagh broke his right shoulder blade, sending a jagged spear of pain through to his breastplate. He tried to roll away from the pain, but as soon as he was on his back, a second blow caught him diagonally across the face, breaking his left cheekbone, flattening his nose, and bursting his right

eye in its socket. The blood flooding into Zoran's throat began to choke him, but before the blubbering sound could reach his mouth, a third blow fractured his skull at the hairline.

As the pain mercifully sloughed away, and the last conscious thought flickered through his brain, Zoran Draskovic regretted not staying on his stomach, so he at least could have died watching the river he'd labored so hard to save.

1

JESUS MARY, THOUGHT MAIREAD O'Clare for about the hundredth time since September. I'm in with the assholes.

From her seat, she watched the fat senior partner waddle around the law firm's conference room, the big one on the thirty-eighth floor with a view of Boston harbor through a wall of windows stretching from plushly carpeted floor to acoustically tiled ceiling. His name was Hadley Burgess, a North Shore scion in his fifties with a horsy face and straight hair the color of nicotine except for some white wisps around the ears. Burgess was the head of Mairead's department, Litigation, and he now droned on about the importance of designing formal discovery documents—like Requests for Production of Documents—with the broadest scope possible. Most of the other chairs around the elliptical and polished cherrywood table were occupied by the twenty-some twenty-somethings who were in Mairead's "associate class" at Jaynes & Ward, meaning they'd all been hired in the same year. This was the monthly orientation seminar that all new associates had to attend, and the fact that the firm postponed the Litigation orientation to January—the fifth such Monday—sent a clear message that her department ranked pretty low on the Jaynes & Ward totem pole.

But it also said a lot about the "vision" of the firm's Managing Committee that even Litigation associates who'd spent September through December actually *doing* basic courtroom work still had to sit through a two-hour orientation *on* basic courtroom work.

Well, thought Mairead, not exactly "courtroom" work. She herself had yet to appear in a real legal arena. Instead, the junior partners she worked

for kept her drafting waves of dense discovery documents in a shared, windowless office. Which reminded Mairead of how far from her bunk bed in the Catholic orphanage any windows had been.

And which should be a lesson learned, young lady, said Sister Bernadette's voice inside Mairead's head. *As long as you have to sit here, you may as well enjoy the view.*

And a whale of a view it was, too, even if a bit . . . sterile? The silvery tip of the Custom House tower glowed like a metallic pyramid, its clock finally working again. Across the harbor, Logan Airport hosted constant arrivals and departures of planes in a welcomed, if somewhat monotonous, sequence of genuine activity. And beyond the runways lay Deer Island, its enormous sewage tanks shaped like the antique milk bottles that served as "decorations" on the shelves in the nuns' kitchen back at the—

"Ms. O'Clare?" said Hadley Burgess, now sitting at the head of the conference room table, his thick brows arching and his pudgy lips pursing.

Mairead blinked away the daydream. "I'm . . . I'm sorry?"

Burgess closed his eyes for just a moment. "I believe I asked for your assessment of the issue, given your current skill level after *months* of litigation experience at Jaynes and Ward."

Even without Burgess stressing the "months" part, Mairead would have felt herself reddening in the cheeks, the way she imagined others thought her arms must feel all the time. There were a few coughs and shifting of butts on chairs around the table, but no one else spoke.

"Ms. O'Clare?"

Mairead glanced down at her hands, as though the answer to Burgess's question were outlined in the port-wine stain that covered them from the cuticles of her nails to the cuffs of her blouse.

And, under the sleeves themselves, up past her elbows.

Finally, she said, "Mr. Burgess, I'm really sorry, but I didn't hear your question."

Another closing of his eyes, longer this time. "Was I not speaking loudly enough to reach you?"

The associate next to her, a Latino guy from Stanford and also in Litigation, began to say, "I don't think Mairead's ever worked on a—"

"Mr. Perez?"

A moment before the Latino said, "No, sir. Ramirez, John Ramirez."

"Of course. Mr. Ramirez, should Ms. O'Clare ever appear in a court-room, she'd have to fend for herself, don't you think?"

Mairead looked up from her hands and obliquely into the withering stare Burgess was directing at the associate who'd tried to help her.

Bringing the heat back where it belonged, she said, "Mr. Burgess, I wasn't paying attention. My fault, and I admit it."

The head of Litigation marched his stare a few degrees so that his and Mairead's eyes locked. "Perhaps, Ms. O'Clare, you'd like to excuse yourself for a few moments, regain some composure."

"I'm composed enough," said Mairead, trying to blunt the edge she sensed creeping into her voice. "I was just bored."

Mairead heard several sudden intakes of breath and one squelched male laugh, but from the way Burgess rocketed his glance around the table, the squelcher didn't give himself away.

Then Hadley Burgess hunched stiffly forward in his chair. "Ms. O'Clare, I want you to absent yourself from the balance of this seminar, for whatever reason you prefer."

Using legs strengthened by twelve years of organized ice hockey, Mairead O'Clare pushed her chair back from the table, sorry only that the plush carpeting kept that decisive action from making any noise at all.

"HEY, like, thanks for showing the rest of us how to fuck the duck."

Mairead looked up from her computer screen and into the face of her officemate, a Litigation associate named David Spiegel from Columbia. Tall, doughy, and already stooped, Spiegel wasn't the most pleasant of compan-ions, and Mairead thought he'd probably make a good Burgess in another thirty years.

But right then, she waved him off and returned to the e-mail thank-you she was composing to John Ramirez for trying to bail her out at the orientation.

Even so, though, Mairead couldn't help but notice Spiegel collapsing into his chair, catty-corner from hers, the way all the new associates' offices were arranged. So each could keep an eye on the other. After a year or two,

they'd been told, everyone would have his or her own office because more-senior associates "leaving the firm" would result in open singles, some even with windows.

Spiegel said, "You hone those interpersonal skills at New England?"

Mairead just glared at him. She'd afforded New England School of Law by working two part-time jobs, but the reason she'd gone there was its heritage. New England had started life in 1908 as the first institution in the country organized to allow women to study law at a time when the Supreme Court of the United States still deemed it constitutionally acceptable to deny an entire gender any opportunity to enter practice. The place had been called Portia Law School back then, after Shakespeare's female lawyer, but even though its name had changed to reflect a coed student body and regional attraction, Mairead had known about New England from Sister Bernadette, who'd attended before entering the convent. And the Boston law school, like her college before it, had given Mairead that sense of family she'd yearned for but never really found inside the orphanage.

A pity that schools make you graduate, young lady, said Sister Bernadette's voice.

"Hey," from Spiegel, "what're you gonna do, just sit there and wait for the executioner to, like, come for you?"

Mairead realized she'd continued glaring at her officemate without really seeing him for a while. "David, I haven't decided yet."

"Yeah, well, my guess is, somebody's gonna decide for you."

Reluctantly, Mairead felt herself agreeing with him. She'd gotten this job after working her first summer as a research assistant for one of her professors and her second summer as kind of a hospice aide for Sister Bernadette through the nun's final illness. Jaynes & Ward pretty much hired only from the thirty schools that hyped themselves as being in the top ten nationally, and even then just from the class of summer associates who'd auditioned for three months prior to starting their senior year. But Mairead knew that the professor she'd worked for—Susan Gunnarsen—had interceded for her with Hadley Burgess at the firm, and given that Mairead'd been number three in her class, Jaynes & Ward had offered her a shot.

Only now, as David Spiegel had so tastefully put it, Mairead had gone and fucked the duck.

Her officemate gathered up a thick accordion file from the floor by his feet. "Well, I think I'll let you face Jabba the Hutt alone."

Mairead was about to reply when the telephone next to her hand rang loudly enough to make her jump a little.

"MR. Burgess, Ms. O'Clare."

He looked up as his secretary's words were still hanging in the air, the door closing behind the young associate with the oh-so-bizarre blotches on her hands. And forearms, Hadley recalled from the New Associates Picnic at the managing partner's summer house the weekend before Labor Day. Thinking of the picnic reminded Hadley of what a nuisance it was, actually, having to cut short one's own precious vacation.

And for what? No greater purpose than welcoming a devouring horde of overpaid, ungrateful brats to a prestigious firm whose provenance only a handful of them could begin to appreciate and whose providence only two of the twenty-three would probably ever know as equity partners themselves.

But Hadley rather doubted Jaynes & Ward would be reaching that stage with this one. "Take a seat."

He watched O'Clare settle into a client chair. Before Hadley could begin, though, she said, "You wanted to see me, Mr. Burgess?"

Pity, that forthrightness—which might be so effective in appellate argument—coming across as rudeness in an office conference. And that's when Hadley realized he hadn't spoken with O'Clare individually since welcoming her to the firm months earlier. Another pity, though in a different sense. And not just because this one seemed among the few her age to be spared that treacly Valley Girl lilt in the voice. No, it was more the pity because, really, if paper bags were just slipped over O'Clare's arms, she'd teeter on the verge of beauty. About five-foot-seven, weight nicely proportional, including the high—but not huge—breasts. Auburn hair and fair skin, with those freckles the Irish seem to sprout if they even *think* about the sun. Big,

piercing blue eyes, assuming no contact-lens enhancement. Certainly no enhancement to the shapely legs—if rather more athletic than feminine, but what with girls persisting in sports well beyond the point of—

"Mr. Burgess?"

You should never have listened to Susan Gunnarsen, classmate or not. Probably will even owe the pushy bitch the courtesy of a telephone call . . . afterward.

Hadley glanced at the file in front of him, struggling to recall the overly ethnic name this . . . "Uh, *My*-rat, correct?"

"No, sir. It's 'Muh-*raid*,' the Irish pronunciation."

Burgess frowned. "But my wife has a friend from Canada with your spelling, and she says it—"

"The Scottish way."

"Scottish?"

"Yes. As though the spelling was M-y-r-a with *a-t*."

Hadley took a stab at lightening things up a bit. "Well, I suppose that's better than 'My *rat*' with a space, eh?"

The girl's mouth twisted, but ambiguously.

Hadley cleared his throat. "On to the matter at hand, then." He looked back down at the file for an answer he already knew. "You came to us from New England?"

"Yes."

Best to skip secondary school and college. "And have you been happy at Jaynes and Ward, Muh-*raid*?"

Another twist to the girl's mouth. "Not really."

Hadley feared he'd somehow misheard her. "What?"

"I haven't been very happy here."

"You . . . haven't?"

"No." O'Clare seemed to struggle with something. "I worked hard to become an attorney because I wanted to make a difference in people's lives, in a courtroom where they sought justice. And I thought that a large-firm environment would give me the chance to learn from other professionals trying to do those good things."

Hadley felt a grunt of contempt rise in his throat but tamped it down like tobacco into the bowl of a pipe. "Our clients think we do rather a fine job by them."

O'Clare now softened her tone a bit. "And they should, because—technically—everybody at Jaynes and Ward is a fine lawyer. But I'm not talking about professional competence."

O'Clare crossed her legs, and Hadley found himself wishing his desk wasn't in the way of his view. Athletic calves, yes, but still awfully—

She interrupted his reverie with, "I'm talking about personal satisfaction, Mr. Burgess."

For just the briefest of moments, Hadley wondered if a double entendre was being extended, the sort that in the good old days one could pursue without fear of femi-Nazi partners in the firm screaming "sexual har—"

The girl seemed to read his mind. "In the sense of job satisfaction. Being a social engineer, genuinely helping real people."

Good Lord, thought Hadley. How did this one ever get an *inter*view with us, much less an associate's position? Then he remembered that telephone call to him from Susan Gunnarsen, and Hadley realized he was suffering from a wound that had been at least partially self-inflicted.

But one that could nevertheless be stanched, and quickly.

"Mah-*reed*, I think—"

"I'm sorry, but it's still 'Muh-*raid*.'"

Very well, no more Mr. Nice Guy. "Perhaps you'd be happier else-where."

"I don't think so, Mr. Burgess. Litigation is the only department here that would teach me how to—"

"Actually, I meant elsewhere out*side* the firm."

A canting of her head. "Just because I didn't pay attention to you talking about things I'd already learned?"

"Your outburst in the conference room would never be forgotten by the other associates." Hadley cleared his throat again. "Nor by me."

The girl finally closed those piercing eyes, if only for a moment. "I have a lot to think about."

"Indeed you do," said Hadley Burgess, launching himself out of his chair less from courtesy and more to get another glimpse at those rather special legs before their owner could rise herself.

MAIREAD O'Clare walked down a macadam path of the Boston Common behind the Park Street subway station. The sixtyish air of a January thaw felt almost like a refreshing breeze, but she still was glad to have put on her coat before taking a break to decompress after the session with Burgess.

And to think, young lady, said Sister Bernadette's voice inside Mairead's head, *about who you are and where you're going.*

Mairead spotted an empty bench, but it stood diagonally across from one on which a middle-aged man in a rumpled business suit was feeding pigeons out of a white bakery bag in his lap. Several of the birds were up on his thighs, pecking at bread crumbs in the pleats of his pants.

Mairead paused. She could change direction and head for her studio apartment on Beacon Hill, but Mairead really wanted to do her mental sorting somewhere she felt . . . unfettered. And besides, Pigeon Man looked harmless enough, so Mairead sat down on the curved, wooden slats of the empty bench.

All right, young lady: Life assessment time.

Just like back in the orphanage, where I fended for myself, there not being enough good nuns—or even bad ones—to really match up for surrogate mothering. And each time a kid in my dorm was adopted, I dropped another set of potential parents further away from adoption myself. Until I realized nobody was ever going to choose the now not-so-little girl with the purplish-red skin covering—

No, Mairead, said Sister Bernadette. *That's not the road to go down.*

Okay, back up and focus on the positives, then. I'll be only twenty-six next birthday. I've survived abandonment by my "natural" parents, who Sister Angelica in a hissy fit once said left me at the convent's doorstep because of the "stigmata" on my hands and arms. Said it loud enough for other kids to hear and to start calling me "Stiggie" to my face. Until I beat them up, after which they still called me that behind my back.

But you survived them, too, Mairead. To play center on the boys' hockey team in high school and a league championship women's team in college. And to graduate law school magna cum laude and land a job with one of the most prestigious firms in Boston.

For four months anyway. But four months in which I've slaved away with that jerk Spiegel in an office smaller than the Supreme Court once held was inadequate as cell space for two prisoners doing life. My "billable hours" are socked to massive corporate clients, maintaining Jaynes & Ward's pyramid of worker-bee associates at the bottom producing honey-money for the rainmaking partners at the top. And all my goals of "helping people" are a laugh—no, worse than a laugh, a *parody*—of what I attended law school to—

"You don't mind my saying, it's a shame to see somebody so pretty seem so sad."

Mairead looked over to Pigeon Man, not positive at first if he was the one who'd spoken, though the words came from that direction. But, yes, he's staring this way, his lips forming a grin without showing any teeth.

"I'm not sad," said Mairead, unsure why she was even replying. "I'm just . . . weighing things."

"Must be pretty heavy things."

"They are."

"Sometimes," said the guy in the rumpled suit, "it helps to talk them out with somebody doesn't know anything about them. Strangers on a plane, you know?"

Mairead had taken only one airline flight in her life—for an interview with a federal agency in Washington, D.C.—so she wasn't sure exactly what the guy meant. But his brown eyes were mournful, like a cocker spaniel's, so Mairead decided to go with it.

"I took this job?" she said. "A big law firm. I thought I'd become a trial attorney, make some difference in people's lives. But all the partners do is bounce me around like a pinball between bits and pieces of obscure corporate litigation."

A nod from the man. "You wanted to be Perry Mason, but instead you're Ally McBeal."

Mairead blinked. In an orphanage, you watch a lot of TV, so she knew the old series with Raymond Burr. What surprised her, though, was that Pigeon Man would be up on a cool new show.

Then Mairead examined the guy a little more closely. He was definitely past forty—and maybe even fifty, more from the lines in his face than the sandy hair with no gray showing. His tie wasn't snugged quite to his collar, and his shirt was nearly as wrinkled as his suit, which actually had cuffs above loafers that looked less polished than scuffed.

Mairead said, "Or maybe I thought I'd be Ally McBeal learning from Perry Mason."

A pigeon landed on the man's shoulder. "Kind of hard to get that in a big firm?"

"Kind of impossible. And the partners think that once you're onboard, you won't leave because of the 'golden handcuffs.'"

"Meaning the money this firm pays?"

"Eighty-four thousand a year."

The guy whistled softly through his front teeth.

Mairead said, "Sounds like a lot, right?"

"I'd say so."

"Not when a lot of the associates are carrying humongous student loans."

"But you aren't?"

"Uh-uh. I worked my way through law school."

"And college, too?"

"Kind of. I was on a hockey scholarship."

The man smiled. "Hockey."

Mairead somehow liked that Pigeon Man didn't say it as a question. "Anyway, I don't owe anybody a dime."

"Even so, though, you don't much like the people around you at this big firm, huh?"

Mairead blinked again. "How do you know that?"

A shrug this time, though the shoulder pigeon stayed put. "You had good friends where you're working, I don't see you talking this out with me."

He's right, young lady. "Well, even that's not going to be a problem much longer."

"They're giving you the old heave-ho?"

"The what?"

"They're firing you?"

"More laying the groundwork," said Mairead. "I daydreamed this morning while a partner was lecturing to us."

"Lecturing?"

"An orientation seminar, the firm calls it. On litigation."

A small frown. "I thought you said that was the kind of work you were already doing?"

Mairead grunted out a laugh. "The reason I was daydreaming."

Now the guy nodded a third time. "I don't see any rings on your fingers."

Uh-oh, though his voice didn't have the smarmy undertone of a pick-up line. "I don't have any family."

"No husband, or no family at all?"

Mairead decided to trust her intuition. "Raised by the nuns in an orphanage."

The man's eyes closed, but more from pain than the way Hadley Burgess had closed his at the seminar, and the shoulder pigeon fluttered away.

Finally, the guy said, "I know what that can be like."

Mairead felt her head canting to the side. "You lost your parents, too?"

"No." The man bowed his own head. "My wife and daughter."

Ohmigod. "I'm so sorry."

"Years ago. It gets a little easier, time goes by."

The guy now crumpled up his bakery bag with one hand and gently shooed the pigeons off his legs with the other. Mairead sensed that the conversation was ending, but she also realized that—however irrationally—she didn't want it *to* end.

Mairead said, "What do you do?"

The man looked over at her as he stood up—at nearly six feet, taller and more athletic than she'd have predicted. Instead of answering Mairead's question, though, the guy reached into the side pocket of his suit jacket and began walking toward her.

Mairead rose abruptly, instinctively not wanting to be caught sitting down as a stranger—even one with spaniel eyes—approached closely with something in his hand. But all the man fished from his pocket was a business card, which he extended to her, his fingernails clean on what she now saw as hands big enough to palm a basketball, the knuckles kind of lumpy.

He said, "I've got a spare office in my suite, you want to do a space-share."

"A what?" replied Mairead, taking the card.

"Share space with me. I could even pay you something—not what you're getting at that big firm, but I could refer you some cases, and you could help me out on some of mine."

Mairead recited from the card. "'Sheldon A. Gold, Attorney at Law.'"

"I like that better than 'Esquire,' which always sounded kind of phony to me."

She read silently the Beacon Street address, gauging it to be only a few blocks from her apartment. "You're a lawyer, too?"

"Appearances can be deceiving, huh?"

Mairead found her cheeks reddening for the second time that morning. "I didn't mean—"

"You want to learn from Perry Mason? Well, I don't have his track record, but I do mostly criminal defense, so you're interested, just come see me." He reached out his right hand. "Instead of your big-firm golden hand-cuffs, how about a Shel Gold handshake?"

Mairead extended hers, the fingers disappearing into his palm. *Almost like holding a bag of peanuts, young lady.* But the big hand felt warm and strong.

As Gold began walking away on the macadam path, Mairead hesitated, then called out, "But you don't even know my name."

Without turning, he called back over his shoulder. "We talked, and I know you. That's good enough."

There were other people on the path now, so Mairead O'Clare didn't say anything else. But she found herself watching Sheldon A. Gold walk—shamble, really—until he was swallowed up in the crowd milling around the subway station.

"MAIREAD!" said Susan Gunnarsen. "What, it's only January and that sweatshop's already letting you out for lunch?"

"I really appreciate your seeing me without an appoint—"

Mairead watched Gunnarsen flick her wrist dismissively. "Appointments are for students, make sure they prepare toward our time together. Alums, now, are always welcome."

Taking a seat, Mairead felt soothed by her old professor's welcome. And by the cornsilk hair and Minnesota accent out of the movie *Fargo*.

"So, Mairead," Gunnarsen plopping into the highbacked swivel chair behind her desk, "what can we do for you today?"

"I think I just wrecked the chance you made for me."

Gunnarsen frowned. "At Jaynes and Ward, you mean?"

"Yes," and, after her dress rehearsal with Sheldon Gold, Mairead rattled off the situation with Hadley Burgess pretty concisely.

"Bastard," said Gunnarsen.

"Susan, I'm really sorry—"

"Oh, not you, Mairead. I meant Hadley. Thinks he's so 'progressive, don't you know?' That tight-assed snob. Frankly, I was hoping you might have some positive influence on him, while you lasted."

"While I . . . ?"

"Lasted. You didn't really think you'd make *partner* there, did you?"

Mairead's assumed world seemed to be unraveling at a sharply accelerating rate. "Susan, I don't understand."

Gunnarsen came forward, elbows on the desktop. "Look, because of how you spent your first and second summers of law school, Jaynes and Ward is your initial exposure to a large firm. Well, there are dozens more just like it in every major city, the hiring partners and 'recruitment coordinators' wining and dining their twenty or thirty summer associates. For three glorious months, it's ball games and barbecues, pool parties and polo matches."

"Susan, I didn't expect any of that, and I knew I'd have to work hard. It's just—"

"Let me finish, okay?"

"Okay."

"Well, the firm takes its pick of that summer-associate litter, and then hires a few third-year students—like you—to fill out the roster." Gunnarsen leaned back. "And then the marathon begins."

"The . . . marathon?"

"How good you were—how *great* you were—at the last round of competition doesn't matter. It's how well you run the next mile, and the one after that after that after that. Then, at the end of this eight-year Olympic tryout, only two, maybe three of the original associate class will be admitted to partnership."

Mairead did the math. "A ninety-percent attrition rate."

"Exactly," said Gunnarsen. "I wanted you at Jaynes and Ward to polish your legal skills and pump up your résumé. But I never expected anyone as talented and independent as you are would stick in that place."

Mairead tried to smile. "Did you expect me to stick longer than four months?"

Gunnarsen did smile. "Well, here's my advice on that. Think about all the benefit you conferred on Jaynes and Ward—and its clients—by the quality work you did for them. You don't owe the partners there a thing."

"But I feel I owe you some—"

"Then here's how to pay me back. Take what you learned at the firm and abstract from it some lessons to carry away from the experience. After that, lace up your skates and hit the ice for another team that suits you more."

"I've . . ." Mairead did a quick ego check, to make sure that her next words weren't just to save face with a mentor. "I've already got another job offer."

"In the past two hours?"

"It was kind of a coincidence. Like serendipity?"

"Like miraculous. Is it a good opportunity?"

"I don't know much about it." Mairead did a quick gut check now. "But I trust the guy who made the offer."

"Well, as I always preached to you: Analyze with the head, but decide with the heart."

"Susan, thank you."

"For what, common sense?"

"For letting me off the hook on your recommendation to Hadley Burgess."

"Hah!" Gunnarsen hoisted herself from the chair and came around the desk. "Probably did the old bastard good, get a little professional enema."

Then a grunted laugh so like Mairead's own in the Common that she wondered if her old professor had taught her that, too.

"MS. O'Clare," said Hadley Burgess, rising from the other side of his desk but speaking more to her legs than her face, Mairead thought.

Then he glanced at his watch. "A third interlude in the same day is rather straining my schedule."

Mairead sat. "I think it'll be our last ever."

Both the fat man's eyebrows went up. "I beg your pardon?"

"I've thought carefully about what you said this morning, and I'm giving my notice now."

Burgess seemed to need the arms of his chair to steady his landing on its cushion. "Your . . . what?"

"My notice," Mairead said. "I'm leaving in two weeks. Of course, I'll spend the time bringing any associates you designate up to speed on the matters I'm covering for clients."

"You're . . . *leaving* Jaynes and Ward, just like that?"

Mairead couldn't understand the apparent shock. "Well, yes."

Something seemed to flicker behind the man's eyes, then burn through them. "And in two weeks, you say."

"Seems fair to both sides."

"Yes, well, *fair* is hardly the word to use in trashing not only your charitably offered position here but indeed your reputation within the bar as—"

"Mr. Burgess, I just don't want to prolong the agony for either of us."

Mairead, no stranger to blushing, thought the color surging into Burgess's face might just burst through his pores.

"Ms. O'Clare, you are hereby terminated at once. Clean out your office—your desk, your bloody *waste*basket—and be gone by five P.M."

"Mr. Burgess, the firm's clients deserve a professional transition, and I promise you I won't sabotage any—"

"Get out! Get out of my office before I throw you out."

Thinking òf what the man had said back in the orientation seminar, Mairead O'Clare squared her shoulders and rose slowly from the chair. "Mr. Burgess, I'm afraid that might reach beyond your 'current skill level.'"

2

MAIREAD AWOKE WITH A start, too much January sunlight in the room. Her clock radio read 9 A.M., the latest she'd slept on a weekday in over four months.

Then Mairead remembered the prior afternoon and stretched in the long T-shirt she wore as a nightdress. Cleaning out her office at Jaynes & Ward the day before, the file folders fell away like bricks from her shoulders as she put a Post-it on each for the partner involved. What little stuff was Mairead's own—diploma, pen set, matching scissors and letter opener—all fit into one small box that once held photocopy paper, and the box and she fit easily into the cab that took her home.

Once inside the studio apartment, Mairead had settled into her one big easy chair and put her feet up on its ottoman. She indulged in a whole bottle of wine to accompany the frozen dinner zapped in her microwave. But then Mairead turned in early in preparation for hard work on the next task.

The way you always have, young lady, said Sister Bernadette's voice. *Regardless of the task itself.*

As Mairead stretched in bed one last time, she thought about calling some of her friends from New England, let them know what she'd be doing now. But then Mairead decided it made more sense to wait until she had her feet on the ground at the new offices—her direct-dial number, e-mail address—so they could reach her for lunch or drinks after work.

Work with Sheldon A. Gold. And his sad, soulful eyes, from the Common the day before, when he'd made Mairead the job offer.

Well, young lady, the man did say, "Just come see me."

I SHOULD have scoped out his building first.

Standing on the sidewalk near the Boston Bar Association's red-bricked headquarters and the Boston Athenaeum's granite library, Mairead O'Clare closed her eyes once, then confirmed the address on Sheldon A. Gold's business card. The building across Beacon Street staggered up eleven stories, the stonework needing sandblasting and the mortar repointing. Double glass doors sported a layer of soot thick enough to show finger-sketched initials.

Inside the lobby, the ceramic floor tiles—maybe white, originally—had gone to milky-gray, chipped here and split there. Mairead's two-inch heels clacked with an echo in the empty, musty air as she made her way to a building directory flanked by the two elevators. One displayed a handwritten Out of Order sign below the diamond-shaped window in its door, and the directory put her destination on the top floor.

With a sigh she thought best to leave in the lobby, Mairead O'Clare pushed a button that made the working elevator open.

"GOOD morning."

"So far," said a middle-aged African-American woman sitting sidesaddle behind the metal reception desk, a dinosaur electric typewriter on her secretarial pull-tray. The desk was centered in a hexagonal foyer laid with tattered, faded carpeting that might once have had a recognizable pattern to it. Some plastic scoop chairs were distributed haphazardly around a coffee table with dog-eared magazines covering its surface. Mairead could see three heavy doors off the foyer, all closed.

"Honey?" said the receptionist.

Actually, "honey" was the color of the dreadlocks that trailed behind the woman's back, but Mairead focused instead on her face. The skin tone two shades darker than the hair, the scowl scrunching up a broad nose and widely spaced, yellow-brown eyes.

"Honey, you got anything more in your vocabulary past wishing me a nice day?"

"Sorry." Mairead snapped out of her trance. "I'm here to see Sheldon Gold."

The woman glanced at an appointment book open to the left of her typewriter. "I don't see anything written down here."

"My name's Mairead O'Clare."

The black woman just looked up with a "huh?" expression in her eyes.

Mairead spelled her first and last names, then added, "I'm Mr. Gold's new associate."

The receptionist didn't reply. Didn't move her head, didn't even blink.

Mairead plunged onward anyway. "He . . . we weren't exactly certain when I'd be able to start."

"But here you are."

"Right."

"Well, my name's Billie Sunday, spelled *i-e* and like the Sabbath. Shel didn't say boo to me about you, so have yourself a seat there, and I guess you all will talk when he gets in."

Mairead felt that sitting down would mean losing her momentum in this new situation. "Could I maybe see my office while we wait for him?"

Another stare, then Sunday hiked her thumb vaguely toward the three closed doors behind her. "Which of them is Shel giving you?"

Maybe a bad sign, there's more than one open. "He just said he had a spare."

Now Sunday pointed toward a plastic reception chair. "Well then, maybe you should just try that seat on the right, which I can tell you is yours for sure till Shel gets here and says different."

Mairead bristled a little, but after keeping her last legal job only four months, she decided that maybe her next one should last more than four minutes.

"BILLIE, Billie. What a morning, what a—"

Mairead watched the door to the corridor open inward, Billie Sunday at the desk holding up her hand in a stop sign while scribbling another telephone message on a pink pad, the office voice mail obviously down. When not taking calls, Sunday had typed information onto forms she'd rolled into the old typewriter. Mairead couldn't believe that the forms—whatever they were—wouldn't be more easily generated via computer.

Sheldon A. Gold continued through the door, closing it behind him without looking toward the plastic chairs.

Mairead stood up anyway. "Mr. Gold."

He turned, surprise appearing on his face, followed by a warm grin. "My friend from the Common. And it's just Shel, remember?"

Mairead tried to sound professional as the receptionist spoke into the telephone. "I told Ms. Sunday who I was, but she said you never told her about me."

"How could I?" said Gold, shrugging both shoulders under another rumpled business suit, but at least a different one. His right hand was wrapped around the handles of a battered old bookbag, and his left trailed a large container of Munchkins from Dunkin' Donuts.

Mairead said, "How could . . . ?"

". . . I." Gold set the multicolored box on the reception desk, Sunday nodding as she dipped her writing hand inside.

To his new associate, Gold said, "You never told me your name, right?"

Mairead closed her eyes. He was right. Blushing—she *knew* she was—Mairead slowly pronounced and spelled her name for the second time that morning. "Ms. Sunday wasn't sure which office would be mine."

Gold said, "Probably better if you have your pick."

He began shambling toward the middle of the three closed doors. "Come into mine first, though, maybe give you some ideas."

"WELL, what do you think of the view?"

Mairead stopped short. Expecting at best an airshaft and dirty bricks to appear through any windows there might be, she instead saw a beautiful, three-sided bay giving her 180 degrees of Boston westward. The Charles River, winding its mostly frozen way toward the Harvard Square bridge. The gentrified Victorian neighborhood of Back Bay, granite stone buildings split by the hundred-foot-wide Commonwealth Avenue Mall on which stood hundred-year-old Dutch elms. And, in the relative foreground, the sweeping downslope of her own neighborhood, Beacon Hill, with its Federalist town houses of red brick and its soaring church steeples of gold leaf

and white. Unlike the sterile harbor/airport vista from Jaynes & Ward's sky-scraper, this one felt . . . human.

"Mairead?"

"Uh, sorry. It's just . . . beautiful."

"I've always liked it myself. Kind of reminds me who I'm working for."

"Your clients come from Back Bay and Beacon Hill?"

Gold smiled. "Not usually. I meant more working for the community as a whole. The people, you know?"

Mairead hesitated, wondering if he was pressing a button she'd revealed during their talk on the benches. "I can understand that."

Gold's smile lost a little of its candlepower. "Well, this is where I work. Let's give you a look at your choices."

As he did an air-push with his hands toward the office door, Mairead tried to take in as much of her new boss's space as she could. Old wooden shelving recessed into the opposing long walls, the shelves themselves nearly creaking from heaps of dusty books and curling manila files crammed between the levels. Old wooden furniture, too, the arms and seats of the client chairs showing worn spots where elbows and butts must have knit nervously. And in one corner, a freestanding safe that belonged in a Wild West bank. Only, why in the world would he need—

They were back in the reception foyer, Billie Sunday staring at them from the opposite sidesaddle profile in her chair.

Gold said, "First this way."

Mairead turned as he opened the closed door to the left of his. Crossing the threshold, though, she felt it was wrong. Granted, a big step up from her last, windowless space. But while the room had its own bay, the view was more of the office buildings across Beacon Street.

Her new boss said, "You want to see the other one, right?"

Am I that transparent? "Please."

He led her back into the foyer toward the third door. This time, Mairead didn't bother to check on whether Billie Sunday was staring at them.

Gold turned the knob. "You don't like this office, either, I'm afraid we're out of luck."

She loved it.

Stepping into the space gave Mairead the dizzying sensation of being on top of the world instead of just on top of the Hill. The bay window here looked over town houses and churches, one steeple backdropped by the river's dark ice. In the distance, a Red Line subway train inched its way like a choo-choo toy over the arching bridge to Cambridge. Going up on tiptoes, Mairead could even see the roof of her apartment building.

Well, maybe see it.

"Bingo," said Gold.

Steady, young lady. Your whole body's beaming, but you still have to negotiate salary and benefits, so turn ever so slowly. . . .

"It's very nice," Mairead said to Gold's face.

He just nodded. "The furniture's old, but it's solid, and these book-shelves ought to be enough for you. I've got file cabinets down in cold stor-age, you want them. Me, though, I like to be able to keep my eye on the cases, the way I have them in my office."

"I'll try it your way," said Mairead, conceding on something that didn't matter to her. "But we need to talk about terms and conditions."

Gold seemed a little thrown. "Terms and . . . ?"

"Conditions. Of my employment."

Grinning without showing any teeth, he checked his watch. "Tell you what. You move around in here some, get a feel for the place. Let me make a few phone calls, and we'll talk in ten, fifteen minutes. Okay?"

"Okay."

Mairead watched him walk out, closing the door behind him. As soon as it clicked shut, she jumped two feet in the air, spinning in a tight circle with her arms over her head like Sly Stallone did way back in his first *Rocky* movie.

In fact, it took several more spins before Mairead noticed something was missing from this office, too.

"RONA, Shel Gold . . . No, I'm fine, fine, thanks. You? . . . Good, glad to hear it. Listen, Rona, not to beat around the bush, I'm taking on a young lawyer, space-sharing but some salary, and I'm wondering what you're pay-

ing your new associates now. . . . Er, but that's including all kinds of benefits, like health—it's not? . . . Just straight salary, and beyond that is . . .
Right, right . . . No. No, Rona, I don't think so, either."

"EXCUSE me?"

Billie Sunday looked up at the new child standing in the doorway of Vincent's old office and tried to dredge up some sympathy for her. Can't be the
easiest thing in the world, having hands like somebody exposed to an
atomic bomb. "Yes?"

"I don't see any . . . computers?"

Billie tried to fight down her natural response, which would have been
along the lines of "How long you been working here, again?" Instead she
just said, "Computers?"

"Yes." The child couldn't seem to form her next question. "You know,
like for word processing, billing, on-line research?"

Billie lost the internal fight and pointed at the IBM Selectric III she'd been
using since coming on the job for Shel. "This is where most of our words get
processed." Then she pointed in the general direction of the safe behind
Shel's closed door. "The billing gets done upfront and in cash, because the
winners disappear, and the losers are making a dollar a day painting 'Massachusetts' on license plates." Then Billie pointed at the child's shoes. "And
honey, our research gets done a lot more on foot than on-line."

A look of shock. "There aren't *any* computers?"

Billie began to wonder how a body could finish high school, much less
law school, being such a slow study. "My oldest says half the homes in
America don't have personal computers."

Shocked gave way to curious. "How many kids do you and your husband have?"

Billie felt that pang, down deep in her chest. "We had three, but I've been
raising them on my own for a while now."

The child's face grew kind of sad, like there was something hurting inside
her, too. "Well, maybe computers is a topic we can talk about."

Billie sucked in a deep, deep breath, again fighting down what she
wanted to say. That she'd been working *for* a lawyer a lot longer than the

child had *been* a lawyer. That she'd scrimped and saved so her kids *could* have a PC at home, even if it was bought used and took a while to get things done. That lately she'd even taken to bringing Shel's handwritten briefs home with her to type on the computer and get her oldest to print them out at school so the courts—

Then Billie realized the child had asked another question. "What was that?"

"Voice mail," said Mairead, "so I can get phone messages. When I saw you writing on those pink slips, I realized that—"

"Our voice mail is that tape machine over there. Cost twenty-nine ninety-five at the Best Buy. Now, you got any more questions?"

"Just one," the child's voice a little edgy. "What should we call each other?"

Another change of gears. "Say your name for me again?"

She did.

Billie nodded. "I like 'Mairead' if you like 'Billie.'"

The child smiled, all warm and friendly now. "Then let's try it that way."

Billie smiled back just as warm and just as friendly, thinking, Honey, I hope you don't believe you're fooling me.

"So," said Sheldon Gold from the other side of his desk, "I've made some calls."

Mairead nodded, absently this time. She was still a bit stunned from talking with Billie Sunday, though less by the absence of computers in the office and more by the woman raising three children as a single parent on a receptionist/secretary's wages. Mairead herself had always wanted children, but after being brought up in an orphanage, she'd also vowed never to have them until she could afford to provide well for them.

"And here's what I can do, business-wise." Gold leaned back in his chair, the leather of the bustle at the top cracking even wider as his head pressed into it. "Use of the phones and Billie for your typing, plus twenty-five thousand a year and half the fee on any cases I refer to you."

Twenty-five. Less than a third of her salary at Jaynes & Ward.

Gold said, "Plus the office next door you've fallen in love with."

Bothered that he was dead-bang right about that, Mairead tried to stay on course. "Granted it's a nice office, but twenty-five thousand?"

"You told me in the Common you didn't have any student loans to repay."

"That's right, but—"

"And you don't have any family to support."

Mairead said, "At a job interview, you wouldn't have been able to ask me about those things. Or whether I was disabled or—"

"What we had on those benches wasn't exactly an interview."

"Not from my standpoint maybe, but it was from yours."

Gold grinned disarmingly, shrugging with his whole body, and Mairead sensed the man could be magic in front of juries.

"Got me." He came forward in the chair now, but loosely, like himself, instead of stiffly like Hadley Burgess back at Jaynes & Ward. "Okay, so what's your idea of salary?"

She told him.

Gold lost his grin. "Split the difference?"

Mairead waited a moment, then nodded a third time.

He smiled broadly now. "Sounds like we got a deal."

"Not quite."

Gold was already halfway out of his chair. "Not quite?"

"There's still insurance, right?"

"Insurance."

"Health, dental, malpractice . . ."

Mairead O'Clare felt a slight ping of satisfaction as she watched Sheldon Gold sink back into his chair.

WHAT have you done, unleash a monster?

Shel Gold watched the young woman across his desk use her fingers to tick off details of insurance coverages. Frankly, he already carried most of the policies—had them in place, thank God, before Natalie and . . . No, keep focused here.

Mairead was now deep into health insurance. Not surprising, thought Shel, what with the hemangioma that seemed to creep up from her hands

onto their wrists whenever her sleeve cuffs slipped during a gesture she made. Hemangioma, from "heme" meaning blood and "angio" meaning vessel. A doctor friend from the old neighborhood in Chelsea once told Shel about the condition, how it usually was just a small birthmark, like the port-wine stain Gorbachev had on his forehead.

But admit it: This Mairead is different in another way, too. She projects an aura of . . . resolve, that was the word. Shel had seen it in a lot of the girls he'd grown up with, the smart ones that got shunted off by even Jewish parents toward teaching or nursing, something she could fall back on if—God forbid—something happened to the husband/breadwinner. But Shel hadn't seen Mairead's kind of resolve shown by many younger lawyers in the courtroom, and he wondered if it came to her more from the hemangioma side or the orphanage side of—

"Shel?"

"Sorry?"

Mairead's deep blue eyes were like lasers. "All that's left is malpractice coverage."

"Go ahead."

About five minutes later, Shel had made up his mind which case he was going to start Mairead on, but he waited five more until she said, "Well, I think that's everything."

"Okay. Now that we've got your 'terms and conditions' squared away, time for your first assignment."

Mairead blinked. "I, uh, don't have any of my things from the firm over here yet."

"All you'll need for this is your Board of Bar Overseers card, a photo ID, and one pad and two pencils—in case you break a point taking notes."

A curious look. "Notes about what?"

"Client I took on, pretty much *pro bono*. He's being held without bail at Nashua Street, and I want you to interview him."

Shel thought he saw curious grow a little excited.

Mairead said, "Held without bail?"

"Capital case. A homeless man, charged with clubbing another one to death along the Charles River."

Mairead's eyes glowed now. "The news story on TV about the guy who claims he's a hermit?"

"That's him. And Alpha is the only name he goes by." Shel paused. "You remember anything else about the case?"

He watched Mairead shake her head, but slowly, as though she was really trying to bring more back but just couldn't.

"Good," said Shel. "I want you to talk with him before reading the police report or any of my file."

Now a puzzled expression on her face. "Why?"

"Because, you're going to learn how to try cases, you've got to gauge the client on a first impression, not already pigeonhole or stereotype the man or woman in a way that closes your mind to imaginative ways of representing him or her. Or to how he or she's going to look and sound in front of a jury."

Shel could see Mairead was taken aback. Exactly the reaction you'd hoped for, too. She wants to learn from a Perry Mason, show her you've got some things to teach.

"So," said Mairead, "I just kind of meet with him?"

"Toward gauging him, though. Then come back and tell me your take on him, especially as a witness, if we need to call him."

The eyes glowed brighter. "You mean, to the stand during trial?"

"Stranger things have happened."

Mairead seemed to have more questions to ask, but Shel could tell she also believed it was time for her to hop on this first task. Which he liked, judgment-wise.

After Mairead rose from her chair and went into the foyer, Shel decided he'd made a good choice of her as associate and this homicide case as training ground. On the other hand, it probably wouldn't hurt to call ahead, let the jail know she was coming.

Shel was turned to the bay window, phone cradled on his shoulder, when he heard a faint knocking behind him. Swinging around in his chair, he saw Mairead hesitating at the threshold to his office.

"Go ahead," Shel said to her. "Nobody's picked up yet."

Mairead nodded. "Uh, Billie's not out here."

"She's always in by eight, so she takes an early lunch."

Another nod, but weaker somehow. "At the firm, Shel, I worked just on civil cases."

"Not a problem. Call this one *Commonwealth versus Alpha.*"

"That isn't what I meant."

"So . . . ?"

Shel watched Mairead take a breath, then blow it out in a way that ruffled a few strands of her auburn hair before turning into a bleak smile. "So, can you tell me how I get to this Nashua Street from here?"

Shel kept any smile from his face, but he could feel something solid and warm and genuine welling inside him. Then Sheldon A. Gold brought himself up short.

You sad, lonely schmuck, you'd better remember: There's no fool like an old fool.

3

WALKING DOWN THE BACKSLOPE of Beacon Hill past Cambridge Street, Mairead's excitement over having her first case involving "real" people—and a *homicide* yet—was tempered by her shoes already being covered with cement dust from Boston's Big Dig. The construction project had been started before she'd begun her law studies three and a half years before, but the third tunnel under the harbor to Logan Airport was the only part completed so far. Mairead knew it would be a more functional city once the elevated, multilaned Central Artery was dropped below street level. She only hoped that on her new-and-reduced salary she'd be able to afford enough black leather pumps to weather the siege.

Three Jersey-barriered work sites later, Mairead was standing before a modern building that looked to her more like a high school than a jail. Reddish brick and five stories high in some places, with a ramp leading up to the front entrance.

Inside the lobby were banks of orange lockers and rows of black-wire chairs like a bus station. Mairead thought a couple of the people sitting and waiting resembled the rinkrats who would come to watch her play hockey.

Then the uniformed deputy behind a thick glass window said, "Help you?"

She cleared her throat, she hoped of just cement dust. "I'm attorney Mairead O'Clare, here to see a client."

The deputy—not much older than Mairead—gave her a nice smile, saying, "We had a call you were coming. Bar card?"

Mairead fished in her tote bag for her wallet. "Here you go," then realized as she extended the card that there was no opening in the glass for passing anything.

Before Mairead could display any more ignorance, a tray like one under a bank's drive-in window slid out to her. She laid her bar card in it.

On the other side of the window, the deputy retrieved the card and wrote on something Mairead couldn't see. "Ms. O'Clare, some photo ID?"

Mairead was ready this time with her laminated driver's license and put that in the tray, too.

The deputy compared the photo to Mairead. Then he clipped the card and her license together. "Now your bag, please?"

She thought back to what Shel Gold had told her. "I'm going to need a pad and pencils."

"Take them out before putting your bag in the drawer. Or you can use one of those lockers."

Mairead glanced over at the orange bins, then figured the deputy might be safer. Not to mention he really was pretty cute, and it'd give her another chance to talk with him on the way out.

"FIRST time here?" said the deputy, riding up in the elevator with Mairead, her pad, and her pencils.

She'd been looking down at where he'd stamped her hand with invisible ink—even on the hemangioma—before passing it under a special lamp. "Yes, my first."

"It's not so bad, especially compared to the old Bird Cage at Charles Street."

Mairead had no idea what he meant.

The deputy spread his hands. "We've got real conference rooms now, with new tables and chairs. Attorney-client confidentiality assured, but also a panic button on the wall."

"Panic button?"

"In case you need us more than your client needs you."

Mairead could sense the deputy smiling differently—patronizingly—

beside her, and she decided she wouldn't try to talk with him on the way out after all.

"AMAZING country, this. They assign you a lawyer-lass that could pass for your own cousin."

In the eight-by-eight room, a corridor door to her back, Mairead had watched Alpha be led by a different deputy through the door from what sounded like a fraternity house behind them. Her first client—well, *Shel's* client, technically—had dark brown hair that rose less than an inch above and around his entire scalp, making him seem younger than the thirty-five or so she'd have guessed and, until he spoke, maybe a little mentally slow, like the kid with the banjo at the beginning of that old movie *Deliverance*. He was only about five-ten, but blocky, the sort of tough guy who'd try too hard to make the football team when he just wasn't big enough. The eyes on either side of the broken nose were a jumpy green, though, and Mairead thought they'd give a "Don't mess with me" message to anybody bothering to read them.

Which means, young lady, that even if he didn't kill the other homeless man, he might be capable of—

"Even more amazing, I've drawn a lawyer who doesn't herself like to talk."

Mairead laughed in spite of Sister Bernadette's warning in her head, and the man's don't-mess eyes twinkled now, like a kid in third grade about to throw a spitball. The nun's voice, though softer, still said, *Beware, Mairead. He's got more than a bit of the devil in him.*

There being no screening or glass separating them across the table, she extended her right hand to the man. "I'm attorney Mairead O'Clare."

"Ah, a lovely name, befitting its owner." He looked down at her hand, then took it. Warmly, even gently, like Shel Gold had in the Common. "You've quite the beauty marks, don't you?"

"Not how I think of them," Mairead replied reflexively.

"You should, though, you should. They're what highlight your attractiveness, make you distinctive and real."

Steady, young lady. This isn't a blind date. "Mr. Alpha, I—"

"Ah, no. Sorry for the interruption, lass, but it's just plain Alpha, as in 'the first.' I'd thought about using the opening letter of the Gaelic alphabet. But it's pronounced simply *Ah* in the lovely lilt of our Emerald Isle, and therefore regrettably isn't sufficiently well known in this adopted homeland to catch the ear of a likely listener."

Mairead said, "Listener to what?"

"To the creed. Of our New Order of Celtic hermits."

He pronounced it "*Kell*-tick," and Mairead found more of the TV-news story filtering back into her mind. "Making you the leader of this new order."

"The very same. Though given the depths of our ranks so far, I'm currently what you might call self-anointed."

"Meaning, you're not just the first, but also the . . . only?"

"Exactly so. For the time being, that is."

A closed-mouth grin now, but a nice one, like the one the deputy originally showed Mairead downstairs. A demented smile would fit Alpha's words a little better, she thought, but strangely she didn't feel at all afraid of him.

Mairead said, "I've been asked to talk with you about what happened."

"By the older lawyer, that fine Jewish feller?"

She decided to take the religious allusion as description, not slur. "Yes."

"Well," said Alpha, folding his arms across his chest more casually than defensively. "Ask away."

Mairead thought back to her Evidence course at New England, the professor lecturing about initial dealings with real-world clients. "Since I'll be helping Mr. Gold on your case, everything you tell me is confidential."

"Heartening."

Okay. "Let's start with some background."

"Background? Well, lass, I come from a family of tinkers."

"Of what?"

"Ah, and here I thought, despite your Yank accent, that you might have had at least *some* grounding in the heritage."

"My name's Irish, and my parents probably were, but I was raised in an orphanage."

Alpha seemed a bit jolted. "My condolences, Mairead."

"Thanks, but I'm over it."

"Somehow, I think not." Alpha straightened in his chair. "However, you're wanting my background. The tinkers in Ireland are something like the Gypsies, in that we've been moving around the countryside since the Vikings began toughening our gene pool. For centuries, we mended the pots and pans of highborn folk, carrying all we owned on two-wheeled carts drawn by horses. Was a time we were even treated passingly well, aside from accusations regarding an occasional seduction. But now we're persecuted more than tolerated, although I hear the local councils have become polite enough of late to refer to us as 'travelers.'"

This, young lady, is not going to be easy. "Alpha, by 'background,' I meant—"

"More recent events, of course. Well, there's a bit of a story to that, too, actually. We tinkers developed our own language over the years, you see. It's called 'shelte' by some, and 'gammon' by others. We invented it because the kindly English masters who lorded over our country forbade us to speak Irish—what you probably think of as Gaelic—in their presence. Even made our schoolchildren wear 'tally sticks' around their necks, and every time the poor lass or lad would let slip a word of our own lovely tongue, the teacher would cut a notch in that stick, then settle up at the end of the day with a switch whipping across the hands or bottom until the poor child would cry tears righteous as Holy Water."

Mairead put down her pencil. No need to question this guy in a courtroom. Shel can just put him on the stand, and he'll talk until the judge'll beg to let him off, just for the prospect of peace and quiet.

"But Mairead, I don't notice you taking copious notes, so I'm thinking it's my *most* recent past you're really wanting."

"Somewhere around the last couple of months would be nice."

She watched him grin. "I think I'm going to enjoy your representing me, lass."

Picking up her pencil again, Mairead found herself hoping she'd be able to say the same. "How did you come to be in the Boston area?"

"Well, I can't very well give out many details of that now, can I?"

Mairead sensed herself squinting at him. "Why not?"

"Because it's the sort of information that could lead the kindly authorities here to figuring out who I used to be."

"Used to be."

"Before I established our New Order."

Mairead took a breath. "Alpha, as I said before, everything you tell me is confidential."

"Ah, and I'm sure you'd keep your word on that, Mairead O'Clare. However, I'm also sure you'd try to use whatever I told you in your grand efforts to help me, and that might tip the kindly coppers to my past."

"But if you've been convicted of a prior crime, the prosecutor can—"

"Not to worry, lass. The first time I've ever been even fingerprinted was when a fine Chinese officer arrested me this December last."

The first . . . ? "Meaning, you weren't printed when you entered the States?"

Mairead watched Alpha close his eyes and seem to laugh internally. "Very nicely done, Mairead. You've caught me like a hare in a snare. But I'm afraid your cleverness just reaffirms my position."

"What position?"

"Me keeping mum about my background." Alpha became more animated. "You see, a hermit's only duty is to living the present day, pleasing himself with what its hours might bring his way."

"Bring his way?"

"When he leaves his cave in the cliff, lass."

Better and better. "And where is your . . . cave?"

"Ah, in a lovely spot, snug-under an abutment near your River Charles."

Mairead let him give her specific directions to what she wouldn't have called exactly "cliff" country. Then she said, "So, you live under a bridge?"

"Well, lass, not every hermit's cave can be fashioned naturally by the hand of God now, can it?"

"Okay, Alpha, I'll give you the cave part. What I—"

"Ah, lass, sorry to be interrupting again, but nobody 'gives' a hermit anything. That's part of our vocational philosophy, you might say. We take what we need when we need it, like I did with Old Man River's fine overcoat."

The nickname the newscasts used for the decedent. "You admit stealing his coat."

A frown. "Since to a great extent I was wearing that warm garment to save its prior possessor from himself, I think 'acquired' might be a better description."

The even better description "bullshit" leaped to mind, but Mairead kept it there. "Save him?"

"Naturally." Alpha's eyes flashed now. "Old Man River wasn't a well man, and worse, he wasn't exactly beloved by all who made his acquaintance. I'd attribute that to his behavior, I would."

"What behavior?"

"Oh, he'd oft be cursing or pushing or throwing various hurtful objects their way."

"Whose way, Alpha?"

"The 'Blighters,' he called them. Normal enough folk whose idea of enjoying the watershed departed from his own."

Mairead tried to put it together. "So, by 'acquiring' this man's coat in the cold of December, you were actually keeping him from walking around and confronting people who might have hurt him?"

"And did hurt him, I'm guessing."

"Because . . . ?"

"Lass, maybe you should be taking more notes." Now the twinkle returned as Alpha lounged. "I do believe these are motives why others might have wanted the poor soul dead."

"By smashing his head in with your club."

"My Holy Shillelagh was simply handy for the killer."

"Any names?" Mairead turning to a fresh page in her pad.

"Ah, you'd be best off asking the kindly police that one, I think. A hermit doesn't tend to seek out conversation with unfortunates like Old Man River."

Mairead shook her head. All those years in the orphanage, the one thing I wanted was the companionship and support of others in a family structure, and here's this happy-go-lucky charmer intentionally cutting himself off from a version of that.

But while he's eccentric, young lady, said Sister Bernadette, *you don't think he's certifiably crazy. And more, there's something about him, an . . . empathy, perhaps? Like when he seemed touched—even saddened—by your being in an orphanage.*

Go with it. "Alpha, it seems to me that you cared enough about Old Man River to try and save him from being hurt."

"A moral gesture, lass, not a fast friendship."

"You never even followed him or anything?"

"A hermit doesn't think of himself as his brother's keeper."

Mairead found herself running out of questions. "Based on what you've told me so far, I'm not sure Mr. Gold and I will be able to get bail for you."

A laugh. "And who'd be wanting you to?"

"What?"

"I prefer it here."

"Here." Mairead swiveled her head around, as though she could see through the tiny room's walls. "You mean, in jail?"

"This fine new edifice isn't so different from an Irish cliff, and the cells remind me of a honeycomb of caves. As an accused murderer, I'm kept in one all by myself, with a mattress that stays dry, water that runs hot and cold, and three meals a day, all provided free of charge." Mairead watched Alpha run a palm over his brush-cut hair. "Oh, I grant you, the kindly guards scalped me of a nice head of locks as though I was a lamb being shorn, supposedly because those very locks themselves provided a wet-nursery for lice. And the meals here wouldn't put Black Pudding Roisin or Dublin Coddle to shame. But on the whole, solitary confinement in a solid stone environment is a fair version of every hermit's dream come true."

Mairead waited—or waded—through that. "So, you like being where you are."

"I do, though if you could possibly bring me some of my library, I'd be that much closer to heaven on earth."

"Your . . . library?"

"Books, in my cave, and philosophy tomes, most of them. But any you could gather up would do."

"Let me get this straight, Alpha." Mairead tapped her pencil on the pad. "You'd rather read philosophy and feed me little lessons on Irish culture than help in your own defense?"

Grin and twinkle. "I knew there'd be a worthy brain inside that lovely head."

Mairead thought back to law school again. "Okay, then. Maybe the District Attorney's Office will offer some kind of deal."

Another frown. "You mean, ask the kindly prosecutor about me pleading guilty?"

"It's an option."

"Sorry, lass. Not a worthy one, I'm afraid."

"Why not?"

"Because a hermit mustn't lie to those trying to help him."

Mairead flipped back a page on her pad. "I thought you said before that a hermit never seeks help."

"Indeed, and we don't. But when a soul offers that help freely, like you here or the fine construction boss who gave me scrap lumber to build my cave? Why, we stay loyal to the person involved, and that includes not lying to them."

"Alpha, I don't get you."

He spoke more slowly. "You're trying to help me, correct?"

"I'm trying. You're not."

Another twinkle. "But that's my very point, you see."

"What is?"

"You've been dragooned by your kindly justice system into representing me, you and your fine Mr. Gold. And I greatly admire all your efforts. But I'd rather stay the man that I am."

"Which means?"

"I can't lie to you, Mairead O'Clare. I didn't crack open Old Man River's skull for him."

"You're innocent."

"As the driven snow. And I'll not be pleading guilty to a crime I never committed, even if there's no death penalty in your fine state."

Mairead laid down her pencil. "You didn't do the killing, but you won't help us prove that."

Alpha smiled, openmouthed for the first time, only five teeth total left in his jaws. "Now you've tumbled to it."

"SO, what'd you think of our client?" said Shel Gold, settling into the bustle-backed desk chair that had come to fit his body like an old shoe does an arthritic foot.

"*Your* client," replied Mairead O'Clare, looking frustrated as she took a seat in front of him.

"He rubbed you the wrong way?"

"Shel, I'm excited about working with you, especially on a murder case. Honest. But Alpha's impossible."

"How?"

Shel watched the young woman try to keep her frustration from turning into temper. That's all right, though. The ones with no fire, they're hard to light. The ones with fire, they can be . . . adjusted, to burn just right. What poor Vincent—

Mairead said, "Alpha won't even help in his own defense."

"He gave me that line, too." Then the older lawyer paused. "You think our client did the crime?"

Shel watched Mairead. Watched her struggle with something other than frustration this time. Pride, if you're lucky. A passion beyond that if she's one of the truly—

"No," said Mairead. "I don't think he did."

"Because Alpha told you so?"

"Because the man didn't do it, period."

"You sensed that," said Shel.

"I just know it."

"Would a jury 'sense' or 'know' the same way?"

"Your reason for having me visit the guy, to gauge him?"

"Yes."

Shel liked that Mairead took a moment before speaking again. "He's a talker," she said. "A storyteller who paints pictures in the air with his words."

Admit it: Your take on him, too. "But . . . ?"

"But Alpha won't tell me his real name, or anything about his background, other than this fairy tale about being kind of a nomad in Ireland before entering the U.S. illegally."

Shel felt himself perk up a little. "That's more than he told me, though it's consistent with the police not reporting any immigration papers when they searched his cave."

"Oh, and he wants me to stop by there, bring him some of his philosophy books."

Shel suppressed a smile. "The prosecutor—Pereira's his name, and a decent man—told me the Homicide Unit's released the cave as a crime scene, so I think that would be all right." Then Shel shifted in his chair. "Do you trust him, Mairead?"

"Who, Alpha?"

"Yes."

She took another moment. "I believe him, but I'm not sure I trust him."

Shel nodded. "A touch of the snake-oil salesman?"

"Snake oil?"

Shel sighed, but only inwardly. "Like you wouldn't swallow his claims without some kind of proof."

"Exactly," said Mairead. "Only, how are we supposed to find that proof, if Alpha won't help us?"

"There's an investigator I use sometimes." Shel started rummaging through the crapola on his desk, not optimistic about finding the telephone number. "Lives on a boat in the harbor."

"A boat," said Mairead in the deadpan monotone that so many women in her generation seemed to have. Shel thought the attitude might now be taught during some required course in school.

Probably whichever one replaced History and Geography.

"Shel?" said Mairead in a more distinct voice.

He gave up on his desk. "Is Billie out there?"

"Guess she's not back from lunch yet."

Shel nodded again. "Well, you found the jail, it'll be even easier for you to find him."

"Your investigator, now?"

"Yes." Shel gave Mairead the name of a waterfront restaurant. "He's the fifth or sixth parking space toward the ocean."

"What's his boat called?"

"Billie would know, but it's blue and white, a good forty feet long."

"How about your investigator's name?"

"Pontifico Murizzi."

"Spelled?"

Shel went through it for her. "His nickname's the Pope."

Mairead seemed to take that in stride before saying, "And Mr. Murizzi might be able to help us?"

"He might. Used to be on the Boston Homicide Unit."

Shel saw Mairead's eyes widen. "A retired police detective?"

"Kind of retired."

Now a canting of her head. "Why did this 'kind of retired' detective leave the department?"

"I think you should ask him. It's an interesting story."

Mairead, obviously confused, nevertheless nodded. And in fact, as Shel Gold handed her the file on Alpha, he actually envied her in a way, getting to hear the Pope tell his tale for the first time.

"THAT new child's stomping down the hall toward the elevator like she's off to kill somebody her ownself."

In their office foyer, Billie Sunday started taking her coat off as her boss pulled his on.

Shel—with that little homey grin he's got—said, "I think Mairead's going to work out fine for us."

"She coming back today?"

"Not sure. I sent her off to see the Pope."

Billie pictured that spooky man and shivered. "About what?"

"Things she learned talking to Alpha."

Hunh. "Your new child talks to that weird ex-cop the same day as your crazy hermit, she may not be back ever."

Billie watched her boss reach for the Kangol cap he kept on a hook behind his office door. From the way his face sagged just a bitty-bit, she knew where he was going.

"Shel?"

He turned, the cap halfway to his head.

Billie said, "You tell that child about your situation?"

One of his blank looks now, like a toddler who knows he's been bad but isn't sure just how much his momma's found out. "Regarding my owning this building, you mean?"

"Regarding everything, I mean."

Her boss slid past her to the suite door and opened it. "The young woman's first day, Billie. Best to break her in slowly, don't you think?"

As the door to the corridor closed behind Sheldon A. Gold, Billie Sunday said a silent little prayer for the toddler-man with more cross on his shoulders than most had to bear.

4

OVER TWO HOURS AND a monster Starbucks latte, Mairead
read Shel's file on Alpha—including a scary, black-and-white photocopy of
his mug shot with hair both long and ucky. After walking in early dusk to
the harborside restaurant, she made her way down a set of planked steps to
a narrow dock that ran along the wharf pilings. The dock actually seemed
more a catwalk, servicing the sterns of big boats, both motor and sail. To
her surprise, the dock swayed under her feet.

Pontoons, young lady. So it can rise and fall with the tide.

Mairead came upon a blue-and-white sailboat, a guy in his early twenties
using a rag to rub some kind of compound from a can into the woodwork
near the mast. Never great at estimating distance, Mairead thought the vessel might be forty feet long.

"Excuse me?"

The guy turned, his hair short but spiky, with dark roots and a brassy
dye job on the tips. The light from piling lanterns was good enough to make
out handsome—if "pretty-boy"—features.

"What can I do for you, luv?"

English accent, friendly tone. "Is this Mr. Murizzi's boat?"

"The Pope's? No, try this next one on."

The guy inclined his head toward a large motorboat.

"Thanks," said Mairead.

"Right," replied the guy, like one of those comedians on the old Monty
Python shows.

Mairead moved on, thinking it a bummer, the way cute men had to screw up their appearance with the punk look.

The motorboat, also blue and white, was more what Mairead would call a houseboat, calligraphic lettering on its stern reading THE NORTH END. The boat had a wide lower deck facing the dock and at about the same height, with a couple of folding lawn chairs and a little white resin table. There was a ten-rung ladder going up to a bridge with two chairs on posts and a steering wheel mounted into the dash. On the lower deck level, Mairead could see a sliding glass door leading to the cabin area, a drape drawn but with a light on behind it.

"Hello?" called out Mairead.

From above her, the English guy said, "You look harmless enough, luv. I doubt the Pope'll shoot you for going aboard."

Mairead hitched her handbag up on her shoulder, put one hand on the near side of the hull, and vaulted like she was going over the boards from the bench in a hockey game.

She'd just regained her balance on the deck when the glass door slid open and a drop-dead gorgeous, Richard Gere clone in shorts and a T-shirt pointed a big, silver handgun at her.

"Then again," said the English guy. "I've been wrong before."

The man Mairead assumed was Murizzi glanced up at him, then stared at her. "Who the fuck are you?"

She forced some air into her lungs. "Mairead O'Clare. I started working with Sheldon Gold this morning, and he sent me to see you."

"Without any warning?"

"The guy next door said it'd be okay."

"Jocko just likes the sight of other people's blood."

Mairead motioned toward the door. "Well, can I come in?"

Murizzi lowered the muzzle of his weapon, then held back the drape with his free hand so Mairead could pass through. Going by him, she guessed the Pope to be four or so inches taller than her five-seven, which should match up their bodies just right for slow-dancing. And he wore some kind of aftershave that was musky without being oppressive.

This is a business meeting, young lady, said Sister Bernadette's voice. *Not a law-school mixer.*

Mairead would have described the cabin's interior as a spacious apartment's living room if she'd been brought to it blindfolded, especially compared to her studio on Beacon Hill. Some sectional furniture with nubby, oatmeal upholstery and two polished end tables were positioned functionally in the foreground of a breakfast counter and small kitchen. The walls had recessed shelves like the ones in Shel's office, but these held an eclectic library of paperbacks. Given how the temperature had dropped with the sun, Mairead thought the room felt a little chilly.

Murizzi said, "Have a seat."

She saw a book opened facedown on one table, so Mairead took a sectional piece across from it. Then she watched Murizzi lower himself gracefully into the one by the table. In good light, he really *did* look like a forty-something Richard Gere, though the hair was all black and more wavy. But the cheekbones were there, along with piercing brown eyes—no cocker spaniel, this one. More like a vampire, except with olive skin, good muscle tone, and just the right amount of hair on his forearms and legs.

Mairead suddenly realized she was staring.

Murizzi grinned without showing any teeth. "You want to take off your coat?"

"Not yet." *Recover your composure, young lady.* "Aren't you cold?"

"My body temperature runs a couple degrees above normal." Murizzi glanced toward a breakfast counter to his right. "How about something to drink?"

Stick to business. "No, thanks."

A nod. "Anxious to get on with the case, huh?"

Great. Another older guy who can read my mind.

Murizzi changed his expression. "Shel tell you how I work?"

"Just that you were a private investigator."

"Nothing else?"

Mairead decided she didn't want to start her relationship with the Pope by lying to him. "Shel said you were 'kind of retired' from the police, but that you'd tell me your story."

She expected another grin, maybe even a smile. Instead Murizzi closed his eyes for a moment and clasped his hands like a sinner about to pray.

In a quieter voice, he said, "I was on the Boston P.D. for twenty-one years, Homicide Unit the last nine. Never once had a qualm about anybody I put away. Then we nailed this guy solid on a home invasion felony–murder—I mean eyewitness to access, prints, the works. Like everybody else, he kept claiming he was innocent. Twenty years old, but with baby-blue eyes and a blond cowlick, our defendant looked maybe twelve, especially when he started crying about how he knew the victim and wouldn't ever hurt her. We laughed about him, me and the other detectives in the unit. Only even while I was laughing, I had this little worm inside me." Murizzi hiked a thumb toward his belly. "And it twisted around and around every time I talked with the guy, even when I just looked at him. But I didn't do anything about it."

Mairead felt herself wanting to help the man sitting in front of her. "Isn't that why we have trials?"

"What I kept saying to myself, both before and after I testified. And the DA's office got a guilty verdict within two hours of the judge giving the case to the jury."

Murizzi cleared his throat. "A guy goes away—to prison, I mean—and you kind of lose track of him. Out of sight, out of mind, you know?"

"Yes."

"Well, a couple months down the road, our defendant hangs himself. Leaves a note saying he couldn't face the prospect of doing life while being punked—raped—by every hard con in his cellblock." Murizzi's voice dropped almost to a whisper. "Two weeks later, we collar a different guy some homeowner shoots during another invasion. The new boy turns out to have our female victim's car keys from the first case still in his van."

Jesus Mary, thought Mairead, and for a moment wasn't positive she hadn't said it aloud.

Murizzi looked up. "Only the new boy tells us he wants a good deal on his plea bargain, because otherwise he sings to the media about how we got the wrong guy dead. The DA goes along hush-hush, it being an election year and all." Murizzi looked down at his hands. "I put in my papers right after that."

"To retire."

"And to get my private license, to work heavy cases for Shel and a couple other lawyers. But on one condition."

"Which is?"

Murizzi said, "I've got to believe the defendant's innocent."

Mairead processed that, trying not to let her attraction to the private investigator fog her thinking. "Ours is."

She watched the Pope exhale, then lean back into his chair.

He said, "Persuade me."

SHELDON Gold got off the Green Line trolley eleven blocks before his apartment in Brookline. There were closer stops, but on nights like this, when he could leave work early enough, Shel liked to visit.

If they'd let him.

He crossed Beacon Street and headed south until the looming granite building appeared around a curve. It'd been built when the roads were still unpaved, and as the town had to widen them for increased car traffic, the yard in front had grown shallower. Shel knew this because of some old photos in the director's office. But if the front yard was now not enough to be called "grounds," the backyard of the old estate was still spectacular, especially when the maintenance staff brought into bloom the flower beds that bordered the high stone walls.

Admit it: You're unlucky enough to need this kind of place in your life, you could do a lot worse.

Shel reached the entrance, climbing the steps before pushing the button set into the jamb. He took off his Kangol cap and looked up at the security camera, trying to smile for whoever it was had to spend their working hours looking into faces like his. Then there was the sound of a key in the lock on the other side of the door, and five hundred pounds of oak—Shel had actually been there when it took three strong men to rehang it—swung open.

"Mr. Gold, so good to see you again."

Shel nodded to the aide, a plump young woman with mousy brown hair but kind eyes through glasses thick enough to distort her irises. Shel would

have remembered her name, even without the *Doreen* stitched in script on her lemon-yellow jumpsuit.

Funny how the movies show them dressed in white jackets and skirts, more like jaunty garage mechanics than old-time nurses.

Shel said, "Doreen, you weren't here the last time."

"No, I haven't seen you for at least a few weeks, I think."

A part of Shel didn't want the small talk to end, but Doreen turned and led him down the cavernous entry hall, his shoes sounding like the clopping of a horse on the marble tiles while her sneakers only whispered.

At the corridor to the West Wing, Doreen said, "And now to the right," as though Shel hadn't been coming there for nearly twenty years. "And now to the left."

Maybe it reassures people, the first time they visit.

Doreen stopped at a door, normal in size but still solid. "I'll just wait right out here."

"Thank you," said Shel, meaning it. Then he drew in a deep breath and knocked, opening the door without waiting for a reply.

"Shel, darling! I've been wondering where you were off to."

The only person in the tastefully furnished room rose to her feet while muting the boom box next to her chair. The mournful strains of solo piano—Mendelssohn?—still carried to him.

"I had to stay at the office, Natalie. Finish up a case."

He watched his smiling wife wag her index finger at him. "Oh, that's what you always say."

Almost fifty, she still had a face that could break Shel's heart. The first time he ever saw her, Natalie was standing sideways, her face in profile like a Victorian cameo. But full-front was even more so: lush, chestnut hair framing green eyes that turned up just slightly at the corners and full lips parted in a half-smile. Someone—maybe Doreen—had picked out a plaid skirt and apricot turtleneck that hid the needle marks on—

"Well, aren't you going to give your house-spouse a kiss?"

Shel moved toward her, kissing his wife chastely on the mouth while she threw her arms up and around his neck, pressing into him with both breasts and hips.

Natalie broke the kiss but not the embrace, nestling those full lips into Shel's throat below his right ear. "How about a little afternoon delight before Richie gets home from school?"

Shel willed himself not to cringe. "We won't have time."

Natalie let go now, cuffing her husband on the bicep. "Spoilsport." Then, in a different tone, "So, tell me about your day."

Shel followed her to the other chair in the sitting area. They were both barrel-style and made of vinyl—easier to wash, he remembered the director telling him so many years before. The table had no lamp, but the track fixture out of reach in the high ceiling above cast a warm glow that included the queen-sized bed behind their chairs. Which was good, since not much sunlight penetrated the heavy curtains masking the bars on both windows.

"Shel, your day?"

He told her about Alpha, Natalie scolding him for taking on *another* charity case—"I don't know why you keep at this criminal junk." He told her about Mairead, which pleased more than provoked—"Just don't be getting any 'May/December' ideas, mister." He told her about what he had for lunch, and who he spoke to by telephone, and what songs a talented guitarist had been playing on the Park Street Under platform. Just a kid, but—

"Speaking of kids," said Natalie suddenly. "I wonder what could be keeping Richie?"

Shel tried to move her off that. "I think I might get some tickets for the Celtics next—"

"How can you be talking about a *bas*ketball game when our son is missing?"

Her voice was only a little louder.

"Natalie, he's not—"

"Don't you *dare* contradict me! I think I know when my own child is gone."

Now she was shouting.

"Natalie—"

"You were the one, you bastard! Everybody says so. *You* were the one who left Richie in that stroller! *You* were the one who didn't want to bother the police! You, *you*, YOU!"

Shel raised his own voice. "Doreen?"

His wife was on her feet now, fists on hips, full into her fury. "You worthless piece of shit, you motherfucking worthless cocksucker! You lost our Richie, and you won't even admit it to his own *mother*?"

Out of the corner of his eye, Shel had registered Doreen slipping into the room. She now laced her forearms very gently at the crooks of Natalie's elbows, applying pressure just as Shel's wife tried to claw him with nails that were kept clipped to the cuticle against such a contingency.

"I'm going to gouge your fucking eyes out for what you did to our son, for what you did to *me*. Oh, you motherfucker, you're going to burn in whatever hell I can send—"

Doreen said, "I think maybe now."

Shel got up, keeping his distance. "I'm so sorry, Natalie."

"Sorry? Well, cocksucker, *sorry* doesn't fucking cut it. Sorry isn't going to bring Richie back. Sorry doesn't mean *shit*!"

Shel could still hear Natalie after he closed the door behind him.

No, admit it: You can always hear her, wherever you happen to be.

PONTIFICO Murizzi said, "Anything else?"

Mentally, Mairead O'Clare went over everything she'd told him during the prior twenty minutes from both Shel's file and her interview. Everything about why she believed Alpha to be innocent. But, if the Pope really felt as he'd described earlier, what Mairead believed didn't matter.

She suddenly realized that Murizzi was fixing her with those dangerous, vampire eyes.

"No," Mairead said, "I think that's the best I can do."

The man came forward in his chair, working his hands again but more like he was lathering with invisible soap. "Boiling it down, what you've got is a derelict—"

"Homeless man."

"—who has means, thanks to the club; motive, thanks to the victim's coat; and opportunity, thanks to living a ball toss from the killing ground. But no alibi, and no desire to help in his own defense, am I right?"

"You're right."

"And this is what makes you think he didn't do the other—"

"Homeless man. Right again."

"I was still on the job, this'd be a real bunny."

Mairead caught herself blinking. "A . . . bunny?"

"Shoptalk for an open-and-shut case. The Homicide Unit had somebody who fits the bill like this Alpha, we wouldn't spend a lot of tax dollars turning over other rocks."

"Just like the case that made you quit the force. And all the more reason why we need you."

Murizzi's features changed from skeptical to pensive, and Mairead thought he might be coming to a decision. She also sensed that if she lost this argument, there wouldn't be much else she could do to help Alpha on Sheldon Gold's behalf.

Murizzi said, "Let me sleep on it, and I'll get back to you."

Mairead didn't want to push her luck. "Okay if I tell Mr. Gold that?"

"Do you call him by his last name?"

"No."

"Good." Murizzi stood up. "Hate to think Shel was going fogey in his old age."

Mairead rose as well. "What should I call you?" she said, trying not to put a flirty edge on it.

Murizzi extended his hand. She shook with him, feeling a near electric charge ripple up her arm.

He said, "Everybody just uses 'Pope.' I'm used to it."

"But do you prefer it?"

"Yeah," he said, a little begrudgingly as he led her back to the sliding glass door. "Yeah, I suppose I do."

"Well, I'm Muh-*raid,* and I don't have any nicknames I like."

"Too bad."

"Too bad?"

"Right," said Murizzi as they stepped onto the lower deck of the boat. "Nicknames—whatever lays them on you—they can help round you out as a person."

Hitching her handbag again, Mairead vaulted back over the side of the

boat onto the dock, grateful that her earlier trial run let her land a little more gracefully now that the Pope was watching. She willed herself to simply walk away without looking back, but then Murizzi spoke her name like a question.

Turning, Mairead said, "Yes?"

"Sometime ask Shel to tell you his story, too. Okay?"

"Okay."

"And some other time after that?"

"Yes?"

"You tell me yours."

Mairead watched maybe the most compelling man she'd met in the last five years saunter back into his living room and slide the door shut. In fact, she was almost at the harborside restaurant steps before realizing she couldn't remember Pontifico "the Pope" Murizzi looking down at her hands.

Not even once.

J U S T inside the front door, Sheldon Gold let his one-eyed cat stretch its front claws on the tops of his loafers.

So they leave some little marks. He's home alone all day, and maybe this helps him deal with it.

Shel had walked from the Estate—he didn't like to call it an "asylum" or a "sanatorium," even in his own head—to a good deli three blocks past his apartment house. He bought smoked turkey on caraway rye, mustard and lettuce but no tomato: it'd make the bread soggy before he'd get around to eating it.

That was because Shel didn't like to wolf down his food as soon as he got home. Thought it was bad for the digestion. Instead he followed a little ritual, just like his cat with the shoes.

Suit and tie and shirt off. Then an old pair of sweatpants—like he used to wear for his roadwork, winters—and a long-sleeved T-shirt from a "Let's Beat Cancer" race he'd done. Once he was comfortable, he'd go to the fridge, take out the bottle of red wine—he never much cared for white, no character to it—and pour himself the one glass he didn't tell his own doctor about.

Why upset the man with things he'd rather not hear?

Then Shel would sit in his bulbous easy chair in front of the cable TV, which he thought was possibly the greatest advancement for understanding the world since *Encyclopedia Britannica*. On a normal night, he'd turn on CNN, slap his thigh lightly, and wait for the cat to jump up into his lap. The thing's name was Moshe, after Moshe Dayan, the Israeli army leader in the '67 and '73 wars. Even decades later, Shel still could picture the general's television image clearly. Skinny as a rail, hard as a nail, and with that black patch over the eye he'd lost in battle.

Tonight, though, the cat leaped up unbidden into Shel's lap and began to purr. Shel stroked its head, being more gentle on the side over its missing eye. "Moshe, you should be proud of your namesake. Pride can keep you going a long time."

A very long time.

Instead of clicking on the remote, Shel went over his visit with Natalie, like postmorteming a trial he'd lost, trying to see where he went wrong. The director of the Estate—and every doctor that'd ever seen his wife—said there was nothing Shel could do about it, so he shouldn't beat himself up over it. After Natalie left little Richie in that stroller outside the mall store— "Just for a minute, Shel, probably not even thirty seconds!"—she searched frantically alone before her behavior triggered several people into asking what was wrong. By the time mall security—thin in those days—responded, and they in turn called the police, Richie had been gone a good fifteen minutes.

Within a month, Natalie was as gone as their son.

The first doctors—when it happened, almost twenty years back—diagnosed her condition as a psychosis: Being a young mother, Natalie couldn't deal with causing the loss of her small child, and so her mind had made up a version of the story that let her be awake without screaming, a version in which Shel was the negligent parent she could blame.

And, admit it: You might have done the same thing Natalie did outside that store, just rush in alone for a minute.

Only Natalie's delusional version came to replace completely what really had happened. And no doctor was able to break through it. Not by psycho-

analysis, not by drugs, not even by electroconvulsive therapy. The shock treatments did raise Shel's hopes at first. Because Natalie's "remissions"—like she had some kind of cancer in her mind that didn't affect the tissue of her brain—were real, genuine lapses into rationality. But then something would remind her of Richie, and it would be back to the Estate for drugs, with newer names and fewer results.

"Intractable" was a word the latest generation of doctors liked to use. Or preferred to *avoid* using, since the adjective suggested that even the inventiveness of medical science couldn't address a long-studied reaction to an irreversible tragedy.

Shel shook his head, and, as so often happened, Moshe shook his, too.

After the police reached Shel at his office, he spent the first couple of hours as irrationally as Natalie would become. Thinking that maybe—just *maybe*—an incredible but honest mistake had been made, that the new nanny for a two-year-old boy dressed in similar clothing and in a similar stroller had wheeled Richie away without looking closely, perhaps not realizing the error until the first time the child had to be changed. Or, what, at most . . . dinnertime?

The next few days were even worse, as Shel waited for a ransom demand he couldn't begin to cover. When no note or call came, the police, still trying, brought in the FBI, even though there was no evidence of the child crossing a state line. But there never was any evidence, period, not so much as a trace.

Like Richie in person had never been part of their lives to start with. Like all the toys and clothes and just plain stuff in his room were some elaborate . . . hoax, an illusion created to play a joke on two brunts named Natalie and Sheldon Gold.

And, as the months merged into years, even Shel's hope faded. He knew the odds, forced the police to quote them to him using statistics an FBI report provided. Then he clung to just one thin strand of hope. Or of consolation, really. That maybe Richie hadn't been sexually abused, or strangled, or chopped up into pieces because his blood matched some sick child of a rich foreigner desperate for an organ transplant. That instead maybe—again, just *maybe*—whoever took him wanted a son of their own so badly

that stealing someone else's seemed justifiable. That Richie—under a different name, in a different city, through a different religion—was being raised lovingly by "parents," however defined, who cared for him as well as Natalie and Shel would have. Education, sports, ethics.

But finally, even that "just maybe" part of thinking about Richie began to slip away from Shel's mind. To slip away and be replaced by the grief and the frustration and the just plain goddamned un*fair*ness of it all, surging up his throat, threatening to choke him.

At which point, Shel picked Moshe off his lap and held the poor one-eyed cat on his shoulder, like a baby lifted from the cradle. And, stroking its back with his lumpy fingers, Sheldon A. Gold cried so silently he could hear and feel the creature's purring down to the center of his bones.

5

"MOMMA, MOMMA, THE SCHOOL bus is almost here!"

Billie Sunday looked away from the sandwich she was making on the kitchen counter and toward her youngest, William. Only eight years old, he was a worrying child.

She said, "We've still got a good fifteen minutes, William."

"Hey, Mom, that reminds me. How's *my* sandwich coming?"

"About ready to roll off the line."

Billie didn't bother to look toward her oldest, Robert Junior, because she knew with the television on, he wouldn't be looking at her, anyway. The only thing Billie let him watch on school mornings was the *Today* show, because she thought it was important for him to notice that the best brain on the program belonged to the black weatherman.

Then Billie realized she hadn't heard from her middle son, Matthew, for a while. "Hey, upstairs, you almost dressed?"

No answer.

Billie sighed, then cut the sandwich in two—Robert Junior liked to eat half during lunch period and half during study hall, claimed it helped toward sports practice at the end of the day. Wiping her hands on a towel hanging down from the fridge handle, her eyes rested on a photo of the five of them held up by a turtle magnet. Robert Junior, just age eight then himself, stood in front of Billie, his mother's hands on his shoulders. Next to her stood Robert Senior, cradling Matthew, age four, in the crook of his right arm and hefting William, barely six months, in his left palm. Big hands her husband had had, and strong.

Only not as strong as that truck, running the stop sign three weeks after the photo—their last together—was taken.

"Matthew?" Billie called out, loud enough to carry.

No answer still.

She turned away from the counter and crossed to the kitchen doorway.

"Momma," said William, a little wheedly cut to his voice now, "the bus'll be here—

"In thirteen minutes, child. Now hush up."

Billie reached the bottom of the stairs. "Matthew!"

"Comin'," the echo of the bathroom around his reply.

"Well, you're sure taking your sweet time about it. I want breakfast in you before you leave this house."

"I can get somethin' over to the—"

"I can get *something at* the—"

"Yeah, yeah. What I meant."

"Don't you sass me, Matthew. Down here, now."

"Comin'."

Billie thought, Sometimes you just want to strangle . . .

"Momma, Momma, the bus is gonna—"

"Mom, I've got to leave if I'm meeting—"

Of course, I'd need three pieces of piano wire, so they could each have their own.

And, grinning to herself, Billie Sunday turned back toward the kitchen.

WITH less than thirty seconds left in a tied game, Mairead slipped the check of the blocky defenseman who'd pinched up from the point on the power play. Shoveling the puck between his legs, she got half-spun by him grabbing her sweater at the right shoulder blade, just above the curve of her number 9. Earlier in the contest he'd received a cross-checking penalty from the referee for hitting her in the chest with the aluminum section of his stick centered between his hands. Twice before, when the ref wasn't looking, the same defenseman had dodged other, more serious penalties, such as trying to drive the butt end of his stick into her stomach and trying to spear her in the ribs with the blade end. When Mairead heard no whistle this time, she

broke the defenseman's grip on her uniform, yelled, "How about holding, ref?" and tore down the right wing for a short-handed try.

The other team's center, number 14, was the fastest player on the ice, and out of the corner of her left eye, Mairead picked him up just as she regained control of the puck. He was coming across to her side of the rink, trying for an angle of intercept.

Mairead glanced toward the opposing goalie. She'd skated against Sara only three prior times in this dawn league at a rink along the Charles River, but four times while in college. Sara was a conservative net-minder who tended to play stand-up and rarely came out to challenge the shooter.

Mairead had one really good move in her open-ice arsenal: a quick stop and lateral shift, hopefully making an opponent—here number 14—slide right by without poke-checking the puck away. But he was closing with a full head of steam on Mairead's left, so if she misjudged by even a fraction, he'd cream her.

Which was okay. Not because their center was cute, or even small, as he had a good twenty pounds on her. No, Mairead preferred men's rules, which permitted bodychecking, to women's rules, which prohibited that collision style of defense. She felt that taking the body was an integral part of the sport, just like tackling in football and blocking out in basketball.

Number 14, though, underestimated Mairead's speed. Or maybe he just had less gas left in his tank than she did in hers. Because he stumbled trying to slash at her stick, and Mairead was able to hurdle him as he slid by.

Which left just Sara, the stand-up goalie.

Mairead skated toward center ice. One option was to shift right and shoot the puck on her forehand, strong and accurate. Another was to shift left and bring the puck onto the blade backhand, which would be less powerful but also harder for Sara to stop, kind of like a knuckler is harder for a batter in baseball. A third option was to deke either way as a fake, then come in on the opposite hand.

Decision time.

Mairead deked right, as though setting up the forehand. Sara bit on the fake, sliding to her left to line her pads and body up against that goalpost.

Then Mairead executed the move she didn't have to use on number 14, cutting across Sara's field of vision.

As the goalie frantically, futilely tried to maneuver her left-committed body back to the right, Mairead lifted a backhand shot beautifully off her blade and over Sara's right shoulder.

Only to see the puck clang off the crossbar and tumble harmlessly onto the ice behind the net.

"Shit!" said Mairead, as Sara hissed, "Yes!" and the players on the opposing bench banged their sticks against the boards.

The left defenseman, whom Mairead had fooled to start the play, drew even with her. "You try that between-the-skates move on me again, and I'll break your fucking neck."

In two strides she pulled away, turned her head to return the verbal courtesy, and got clocked by number 14, who'd slipped in on her blind side.

Struggling back up, Mairead mouthed silently, "I still like men's rules," but she had to say the words twice before they rang true.

SHELDON Gold bent over the waist-high metal box on the sidewalk and fed in his coins. Pulling on the handle, he got a Boston *Herald,* the city's tabloid-sized paper. Most lawyers he knew read the *Globe,* the long-form paper recently acquired by *The New York Times.* But Shel believed the *Herald* had better crime reporting, which was kind of important to his practice.

And, admit it: You like to be different.

Opening the door to the coffee shop, Shel wished he'd gone jogging before stopping for breakfast. But after his visit with Natalie at the Estate the night before, he just didn't feel like it. Which bothered him, because Shel knew—even without his own doctor telling him—that exercise after a difficult situation helped to stave off—

"Sheldon, my friend. How are you this morning?"

"Fine, Julio, fine. And the family?"

"Could not be better."

Shel wasn't surprised that Julio didn't ask after his family. It had gotten to be second nature for Shel to tell people that he'd "lost" his wife and son years before, just like he'd replied to Mairead during their bench conference

in the park. And for as long as Shel had known Julio, the coffee-shop owner was the kind of mensch who remembered his customers' wounds and avoided them.

After wiping down the Formica in front of Shel's favorite stool, Julio said, "Regular or decaf today?"

"Regular," said Shel, given the night he'd had.

As his porcelain cup with the cobweb of patina cracks was filled, the lawyer turned to a story on bodies being uncovered outside yet another village in the former Yugoslavia.

"Terrible thing," said Julio, jutting his chin at the grainy photo. "Terrible, terrible thing."

"No argument there."

"I tell you, Sheldon, I don't understand why the Europe countries did not do nothing. That was where the World War One started, right?"

"Around there somewhere."

Julio set down his Pyrex pot. "But if those countries just sit and watch, why does our country not do something?"

Shel thought the answer might be as simple as "Vietnam plus no oil production," but all he said was, "I don't know much about military strategy, Julio."

"Yeah, well, Mr. Clinton should have thrown the atomic bomb at the bad guys."

"I kind of hope not, though I know what you mean."

"Only all the other leaders sit on their hands. I tell you one thing, Sheldon." Julio jabbed an index finger at the photographed bodies in the trench. "If those peoples are Catholics or Jews like me and you instead of Muslims that nobody in this country cares about, the Air Force, the Army, *and* the Marines would be over there like that."

Julio snapped his fingers, and Sheldon A. Gold ordered two eggs over hard with sausage and a blueberry muffin.

BILLIE just glanced out the window as Robert Junior got into his friend's convertible, a kid named Carmine whose father actually sold cars. Which always struck her as kind of funny.

Though it shouldn't. Here you still call your firstborn Robert Junior in your head when there hasn't been a Senior around for—how many years?—to confuse him with.

"Momma, the bus will leave without—"

"Matthew!" Billie yelled.

"Right here," said her middle son, so close his answer almost made Billie slice her finger with the sandwich knife.

She looked at him. Robert Junior was slim but strong, favoring his father, while little William was a bit to the heavy side, more like Billie. Only Matthew didn't seem to fit either side of the family very well.

Fact is, if you hadn't borne him knowing he was his father's son, you wouldn't pick Matthew out your ownself as belonging with the rest. Especially the way he's been behaving lately.

Billie had spoken with all of her kids, early and often, to reinforce the code her army-sergeant husband had hammered home to her while she was still just pregnant with Robert Junior. She thought of it as the "three-eighteen" rule: No alcohol, no sex, and—most important of all—no drugs, before age eighteen. After that birthday, they were men in the eyes of the military, so they could make their own choices. But not before.

Only Billie was no longer sure about Matthew. On any of the three counts.

Hugging or kissing her middle son, she smelled for beer or perfume or marijuana. But if he used hard drugs, there'd be no tattletale scent, and that worried Billie the most. So she watched Matthew even more than she sniffed him. Watched his eyes and his coordination, his sleeping habits and his moods.

Only he was out of school three hours each day before Billie got home from work. It wasn't fair to expect Robert Junior to play snoop, and Matthew had gotten too old for the kind of straddle care that she arranged for third-grader William.

So Billie watched her middle son and worried over him.

"There," said Matthew, his eyes staring at her like unblinking buttons. "Okay if I go now?"

Billie refocused on the plate in front of him, just a crust of toast left on it. "Okay."

"Momma, that bus—"

"Your sandwich is next, William. Don't you be sweating the small stuff, remember?"

Her youngest squinched his eyes and crossed his arms in an old man's pout, Billie having to turn away or laugh out loud.

IT'D still been dark on the way to the rink, so Mairead had taken money from the key case she carried in lieu of a handbag to pay the cab from her apartment over to the early morning game. However, when she came outdoors after changing and leaving her hockey gear in a rented locker, the sun was actually out, and the air temperature nearly fifty.

The January thaw *rules*. Thank you, God.

A month before, a teammate had given Mairead a ride from the rink back to Beacon Hill, and, according to his odometer, it was a six-mile jog along the Charles to her apartment. Which felt just about right for blowing off frustation over missing the game-winning goal. Also, the wind was out of the northwest, pushing helpfully at Mairead's back instead of lashing painfully against her face. Shifting the key case to her left hand to make the minor side of her body work a little harder, she began to run.

After the stop-start-sprint cycle of playing hockey, it took Mairead almost a mile to regulate her breathing for fat burn and relaxation. As the new pace began to feel natural, she allowed herself to notice winter things about the river. Two ducks—a green-headed male and a brown female— paddled around a Jacuzzi-sized hole in the yellow crust near the shore. Farther out, some seagulls skidded a little as they landed on more solid ice. A cormorant, black and looking oily, spread its wings while perching on a chunk of stone riprapped up the slope against erosion.

Mairead also began second-guessing her decision to go from Jaynes & Ward to Gold and Associate, wondering if she'd be able to afford a new hockey stick in the near future.

Except the reason you missed that goal wasn't because of your stick being old. You tried a difficult shot without practicing enough lately to make it.

Mairead nodded. Well, now that I've got a more flexible job, maybe I *can* practice a little more. If I can budget rink time and cab fare on what Shel's paying me.

Which made her think of Alpha's case, and the man who might be investigating for them.

Pontifico "the Pope" Murizzi. *I know I should stay strictly professional with him, but wouldn't it be a pisser if I really fell for somebody with a nickname like—*

Young lady?

Mairead nodded again. However, maybe because Alpha had been so recently in her head, she realized that she was approaching his "cave." Using the next half-mile to mull it over, Mairead decided that stopping now would save her a separate trip to pick up the books she'd promised to bring him.

So, when a tatter of yellow tape with POLICE LINE—DO NOT CROSS caught her eye, Mairead slowed to a walk and began climbing the shallow incline toward the stanchions of the overpass.

BEHIND the wheel of his aging Ford Explorer, Pontifico Murizzi inched along in the bumper-to-bumper traffic paralleling one axis of the Big Dig construction. He thanked God he didn't have to negotiate rush hour on anything like a daily basis. When the Pope worked Homicide, the unit was in South Boston, the second floor of an old police garage on D Street, and it was a snap to get there from his boat. Now his former office had moved along with most everything else to Schroeder Plaza, the new headquarters building at the edge of Roxbury. Which would mean crossing downtown traffic every fucking shift to go from home to the job and back again.

Not that the Pope was headed there right then.

No, he'd decided after talking with "Muh-*raid*" that he wanted to know a little more about this Alpha guy before hitting on his old buddies for their take on the defendant. Despite being so young, the redheaded lawyer with the blotched hands had summed up the case pretty well. But you learn one thing on Homicide, it's this: To understand a defendant, to figure out what he might have and might not have done to another human being, you have to visit him where he lives.

And, if he's not living there now, go visit it anyway.

So Pontifico Murizzi tuned his radio until he found a pretty good jazz piece to muffle the frustrating traffic.

"WILLIAM, you got your pencils in that knapsack?"

"Yes, Momma."

Billie Sunday held her youngest's hand a little tighter as she walked him down to the curb for the bus. "And all your books for school today?"

"Uh-huh."

"And you didn't crush that sandwich I made for you?"

"Uh-*uh*."

As the bus pulled up, Billie thought she felt William's grip change a little inside hers.

He said, "Momma?"

"Yes?"

"Everything okay with you?"

Billie smiled internally. One thing her worrier son had inherited from his daddy was that way of sensing when something was bothering her. "Everything's fine, William."

"At work, too?"

"We just hired on a new lawyer in the office. Young woman fresh out of school herself."

William reached the open door of the bus. "Do you like her?"

Billie looked up at the driver, some stitches of impatience tugging at his eyes. The man had a hard enough job from her way of judging things, tolerating somebody else's screaming kids for an hour twice each day, and she didn't want to add a minute to that.

Patting her third son on the head, Billie Sunday said, "Remains to be seen, child. Remains to be seen."

JESUS Mary, thought Mairead O'Clare. Somebody *lived* here?

The first thing that struck her about the cave was how tacky it looked from the outside, the mismatched pieces of lumber cobbled together like a drunk putting Band-Aids every which way on his skin. But she tugged on a few of the planks, and they were attached solidly by nails.

The second thing, as Mairead stepped over some more police tape, was the smell coming out the open door. Sour, a combination of sweat and musk and—

Mairead stopped analyzing it, wanting to retard her gag reflex. Having been in some pretty foul locker rooms over her years of hockey, she'd learned how to seal off the nasal passage at the back of her mouth to keep air from going through the nose and nauseating her. Mairead willed that closure to begin again now, and in ten seconds, she felt shielded enough to move forward.

And into the cave itself.

Pity you didn't think to bring a flashlight, young lady.

Mairead shuffled her feet to scare off any rats or other squatters. It was surprisingly warmer in the cave than outside, maybe some tribute to Alpha's carpentry. Mairead took off her gloves and let her eyes adjust to the dim morning light.

The interior looked pretty much as the police report had described it. A bed—well, two mattresses, one on top of the other, with cinder blocks spaced underneath to lift everything off the damp ground. Dirty blankets lay jumbled on the bed, and underwear—which she had *no* intention of touching—hung from nails in shelves crammed with books.

The man might be in jail accused of murder, said Sister Bernadette, *but he didn't lie to you.*

Mairead moved along the rows of volumes, almost all hefty hardcovers. The jackets with dark print on pale backgrounds were the easiest to read, though even for these, she had to strain her eyes or pull a book off its shelf to get a more direct ray of light on it. *The Cerebral Symphony,* by William H. Calvin. *An Inquiry into the Good,* by Kitaro Nishida. *Paradigms Lost: Images of Man in the Mirror of Science,* by John L. Casti. *The Power of Place,* by Winifred Gallagher.

Mairead stopped at the last one, realizing it was the first showing an Irish-surnamed author. Then she skimmed the spines of three more, by Margenau, Staguhn, Durckheim.

Your Alpha seems quite the eclectic intellect.

Mairead gathered the first four volumes, figuring that about seven pounds of books ought to keep Alpha going awhile. She'd just stacked them under her left arm when she heard, "Thought I saw somebody a-coming in here."

Not Sister Bernadette's voice. Definitely.

Mairead whirled around. The man in the doorway was tall and skinny, his black pants and boots caked with mud. He wore a quilted jacket, the sleeves cut off and wispy puffs of stuffing showing like feathers against the dark shirt underneath. A baseball cap of some kind kept Mairead from seeing much of his hair, but it looked short and almost blond around the ears.

She took a step toward the door. "I was just leaving."

The man moved nearer, close enough for Mairead to smell him. If the cave was damp and sour, the new arrival gave off a more active scent. That of a hunter.

"What do you have there, missy?"

With more words, the Southern lilt in his voice grew softer. Mairead said, "Alpha asked me to bring him some books."

"The Hermit asked you?"

The man crossed his arms and cocked a hip. Mairead had seen the pose often enough. On the ice, in bars, even at museums. A macho posturing that read, "I'm coming for you, sweetmeat."

"My name's Rex, missy, and I sure don't remember the Hermit saying a little librarian would fetch his books for him."

Mairead tried a tougher tone. "I'm Alpha's lawyer. He's in—"

"His lawyer?" Rex changed his own tone markedly. "Sorry, I didn't know. Look, maybe I can help you out a little here."

"With what?"

Rex moved toward the bed, and Mairead circled away. If they'd originally been standing at six and twelve on a clock face, now they were at three and nine, with Mairead that much closer to the door, though she figured Rex was still within lunging distance if he had any quickness to him at all.

Rex sat down on the mattress as though it were a couch, his face now in the best light for Mairead. The wrinkled skin was layered with grime, the eyes squinty. He had a vivid white scarline through one eyebrow that continued up at a diagonal to his hairline, just visible under the kiltered brim of his filthy cap. The scar seemed to distort Rex's features, and Mairead could feel her fight-or-flight reflex building.

However, what he said was, "I can maybe help you with who killed that pain in the butt."

"Zoran Draskovic?"

"His real name was something foreign like that." Rex grinned. "But everybody just called him Old Man River."

The books were getting a little heavy, so Mairead shifted them to her other arm. "You knew him well?"

"Well as anybody." Rex stretched his legs a bit. "He wasn't what you'd call overfriendly."

Alpha's description of him, too. "You ever see Mr. Draskovic argue with anyone?"

A grunted laugh. "Be a sight easier to tell you who he *didn't* fight with. But the cops went after the Hermit account of the winter coat and his nightstick being used to kill the old fart."

Rex appeared pretty well informed for a man scratching out an existence along the river. "What do you know about the coat?"

A shrug. "Just what everybody heard, I reckon. Old Man River had himself a winter coat from Russia or some such place, and the Hermit took it from him."

"Which I'm guessing made Mr. Draskovic angry."

"Angry? He was a-ranting and a-raving about it to anybody who'd listen, and a lot that wouldn't."

Desperate for some wedge she could drive into what was sounding more and more like a dream case for the prosecution, Mairead said, "You ever see them fight?"

"Who, now? Old Man River and the Hermit?"

"Yes."

"Wasn't much of a fight, but yeah, I seen them tussle some. Only Old Man River didn't stand a chance against the Hermit."

"Tell me what you saw."

Rex started to get up. "Be easier to show you . . ."

"No," said Mairead. "Just in words, like we were in court."

Rex grinned again. "Sure. The Hermit'd take the coat, and Old Man River'd snitch it back. Then—"

"Wait a minute. This happened before?"

"What did?"

"The night of the killing wasn't the first time that Mr. Draskovic tried to take back his coat?"

"Hell's bells, no, missy. They were always a-scuffling over it. Old Man River trying to punch the Hermit and grab the coat, the Hermit holding him off with one hand, and just plain having hisself a good old time, laughing like the Irish do."

Before Mairead could ask another question, Rex said, "With that hair, you Irish, too?"

Give a little to get a lot. "Yes. But you said before that Mr. Draskovic would 'snitch' the coat back?"

"Right, right. When it was a warm enough day, the Hermit'd leave the coat here instead of wearing it all the way down to the construction place."

Mairead remembered Alpha mentioning it.

Rex waved his hand expansively around the cave. "The Hermit claimed some foreman gave him all this wood, but I'd bet that Irishman stole it just like he stole Old Man River's coat."

"Rex, where is this construction place?"

After he described it by landmarks Mairead could picture, she said, "Anybody else have reason to fight Mr. Draskovic?"

"Sure thing. Like I said, he was a pain in the butt. Yelling at college kids just out having a few drinks—snotty kids, though, no sense in them of sharing with others less fortunate. And then there's this old sailor guy."

"Navy?"

Another shrug. "Maybe one time. But he's got the look of a rich fart about him. Anyway, the sailor would bring his boat too close onto shore, and Old Man River'd pitch a fit, a-cussing and a-throwing rocks. The sailor'd cuss him right back, only with more 'refined' swear words. You ask me," and Rex's voice seemed to go down an octave, growing a smarmy edge to his words, "the rich fart's the one who might do something he ain't supposed to, figuring his money'd let him get away with it."

Mairead's antennae went up.

"Of course, they's a lot of us can get away with stuff, and I ain't never had an Irish girl with hands redder than her hair."

Mairead could feel the adrenaline rush. "I'm walking out of here right now. And you're not."

"Oh," Rex flexing a little on the edge of the bed, "I figure to stay here. Or maybe come right back to this mattress, with you in tow and a little more considerate of my needs."

Keeping her eyes on him, Mairead took a step toward the doorway. As she'd feared, Rex bounded up from the bed. Mairead banked on him expecting her to back up some more or turn to run.

Instead, she took a stride toward Rex, throwing off his timing, his hands still wide apart. And with all the strength in her major arm, she shot-putted Alpha's four philosophy books square into Rex's face.

He cried out and toppled backward onto the bed, the books scattering on the ground.

Mairead turned now and ran, tripping on the primitive door sill and sprawling in the mud outside the cave. Thanks to hockey, her head was swiveling before she got up, but Mairead also had felt something twist in her left ankle.

Rex came raging through the doorway, blood flowing from his lower lip. He lurched forward, missing a grip on Mairead's good ankle as she used that foot to push herself up from the mud. Rex stumbled, giving Mairead precious seconds to scramble down the slope, almost hopping on her right leg.

She was relieved to hear Rex's voice no closer when he yelled, "You think the pen's mightier than the sword, missy? Well, I'm telling you, Rex's sword's mightier, and you'll be feeling it soon enough."

Gaining the macadam path, Mairead slowed to a fast walk, trying to favor the bad ankle while putting as much distance as she could between her and Alpha's cave.

"NEED any help?" said Pontifico Murizzi, arms folded in front of his chest, rolling his left shoulder around a stanchion about ten feet from the derelict who'd ID'd himself as Rex.

Drawing a dirty shirtsleeve across his bleeding lip, the tall guy turned toward the Pope. "Who's asking?"

Casually, Murizzi moved closer. "Rex, you really want to know my name? Or what a badge lets me do for a living?"

"Shit, man," the derelict backpedaling a little. "I didn't try nothing. She started it with—"

The Pope closed the distance between them. "Just couldn't resist you, is that it?"

"I'm telling you, I didn't try—"

"Tell me something else," Murizzi now less than a stride from the tall man but keeping his hands at his sides. Expecting the rank body odor, the Pope didn't flinch. "What do you know about the night this Old Man River died?"

"I don't know—"

A backhand slap across Rex's face.

The scuzzball winced. "Hey, man, I got rights, you—"

A forehand slap this time.

"Fuck," whimpering now, both hands going to his face, but purely defensively.

Murizzi waited a few seconds, letting the derelict wonder what might be coming next. "Now that we're communicating, answer my question about Old Man River."

Rex opened up, almost gushing. He went to a soup kitchen. He came back to all the "commotion" of bubble lights and TV vans. He was told by a uniform in earmuffs to "go home, but man, I already *was* home."

The Pope said, "Before that."

Rex told him about all the fights between "the Hermit," as he called Alpha, and the deceased. Prodding, Murizzi found out no weapons were ever involved. In fact, it sounded like this Alpha made the coat thing more into a game of keep-away.

As Rex nervously shifted his feet, the Pope spotted something brown near them. He moved toward it as the derelict backed away.

A key case, on the line of flight that Mairead had taken.

Murizzi bent down, picked up the leather case, keys jingling. "I take it these aren't yours."

"Never saw them before."

The Pope flipped the keys back in their case and pocketed it. "All right, where're you crashing now?"

Rex pointed at the open door. "Your cop tape was down, so I figured somebody oughta get some use out of the place."

"Like by trying to rape that woman with the red hair?"

"I told you, she's the one—"

"Okay, Rex. Let's say we did this all formal, through the proper channels."

The derelict looked back, suspicious now.

The Pope said, "She swears out a complaint, I take you in. There's an arraignment, the attempted rape's knocked down to sexual assault, and you go with a plea—because you sure as shit aren't gonna get anybody to believe she came on to you. And you probably have enough of a record to do hard state time instead of soft county. How am I doing so far?"

More suspicion. "It's your story, man."

"But there's a simpler route. You tried to victimize that woman—what, fifteen minutes ago? Let's say we settle the whole thing right here and now."

Rex shook his head. "I don't have no money to—"

"Not money, scuzzball." A beat. "I break your finger."

The derelict's eyes got big.

The Pope said, "I break the middle finger on the hand you don't use to write with. Or pick your nose with or wipe your ass with. We still communicating?"

"You're . . . you're gonna break my finger because of—"

"Your bad behavior as a citizen. Now, I can bring you in to take your chances, or I can end things here. Which'll it be?"

"Aw, fuck me, *fuck* me."

"Rex?"

Slowly, the tall man in the filthy clothes extended his left hand waist-high in a nonthreatening fist, the middle finger out and trembling. Then he closed his eyes and clamped shut his jaw.

JULIO said, "You want anything else, Sheldon?"

"Just a glass of water."

"You got it."

Shel Gold watched as Julio glanced around at the other customers in the shop before reaching under the counter for a liter of bottled water. Shel knew that the owner generally drew straight from the tap, maybe with a few ice cubes. But for favored patrons, he'd uncap—

"The good stuff," said Julio softly, pouring six ounces.

As always, Shel waited for Julio to serve another customer before reaching into his pocket for the anonymous plastic vial. You could buy them at CVS for seventy-nine cents, and—thanks to his health plan—the pills in the vial didn't cost that much more.

The ones Shel'd started taking after Natalie went to the Estate.

The psychiatrist back then told him there weren't many choices for treating depression. Prozac, Zoloft, a couple of others. Originally, Shel figured to be on them just for a while, get a boost back to normality, then wean himself off. Because of the side effects, you see. Some nausea at first, though that goes away pretty fast, especially if you pop the little buggers with your first meal of the day so they get buffered by the food. Worse side effect for most—and for Shel—was impotence.

Admit it: Not that you were exactly overwhelmed by opportunities for erections.

In fact, each time Shel discontinued the Zoloft because he was feeling better, he'd eventually spiral downward again—what his doctor called "chronic clinical depression"—and the pills took longer to hoist him back out of the abyss. Over the years, new drugs would come on the market, boasting of no—or anyway different—side effects. The shrink had Shel try them, but the problem was that, for everything except sex, he functioned best on Zoloft. It was his body's magic bullet, and Shel had resigned himself to taking it till the day he died.

A simple choice, really. A life of lying in bed staring up at the ceiling—with no capacity to work or socialize or enjoy something as simple as reading a book—versus a life of living and working in the real world, only with no capability for sex.

Not exactly a pleasant dilemma, but nevertheless a real "no-brainer," as he'd heard Billie Sunday's oldest son once say.

And admit it: There're plenty of people worse off than you.

At which point, a video of Natalie replayed in his head.

SHIT, shit, shit.

Mairead O'Clare kept the words inside, but she wanted to explode. The adrenaline rush had worn off, and her left ankle hurt every time that foot hit the macadam path between Storrow Drive and the river. Except the pain wasn't why she was cursing.

Digging in a pocket for her gloves, Mairead couldn't find her key case.

Sister Bernadette's voice began damage control. *The only ones in the case were your downstairs building key and your upstairs apartment key. Since you carried no identification with them, nobody finding the case can trace you to Beacon Hill and use them for burglary or worse. Once you arrive at the building, the super can let you in, and you'll have new keys made. And, since you'd already taken a cab out to the skating rink, there was less than ten dollars left to lose.*

Yeah, only it'd be a whole lot easier to take a footbridge to Beacon Street and hail a cab instead of hobbling all the—

Mairead heard an engine behind her just as a horn tooted three times. Except for State Police cruisers that patrolled and Metropolitan District Commission trucks that pruned and cleaned, vehicles weren't supposed to be on the river paths. Glancing over her shoulder, Mairead didn't see anything official about the white SUV gaining slowly on her.

Still, after going a round with that jerk Rex, you're not going to fight a car.

Mairead stepped off the path to the right, her bad ankle twinging on the uneven earth. Instead of speeding up and passing, however, the two-door Explorer slowed to draw even with her.

The window on the passenger side was open. Through it, a voice Mairead recognized said, "Give you a lift?"

The perfect end to a perfect morning. The man of my dreams sees me looking like I just finished mud wrestling.

Mairead ran a hand over, if not through, her hair. "What brings you here?"

Pontifico Murizzi rolled his lower lip out, like a little kid feigning inno-cence. "I was driving on Storrow over there, and I thought I saw you limp-ing. So I pulled off at a curb-cut through the guardrail and came back."

Mairead looked east and west along the path. A mother jogging with her toddler in one of those canvas carriages you push in front of you. An older couple, walking hand in hand but frowning at the vehicle in their way.

Mairead said, "Private cars aren't supposed to be here."

The Pope leaned over and opened the passenger door. "Then get in so I won't be."

Fate, young lady. Best to just trust and accept.

"Thanks," said Mairead, using her arms and right leg to heave herself up and into the high-riding vehicle.

After Murizzi began driving again, Mairead turned to him. "So," she asked. "Are you going to help us with Alpha?"

The Pope grinned a little, and Mairead felt her heart literally flutter, like that puck she'd shot off the crossbar.

Pontifico Murizzi said, "Maybe I already have," and from his right pants pocket he produced her key case.

6

AS MAIREAD O'CLARE LIMPED through the suite door, Billie Sunday looked up from the reception desk, honey-colored dreadlocks shimmering, and extended her hand. "Message for you."

Mairead took the pink slip. John Ramirez, from Jaynes & Ward. Now what could he—

"Shel wants to see you, too," said Sunday, glancing down at the switchboard. "But he's on the phone now."

"Can you let me know when he gets off?"

The receptionist/secretary turned back to her typewriter. "I'll give a holler."

As Mairead moved toward her office, she heard over her shoulder, "You hurt yourself?"

A white lie seemed best. "Hockey game."

Sunday didn't reply.

Easing down to her desk chair, Mairead dialed Ramirez on his direct line. He picked up during the second ring.

"John, it's Mairead."

"Hey, how're you doing?"

"Fine." She resettled herself in the chair to ease the pressure on her ankle, which she'd iced during breakfast at her apartment and then—gingerly—tried to loosen up by walking to the office. "Jaynes and Ward struggling without me?"

"I know I am." Mairead thought his voice sounded funny. "Uh, look. A couple of us think you got a total bummer of a deal. We want to take you out for lunch."

"Lunch?" She was surprised, but pleased. "You fix on a date?"

"Today."

Mairead listened as Ramirez went on about conflicting deadlines facing him and the other two associates, neither of them David Spiegel. She agreed to meet all three at P.J. Clarke's, a loud bar near Quincy Market.

"See you there," said John Ramirez, hanging up.

As Mairead cradled her own phone, she heard Billie Sunday's voice. "Shel's off his line."

PONTIFICO Murizzi found a space on Ruggles Street, feeding the meter so his Explorer wouldn't get tagged. Then he walked around the corner to the new Boston Police Headquarters.

The building in Southie where Homicide used to be looked like a police station out of a cheap, black-and-white movie. Shroeder Plaza, though, named after two brothers killed in the line of duty, looked more like a museum of modern art.

Headquarters filled most of the city block at the edge of the predominantly black part of town. The twin buildings were made of granite in shades of gray, with turquoise borders under the smoked-glass windows. Between the two wings, an office bridge spanned a cement patio, security cameras prominent.

At the main entrance, the Pope was glad to see the tall poles still flew the silhouette pennant of POW-MIA next to the Stars and Stripes and the Commonwealth's state flag. Then he remembered that the building, originally constructed for the Registry of Motor Vehicles, had been evacuated after many employees claimed they were sickened by the air inside.

Good enough for cops, though, Murizzi thought.

The lobby had gray granite walls, too, with chromed pillars and indirect lighting. Across the way were the booths labeled "Licensing Unit" (which handled firearm identification cards and gun permits) and "Hackney Carriage Unit" (for cabs and limos), short lines of applicants in front of each.

The Pope walked up to a security desk. He recognized the uniform behind it, but couldn't put a name to the face.

"Hey-ey-ey, the Pope. Back for a visit?"

"First time here, tell you the truth."

"No?" The guy came up with a clip-on guest pass. He said, "You want Homicide, it's two-N."

"Two-En?"

"Two for second floor, letter 'N' for north wing, which is where we are now."

Feeling vaguely stupid, Pontifico Murizzi thanked the uniform, took the pass, and got aimed toward the staircase.

"WHAT happened to your leg?"

"Ankle," said Mairead, watching the concerned expression on Shel Gold's face.

"Ankle, then."

She sat in a client chair in front of his desk. "Hockey."

Shel nodded. Mairead again found herself liking the fact that he didn't question what she did for fun, even if she wasn't exactly telling him the truth.

He shoved a piece of paper over to her. "I got a call, this assistant clerk friend of mine named Chet at the BMC."

"Bee . . . ?"

"Boston Municipal Court. A woman's up for arraignment. Chet wanted me to represent her, but I've got a divorce thing on that'll go past second call."

Mairead wasn't sure what "second call" meant, but the handwriting on the paper read "Talina, A&B/DW, Rm 403." She said, "Talina's the name, and assault and battery's the charge?"

"With a dangerous weapon."

The "DW" part. "You want me to go?"

"Right. The main issue should be bail, though try for Personal Recognizance."

"Meaning, no bail."

"Just her promise to show up for trial."

Mairead weighed it. "Why did this clerk call you?"

Shel Gold almost smiled. "Chet thinks there's something funny going on, but he can't exactly represent her himself."

Made sense. "Shel, remember when I had to ask you about where the jail was?"

He actually smiled this time. "You've never been to the BMC, either? Well, look on the bright side."

"Which is?"

"After this morning, you won't have to say that again."

"POPE! Long time."

Murizzi waited for Artie Chin to come around the counter in Homicide. The rug beneath their feet was tweedy, like indoor/outdoor carpeting, some rust-colored chairs for waiting. As Chin approached, the Pope could see his badge, worn on the front of his belt, gunhand side, the words "Boston Police" emblazoned across the top, his rank of "Sergeant Detective" on a band beneath it, and his badge number under that.

"Artie, if I'm interrupting anything . . . ?"

"Interrupting? I haven't seen you since. . . . Well . . ."

"Since," said the Pope mercifully, picturing his kind of impromptu retirement party.

"So," said Chin. "What can I do you for?"

Murizzi looked into the eyes of his old friend. Artie Chin hadn't been the first minority in the unit, but he was the first Asian, and he'd taken heat for it. All of five-six in new shoes, he could be mistaken for a fireplug. Crew-cut hair he'd kept the same length since his hitch in the Marines and bulging cheeks, so much so that his nickname in the Academy had been Squirrel. A good investigator, though, and invaluable once the gangs in Chinatown had started banging on legitimate businesses with kidnapping, home invasion, or just plain murder-for-hire.

And a good friend, one who knew the whole truth about—

"Pope, you okay?"

"Fine, Artie. Just fine." Murizzi altered his tone a bit toward the business side. "I might be in for the defense on this homeless killing."

"Draskovic, the Old Man River guy?"

"Right."

Chin frowned. "And you want me to talk with you about it."

"The general idea."

"You here as an investigator for the accused or as my old best bud?"

"Both, I guess," said the Pope.

Chin lost the frown. "You know, that's a pretty good answer."

"EXCUSE me, Room four-oh-three?"

The bailiff in the blue uniform shirt jerked a thumb behind him, and Mairead O'Clare walked into a modern form of bedlam.

Except for the judge's bench, there were people everywhere in the courtroom: bar enclosure, gallery pews, even the aisles. Some were in suits, some in jeans, some barely dressed at all. Vertically integrated in terms of age, more minority than white, they were talking and yelling, laughing and crying. As far as Mairead could tell, the bailiffs had given up hope of keeping strict order, just watching like bouncers in a bar for a real problem to flare.

She edged her way through the crowd in the aisle until she reached the picket-fenced bar enclosure, then went through to the little kangaroo pouch in front of the judge's bench. Four different lawyers—based on dress code, anyway—were trying to get the attention of a beefy man wearing a tie and dress shirt but no jacket. He wasn't more than thirty-five, Mairead thought, but he wore his black hair parted in the center and slicked back, like some old photos she'd seen of the passengers boarding the *Titanic* when the movie came out. A man Mairead's age sat to his left, entering information into a computer.

One of the lawyers was waggling a file under the beefy guy's nose with her multiringed left hand. "Chet, I got to have a—"

"Zelda, please. All in good time, all right?"

"But 'time' is what I don't have. I'm due in a trial—"

"Session at eleven. You told me, and I'll try, okay?"

The woman railed on, burning her goodwill, Mairead thought. She also found herself liking Chet, who seemed to stand as a stolid beacon of calm in the hurricane swirling around him.

Standing patiently, Mairead waited until the storm washed away from the clerk, then said, "Excuse me?"

Chet looked at her hands, then focused on her face.

She held up the piece of paper with Talina's name on it. "I'm Mairead O'Clare, from Sheldon Gold's office. He asked me to—"

"Right, right. Her last name's Dongg, with two *g*'s."

Mairead closed her eyes. "Tell me she's not a prostitute."

Chet's voice said, kind of sadly, "I can tell you anything you want, but that won't change what she does for a living."

Mairead opened her eyes. "I'm supposed to—"

"Represent her for the arraignment, right. But I'm thinking maybe you'll want to apply for a cross-complaint."

"Cross-complaint?"

"Yeah. After you talk with her, maybe you'll want to ask for a hearing in front of an impartial clerk magistrate, maybe get her john hauled in for A and B himself."

Mairead got the hint. "Where is she?"

Chet's eyes crinkled at the corners, and, despite his being only a decade older than she was, suddenly Mairead had the disquieting sensation of talking with an unknown grandfather.

He said, "Your first time here?"

"Kind of my first time anywhere."

Chet gathered a couple of forms and handed them to Mairead before glancing around and calling out toward one of the court officers. "Ike, can I see you a minute?"

"NICE," said Pontifico Murizzi, meaning it.

Artie Chin had led him to an alcove with three comfortable desk chairs and computer monitors on the shelves of a hutch with not so much as a scratch on its veneer.

"Each squad in the unit has its own space like this. And with all the units being in the same building now, there's less phone tag and no wasted time driving to visit Ballistics or ID Imaging. In fact—you been in the cafeteria downstairs?"

"No."

Chin nodded. "Well, you won't believe it. High ceilings, burgundy and slate tiles, chairs upholstered like a kaleidoscope."

"And designer coffee, too?"

"Yeah. No more 'Fill your belly at Bernie's Deli.'"

Murizzi laughed, remembering hefty if hasty lunches at the place near the unit's old location.

Chin said, "But the reason I brought up the cafeteria: When everybody's in the same building, you can have conferences over lunch. Or maybe you hear a lab tech say something that clicks with you, and bing, the squad makes a case while the two of you are sipping Frappuccinos."

The Pope smiled, but he shook his head, too. After leaving the department, he'd visited Homicide over in Southie and felt like he still belonged. Shroeder Plaza, though, seemed alien to him, like the city had torn down his high school and taken with it the connection he had to it.

"So," said Artie Chin, "you want a designer coffee, or you want to get started?"

"THANK you," said Mairead to Ike.

The court officer nodded. "Yell when you're ready."

Mairead approached what he'd called the Women's Lockup, a holding cell with three stools on this side of the bars. A number of women stood inside, several dressed in wildly hued hot pants and halter tops. January thaw or not, Mairead found herself hoping they'd had coats when arrested. She figured the wrist and ankle shackles had been added afterward.

Determined not to announce her client's last name unless she had to, Mairead raised her voice. "Talina?"

A couple of the women looked at a third wearing a dark purple miniskirt and a lavender tube top. She seemed Amer-Asian and even exotic—lustrous black hair in a sideways ponytail, eyes whose slant appeared enhanced by makeup. But her face was terminally weary, and she held a pair of killer platforms in one manacled hand while massaging a fishnet-stockinged foot with the other.

Mairead felt a pang of empathy. Back in the orphanage, some of the older girls would hit on her. "Aw, join in, Stiggie," they'd taunt, using the nickname they knew she hated, "we're only talking a finger-fuck here."

The woman holding the platform heels said, "Who're you?"

Mairead snapped herself back. "I'm your lawyer."

One of the women who'd looked at Dongg now hooted. "Hey, Tal, her hands be blushing over coming back here with us felons."

Talina ignored the jibe. "You my lawyer? Clerk say he get me a good Jew."

"I'm here instead. Can we talk about it?"

Somewhat to Mairead's surprise, the other women drifted away from the front of the holding cell, making some room—and even a modicum of privacy—for Talina at the bars. Mairead wondered whether the deference was born of pecking order or "do unto others" for when their own lawyers would be visiting.

Talina duckwalked in the ankle shackles to the bars, her toes pointed outward a little. "So talk."

"I understand you're charged with assault and battery. Can—"

"A and B with a dangerous, lady-lawyer. There a difference."

"Yes, there is. Can you tell me the details?"

"Details." Talina made a noise that wasn't quite a laugh. "Yeah, well, the details are, this john want a rough ride, and I say for double, and he say okay."

"His name?"

"Tell me Jason, but I figure that so much bullshit. When we get to the station, the cops take his driver's license. It say Josh Brewer, so I call him JJ."

"What happened before you got to the station?"

"Well, we in his car first, but then JJ get a lot rougher than rough, so I hit him with a brick."

"A brick?"

"Yeah. I was working a corner by the Big Dig when JJ pick me up. We in his backseat on account of what he want."

"Which was?"

Talina's eyes glittered. "Delivery inna rear."

It took a beat to register with Mairead. "Anal intercourse."

"You lady-lawyers." Now a genuine laugh from Talina. "Try living in the real world, okay?" Then she suddenly got more serious. "A john want to go back door—or front door, these days—he gotta wear a condom. Only when JJ get his mojo working, he pull this thing out from under the seat."

"Thing?"

Talina glanced away, and for just a moment, Mairead realized how scared the woman must have been, for the memory to crack through the tough surface. "Galliano."

For a second, the astronomer Galileo flashed through Mairead's mind before she said, "The liqueur?"

Talina came back, her eyes ablaze with what looked like contempt. "No, lady-lawyer. Not the liqueur. The fucking bottle it come in. You ever see one?"

Mairead could picture it, from a Senior Week party at law school. Absurdly tall, tapering from bottom to top.

"That butt-fucker JJ ram that thing up my ass!" Talina spitting the words. "You know how bad you can bleed from that? You know how hard it is, you in pain and you moving and trying to get him the fuck off you and that bottle the fuck out of you and then you think, what if the fucking glass *break* inside you, and you got all the fucking edges tearing the shit out of—"

Talina made another sound and turned away, only to realize, Mairead thought, that the other women in the cell were staring, so she turned back, raising her cuffed hands to swipe across her eyes and then under her nose.

Talina said, "So, I get JJ off me, and his fucking bottle out of me, and I bust out the car door onto the street. And he after me again, saying he pay his money and he gonna get what he buy. And JJ catch me and bend me frontways over this—what do you call the stone construction things, the cranes move them around?"

"A Jersey barrier," said Mairead, quietly.

"Yeah, so he bending me over this Jersey stone, and I can feel him back there, with his bottle again, but I feel this brick under my hand, too, and so I go like this"—Talina as a bride tossing the bouquet over her shoulder—

"and I get him in the face. And he let go just as the cops pull up, lights so bright I can't see for shit."

"Where was the brick?"

"Still in my hand."

"Why?"

"Why?" Talina lifted her arms so violently, one of the platform shoes fell to the floor of the cell. "Because I not sure he finish, and I sure as shit can't run away in these." She thrust the remaining heel in her hand toward Mairead's face. "So tell me, that happen to you, what you do?"

Mairead thought back to being in Alpha's cave with Rex, shot-putting the books into his face. Then she called for Ike the court officer before Talina told her no, lawyers could just walk away.

"CIRCUMSTANTIAL, Artie," said Pontifico Murizzi.

"We've made cases with less."

The Pope ticked off points with his fingers. "You figure this Alpha guy killed Draskovic over a coat."

"It was early December, winter coming."

"Only," said Murizzi, inclining his head toward the file on the writing surface of the alcove's hutch, "according to the uniforms responding, the deceased still had the coat on."

"Figure Alpha panicked when he realized the vic was dead."

"What about blood alcohol?"

Now Chin tilted toward the file. "On your guy, point-oh-four. Sober enough to drive an MBTA bus."

"But Alpha was tested—what, eight hours after the fact?"

"Pope, I can't make the vic's body get found, all right? When the joggers stumbled over him and called it in, Draskovic was stiff as a carp on that riverbank there. And your guy, when we hauled him in an hour after that, blew almost the same on the Breathalyzer as his blood showed in the lab."

"So, as far as you're concerned, this Alpha's cold sober when he catches the vic repossessing his winter coat, chases him down, and bludgeons him in cold blood with that Irish walking stick."

"Not 'that' Irish walking stick. The *accused's* Irish walking stick. Thing's heavier than a baseball bat, but about as good for bashing in a skull. And how many other people are going to know Alpha's got the thing in his cave or whatever he calls it?"

Murizzi said, "How about this other homeless guy?"

"Rex. Born Roderick Thorne, with an *e* at the end. Guy sounds like he should be in the House of Lords along the Thames instead of scrabbling away on the banks of the Charles."

"What about him?"

"Record reads petty theft and sex crimes, some of it violent. But nothing close to *mano a mano* with a guy like Draskovic, who was nearly as big as your boy Alpha. No, I interrogated this Thorne myself. He's a wuss."

"Maybe not with a club in his hands."

"Besides, he doesn't have a motive for wanting the vic dead."

"What about the decedent's background? Draskovic, first name Zoran. Sound like any names you've seen on the news recently?"

"What, you mean the Yugoslavia stuff, a political hit?"

"Or a carryover feud."

"Be a hell of a coincidence, Pope. Granted our vic maybe was Serb or Croat or even Muslim, but somebody's going to hunt Draskovic down over here, then use opportunistically whatever weapon happens to be available for the job?"

Murizzi didn't much like playing it that way, either. "What about all the people this guy pissed off?"

"The vic was a pain in the ass, but pretty harmless."

"Didn't you tell me he used to throw rocks at people?"

"Yeah, and if somebody punched Draskovic out two seconds later, I wouldn't have been surprised. But the college kids he went after the most, they don't strike me as enterprising enough to come looking for him on a cold winter's night."

"Names?"

Chin shrugged, then opened the file and read them off. Three males, the same dorm address for two, an apartment on the third.

"Artie, anybody else?"

"On the rock-receiving end? This guy named Hayes, Winston."

"Hayes being his last name?"

"Right. Rich environmentalist, a Beacon Hill manse."

"He's an environmentalist," said the Pope, "I'd think Draskovic and him would've hit it off."

"Seems our decedent thought otherwise. Hayes used to park his sailboat—is that the right word, 'park'?"

Murizzi smiled. "Depends. Could be 'moor,' or 'anchor,' or even 'run aground.'"

"Yeah, yeah. More like run aground. Draskovic used to go apeshit, this Hayes nudged his boat into the fishies' spawning beds."

"Anything to it?"

"What do I look like, a game warden?"

Murizzi actually laughed. "Address on Hayes?"

Chin reeled it off. "That do you?"

"For now," said the Pope. "Thanks."

A nod, then an awkward silence before, "So, how're things going in the social-life department?"

Murizzi appreciated his old friend asking the question. Even the way he phrased it. "Couldn't be better, Artie."

A look that the Pope found hard to read.

"I'm glad," said Sergeant Detective Arthur Chin. "Really."

MAIREAD watched Chet the clerk nod at the defense attorney who'd just spoken into the microphone near the left side of the bench. The judge's name Mairead hadn't caught in the noise of a hundred people standing when he'd entered the courtroom.

Chet cleared his throat before, "Talina . . . Dongg."

Now Mairead heard a hundred people laugh as a bailiff yelled what sounded like "Custody!" and Talina was brought through the door from the lockup to a raised box that the judge had referred to earlier as "the dock." Talina shuffled, the rattling of her chains carrying back to her lawyer sitting in the audience.

Then Chet said, "Attorney O'Clare, your Honor."

"Here, Your Honor," Mairead standing and moving into the bar enclosure as the words *Your first court appearance, young lady* rang in her head.

"Counselor, I'm not taking attendance in kindergarten." Laughter again. "I would, however, appreciate a statement of your full name for the record, since I don't recognize you."

Arriving at the microphone, Mairead heard Talina say "Great start" in a stage whisper.

Frowning, the judge glanced over at the dock. Mairead quickly spelled both her names.

"Very well," he said, writing something down. The judge was balding, with those little granny glasses perched halfway down his nose like Gary Oldham in *Bram Stoker's Dracula*. But now he looked over the frames, first toward Talina, then at Mairead. "A plea of not guilty is entered, but you're aware this is a serious charge?"

"Yes, Your Honor."

"And that I'd have to consider imposing a substantial bail."

"Great," said Talina, a little bit louder.

The judge turned once again, now clearly annoyed.

Mairead used the extra few seconds to think. *Maybe he wants you to plead her guilty, young lady. Otherwise, he'll set bail so high, the poor woman will rot in jail until she* does *confess.*

Mairead tried unsuccessfully to make eye contact with Chet before saying, "I don't think bail is necessary here, Your Honor."

"You don't?" replied the judge, sarcasm dripping from both syllables, a peripheral sense of Talina rolling her eyes in the dock and saying "shit."

Mairead spoke into the microphone. "No, sir. In fact, we'll be applying to the clerk/magistrate for a hearing on a charge of assault and battery against the complaining party."

Still no eye contact from Chet.

The judge looked down at his papers. "You mean the victim, Mr. . . . uh, Joshua Brewer?"

"Who attacked my client in his car—"

"After she enticed him to pick her up on a street corner." The judge

heaved a great sigh. "Best save your guns for the cross-complaint. Ms. O'Clare, I'll hear you now on bail."

Mairead had been practicing in her head while sitting in the gallery. "Your Honor, my client has lived in the Boston area for almost ten years. She has very few arrests on her—"

"Sheet, yes. But most of them are for prostitution."

"That's not relevant, Your Honor. What is—"

"You mean it's not material, counselor. 'Material' means whether or not a fact matters; 'relevant' refers to whether competent evidence proves or disproves a material fact."

Great, thought Mairead, back in the classroom again. "Either way, Your Honor, what's important is that my client has never failed to appear for trial."

The judge's eyes skimmed papers that he now turned from time to time. "From the record before me, she's had only one trial date. In fact, it seems she's otherwise always pleaded." The judge turned to a pudgy assistant DA who'd been standing most of the morning as Mairead waited for Talina's case to be called. "Recommendation?"

"Five hundred dollars," was the reply.

Talina said "fuck," very distinctly.

As the judge whipped his head toward the dock, Mairead said, "Your Honor—"

"Silence!" He pointed an index finger at Talina. "And one more expletive from you, Ms. . . . . defendant, and I'll impose a few days of criminal contempt for disrupting my session."

Mairead felt her first court appearance turning to ashes.

"Five hundred dollars, cash or equivalent." The judge actually raised and pounded his gavel. "So ordered."

"Hand job," said Talina as a court officer tugged on her elbow and told her to shut up.

Mairead addressed the dock. "We'll still apply for the cross-com—"

The judge boomed. "Ms. O'Clare, a courtroom in session is *not* the place for attorney/client . . . intercourse." He paused ever so theatrically for the new laughter to die down before saying, "Next case?"

"MR. Hayes will see you, sir," said the guy Pontifico Murizzi took for a butler, though instead of wearing a black monkey suit he had on a camel-hair sports jacket and chocolate slacks. The Pope had flashed his ID at the butler and given him a business card when the guy answered the door of the five-story mansion on the flat of Beacon Hill. The butler made Murizzi wait out in the chilly air while he checked with his boss.

Now the Pope was led up a wide, central staircase that curved to the right. Art Deco style, if he remembered what someone had once tried to teach him about appreciating such things.

At the head of the stairs, the butler opened a door, then did more a nod than a bow as Murizzi went by him.

What the Pope saw: a room full of leather furniture the color of oxblood shoe polish, with dark tables and a huge desk, all resting on an elaborate Oriental carpet. Large books sat on built-in shelves, the wall space between them filled with etchings of old clipper ships and photos of modern racing yachts.

A man with big bones stood from a wingbacked easy chair beside the desk. His broad shoulders stooped a little as he reached his full height of maybe six-three. Probably pushing seventy, he still had mostly black hair, with just dabs of white for sideburns. Blocky face and heavily lined in the forehead above bushy eyebrows and clean-shaven cheeks, but a density in the eyes themselves that made Murizzi think those lines had come less from booze and more from thinking about things. The man he took for Winston Hayes was wearing a yellow dress shirt, beige cardigan sweater with elbow patches, and brown wool pants with little holes in the fronts of the thighs.

Probably live ashes from the pipe that stayed clamped in the man's mouth as he said, "I must say, I've never met anyone named Pontifico before."

The Pope looked around the room before moving to a matching wing-backed chair. "That why I got to come up here?"

"Yes," said Hayes. "Yes, as a matter of fact, it is."

"Makes us even, then."

"Even?"

Murizzi settled into the leather. "You're my first Winston."

A mulish laugh that came out "huh-huh-huh" as Hayes dropped back into his own chair and reached for a box of matches on the desktop. "Pontifico, I think we'll get on famously."

The Pope watched Hayes make a religious ritual out of lighting his pipe, plumes of blue-gray smoke rising.

Then Murizzi said, "You know why I'm here, Mr. Hayes?"

"No idea, but . . ." He waved out his match. ". . . I'd love to be able to say 'Pontifico,' so why don't you call me Winston?"

If it opens him up, why not? "I came to see you about Zoran Draskovic."

"Lord, my first Zoran, too. Though I don't know the chap."

"He was a homeless guy they called Old Man River. Got killed along the Charles last month."

"Oh, yes." The mule laugh again. "A blessing for us all."

"Draskovic dying?"

"Pontifico . . ." Hayes paused, seeming to enjoy pronouncing the name as much as sucking on his pipe. "The wretch was rather a pain in the collective neck."

"Mind telling me how?"

"Let me count the ways." Hayes actually took his pipe from his mouth, holding it by the bowl. "Zoran cursed, Zoran stank, Zoran ranted, Zoran threw sticks and stones—literally. And some misguided reading of our federal or state constitution seemed to prevent the police from simply carting him off."

Winston, three years ago, you'd have been a man after my own heart. "He ever hit you with one of his sticks or stones?"

"My person, no. But my boat is—was—a different story." Hayes came forward in the chair, its leather upholstery squeaking a bit. "You see, Pontifico, I occasionally would scud my small river dinghy over mud banks he believed sacred."

"Sacred?"

"For the spawning of . . . carp."

"The fish."

"The *trash* fish. Primitive creature, the carp, now—with the kind of dank, unappetizing flesh that comes from living over those very mud banks. Of course, the Chinese love them."

And Artie Chin must love you, Winston. "Did Draskovic?"

"Did . . . ?"

"The carp. Did Draskovic eat them?"

"Oh, good heavens, man, no." Back to the pipe. "No, rather the opposite. Our Zoran believed he was divinely ordained to save the creatures. And the river they swam in, for that matter."

"Environmentalist?"

"Huh-huh-huh. Only if you'd count a madman who raves on street corners a poet." Two deep puffs. "No, Pontifico, our heroic crusader was simply another homeless crazy, just more of a pain than most, as I said."

"What'd he do to your boat?"

"Dinged it rather badly with some of his rocks. The man was hardly major-league material, but my boat's custom-made from staves of lovingly bent cedar, and I had a devil of a time getting it repaired."

"Expensive, too, I bet."

"Indeed, Pontifico, indeed. And there was the dratted inconvenience of not being able to sail when the spirit moved me."

Murizzi had long ago discovered that even the rich—maybe *especially* the rich—were willing to kill over money. "Mind telling me where you were that night?"

Hayes seemed to freeze in mid-puff. "What . . . 'night'?"

"When Draskovic was killed."

The dense eyes began to burn a little more than the tobacco in his pipe. "You can't be . . . You suspect *me* of killing that miserable . . . toad?"

"Somebody did."

"And the police caught him. Another derelict, as I recall."

It somehow bothered the Pope that he himself had used the same word to label both Draskovic and Alpha. "There's some question about that."

"Ah, I see now." Hayes picked up a business card lying on the corner of the desk nearest his chair. "Pontifico Murizzi, private eye, is working for the accused defendant, correct?"

The Pope thought that last part was a little redundant, but he said, "Or deciding about it."

"Yes, well, I suggest you devote yourself to more fruitful endeavors, then." Hayes leaned over his desk and used the palm of his hand to spank out dead tobacco into an ashtray. "And, since you brought up the term, allow me to tell you something about 'environmentalism' as well. Two hundred years ago, my family made its fortune building and running the mills upriver that polluted the Charles so thoroughly. As a boy, I saw fish—largemouth bass and other *real* fish—floating dead on the surface with three eyes in their heads. Waterfowl with their bills glued shut from trying to eat unimaginable gunk or with those same bills virtually dissolved by simple, constant contact with the bilious liquid they were supposed to be able to call home. Well, I—and many in my generation from other established families—did something about that, Pontifico. We actually spent money to raise petitions, lobby legislators, finance clean-up operations. And it worked. Our efforts finally paid off to the point that now when I sail, I see sports fishermen catching largemouth bass as far downriver as the lagoon at Fairfield Street, not ten city blocks from where you're sitting now. College students actually windsurf across the chop, unafraid to fall into the very water that once would have required them to receive tetanus shots upon—"

"Speaking of college kids," said Murizzi, sensing that his time was running out, "I hear that some of them used to harass this Draskovic."

"Harass? Pontifico, I won't say that I entirely agree with citizens drinking rowdily in public, but boys will be boys."

"They do anything 'rowdily' besides drink?"

"Against the derelict Draskovic, you mean?"

"What we're talking about here."

Murizzi watched Hayes actually pause, seemingly as much to think as to reload his pipe. "Well, yes, I did see some of them once take umbrage against him rather more physically."

When's the last time you heard a real person use "umbrage" in a sentence? "Can you tell me about it?"

"Not much to tell, really." A few start-up puffs again. "I was sailing near where three of them were sitting on a rotting dock, drinking. One smashed a bottle—rather intentionally, I'd have said—against a rock at the water's

edge. That's when Zoran hurled a stone at them, striking another boy, who was wearing a hooded anorak, yellow."

"And after that?"

"The boy who was struck jumped up from the dock and chased after his assailant. Difficult for me to see—the wind and my position dictated I tack just then—but when I could crane my neck enough to see them again, the boy seemed to have somebody on the ground and was kicking rather forcefully."

"Kicking Draskovic, now?"

"I was a good fifty yards away by that time." A long drag on the pipe, a few tiny embers hopping out of the bowl and dropping onto his thighs. "I could see the boy's yellow anorak, Pontifico, but not who was on the ground."

"And when was this?"

"Oh, rather late, sailing-wise. On toward Halloween."

So, about a month before Draskovic was killed. "Anything else you can think of?"

"Just one supplemental. I was too far away to see well, but—you know how sound travels over water?"

Murizzi thought about his houseboat on the harbor. "I do."

"Well," said Hayes, "another boy yelled over to the one in yellow. The words were"—an embarrassed rumble in the chest—". . . 'Leave him the fuck alone and let's get back to Van Cleeve.'"

The dorm Artie Chin mentioned as an address. Murizzi named the school.

"I'm impressed, Pontifico. Van Cleeve *is* a residence hall near the river." A look of distaste crossed Hayes's features. "A newer building, however, and rather banal, architecturally."

Even with that qualification, though, Pontifico Murizzi thought Winston Hayes looked pretty pleased with his guest.

MAIREAD false-started twice toward P.J. Clarke's before finally deciding that, no matter how bad a morning she'd had at her first appearance in court, a person still had to eat lunch, and she might as well get treated to it. Plus, Mairead had started the ball rolling on her—well,

Talina's—application for a cross-complaint against Joshua Brewer, and that simple step made her feel a little more professional. Not to mention she'd love to see the look on the guy's face when he got ordered to appear as a potential defendant. Chet the clerk—once outside the presence of the judge, his young-grandfather demeanor returned—said the notice to Brewer would go out that afternoon. And there was even a possibility that somebody would post bail for Talina, since Chet said it had happened before.

Exiting the courthouse complex, Mairead jaywalked through traffic, crossed the red-bricked plaza called Government Center, and took the stairs down past City Hall. After dodging a few more vehicles, she kept Fanueil Hall on her left and found P.J. Clarke's just on the south side of the Quincy Market area.

The bar part was packed, even on a Wednesday at 1 P.M. She moved through it slowly to the dining room, spotting John Ramirez in a booth. He waved to her, but when she arrived, there was only one other associate from Jaynes & Ward at the table.

Mairead said, "Where's Timmy?"

Jenna, the short-haired blond lawyer sitting on the bench opposite Ramirez, said, "Burgess yanked him for some last-minute brief on a discovery issue. Timmy'll be there till dawn tomorrow."

"Bummer," said Mairead, remembering what it was like as she slid in next to Jenna.

The waiter came over immediately. There already were two draft beers on the table, and Mairead asked for a third. While there was never any express policy at Jaynes & Ward about drinking at lunch, every associate knew it would be careericide to order alcohol when out with partners, regardless of what the older lawyers might slug down.

Something you'll not have to worry about again, young lady.

"So," said Mairead, "what else is shaking at the glue factory?"

Both of the other attorneys moaned, Jenna complaining about having to wade through twenty depositions in a municipal bond lawsuit originally filed when she was in seventh grade. Ramirez had three major things going for corporate clients, all *molto* boring except for a patent question on a radar device that could probe for earthquake victims buried under rocks.

Then Ramirez hunched forward. "But we're here to honor you for pulling the rip cord. How's the new job going?"

"It's different."

"Like, how?" said Jenna.

"Well, today I represented a prostitute who—"

"Get out of town!" said Ramirez, amazement flooding his face.

"No, really."

Jenna ran an index finger around the rim of her mug. "Was she, like, you know . . . gross?"

"I wouldn't say that, no. More . . . used? She's not stupid, but she seems maybe caught up in the life?"

"'The life,'" said Ramirez just as Mairead's ale arrived. He lifted his mug, and all three clinked together. "Well, here's to a life, any life."

Jenna licked foam off her upper lip. "Yeah, like, tell me about it. I've had three dates in four months. Oh, I get calls from guys—even a couple who aren't total dweebs—but after working all week, I just don't have the energy to *have* a life."

Ramirez turned to Mairead. "So, how about you? What's perking other than the prostitute?"

Should I or shouldn't I? "Well, I met this neat private investigator."

Jenna stopped with her mug halfway to her mouth. "Magnum? Tell me he looks like Magnum."

"Sort of, but not as tall. And he lives on a boat."

Ramirez, deadpan. "A boat."

"In the harbor. But it's more like a one-bedroom apartment."

Jenna looked at Ramirez, then spoke in a singsong voice. "Mairead's been in his bedroom."

"No, for your information, I haven't. I just know there must be one, because I didn't see any bed from his living room."

Ramirez said, "I thought sailors slept in hammocks."

"No." Mairead laughed. "I don't see the Pope in a hammock."

Jenna coughed into her beer. "The . . . Pope?"

"His nickname."

"So," said Ramirez, "how did you meet this guy?"

"I'm trying to get him to help us on a . . ." *String it out, young lady* ". . . case of ours."

Ramirez smirked, but not unfriendly. "What, a divorce?"

"No, though my new boss does those, too." Time for the hammer. "This is a homicide."

"Homicide?" said both like a Greek chorus.

"Murder one."

"You *have* to be shitting me," said Jenna.

"My hand to God."

Ramirez seemed stunned. "Who did this guy kill?"

"Allegedly kill. I don't see him murdering the victim here. Our client's too . . ." Mairead searched for the right word. "He strikes me as too honorable."

"Strikes you?" said Jenna, glancing at Ramirez before coming back to Mairead. "You've actually, like, *met* the guy?"

"Interviewed him. Over at Nashua Street."

"Where?" from Ramirez.

And Mairead could feel some pride and confidence flowing back into herself as she described for her two former colleagues things she realized they'd probably never experience.

7

"... AND MY CLIENT wants the marital home she's slaved to—"

"Slaved? *Slaved*?" said Little Benji Schwartz, on Sheldon Gold's side of the conference table but leaning hard on his elbows toward the attorney representing Mrs. Schwartz. "If Hedda's worked an eight-hour day in her whole life, I wasn't around to see it."

"No surprise there," Hedda sitting diagonally across from Little Benji while folding her arms under her ample breasts, lifting them like a flesh-and-blood Wonderbra. "You weren't around all that much, period."

"Everybody, please," said Shel, using his thumb and index finger to massage the bridge of his nose. He'd felt this headache coming on at the beginning of the divorce settlement conference.

No, admit it: You started getting the headache just *thinking* about this morning.

The truce Shel called was briefly observed by the other three people in the room. Christina Medina, thirtyish and petite with brown hair and hazel eyes, was the lawyer Hedda had hired. Shel, checking out his opponent, had received telephone reports that she was tough but fair. And, in truth, Hedda herself wasn't being unreasonable, especially given the length of the marriage (twenty-two years), the fact that she'd never worked outside the home (a source of pride to Benji, Shel knew), and the . . . awkwardness of presenting evidence in court of his client's income stream, given the man spent most of his working hours in other people's houses.

Burglarizing them.

Shel had met Benjamin Schwartz the second day of kindergarten and liked him from the start. Not the kind of kid who'd become your best friend, maybe, or even one you'd nudge toward your sister. No, Benji was scrawny at five years old and never much filled out thereafter, his Adam's apple the most prominent thing about him below his eyes, which bulged some and moved kind of funny, even independently, like a gecko's. Shel and Benji both graduated, in some sense of the word, into a neighborhood gang run by Benjamin Friedman. Once they hit middle school, Friedman insisted on being called Big Ben, and Schwartz got stuck with Little Benji. Shel had a nickname, too, Golden Boy, though that had less to do with his last name and more—

"Shel," said Medina, "are we all calm enough now?"

"I think so, Christina." Shel took a breath, knowing his client wasn't going to like his next sentence. "While a judge might look favorably upon Mrs. Schwartz's position here, I—"

"Her *position*?" said Benji. "What's with 'her position'? Every dime went into that house was money I earned."

"From stealing," offered Hedda, raising her breasts another half-inch.

"Yeah, well, I don't remember you complaining about me putting food on your table and clothes on your back."

Medina seemed to read from the pad in front of her. "Mr. Schwartz, I'm sure your attorney has explained to you why this case really ought to settle."

Shel liked the way Medina used and pronounced the word "attorney," like she was trying to get through Benji's thick skull the respect Shel's own judgment should receive.

Only that wasn't the way his client took it.

Little Benji snapped his head so sharply, Shel thought he could hear the vertebrae cracking. "What, you been telling this shark what we talked about?"

"Benji," said Shel, squeezing his nose again. "First, Ms. Medina is not a shark. She's just doing for her client what I'm trying to do for you. Second, it's pretty obvious that she's—"

"Cruising the shallows, looking for an easy meal. Just like a shark. Only I'm not gonna be the one ends up in her jaws."

Shel watched Little Benji's eyes move independently, and he knew his boyhood friend was about to rabbit.

"Benji, please, we need to finish this."

The man shoved back his chair and darted to the conference room door. "Oh, I'm gonna finish it, all right."

Shel Gold let the breeze created by the slammed door wash over his face, but the sensation didn't help his headache much.

LEAVING P.J. Clarke's, Mairead O'Clare realized how much lunch with her former colleagues had lifted her spirits. They were still mired in drudge at Jaynes & Ward, while she was doing things that were genuinely exciting.

Like visiting a construction site.

Mairead walked farther down State Street, navigating by Rex's landmarks and watching for a sign reading "Cornerstone." She spotted it just before the Big Dig street-level wall.

The lettering said, GENERAL CONTRACTOR: CORNERSTONE CONSTRUCTION, INC., on a marquee with owner and architect given top billing. The structure was a half-rendered office building, the site a beehive of structural steel, concrete, and mud.

Trying to erect as much as a shed in this city must be a nightmare with all the road disruption, so maybe it doesn't screw things up that much more to be building a skyscraper.

Mairead reached a chain-link fence with concertina wire in rolls at the top. Trucks lumbered through a wide, open gate, but there was a person-sized door near a little glass-windowed sentry box inside the fence, so Mairead went to the guard standing there.

The florid-faced man of maybe sixty said, "Help you?"

"I'm attorney Mairead O'Clare." She opened her wallet to show her Board of Bar Overseers card. It was just a thin piece of white laminate with a signature and some small print, but Mairead felt vaguely official, like a police detective flashing her badge.

"So?"

"So, I'd like to speak to the construction supervisor about a client of mine who used to come here."

A frown. "This client used to work on the site?"

Mairead felt her momentum slipping. "Maybe if I could speak to the supervisor?"

The guard kept frowning but went into his little sentry box for a cell phone. Mairead saw his lips moving, then his head nodding. Rather than coming back out, though, he just spoke to her through the open doorway. "Somebody'll be down for you."

"Thanks." Mairead checked her watch, then turned to study her surroundings a little more carefully.

It was going to be over thirty stories, though Mairead stopped counting upward at twenty because only the steel skeleton rose above that. Below the twentieth floor, a lot of human movement was visible, the workers walking or bending or suspended from ropes with all kinds of tools in their hands. Others, on the ground, were guiding crane operators lifting batches of pipe and slabs of plywood off flatbed trucks and toward the floors above. Everybody wore hard hats and looked dusty, wearing surprisingly light clothes. The wind whipping off the harbor half a mile away caused big sheets of plastic to clap sharply against the columns between which they were tied.

Be thankful you never had to do outside work, young lady. It's lovely in the summer, but once this thaw leaves us, February and March will be brutal for the poor—

"All right, what's this about?"

Mairead turned toward the voice, apparently belonging to one of two men walking her way from a trailer near one wall. The lead man wore a business suit and hard hat, though he now had the helmet in one hand while he ran his other through the compressed, shortish blond hair on his head. He was about six feet tall and trim, striding with purpose and blocking most of her view of the man behind him. As the lead man got closer, Mairead could see he was good-looking in a Madison Avenue, android kind of way.

The trailing man was shorter and more solid, and while he wore a suit, too, Mairead got the impression he'd be happier in more casual clothes. Taking his hard hat off, he revealed thinning brown hair and a face you wouldn't look at twice on the subway because it was neither handsome nor threatening.

The lead man said, "Come on, I don't have all day."

Mairead extended her hand. "How about introductions first?"

The first man took her hand, briefly and without any semblance of courtesy. The rear man shook firmly with her, saying, "This is Mr. Pratt, president of Cornerstone. I'm Al Wyckoff, chief of security."

Security, thought Mairead, though she addressed Pratt. "And your first name, sir?"

He huffed out a breath that apparently meant to display impatience. "Severn, spelled S-e-v-e-r-n."

Mairead liked to empathize with other people who felt compelled to spell their given names, but she decided against that with Pratt. "I'm Mairead O'Clare. My firm represents the defendant accused of murdering Zoran Draskovic."

Pratt waved away her opening. "Means nothing to me."

Persevere, young lady. "He was a homeless man, clubbed to death along the Charles."

Wyckoff looked at her thoughtfully. "By the other bum?"

Mairead let it pass. "The police arrested my client, who goes by the name Alpha. I understand he used to get wood from here to build a shelter for himself under a bridge."

Pratt bristled. "In other words, you represent a thief who stole from me."

"I'm told that the wood was scrap."

Pratt's hackles rose higher. "Cornerstone doesn't provide free samples. If we did, they'd scavenge us to death."

"Look, I don't want to get anybody in trouble, but it'd be a real help if I could confirm this part of my client's story."

"You're saying this man took wood—whether scrap or not—from my construction site, and you expect me to—"

"I also understand that the wood was *given* to my client."

Pratt nearly yelled in Mairead's face. "Nobody on one of Cornerstone's projects would ever . . ."

She saw Pratt's eyes change as his head dropped. Then he turned to Wyckoff. "Tomlinson?"

Wyckoff looked Mairead straight in the eye before shrugging once. "A long shot, even if she is telling the truth."

Mairead said, "Who's Tomlinson?"

Pratt turned back to her, no longer yelling but not any friendlier, either. "Donn—with two *n*'s—Tomlinson was a project unto himself. A black I took on out of prison. 'Rehabilitated,' I was assured. Well, I gave him steady work, even promoted him to foreman. Then Tomlinson stole from me, robbed me blind on copper piping, electrical fixtures, even tools. And after all I'd done for him, the bastard didn't even have the guts to own up to it."

Mairead processed that. "He pleaded not guilty?"

Wyckoff shook his head. "The guy disappeared. Poof. Ran out on his wife *and* us just as I was making a case against him."

"And right before we really needed him," said Pratt, gesturing, "to oversee the pouring of those slabs toward the street. But if he'd hung around, I would have prosecuted. Nobody cheats me. Not Tomlinson, and not a bum like your client."

Mairead felt her own temper flaring. "My client's homeless, Mr. Pratt. That doesn't make him a bum."

"The beauty of America," said Severn Pratt, obviously ending the conversation by whisking his hands at the sleeves of his suit. "We can all express our opinions freely." He didn't bother looking at Wyckoff before saying, "Al, get her business card, then meet me back at the office."

"You bet."

When Pratt was out of earshot, Wyckoff reached into his coat pocket and came out with a blue vinyl card case. "This is me."

Mairead read the card. It had all the information he'd already given her, except that his full first name was Alvin. It also listed an address for Cornerstone about twelve blocks away.

Wyckoff said, "How about yours?"

Mairead was ready for that one. "I'm just having more of them made up, but I can write out my office address and phone for you."

Wyckoff gave her another of his cards, and Mairead block-printed her name and Shel's details on it. Wyckoff read the specifics aloud. Then he lowered his voice. "You want, I could check on things for that night, but I don't recommend it."

"Wait a minute. What night?"

"The night that homeless guy got killed."

Mairead felt her head canting to the left. "How would you remember when that was?"

"Because it was the night in early December that Tomlinson never went home, and the two events stuck in my mind when I read the *Globe* the next morning. Only that's also the reason I don't recommend my checking on things."

"Okay, I'm lost."

Wyckoff leaned in a little closer. Even in the open air, Mairead got a whiff of minty breath. "If your guy—Alpha?"

"Right."

"If this Alpha was running a scam with Tomlinson, you might not want to know whether your guy was on-site the night before his coconspirator stops showing up for work."

The light dawned. "You think Alpha could have done something to Tom—"

"Hey, counselor," said Alvin Wyckoff, "I may be head of security for the company, but all I really know is what I read in the papers."

PONTIFICO Murizzi was trying to remember that line from something he had to read in high-school English. It went something like, "What a pity that youth is wasted on the young."

As the Pope oriented himself on campus, he thought that most of the young he saw were also wasted. He'd never worked Narcotics, but he remembered the late sixties and early seventies, the bars in Kenmore Square and Harvard Street, the kids getting their first taste of beer or harder stuff,

puking their guts out. Or worse, poisoning themselves so badly even the hospitals couldn't pull them back to life. Murizzi had kind of hoped that, thirty years later, things would have changed for the better, but all he could see for sure was that appearances had gotten worse.

The kids the Pope moved past wore metal shit through their ears and eyebrows, noses and lips. The ones who weren't "grunge" had enough black clothing on to make a ninja movie.

Murizzi found "Van Cleeve" carved into a piece of granite the size of a railroad tie over a double door. He was prepared for the dorm to be coed, but the Pope was surprised that the actual floor he wanted seemed to have both men and women living on it.

How do they divvy up the lavatory?

Murizzi found room 512 at the end of the corridor, a scent of marijuana in the air. The door was closed, but when he knocked, a blurry voice said, "It's open, dude."

The Pope tried the knob and stepped into a large room with two of everything: beds, desks, chairs, half-raised windows, even bolt-on, snake-neck lamps. Oh, and two kids as well, lying faceup on each of the perpen-dicularly arranged beds, their heads almost touching as one passed a joint to the other.

"Whoa, dude," said the Passer. "Like, who might you be?"

Shades of the sixties, thought Murizzi, and shook his head. Their stash, open to the world in a clear plastic bag on one desk, looked to be a good double handful. The Pope briefly wondered how they measured out the weed nowadays.

"My bud asked you a question," said the Receiver, a little dreamily through a sweet, lingering haze.

Murizzi pulled over a chair, reversed it, and sat smoothly, his hands on the curving back, his chin resting on tented fingers.

Passer got up onto one elbow. "What's the matter, you deaf?"

The Pope was just taking it all in: the moment, the room, the assholes.

Receiver now copied his friend's posture. "We gonna have to throw you out of here, or what?"

Murizzi stood back up, then in one stride was at the desk with the mari-

juana bag. Hefting it in his left palm, he took another stride, his hand and the "brown-green vegetablelike substance" extending a foot out one of the half-open windows.

Both boys came full upright, Passer a little steadier on his feet than Receiver, who managed, "The fuck you doing, dude?"

"Names," said the Pope. "Start with yours."

The two kids exchanged a glance. Passer said, "You can't just barge in here and threaten—"

Murizzi shook the plastic bag a little, and a thatch of grass the size of a pocketknife went fluttering away.

"Shit, dude," said Receiver, rubbing his eyes in disbelief. "You know what that costs?"

"It's already cost you your names."

Another exchanged glance. The two kids weren't shrimps, but there was something indecisive about them that the Pope didn't think came from the roaches. More like neither was ready to lead.

"Last chance," said Murizzi.

"Jeff," admitted Passer, who had a butch cut and a short-sleeved sweatshirt over baggy jeans. "Jeff Glennon."

"Rick." Receiver had a pageboy chopped at the ears and a long-sleeved T-shirt over basketball shorts. "Rick Dorsey."

"Okay, Jeff and Rick. Here's the drill. I ask a question, you answer it, or you can go chase your pot with butterfly nets."

When they didn't reply, the Pope said, "You remember harassing a guy on the river?"

"The Charles River?" said Jeff.

"There another one within walking distance?"

Rick waved his hand toward Cambridge. "I remember harassing a guy who wouldn't let us alone."

"Tell me about it."

Jeff glanced at his friend, but got no evident direction. "Not much to tell, dude. We were just, like, sharing a handle, and this homeless geek—"

"A handle?"

Rick seemed heartened that Murizzi didn't recognize the term. "Those big bottles of Jim Beam have the handle on the side you can chug it by, like a fucking hilly-billy with moonshine."

Lovely image. "Go on."

Jeff said, "So this geek comes up to us, tells us not to break the bottle, account of hurting the fish and ducks."

A sincere voice, but Rick put in, "Yeah, right. Like we'd give a fuck."

Rick's attitude seemed contagious. "Yeah," said Jeff, "so we tell this geek to hit the pike before we mess him up. Only instead of leaving like any sensible shithead, he starts throwing stones."

"How big were these stones?"

"The fuck should I know how big? We didn't stop to—"

The Pope shook the product bag a little. "How big?"

Rick said, "Like maybe plums to baseballs, okay? We were trying more not to get killed than to measure them."

"Then what did you do?"

Jeff started with, "Mitch decided we—"

Rick cut him off. "Yo, Jeff. Not cool. Definitely *not* cool."

Murizzi had the third kid's name from Artie Chin in Homicide, but you build an interrogation by getting more than you give. "How cool would it be to say good-bye to the rest of your stash here?"

Jeff said, "Ah, dude, come on, huh? We been answering everything you asked us."

"Until Mitch popped into the conversation. Now, who is he?"

Rick and Jeff looked at each other again. The Pope began to think who'd go to pee first might require a summit meeting.

Jeff looked back to Murizzi. "Mitch Gerber."

"Like the baby food?"

"What?"

"Skip it. What did Gerber decide you should do?"

Jeff balked. Rick jumped in with, "Nothing. Just that we should come back to his place."

From the way Rick said the last phrase, the Pope didn't think the kid

meant Dorm Van Cleeve, which might explain the apartment address Chin also had given him. "Gerber lives off-campus?"

"What's it to you?" Rick trying to rally a little.

Murizzi shook out another thatch of weed.

"Aw, dude," said Jeff. "Come on. Please?"

"Gerber's place."

Jeff gave up the apartment address the Pope already had. Rick was looking glad that *he* hadn't revealed Mitch's crib.

"Okay, now," said Murizzi. "What did Gerber really decide to do after the homeless guy threw his stones at you?"

Rick shrugged. "We kind of chased the guy down."

"And?"

"And," said Jeff, his eyes studying his bare feet on the floor, "Mitch kind of stomped him."

The goal of any interrogation: Divide and conquer.

"That all you guys ever did?"

Rick said, "You mean the rich prick?"

The Pope tried for poker-faced. "Which rich prick?"

Jeff looked up now. "A sailing dude, always yelling at us, too. So once in a while, we'd throw some shit at his boat."

"What kind of shit?"

"Stones, like the homeless geek," said Rick. "And bottles." Then a wise-guy grin. "If they were empty, of course."

Winston Hayes must have forgotten to mention that. "You citizens do anything more to the homeless guy?"

"Fuck, no," said Rick, like he was on a roll now. "He knew not to mess with us anymore."

"How about we go visit Gerber, ask him the same question?"

As Jeff said, "We can't, he's home," Rick said. "Went to the hospital because his dad, like, infarcted."

"His father's had a heart attack?"

"Yeah," said Rick. "The blood-clot breakdance, you know?"

Murizzi ran that. "Any idea what might have brought it on?"

Rick grinned broadly. "Him fucking Mitch's thirty-year-old stepmom three times a day might do it. What do you think?"

The Pope thought he might shake out the rest of the marijuana like dust from a vacuum bag. But then it occurred to him that he might need these charmers again.

And so Pontifico Murizzi tossed the marijuana back onto the desk and wished Rick and Jeff a nice magic carpet ride.

IT'S LIKE FALLING OFF *the horse, young lady. You need to get right back on and ride.*

Mairead agreed with Sister Bernadette. But given the setting January sun, she just wanted to be done with her mission before dark, even though fingering the new flashlight in her tote bag.

The left ankle was still a little tender, so Mairead took a cab to the point on Storrow Drive closest to Alpha's cave. Retracing the route she'd jogged that morning, she spotted the shreds of yellow police tape again. Taking a deep breath, Mairead started climbing upslope.

The cave's door was open. Mairead stopped twenty feet from it and looked around, but didn't see anything. Or, more important, anyone. Taking out the flashlight, she went up to the entrance.

Before turning on the beam, Mairead waited at the doorway and listened. No distinct sounds of movement, but a slow, rhythmic bubbling of air reached her, she thought from the area of the bed.

Like somebody breathing through a stuffed nose. Mairead flicked on the flashlight.

"I don't have nothing! Don't shoot, please don't shoot."

He thinks I'm police.

Mairead watched as Rex writhed in the circle of light, almost as if it were burning him. He was lying faceup on the bed, his forearms protecting his eyes, the hands open and seemingly empty.

But a glint of metal coming off one of them.

No fear, young lady.

Lowering her voice, Mairead said, "Drop the knife."

"I don't got no knife, officer."

"I can see it from here."

"It's not a blade, honest. It's a splint, on my finger."

Mairead took a step into the room, swinging her light left and right in quick arcs. Just the two of them in the cave.

She said, "Stay where you are."

"I'm not moving. Just please don't shine that light in my eyes no more."

Mairead figured she couldn't pull off the impersonation forever. In her normal voice, she said, "It's me, Rex."

"You?" as a genuine question.

Mairead shined the light up into her face, hoping it would look menacing to him, like back in the orphanage when she and the other kids would play at being vampires. Then Mairead put the beam on Rex's body rather than his face.

He said, "How come you're back?"

"I still need those books for Alpha."

Rex sniffled, ran a forearm under his nose. "They're still here on the floor, from when you busted my face with them."

Running the light down briefly, Mairead saw he was telling the truth. "What happened to your hand?"

"Ask your cop friend," said Rex in a whiny tone.

"Who?"

"Your cop friend, the guy shadowing you. He was on me almost before you was out of sight."

He must mean Mr. Murizzi, young lady.

"And my friend broke—"

"My finger. On purpose. Punishment, like. For me trying to get it on with you."

Mairead felt a little tearing sensation inside her chest. A part of her was angry that the Pope didn't think she could take care of herself. Another part was vaguely flattered that a knight in shining armor wanted to come to her rescue. And a third part of her was glad to realize she'd been angry first.

"Of course," said Rex, smarmy now, "if he ain't with you—"

"You need any more fingers broken, I'll do them myself." Mairead's eyes had adjusted to the dimness around her flashlight's beam, and she shined it square in Rex's face again.

"Hey, don't," his forearms going back up protectively.

Bending over, Mairead used her free hand to rake the books on the floor toward the door. One had a broken binding, probably from her shot-putting the stack at Rex, but she gathered it up anyway.

Then Mairead thought of something else. "The wood for these shelves and doors?"

"What about it?" said Rex through his forearms.

"This morning you told me Alpha claimed he got the scraps from a fore-man at the construction project."

"Right."

"But you thought he was lying."

No response.

"Rex, talk to me here."

"Aw, I was just funning with you. We both got stuff from that colored guy, Tommy."

"Donn Tomlinson?"

"He just said to call him Tommy."

"So, Alpha didn't steal the wood."

"I don't know, did he steal *any* of it, but Tommy sure give us bunches of the stuff."

Mairead felt a little better, wondered if the reason was confirming at least one detail of Alpha's story, however minor.

"Okay, Rex, I'm leaving now."

"Just don't be expecting me to escort you no place."

"I think I can manage on my own."

"SHELDON, isn't it?"

The woman who opened the massive front door to Benjamin Friedman's home stood in marked contrast to the two no-necks who'd frisked him at the gate down the driveway. She also was someone Shel had met at a barbe-cue the prior summer. Big Ben's lady friends usually didn't stay around for

such a long time, and Shel couldn't bring back this one's name. But they were all cut from the same pattern: willowy, blonde, and mid-twenties. Almost like there was a period in Ben's life that he was trying to repeat, over and over and over again.

Admit it: You can think of worse delusions.

The woman extended a long-fingered, long-nailed hand. "I'm Tiffany."

"Good to see you again."

Following her back toward what Shel remembered as "the Florida room," he thought Tiffany might have been somebody Big Ben met down in Boca Raton. She had the figure for it, in a red fleece pullover and white jeans that were so tight, Shel could actually see the outline of a silver dollar in her back pocket.

It took a few more steps to register that what he was seeing happened to be a condom.

"Ben, Sheldon's here."

She said it in a bright, surprised tone, though Shel had called before going to the house, and he was pretty sure the no-necks also would've let their boss know he'd arrived.

Big Ben Friedman was stretched out on his back in a woven lounge chair against a stucco wall, like Shel imagined a villa in Italy might have. The other three walls and roof were all glass, bathing the man with dying sunlight. Big Ben wore a royal purple robe, with matching flip-flops on his feet and a matching pair of small, opaque tanning goggles that covered only his eyes and a fraction of his nose. The hands were folded across his belly, as though he were lying in state, and the crow-wing hair bordering his forehead looked like rows of black cornstalks.

From the way they did the transplant, Shel had always assumed.

Without taking off the goggles, Big Ben said, "Golden Boy, sit, sit."

Shel went to a chair that looked out toward the tree house Big Ben had built for his two sons in the long ago. Shel sat so as not to block any of the available light from reaching his friend.

Still blindered, Big Ben pointed back toward Tiffany. "You want something to drink, eat?"

Shel said, "Some ice water, maybe."

Tiffany turned and left without being asked.

"So, Golden Boy, it's January and you're not wearing an overcoat?"

Shel glanced down at his suit, then over to the lounge. "There're holes in those plastic things?"

Grinning, Big Ben pointed toward his ears instead of his eyes. "You love the sun the way I do, you gotta protect your sight, but your hearing, it gets better. You compensate, like some poor blind bastard." Now he pointed toward Shel. "And, with you sitting down in that chair, I could hear your pants instead of a winter coat. Different sounds."

Tiffany came back with a tall glass of ice water on a saucer, single wedges of lemon and lime on the china. As soon as Shel thanked her, she leaned over to Big Ben, kissed him once at his cornrowed hairline, and then was gone again.

About the time that Shel could no longer hear her footsteps, Big Ben said, "Best piece of ass I've had in ten years." He brought his hands to his chest, as though hefting breasts. "And all original equipment, too. Not an after-market part on her. Plus, she even knows how to behave: naughty in the sack, magic in the kitchen, and like a Wellesley girl with my 'business guests.'"

Shel nodded, then realized Big Ben might not be able to "hear" that. "I'm glad for you."

"So, Golden Boy. What brings you here?"

Shel inhaled. "It's Little Benji."

"That *mamzer*? He still double quick and triple slick?"

"He's not in prison."

"Unless you count his being married to that stevedore."

Shel wondered if maybe Big Ben knew more than Benji's lawyer about the situation. "Actually, that's kind of why I'm here."

"What, he finally grew the balls to kill Hedda?"

"I'm afraid he might be in the process."

"Meaning what?"

"They're getting divorced, but it's not going so well."

Big Ben reached up to his face with one immense, hairy hand and removed the tanning goggles before craning his neck forward. "Let me guess. You're representing him?"

"I am."

Big Ben shook his head. "When we were kids, Shel, you always boxed on the undercard. Shel 'Golden Boy' Gold. Hands of stone, before that '*no más*' guy got the label. But you never were the main event. And, doing penny-ante criminal shit and divorcing B and E artists like Little Benji, you're still on the undercard."

Shel willed his hands not to clench. "I'm comfortable."

"Comfortable? Let me tell you, where you are isn't comfortable. This, with Tiffany and an indoor pool and Jacuzzi and Boca three weeks every winter month, this is comfortable. What you got, Golden Boy, what you put yourself through with Natalie over in her loony bin, that is not comfortable."

At the mention of his wife, Shel felt the fists forming, but he gestured with his hands instead. "To each his own, Ben."

"You're hopeless, you know that? You give out advice like a lawyer, but you can't take it."

"About Benji?"

"All right, all right." Big Ben put the goggles back over his eyes. "Little Benji. So talk."

"I'm really worried he might do something to Hedda."

"He tries to fuck that gargoyle, *he's* the one should be worried."

"I mean it, Ben. The divorce negotiations aren't going well, and it's upsetting him. I think he might try to kill her."

"So what do you want me to do about it?"

"Have a talk with him."

"A talk."

"He always looked up to you. We all did."

"Now the butter knife, huh?"

But Shel could see his old friend was still flattered. "What's true is true, Ben."

Some wiggling of the lips under a nose that was a mite narrower than the one Big Ben was born with. "So, a little talk with Little Benji."

"I'd really appreciate it, Ben."

"Hey, what are friends for, right."

Shel sensed it was time to go, but he had a question that had always bothered him. "Ben?"

"What, the talk's not enough?"

"It's enough. Different matter."

"Which is?"

"Granted you have the security at your gate, and probably all kinds of alarms in the house. But aren't you kind of . . . vulnerable, just lying out here?"

The lips spread into a grin, and Big Ben lifted his left hand from his belly in a "how" sign. Then he folded all his fingers except the index, pointing that one at the wall behind him. Shel saw a little dot of red light appear on the white stucco.

"That's a laser sight, Golden Boy. When I raise my hand, the sniper in the tree house aims that dot at your head. I drop my hand instead of pointing like so, what was left of your brains would make poor Tiffany have to redecorate in here."

Sheldon A. Gold didn't so much as twitch until Big Ben Friedman returned his hand slowly to his belly.

"AH, and to what angel do I owe the blessing of *this* visit?"

Mairead reached across the little table and shook Alpha's outstretched hand. "I was trying to bring you some of your books."

A cloud crossed Alpha's face as he sat down and the guard behind him closed the jailside door. "Trying, you say?"

Mairead nodded. "They impounded all four downstairs. After somebody inspects them, I think you'll get them."

Now a crinkle of a grin at the corners of his mouth. "Four? That would have been a burden to you."

"No, but . . ."

Alpha's jumpy green eyes asked the question.

Mairead said, "One of the bindings got broken."

"The bastards."

"No, not the guards. I did it," and she briefly related her first visit to the cave and encounter with Rex.

"It's a lucky thing that I'm incarcerated, then, for I'd have killed him for trying to hurt someone trying to help me."

First the Pope, now my client. Men, always thinking in terms of revenge.

Alpha paused. "Only, if you hurled my poor books at the wormy bla-guard, how did you get them back?"

Mairead summarized her second visit, leaving out the broken finger and the construction site information.

Alpha grinned. "You've got genuine courage, Mairead, and I'm lucky to have you on my side."

He might have fewer teeth than fingers, but there's something about this guy . . .

Business, young lady.

Mairead shook her head. "Alpha, both you and Rex told me you got wood at the construction site, for your shelves and all."

"At least he wasn't lying to you about that."

"From somebody named Tommy?"

"Aye. Short for Tomlinson. A fine black feller who understands the status of being down and out."

"I went to the site."

"I'm impressed you're going to so much trouble for—"

"And they told me Mr. Tomlinson is missing."

The cloud that had crossed Alpha's face came back. "What's that?"

"The people who run the construction company—Cornerstone—said they thought he was stealing from them."

"Stealing?"

"And not just scraps of lumber. Real expensive stuff. They think Mr. Tomlinson took off as a result."

Alpha's cloud began to rain, and he quickly passed a palm across his eyes. "And when was this, lass?"

"That I spoke to them?"

"That Tommy went missing."

Mairead took a breath. "He didn't show up for work the morning after Mr. Draskovic was killed."

Now Alpha closed his eyes.

Mairead gave her client a moment, then said, "Alpha?"

"Yes," eyes still closed.

"I need to know if you had anything to do with Mr. Tomlinson disappearing."

The green eyes flapped open. Jesus Mary, like a monster in a horror movie coming back to life.

And the eyes were different, now. Or the look in them. And Mairead realized that for the first time, she was a little afraid to be alone with the man.

Steady, young lady. Steady.

Alpha said, "After talking as we have, you'd ask me that?"

Mairead quelled her welling fear. "Just doing my job."

He nodded, but less like agreement and more like "so that's it." Then Alpha spoke very slowly. "Lass, I think you might want to be having a talk with your Mr. Gold."

"A talk?"

"Aye. On the importance of trusting your clients."

Mairead found herself bristling a little now, as she had with Hadley Burgess back at the firm. "As in trusting the man who won't even tell me who he is?"

Alpha's eyes burned slightly brighter, like emeralds in the sun, then cooled as he smiled that gap-toothed way. "I've told you who I am, lass. A hermit of the New Order. What I won't tell you is who I was." Then he lost the smile. "But I will tell you something else."

"What's that?"

"I'll help you."

"Help me?"

"On the defense you're struggling to mount for me."

Mairead felt suspicion now. "Not to be rude, but how come?"

"You talked before about 'doing your job.' Well, I agree with you. There's a job to be done, all right, and we each have to be contributing toward it."

"And what's your part, Alpha?"

"I'll have to be thinking on that, Mairead O'Clare. I'll have to be doing some very serious thinking on that."

A S the sun dipped behind the office towers to the west of the harbor, Pontifico Murizzi bounced a little on the floating dock—called a "camel"—feeling anticipation build. He tried to move quietly as he drew near the schooner that adjoined his houseboat.

But Jocko, the young man with the blond-tipped hair, looked up from his polishing. "So, mate, how did your day go?"

The Pope reached the gunwale of the sailboat. In a soft voice, he said, "Not half as well as my night will."

Jocko smiled warmly. "Be over in an hour, luv."

9

I SHOULD HAVE KNOWN the ankle would tighten up.

The next morning, Mairead trudged up Beacon Hill toward Sheldon Gold's office, favoring her left leg.

Walking should at least loosen up the joint, young lady. But no more hockey for the immediate future.

Which was just as well, actually, given the amount of time Alpha's case would require, even if he was finally willing to help in their defense of him. But his philosophy of life—shunning contact with other people—still puzzled Mairead. And troubled her, too. Maybe because for so many years in the orphanage, she'd just marked time, hoping against hope—and experience—to be adopted into a real family, start a "real" life. And then here was Alpha, well into *his* real life, actively avoiding just that, even contact with the other homeless people around him.

Which reminded Mairead of Rex, of the Pope "avenging" her.

The anger rose again, but really only like a footnote in a law review article she'd edited back at New England. Mairead knew she was right to resent the way Murizzi had interfered, and if they were to be working together on Alpha's case—and maybe in the future as well—she decided to approach the private detective about what he'd done.

And besides, it does give me a reason to see him again.

Smiling as she daydreamed about dating the Pope, Mairead felt a little spring in her step, even from the bad left ankle.

———

PONTIFICO Murizzi awakened, fearing at first that he'd disturbed Jocko, who was sleeping with his head against the Pope's left shoulder. The Brit's hair, appearing spiky and stiff from a distance, actually felt quite pliant, but it still tickled a little against the skin, and Murizzi wondered if that sensation was what had brought him out of dreamland.

Sensations. And dreamland.

Without moving his head, the Pope let his eyes rove down Jocko's body, from the rings through his left ear to the nape of his neck down to the calf and foot, the only parts of the man's body outside the blanket on Murizzi's big bed.

Christ, this guy gives you pleasure.

"I'm a genuine rarity, mate," Jocko had said to him, that day two months before, the big schooner docking in the slip beside the Pope's houseboat. "A Brit with good teeth who can cook."

Murizzi laughed now, but only in his mind. The smile that Jocko had flashed with the "rarity" line, a smile that said, "I'm gay, and I'm guessing you are, too."

They'd had dinner together that same night, Jocko describing life as a "boat jolly," his takeoff on "boat dolly," an expression the Pope had heard hetero males using with a leer when talking about the live-aboard women who did everything on boats plying the Caribbean.

With "everything" often including the skipper/owner.

Which bothered Murizzi, the times he thought about it. It was one thing to insist on safe sex—the condoms, the mouth-dams. That seemed to him a matter of survival, like wearing a Kevlar vest to serve a fugitive warrant. It was another to picture this beautiful twenty-three-year-old boy on his knees in front of the main bunk on the schooner, bringing off a fat, hairless—

Jocko stirred a little, his lips moving as though he were talking in a dream, though no sound came out. Murizzi held his breath until his lover's face resettled against his shoulder.

Then thought again. The fuck are you to sit in judgment on the way this guy gets by? Is what you're thinking any different than what the other uniforms must have wondered about you? When they'd tell a fag-bashing war story, and only "the Pope"—and some of the newer women—didn't laugh.

Murizzi caught himself just before shaking his head. No, you did the right thing. Coming out back then wouldn't have helped anybody. Even that wrong kid who hanged himself after being convicted of a murder he didn't commit. And learning just what kind of a life that life in prison would make him live.

No, you couldn't correct that mistake once you'd made it. But you can do what you're doing now.

Murizzi laughed again, still just in his mind, only in a different, "fuck me" kind of way. You were a doctor, you'd probably work against AIDS. A lawyer, probably against discrimination based on sexual orientation. But being an ex-cop—a homicide detective, no less—what you can do is work against any other poor sonuvabitch going away for something he didn't do.

Like this screwy derelict Mairead's got under her skin.

Pontifico Murizzi tried to imagine the intense young woman probably being turned down by most men on account of her stained hands, and he cringed just enough to awaken Jocko from whatever dream the beautiful boy was having.

"MAIREAD," said Shel Gold. "Good morning."

She watched him walk to Billie Sunday's reception desk and hand over a form he'd filled out in handwriting. Billie gave Mairead a pink phone message.

"From Talina," the black woman said, her expression and tone both flat as a pancake. "Didn't leave a last name."

Mairead read the message silently. "Made bail. Three o'clock at your office?" There was no phone number. "Well, I guess I'll be seeing her at three."

Shel started back to his office, but then Mairead felt him on her heels as she entered hers.

He said, "How's the Alpha case coming along?"

Mairead dropped her handbag on the desk. When Shel settled into one of the client chairs, she plopped into hers, the left ankle happy for the rest.

Mairead said, "I went to the construction site—where he got the wood to outfit his cave?"

Shel nodded.

"Well, the president of the company and the head of security there both suspect the employee who gave Alpha the lumber scraps of stealing more valuable stuff as well."

She saw her boss's sandy eyebrows go up, his forehead wrinkling in what Mairead took to be curiosity.

"And," she said, "this employee has taken off somewhere."

"Taken off? As in . . . disappeared?"

"Or been made to, the night Draskovic died. Only when I asked Alpha about it, he got kind of huffy."

"Huffy."

"But he did say he'd start helping us on his case."

"Well," said Shel, "that's a start." Then he glanced out toward the reception area and spoke more quietly. "You're seeing this Talina today?"

Mairead pointed at the pink message slip. "So she says."

Shel stood, but kept the same quiet tone. "Do me a favor?"

"What?"

"Try not to have her around Billie too much, okay?"

"Okay," said Mairead. But Shel Gold wasn't out of her sight two seconds before she wished she'd asked him why.

T H E derelict's shelter under the bridge didn't improve with age. Or a second viewing.

Pontifico Murizzi stood outside the open wood-patch door. When he'd happened upon Mairead and Rex the morning before, he was too late to hear anything they'd said to each other. But watching her scramble to get away, it wasn't hard to figure out what had almost gone down.

But the woman had pride—the Pope had seen that in her when she came to his boat—and he wasn't about to play macho man, rescuing her when she'd handled the situation well enough to escape on her own.

Which didn't mean the lowlife hadn't deserved what he got.

Now, though, Murizzi listened outside the door, keeping his eyes closed so they'd adjust to the dimness inside before he entered. After a full two minutes by his count, he'd heard no sounds of movement or breathing. Carefully, he eased his head around the rough jamb and opened his eyes.

Empty, except for some filthy bedding and clothes. And a lot of books.

Anxious to catch up to Mairead in his truck the day before, the Pope hadn't really inspected the cave. This time, he brought some volumes out into the daylight to read. Or at least to skim titles, authors, and a little of the hype on the jackets.

Only there wasn't much hype at all. They were all egghead books on philosophy and ethics, religion and metaphysics—which Murizzi always took to mean, from the contexts in which he'd heard the word, some kind of science that wasn't based on hard facts.

Which made no fucking sense to him whatsoever. But it did make this Alpha something other than a run-of-the-mill scuzzball.

The Pope knew the crime scene techs would have combed the place, especially with the killing ground itself only yards downslope. But he still flipped through every book, shaking each by its binding, see if anything fell out. Then he tossed the bedding, some ditty bags and some shopping bags. A few had articles from the *Herald* or the *Globe,* more philosophy or ethics, including three on "hermits," which was how Mairead had characterized the guy to start with.

Finishing up, Murizzi had that "kiss your sister" feeling of a tied game: He'd confirmed some of what he'd already been told, but hadn't found out anything new about Alpha. Spotting two more derelicts scavenging along the riverbank with green trash bags slung over their shoulders, he walked down toward them.

"Hey?"

The two turned to him. One was tall, stick-skinny, and black. The other was short and squat, with bad acne.

The Pope thought the second derelict's features made him look as though he should be chewing whale blubber. "You guys collecting returnables?"

The black shifted the trash bag on his shoulder, accompanied by the slight chiming sound of glass resetting. Which probably meant the Eskimo had the aluminum cans.

Murizzi motioned. "You get a nickel for those, right?"

The black nodded. "Ain't hardly worth stealing."

The Pope understood what he said, but more what he meant. "I'm not in the market." Taking a five from his wallet, Murizzi creased the bill like a pup tent. "A day's worth of returnables for whoever knows where a guy named Rex is flopping now."

The black and the Eskimo stared at the money before glancing at each other, which the Pope took to be an encouraging sign.

The black said, "If we both know, does the five grow up to be ten?"

Murizzi admired his guts. "Only if you chant it, together."

The Eskimo blinked, "What you say, man?" in an accent the Pope thought was Spanish.

His taller partner took over. "Rex, he done bugged out."

Shit. "Where to?"

"Didn't say. Just was bitching and moaning 'round the fire last night about this cop."

"Cop?"

"Plainclothes. Came around here yesterday sometime, roust the man. Even broke his finger."

In other words, you. "And Rex said he was leaving?"

"He white trash, just say he gonna make himself scarce for a while, you know? Lay chilly someplace else."

When Murizzi didn't reply to that right away, the Spanish Eskimo said, "Give us the money, man."

The Pope looked at him. "I asked where Rex is. All you've told me is where he isn't."

The black pulled on his chin with his free hand. "Seems to me that be worth five anyway, save yourself the time you would of wasted here, hanging for him."

Pontifico Murizzi felt a grin spreading upward from his chest, but he gave the black guy the five and turned before either of the derelicts could see the expression reach his face.

10

OH, HONEY, DO I have *your* number.

Billie Sunday watched as the Asian—no, probably part-Asian—girl made a fashion-model turn out of closing the door to the office suite. Which went with her fashion statement of fur jacket, tube top, leather pants, and platform shoes.

"Talina," said the girl. "Here to see Mairead."

Billie glanced down at her switchboard. "She's on the phone. You want to sit, I'll let her know you're here when she gets off."

Billie watched the girl smile like you do at a child by the sidewalk selling lemonade from a pitcher, then sashay over to the reception chairs. Only there was something wrong with her stroll, like the girl was in some pain. And . . . there, as she sat, a tightening of her face and a hand going halfway to her rib cage.

Billie remembered back to that period in her own life. A "hooker," they'd have called her in Boston. But down in D.C., hanging out in bars and worse around the Army base, she heard "whore" and "pros" a little more often.

Until Robert Senior picked her up one Friday night when she was half in the bag from cheap bourbon and good heroin.

Brought her back to his apartment in the base housing. Sat up with her babbling and carrying on till she came down from the booze/drug high. Held her when she felt the jones of withdrawal eating through her brain and soul. Talked her past the sweats and the screams and the shits until she was

cleaned out and clean off. Then helped her stay that way, with his love and support.

Till that drunken driver took Robert Senior away from their growing family. Billie had been working for Shel six years by then, and the settlement he got for her was enough to pay off the mortgage and provide for the children's eventual college.

But not enough, not nearly enough, to bring back the man who'd brought *her* back from—

"She off the phone yet?"

Billie glanced over at Talina, who was fussing with one of her dragon-lady fingernails. "Yeah," the button for Mairead's line dimming as another lit up. "Attorney O'Clare can see you now."

"BEN, thanks for calling."

"Might want to hear what I have to say first, Golden Boy."

Shel looked at his office phone like it had betrayed him. "What do you mean?"

"I dialed up Little Benji like you asked. I did some soft-shoe first, you know? Bruins looking good, Celtics suck again. Like that."

"Good strategy," said Shel, just for something to say.

"Yeah, I thought so, too. But then I get to him and Hedda, and the guy goes berserk on me."

Something cold seeped into Shel's chest. "About what?"

"About what? What do you think, about what? Little Benji's screaming at me on how all Hedda cares about is how much money her shark of a divorce lawyer can wring out of him." Big Ben Friedman made a noise on the other end of the line that sounded to Shel like a chuckle. "I tell you, Golden Boy, I don't know how you stand to represent guys like him."

"But were you able to get through to him about not doing anything stupid?"

"Get through to him? Shel, you been listening to what I've been saying to you here? Little Benji was yelling so loud, I had to hold the phone away from my ear." A change in tone. "One thing got through to me, though."

"What's that, Ben?"

"Just before he hangs up—on *me*, Golden Boy, on me—the little *mamzer* says, 'I'm gonna steal a certain piece of iron as a going-away present for a certain piece of ass.'"

"Oh, God," said Shel, dropping the phone onto his desk as he launched out of his chair.

"Hey, Golden Boy," came Big Ben Friedman's voice from the receiver. "You still there?"

But Sheldon Gold barely heard the words, being already halfway into his suit jacket and halfway through the office suite door before even Billie Sunday realized he was leaving.

PONTIFICO Murizzi pulled his Ford Explorer into the lot of the State Police barracks at the Charles River locks near the Museum of Science. The visitor spaces were all full, so the Pope put his truck into a reserved one and flipped down the visor with his PBA shield on it. Then he walked around the old building of yellow masonry and entered in front.

"Help you?" said a female from behind the counter, only her head and neck visible over it as she sat at a desk.

"Pontifico Murizzi. Used to be on Boston, now I work private." He took out his investigator's license.

She didn't get up to look at it. "And?"

"And I'd like to talk with a trooper who's had contact with the homeless people who live along the Charles."

A tired smile. "Tougher to find one of us who hasn't. But I suppose I'll do."

The woman stood up. Granted she probably had some kind of boots on with the uniform, she still went a good six-two. With light brown hair held off her neck with a scrungie and dark brown eyes that seemed to care. "Come on."

Once in a little office that reminded the Pope of the old Homicide Unit in Southie, the trooper said, "Wilkins, Pamela."

Murizzi sat in a chair across from the one she took. "Seems to me we had a chief justice by that name."

"Two, actually. Father and son. I'm so distant a cousin, I hardly count."

The Pope thought otherwise. After they put me in the nursing home, I'll see her face on the news, heading the Department of Public Safety, maybe.

"So, Murizzi, what's your thing with the homeless?"

He considered telling her she could call him the Pope, then was a little afraid Wilkins wouldn't recognize the nickname as meaning anything. "I'm helping the defense in the homeless killing, early December."

"Draskovic. Or Old Man River, which he kind of liked."

Felt like an opening. "You knew the guy?"

"Yeah." Wilkins glanced over her shoulder. "You were on the job, you know about the jurisdictional stuff around the river?"

"Sometimes you guys have it, sometimes Boston on our side or Cambridge on theirs."

"Right, right. Well, your guy Alpha's digs are in Boston, but our decedent was found just to the Boston side of our line."

Murizzi had figured that'd be the case for Boston Homicide to catch the killing. "Only the homeless spend a lot of their time on your side of the line."

"Scavenging. Or just walking off their demons."

"So you end up dealing with them."

"We do." A sigh. "Usually it's just panhandling, the guys hitting up yuppie sunbathers for quarters in the summer. But the decedent was something else."

"Like how?"

Wilkins went over things the Pope already had learned from the college boys who liked to drink and Winston Hayes who liked to sail.

Murizzi said, "How about my guy Alpha and Draskovic?"

"They didn't get along too well, either. Mostly squabbles over this and that."

"Including Draskovic's coat."

Another sigh. "I must have come on them six, seven times. Old Man River yelling at Alpha to give him back his trench coat. Alpha kind of teasing him, like a game during recess in the schoolyard."

The Pope's impression, too. "Alpha was bigger?"

"Not by much, but younger and stronger both. Only he didn't really try to hurt Old Man River, the times I saw. More like the struggles over the coat were physical, but not violent."

"Like the schoolyard."

"Reason I used the simile."

"Simile."

Her cheeks colored. "I was an English major in college."

"Me, I think Ross Macdonald did similes the best of anybody."

A different look from Wilkins now. "Name two others."

"John D. in the Travis McGee books, Linda Barnes in the Carlotta—"

"Stop, Murizzi. You're frightening me."

But Wilkins was smiling as she said it.

The Pope came back on point. "You think my guy could have done the murder?"

Her eyes closed. When they opened again, the caring look was back. "Alpha was a pain in the ass, but he has a brain, and some kind of honor, too. Do I think he *could* kill? I'd say yes. Do I think he'd kill over that coat? A solid maybe."

Best you could hope for, probably. "One last thing. You also know a homeless guy named Rex?"

"Unfortunately. A real sleaze."

"Seen him lately?"

"Not yesterday. You want to talk to him?"

"Yeah."

"Well, I'll keep an eye out. Give me your phone number."

Pontifico Murizzi looked at her just a bit differently.

Pamela Wilkins smiled back at him. "So I can let you know if Rex turns up."

"NOW you want to plead guilty to assaulting Joshua Brewer?"

"That's what I said. Want me to say it again?"

Mairead leaned back in her chair, looking over Talina's head through the open door to the reception area, but thinking only about the woman sitting in front of her.

My first client all to myself, and she has a change of heart.

Mairead said, "But I already applied for a cross-complaint. Notice went out to this Mr. Brewer, ordering him—"

"Don't I fucking know it. I never told you to do that."

Mairead shook her head. "Talina, we talked about all this. Even the clerk, Chet, recommended—"

"Chet, he live in the court. I live on the fucking *street*! He bail me out, but I can't go—"

"Wait a minute. Chet was the one—"

"Bail me out, like before. Only this time, he say he can't take me home because his mama be there."

Mairead sighed on the inside. *No wonder that man wouldn't make eye contact with you in the courtroom, young lady.* "And so you want to plead guilty."

From closer than her reception desk, Billie's voice said, "What she really wants is to not get beat on anymore."

Talina turned in the chair and started to rise. The necessary twisting of her torso seemed to make her grunt, a hand going to the right side of her rib cage.

Mairead said, "Talina, are you okay?"

Billie came into the room. "Hit you where it doesn't show, right?"

Talina flared. "The fuck you know about it?"

"Been there, child."

Jesus Mary, thought Mairead. No wonder Billie was so touchy about her husband if he abused her.

Now Talina nodded, a couple of tears running down her cheeks as she stayed on her feet.

Billie braced Talina as the younger woman eased back down in the chair. "And that tube top, it helps some with the pain, like taping the ribs."

Another nod.

"But not much," said Mairead, thinking back to tearing some cartilage there in a high-school hockey game. For a good month afterward, it had hurt even just to breathe.

Talina began both crying and speaking. "JJ get this paper from your court, and he come with his friend. They take me behind this old building.

His friend hold me, and Brewer beat me bad. Then he go to his car and come back with . . . his bottle again."

Mairead could feel anger growing in her chest, like when a smaller teammate gets picked on by a bigger opponent.

Billie said, "What kind of bottle?"

Talina sobbed, and Mairead said, "I'll tell you later."

The black woman looked back at the Amer-Asian one. "They tell you, 'Give up the assault charge, or we hurt you worse.'"

A weak nod. "Next time, my . . . face."

Mairead found herself looking up at Billie.

The widespread, yellow-brown eyes held less anger than determination. "We're gonna take ourselves a field trip."

"A what?" said Mairead.

"Call it a conference, then. But 'out of the office.'"

"SHEL," said the voice from behind the closed front door of the small house. "What the hell are you—"

"Hedda, can I come in, please?"

"Why?"

"Hedda, please?"

"My lawyer said I didn't have to talk to anybody. Not that little shit Benji, not you."

"And you don't. But I'm standing at your door on a winter day without a topcoat on, and—"

"The Weather Channel said it's fifty-five out."

"It's still January, Hedda. Please?"

"All right, all right."

Shel Gold heard the dead bolts get thrown, one after the other. Trust a career burglar to have good locks, anyway.

When Hedda Schwartz opened her door, Shel moved through into the tiny foyer, a closet to his left built for the days when families could afford only one outer garment per person. The living room was both stuffy and overstuffed with lamps, knickknacks, all kinds of kitsch. Shel wondered briefly if Little Benji would bring home a souvenir from each place he hit.

"All right, so you're in." Hedda sat down like a grim Buddha in a doilied armchair while Shel tried the couch and immediately regretted his choice. "Only I'm not gonna be a good hostess and offer you coffee. I want you to say what you have to say and be on your way."

Admit it: You never noticed this streak of poetry in the woman before. "Hedda, it's kind of awkward, ethically speaking, for your husband's lawyer to be talking to his wife."

Shel could see the exasperation building inside her, like a volcano about to spew molten lava over everything around it.

Hedda said, "Then why in hell *are* you here?"

"I want to wait with you until Benji arrives."

"Benji? What are you, going soft on me? The little shit hasn't been around here in months."

Shel Gold shrugged and tried to settle into the uncomfortable couch. "I think today might be an exception."

A S Pontifico Murizzi reached the stoop of the apartment house in a student-ghetto block of Brighton, a lithe young woman was leaving through the front door, holding it open for him.

"Thanks," said the Pope.

"Who are you coming to see?"

He gave it a beat before, "Mitch Gerber."

"Ah, the musclehead." Coy smile. "Enjoy."

Murizzi grinned as she moved like a young colt down the path toward a taxi.

Inside the door were a bank of mailboxes with little labels below push-buttons, Gerber listed as 3C.

No need to disturb him twice by hitting the buzzer.

The Pope climbed two flights of worn stairs to the third floor. There was no brass letter on the third door down the hall, but the "A" and the "B" earlier let him use the process of elimination.

While the paint on 3C was peeling a little, Murizzi was pleased to see no peephole. He put his ear to the door, heard the sounds of straining, followed by the bouncing of what he would have guessed were barbell weights

even without the young woman's "musclehead" remark at the building entrance.

The Pope knocked on the door.

From inside, a muffled, strained "Go . . . away."

Murizzi said, "I'm from downstairs. Your fucking weights are making my ceiling bulbs break."

"Fuck you, dude."

"Open this fucking door, or I'll kick it in."

"Fuck you and your bulbs and—"

Murizzi started kicking.

In between the impacts he made with his shoe, the Pope could hear movement from inside. Then just one lock turned before the door was yanked open and a sweaty, smelly, bulky college boy in a singlet and torn gym shorts yanked open the door.

"You fucking—"

At which point, Murizzi remembered what Jeff and Rick had described this kid doing to Zoran Draskovic. The Pope shot the stiffened and extended middle three fingers of his right hand into the boy's throat just below the Adam's apple.

Both the sweaty palms, wrapped in some kind of tape, went toward the injured area, and the kid began gasping and backpedaling. The Pope walked through the door and closed it.

The boy had gotten as far as his weight set, coughing now as he took his left hand off his throat and reached down below a padded bench for a small dumbbell, maybe a four-pounder. Getting the general drift of the kid's intention, Murizzi came up fast, slashing down with the edge of his own hand at the kid's wrist. No cracking sound, but the college boy dropped the weight.

Onto his own foot.

With the kid's other hand still at his throat, hopping on his sound foot made him tumble over hard onto the rubber mat covering part of the living room floor.

Finding a small dry part of the bench, the Pope perched on it. "I hope you're Mitch Gerber."

"My . . . uncle's . . . a . . . lawyer. . . ."

"You don't shut up and answer my questions, he'll be probating your estate."

Murizzi waited until a coughing jag subsided. Then, "I want you to tell me what went on between you and the homeless guys down by the Charles."

"Fuck . . . dude . . ."

"Mitch, that's not very responsive."

Gerber took a longer, sustained breath. "We were just . . . drinking, and this one geek . . . starts screaming at us."

"For doing what?"

"Aw, we busted . . . a couple bottles, maybe."

"And busted him up, too."

"He was a pain in the ass, dude. . . . A bum who bothered everybody. . . . We were doing the world a favor."

"Ever see anyone else doing the same kind of favor?"

"What, stomping the geek?"

"That's the question."

Gerber paused. "Yeah, this other homeless bum . . . had—ah, shit that still hurts—his coat . . . or something, used to hassle the geek about it all the time."

Don't assume a conclusion. "There a name for this other guy?"

"Alf, I think. Like the space-alien show when I was a kid."

"Any accent?"

"Irish, maybe."

Alpha, definitely. "You said this Alf hassled the other guy."

"Right, right."

"Ever see them actually fight?"

"Fight. You mean, like *really* stomping?"

"Yeah," said Murizzi.

"No. Just kind of arguing and maybe wrestling a little." A swallow. "Why'd you have to punch me in the throat, dude?"

"I wanted your undivided attention, Mitch. Aside from this Alf, any other people hassle with the guy you stomped?"

"How the fuck should I know? We were down there by the river drinking, not doing a sociology project."

"What about a guy named Rex?"

"Total blank, dude."

"You and your friends still drink at the river?"

"Not since the geek got killed. Bad karma, you know? So we been frying other fish."

Shaking his head, the Pope was very glad his job no longer involved worrying about the little gang's "other fish." But, leaving the apartment, Pontifico Murizzi felt fairly strongly that if the followers Jeff and Rick probably wouldn't kill someone like Zoran Draskovic, Mitch Gerber very well might, and so it wasn't entirely a wasted visit.

11

"IT'S ME, TALINA."

"IT'S ME, TALINA."

Mairead O'Clare couldn't understand the tinny reply that came over the apartment tower's intercom in front of Talina's lips, but the security door buzzed, and Billie Sunday pushed through it into the lobby. Mairead didn't see anybody—doorman or resident—as the three of them moved toward the bank of elevators.

Mairead repeated the same thing she'd said as they'd walked downhill from Shel's office toward the waterfront. "I still think we should have some kind of plan."

"Have to play it by ear," replied Billie again.

Talina didn't add anything, but Mairead saw her shiver despite the fur jacket in a way that probably had nothing to do with the weather.

The doors opened on the twelfth floor, and Talina turned left. The three women were alone in this corridor, too.

When Talina stopped and pointed at 12F, Billie mimed a knocking motion before standing to the lock side of the jamb. Mairead took the hinge side, Talina in the middle at the peephole, rapping her knuckles against the wood.

The big door swung open, a male voice saying, "Just can't get enough of it, can you?"

That last word was still hanging in the air as Mairead watched Billie barge through the door as though she were crashing the net in a hockey game. Mairead had barely stepped in front of Talina when Billie clouted the

medium-sized, balding man wearing just sweatpants with the flat of her right hand.

Joshua Brewer staggered backward, his left hand coming up toward the side of his face. His mouth was just opening when Billie clouted him with her left.

Better do something, young lady.

"Billie—"

"No," said the black woman, pushing both palms into the bare chest of Brewer, driving him backward toward the sliding glass door to a balcony. The man tried to fend her off, but she cuffed his forehead with the heel of her right hand, and he kept moving.

Brewer got as far as "What the—" before Billie ripped open the sliding glass door, its metal frame banging against itself, and pushed him onto the balcony. Mairead registered his bare feet on the brown tiles just as his soles lost contact with them.

Jesus Mary.

Mairead realized that Billie, who had squatted suddenly, was now rising with the backs of Brewer's knees on her shoulders, her hands on the tops of his thighs. The man's waist was barely on the stone railing of the balcony, his torso and head dangling over it.

"Billie, don't!"

"That depends on Mr. Big Dick here."

Mairead felt Talina come up from behind and grasp her right hand in both of hers.

"T H E fuck are you doing here?"

Sheldon Gold had answered the banging on Hedda Schwartz's front door. Little Benji stood on the stoop, an amazed expression on his face, the gecko eyes roaming independently. His left hand was balled into a fist and raised to hit the door again, his right hand stuck deep in his overcoat pocket.

Shel said, "I thought you'd be coming in the back way, diddle the lock."

Little Benji seemed still to be in shock. "Not with all the Schlages I put on. Take an hour, even for me."

Shel nodded. "Let's talk, okay?" and turned away in the small foyer toward the living room. Moving slowly, he heard Little Benji close the door behind him without slamming it.

A start. But only a start.

Shel had debated whether or not Hedda should stay on the easy chair or be in a bedroom or somewhere else. In the end, it didn't matter, as she refused, in her words, "to retreat in my own home,"

Still, Shel kept his body between hers and Little Benji.

The wife spoke first, arms folded under her ample breasts. "There's a court order against you—"

"I paid good money for this—"

"Money you *stole* from innocent—"

"I didn't hear you complaining about—"

"Enough!" shouted Shel over them.

Both spouses shut up, staring at him.

Admit it: They probably never heard you yell before.

Shel didn't want to lose his tiny advantage. "You two have been over all that. Truth is, *we've* been over all that. And it's time everybody got past it."

He turned toward his client. "Let's sit down, okay?"

Little Benji backed against a chair, near tripping into it.

Shel was glad Hedda didn't laugh, because his lifelong friend's right hand was still in that coat pocket.

Shel spoke to her as he retook his own seat on the umcomfortable couch. "You knew before you married him what Benji did for a living."

"I swear I had no—"

Shel spoke gently. "Hedda, I introduced you two, remember?"

She blinked a few times and uncrossed her arms, which Shel took to be good signs.

"My exact words: 'Hedda, this is my friend Benji. He's on the scrawny side and a thief, but not a bad guy.'"

"With friends like you . . . ," said Little Benji, but kind of nostalgically.

Another good sign.

Shel said, "And that kind of . . . intrigued you." He gave her a moment before a whispery, "Didn't it?"

"Yeah," like she was losing a tooth. "Kind of."

Shel turned to Benji. "And you felt secure with Hedda?"

"I didn't—"

Shel interrupted. "You spent a lot of nervous time in other people's houses. Hedda soothed all that away, remember?"

Little Benji started to say something, then wet his lips before making a croaking sound with "Yeah. Yeah, she did."

Shel felt his stomach untie its knot, but tried not to show anything in his voice. "Only now you've both reached a point of moving on. To other things, other people. Am I right?"

He watched the two of them, partners in time—if not in crime—stare at each other, maybe communicating more without talking than they had in their last few years of bickering.

"Yeah," said Hedda and Benji, simultaneously.

Shel lived the moment before saying, "So, what you do is let Christina Medina and me as lawyers split things so they're fair, and you both walk away without hating each other for recognizing the inevitable. We have a consensus here?"

They both nodded.

Get out while you're ahead. "Thanks for the hospitality, Hedda."

"Good seeing you again, Shel."

Shel rose and moved to Little Benji, a bit afraid he'd have to help the man out of his own chair. But the burglar made it to his feet and preceded his lawyer to the foyer.

Before Benji could open the door, Shel tapped him on the shoulder. The man turned halfway, and Shel patted the right coat pocket, feeling only a hand, not metal.

The gecko eyes started roaming again. "What, you think I'd shoot up my own house?"

"It's not your house!" from the living room as Shel Gold quickly opened the front door and ushered Little Benji Schwartz out onto the stoop.

"NOW," said Billie Sunday to the john, hoping he wasn't going to shit his pants almost in her face, "we need to talk."

He didn't look to be in the kind of shape to do a sit-up from where he was, but he managed to crane his neck some, eyes showing a lot of white. "You fucking bitch, you're—"

Billie stepped forward with her right foot, just a bitty bit, but a little more of the man inched over the edge of the railing, his fingernails scraping against the stone without getting any kind of hold on it.

"All right, all right," he squeezed out. "We'll talk."

Billie steadied her stance.

Be glad this john's just a middle-sized one, because you don't know for sure Mairead has the stomach for helping you much, especially since the girl's main contribution so far amounts to just bleating out your name from time to time.

Billie said, "You've been beating on this poor child."

"She's a fucking hooker, tried to—"

Billie's left foot shuffled forward.

"Okay, okay," said the john, not craning his neck anymore but looking down without seeming to enjoy the view.

Billie said, "She's a human being, trying to make her way. Which doesn't give you or your friend the right to whale on her."

"Fine, I won't—"

"Not so simple. Now, here's what we're going to do. First, you drop the assault charge against Talina. Then, she drops hers against you. After that, you and your friend stay away from her." Might as well get some use out of higher education, so over the shoulder with, "Anything else?"

Mairead said, "And he doesn't send anybody else after Talina."

"All right, it's a deal, it's a deal."

"One more thing." Billie shrugged her shoulders, more to balance the man's weight, but he screamed a little, and Billie breathed through her mouth in case he soiled his ownself. "You never met the two of us with Talina, or there'll be a dozen more of us come after you the next time. And it won't end on *this* floor of your nice apartment building."

The man snuffled a little. "I understand."

"I hope you do." Billie Sunday stepped backward gradually, drawing him away from the edge. "I really hope you do."

AFTER leaving Mitch Gerber, Pontifico Murizzi stood on the sidewalk by his Explorer, calling in with his cell phone for any voice mail. There was one from Jocko, punning about what a good time he'd had the night before. Saying, "Oh, and luv, we can do dramatic readings from H. G. Wells's book *The Shape of Things to Come,*" Jocko's tone hinting at even better times "a-head."

Smiling, Murizzi waited for the next message.

Simple check-in from Sheldon Gold on the Alpha case, sounding kind of relieved, though some asshole in the background kept whining about why he should have to split a house *he'd* paid for. The Pope made a note to call the lawyer back.

The third message was from Trooper Pamela Wilkins. She suggested Murizzi meet her and Sergeant Detective Artie Chin at the bridge downriver from Alpha's cave. The Pope pictured where she meant, figuring that he could walk to it faster than driving.

Pontifico Murizzi also figured his return call to Sheldon Gold maybe should wait awhile.

TALINA said, "Okay, I owe you."

Mairead watched Billie Sunday shake her head outside Joshua Brewer's apartment tower. "Don't owe us anything except for the court papers." Billie reached into her slacks, brought out a business card. "Might want to hold on to this, though."

Talina read the card aloud. "Halfway House?"

"A place for giving you some time and space. People there'll talk to you, help you work things through."

Talina's face came up toward Billie's, a skeptical look in the smaller woman's eyes. "You get help there?"

"I get help by trying to give it, child. Might be the same could work out for you."

Mairead expected Talina to tear up the card or vamp some other gesture. Instead, the card went into a pocket of the fur jacket, and Talina reached up and hugged Billie around the neck. Then the Amer-Asian woman turned to Mairead and shook her hand. "Thanks, lady-lawyer. I mean it."

Then Talina walked off, but not the way she had in the holding cell or coming into Mairead's office. This time she moved like a little girl on her way to a puppet show.

Quietly, Billie said, "That one has a chance."

Mairead thought she'd better bring it up now. "Billie?"

"Yes?" Expression blank.

"I didn't join the office to go off on vigilante raids, and what we did up there was no different before the law than what Brewer did to Talina."

Billie faced Mairead. "Everything's based on rules, honey. Rules for my boys, rules from your law school, even rules that fancy law firm had, training you while it was draining you." Billie made a sweeping gesture. "But on the street, sometimes you have to make up your own rules, see to it that the victims come out of things all right."

And with that, Billie Sunday turned in the direction of Sheldon Gold's office building and began walking back uphill.

12

SHELDON GOLD LOOKED AROUND his office suite. The lights are on, but nobody's home.

Admit it: Given what you thought Little Benji had in his coat pocket, you should be happy to be anywhere at all.

Taking a deep breath, Shel went over to the tape machine and replayed the messages. Nothing pressing.

He shucked his suit jacket and sat at his desk. Tried to do some paperwork, found he couldn't maintain his concentration. Not hungry for food nor eager for coffee.

Then he realized what he did want to do.

Taking a deeper breath, Shel Gold got up, put his jacket back on, and left a note for Billie that read, "Gone for the day."

PONTIFICO Murizzi guessed right about which pedestrian ramp to take across Storrow Drive to the riverbank. As soon as he climbed the steps to it, however, he wished he'd been wrong.

The Charles itself was dark, the ice a dull gray, openings in it caused by the January thaw like black pockmarks of water in a tired old face. The vehicles parked at odd angles near the bank contrasted sharply with that background, almost like a carnival against a prison wall.

Two State Police cruisers were bookends to the others, the staties' roof racks of bubble lights strobing an eye-closing blue in their irregular rhythms. In between the cruisers were an unmarked sedan with a single bubble flashing on its dashboard and an ambulance with two EMTs in brown uniforms

lazing around it, one smoking, the other drinking from a bottle of cola. It was the last vehicle, though, that sank the Pope's heart.

A white minivan with the royal-blue lettering of the chief medical examiner.

Murizzi descended the steps on the river side of Storrow. An assortment of civilians stood outside the yellow POLICE LINE—DO NOT CROSS tape looped tree-to-tree. A woman on Rollerblades with her dog, three kids holding skateboards under their arms, several joggers wearing spandex tights and running in place to stay loose.

At least Mairead wasn't one of them.

A trooper came over. The Pope showed his ID, and the tall man nodded, lifting the tape marking the crime-scene perimeter.

As the statie walked Murizzi past the vehicles, the Pope closed his eyes to slits so as not to lose his vision to their lights. Once past them, he took in the familiar sights.

A detective—probably State, since Murizzi didn't recognize him—interviewing an elderly couple, the woman holding the man's hand. Techies from the Boston lab—closer than the State's in Sudbury—inching their way around patches of grass and bare ground. Finally, in the center of things, Sergeant Detective Artie Chin, standing next to someone on their knees beside a soggy lump of clothes, Trooper Pamela Wilkins towering over all of them.

Wilkins looked at the Pope. "You got my message."

"Maybe fifteen minutes ago."

She inclined her head toward the detective conducting the interview. "That nice couple found Rex for you."

Nodding, Murizzi sat on his haunches, partly to look more closely at the body, mostly to hide the little shiver he felt starting at the base of his spine. "Artie, how you doing?"

"Oh, good, Pope. Real good," said the homicide detective without the ghost of a grin. "River's lovely this time of year, don't you think?"

"My favorite." Murizzi addressed the woman who seemed to be keening over the body. "Drowning?"

The assistant ME clucked her tongue. "Don't see any trauma so far, besides this splint on his finger."

The Pope felt Wilkins leaning over him.

She said, "He didn't have that the last time I saw him."

Murizzi could tell by Rex's features that he'd been in the water for a while, so he didn't insult the ME by asking her for a range on time of death.

Chin said, "Wilkins tells me you talked to this guy."

The Pope rose. "Yesterday morning."

"He have that splint on him then?"

"No," said Murizzi, truthful even though misleading.

"The guy mention anything about somebody being after him?"

The Pope looked at Chin now, thinking his old friend was kind of taking the play away from the trooper.

Chin said, "Wilkins also tells me this Rex had been around awhile." A gesture toward the pockmarked river. "Long enough to know he shouldn't be making snow angels on yellow ice."

Murizzi spoke to Wilkins. "You giving this one to Boston?"

A shrug. "Not my call. But it does seem to me Rex's death might be related to Draskovic's."

And so it would make sense to have both investigated functionally by Boston Homicide, regardless of where this particular body might have been found jurisdictionally.

"Pope?" said Chin.

Murizzi turned toward him, starting to feel a little like a suspect, trying to separate what the two officers were saying to him from what he was feeling inside. "You think he got pushed?"

Chin's turn to shrug. "Or got chased and took a chance."

The Pope turned toward the black hole in the ice in front of them. "Pretty cold, you chase a guy and then watch him drown."

"Or just pass out," said the ME. When nobody else spoke, she added, "Hypothermia. Water's only thirty-six degrees. I give him two, maybe three minutes before he just goes to sleep, depending on his adrenaline—or alcohol—level at the time."

Murizzi closed his eyes. Did you somehow trigger this?

Chin said, "Pope, Denver's had a rash of homeless killings. Whole city out there's in a panic, on account of the investigators figure it's more than

one guy getting his jollies from it. When the media here finds out we've had a second one . . ."

Murizzi had seen it before: Piece-of-shit cases going high-profile with the magic words "serial killer."

"So," Chin real solemn, "you got anything to share?"

The Pope gave it a beat before, "Nothing but dead ends."

Wilkins looked down at the body. "No pun intended."

After telling the two officers he'd stay in touch, Murizzi began walking back toward the pedestrian ramp. Ordinarily, he'd have taken the river's macadam path, fresh air as opposed to exhaust fumes. But now the Pope wanted people around him. Walking, driving, even just waiting for a bus.

But living. Surviving another day in their lives.

As he reached the top of the ramp's steps, Pontifico Murrizzi decided he should call Shel Gold's office, let Mairead know about Rex being dead. He also decided this change of circumstance warranted a couple more visits.

MAIREAD followed Billie into the office suite. As the older woman reached her desk, Mairead could see just one message blinking on the tape machine.

Billie picked up a note. "From Shel. 'Gone for the day.'"

Mairead pushed the play button on the machine. The Pope, saying Rex had been found dead along the river, apparently drowned, but that he'd get back with more details.

Mairead moved numbly into her own office.

"Was that who I think it was?" called Billie.

"Murizzi," managed Mairead.

"You all right in there?"

"Fine."

Mairead used the edges of her desk to move around to her chair, almost falling into it.

Young lady, you don't know how it happened.

Mairead wanted to believe that, postpone judgment.

And guilt.

But the thought wouldn't go away. *He broke the man's finger for trying to hurt you.* Would the Pope stop at that?

Or could there be another explanation? Maybe even a connection to Old Man River's death, since both men were homeless and found dead along the Charles?

Mairead O'Clare needed to see the Pope, face-to-face, decide for herself about him. But she also needed more information first, and she could think of only one person who might provide it.

"SHEL, where have you been?"

"I had some things at the office."

Sheldon Gold watched Natalie rise from her easy chair. It was a little soon for another visit. He knew it, and the staffer—not Doreen—who opened the front door of the mansion for him confirmed it. But after the scene at the Schwartz house, Shel needed to share his feelings with somebody who'd understand.

Somebody who'd known him most of his life.

"So," said Natalie, giving Shel a theatrically elaborate hug, "what 'things at the office'?"

"You remember Little Benji, the—"

"Thief and burglar with the lizard eyes? You're not still representing him?"

"Just on his divorce. Hedda—"

"And Benji never had any children, now did they?"

Uh-oh. "Natalie, please?"

"No children they could *lose,* like you lost our son."

"Natalie—"

"You goddamned fucking son of a bitch, you left him. . . ."

Shel closed his eyes and, as he called out for the staffer, tried to close his ears as well.

"SIR, Mr. Pontifico Murizzi."

The butler—in a different sports jacket—closed the door to the roof deck behind him. Sitting bundled up like a Green Bay Packers fan in a white resin

chair, Winston Hayes lowered his field glasses, twisted his blocky head around, and said, "Come, Pontifico. Join me in the celebration."

There was another resin chair—Christ, wouldn't you think the rich could afford better? Or, maybe that's why they were rich.

Murizzi dragged it over to where Hayes was, facing westward. The setting sun gave the horizon and the distant bridge it touched a pink and gray smudge. In the relative foreground, though still more than a mile away from the Beacon Hill mansion, the Pope had a bird's-eye view of the scene he'd just left.

"Another miscreant meets his end," said Hayes, grinning from white sideburn to white sunburn, like a little kid at the circus.

Which reminded Murizzi that even he himself had thought of all the flashing lights as a carnival.

The Pope sat. "How do you know who they're dealing with?"

"These are superb binoculars." Hayes slipped the strap over his head and handed the glasses to Murizzi. "Have a look."

The Pope tried to find Artie Chin and Pamela Wilkins. Christ, you even recognize their faces. Just to be sure he wasn't fooling himself, he swung over to the trooper manning the yellow tape.

You never met the guy, yet there he is, clear as day.

As though reading Murizzi's thoughts, Hayes said, "Something in the binoculars actually can enhance the available light, Pontifico. Amazing, eh?"

"Yeah, Winston. Amazing." The Pope swung back to Chin and Wilkins, but even the Rolls-Royce of lenses couldn't penetrate the bodies of the people around the corpse of Rex.

Murizzi returned the field glasses. "You know the guy?"

Innocence from the old, patrician face. "The guy?"

"The dead one."

"Oh. No, but I'm sure it's one of those homeless again."

"Again."

"Counting the madman who got his head bashed in."

"Right."

"Why?" said Hayes. "Do *you* know who it is?"

"You nailed the homeless part. His name was Rex."

"How ironic."

The Pope just stared at him. "Ironic?"

"Yes. Rex in Latin means King, as in Tyrannosaurus rex."

That's what Hayes reminds you of. A dinosaur, tall and stoop-shouldered, keeping an eye on his part of the jungle.

"Pontifico?"

"I was thinking more that you might know this Rex yourself."

"That *I* would . . . But why? And how?"

The Pope said, "He hung around the same vicinity—"

"Vi-*cin*-ity. Oh, what a wonderful crime word—"

"—as Draskovic and Alpha."

"Ah, then perhaps *they* knew him."

"Perhaps," said Murizzi, with he hoped a little irony. "Mind telling me where you've been today, Winston?"

"Not at all. I awakened around seven. Ate a hearty breakfast. Spent the morning watching CNBC's business news on the cable and communing with my broker by telephone. Worked out at my health club, followed by a massage, followed by lunch at my eating club. Since returning, I've been up here in the remarkably fresh and tolerable air for January, reading"—from between his legs, Hayes pulled a hardcover with Jeffery Deaver listed as author—"and sipping . . ." The book went back, and a leather-covered flask came out from the same place.

When Murizzi didn't reply, Hayes gestured with the flask. "I'd offer you some, but I'm not sure how sanitary it would be for both of us to drink straight from the bottle."

When Murizzi still didn't say anything, his host smiled. "I'm rather disappointed in you, Pontifico."

"Why?"

A gesture toward the crime scene. "Given the scads of people who use the riverbank, you must believe someone would have seen this Rex enter the water if it had happened during daylight. Therefore, I'd guess he must have gone swimming before dawn, yet you haven't asked me a thing about my whereabouts then."

Maybe, you rich fuck, because you never would tell me what you were doing the night Draskovic died. "Okay, Winston. Where were you last night?"

"Ah, the advantages of competent legal counsel. I had to answer to the police but I don't have to answer to you." Hayes turned back toward the crime scene and raised his field glasses. "Good evening, Pontifico."

"Good evening, Winston," said the Pope, squelching a desire to throw the smug, rich shit off his roof deck.

"SORRY to harp, lass, but I've still not received my books."

"I'll ask when I go back downstairs."

Mairead watched Alpha nod a thank you. His brownish hair seemed to be getting darker as it grew, now nearly long enough to part.

"So," said her client, "what brings you back to me so soon?"

"Rex is dead."

Mairead wanted to hit him with it. Gauge his reaction.

Oh, young lady, look at that smile.

Alpha said, "Well, I can't say I'm sorry to hear it."

"Because . . . ?"

"Because of what he tried to do to you, someone who helped me. Can't you see justice when it's staring you in the face?"

A harsh edge that Mairead hadn't heard before. "Could it be connected to Mr. Draskovic's death?"

Alpha leaned back, crossing his arms. "It's plain that you think that, otherwise you'd not be back here tonight."

"It's only five P.M."

A sad grin. "I'm in jail, lass. Hard to tell the difference between afternoon and night, when you've not much to do."

"I said I'd ask them again about your books."

"I'm not blaming you for anything. It's just that even a hermit likes to get out and about from time to time."

He's deflecting you, young lady.

Mairead said, "So, do you think Rex's death—"

"Is tied somehow to Old Man River's?" Alpha looked up, toward the ceiling. "I'd bet the other way, I think."

"Why?"

"I don't see Rex killing the poor devil with my shillelagh. He was fair scared of me himself, and I don't see Rex snatching anything of mine. And besides, that'd still leave the question of who killed Rex."

Mairead felt a little hollow place open up inside her. "I never said he was killed."

"Sure you did."

"I just said he was dead."

Alpha shook his head. "And in your next breath you implied his passing might have something to do with Old Man River's, which we know was cold murder." Now Alpha stared at his lawyer, the green eyes more beady than jumpy. "I keep telling you, lass. You must trust in your clients."

The hollow place began filling with bile. "The last time I was here, you told me you'd help in your own defense. Do you know of any way Rex's killing could be tied to Mr. Draskovic's?"

"No."

"Ever see them fighting?"

"No."

"Even arguing?"

"No."

"Ever hear one or the other say anything threatening?"

"No and no."

Mairead found herself biting her lower lip in frustration.

Alpha seemed to soften, coming forward a little in his chair. "I'm sorry, lass. It's just that . . ." For the first time since she'd met him, the man seemed to be uncertain of himself. "I've not been off the booze for such a long stretch in decades. It was a nightmare at first—back in December, after they put me in here but before I had the pleasure of meeting you—and I guess I'm still not over it. Plus, without my books to soothe me . . ." He shook his head again, but less to disagree, Mairead thought, and more to clear it. "You're asking me good questions, but maybe not quite the right ones."

She wanted to draw him out. "How so?"

Alpha said, "Rex also got stuff from Tommy."

"He told me so himself."

Alpha's eyes lit up now. "Tommy did?"

"No. Rex."

The light faded back to a dull green. "Right. Well, I'm not saying either one stole anything, at least not Tommy himself. But it might be that you should go back to that construction company, have another talk with the head men there."

Something felt off to Mairead. *I don't know why, young lady, but I think he's trying to manipulate you.*

"And ask them what, Alpha?"

"I wouldn't know, lass." The light reappeared in his eyes like a sun was rising behind his face. "Then again, I'm not the lawyer now, am I?"

13

PONTIFICO MURIZZI ENTERED BUZZY'S, then just stood inside the door, letting himself get a feel for the bar before moving around.

The Pope had started at Mitch Gerber's apartment house, but when Murizzi rang his downstairs bell, there was no answer, and nobody conveniently leaving the building to hold the entrance door for him. The Pope remembered the young woman who'd helped the first time, and he pushed buttons until her voice came over the intercom. She went off her feed when Murizzi declined her suggestion—or suggestive—of a drink, but she did steer him toward a student dive three blocks away.

The Pope began moving among the mostly college-aged kids in Buzzy's, beer sloshing over the rims of their mugs and onto loose flannel shirts and baggy blue jeans. The soles of Murizzi's shoes made a *tick-tack* sound as he walked.

A lot of traction on this floor, probably from the spilled drinks. Something to put in the hopper, there's any trouble.

The Pope spotted Gerber pretty quickly, a beer mug in his right hand, the left arm around a bottle-blonde Murizzi felt even other women would call a bimbo. Two more side steps through the crowd, and the Pope recognized the guys on the other side of Gerber. Jeff Glennon with his butch cut, Rick Dorsey with his quasi-pageboy, the Marijuana Twins from the dorm.

Murizzi made eye contact with Gerber, who squinted a little, then almost missed the bar setting down his mug.

Drunk. Which'll make some of it easier, and some of it harder. The Pope started walking toward him.

Gerber yanked his arm off the blonde, her saying something, him pushing her away at the shoulder and getting a loud, clear "fuck you" back.

Murizzi said, "I've got a couple more questions."

Gerber laughed, kind of transparent in the way he winked at Jeff and Rick while sliding his feet into a boxing stance. The Pope felt the crowd around him start to part, that instinctive herd reaction that says "back off, but stay close enough to watch." Murizzi cut a quick look at the Twins, who each took a step toward their friend, supportive but cautious.

Gerber said, "What, you didn't get my message last time?"

The Pope stopped a full stride before he got to the big kid. "What message was that, Mitch?"

"That I don't like fuckbreaths coming around, hassling me." A tilt of his head toward Jeff and Rick. "Or my friends."

"Just need a few more answers."

"Dude," said Gerber, "what you need is a hearing aid."

The Twins laughed, if a little nervously.

Murizzi decided on a lie. "Probably got my bell rung once too often in the ring."

Gerber's face sagged a little, Jeff and Rick exchanging glances the way they had in their dorm room. "What's that?"

"Mitch, back around the time your papa hosed your first mama, I lasted four rounds against Marvin Hagler."

"Who?" said Gerber, apparently overlooking the insult.

The bimbo's voice chimed in from the crowd. "Marvelous Marvin was only, like, the champion of the world."

The Pope said, "Eventually, yeah. But back then, Hagler was just an up-and-coming middleweight in New England, and I fought him at the old Hynes Auditorium on Boylston Street. He beat hell out of me till the ref stopped it." Murizzi now eased half a step closer to Gerber. "But I lasted four rounds, Mitch. How long do you think you'd last?"

The Pope caught Jeff and Rick taking baby steps backward. Like so

many encounters, it all came down to just how stone stupid—or bluffable—their big friend happened to be.

Murizzi said, "Okay, Mitch. When's the last time you saw that homeless guy Rex?"

"Like I told you, with the bad vibes over the killing—"

"You been frying other fish."

"Right," said Gerber, looking to Jeff and Rick for support.

"Mitch," the Pope getting into his face as much as their difference in height would allow, "I don't believe you."

"Hey, dude, I don't care what—"

"You'd best start caring. All three of you. He's dead."

"What?" from Jeff or Rick, but when Murizzi turned toward them, Jeff's mouth was the one hanging open.

The Pope pointed north. "Somebody drowned Rex in the river."

"Not likely," said Gerber, uncertainly. "River's frozen."

Maybe he was telling the truth about not being down there recently, but the Pope still wasn't buying. "The thaw's melted big holes, and the ice around them is pretty rotten. Easy enough to push somebody in, hold him under long—"

"Nobody pushed the guy," said Jeff.

"Shut up, fuckbreath," Gerber starting to flex. "Just shut the fuck up."

"Mitch?" said Murizzi.

"Yeah?"

"I want a partner for this interrogation, I'll ask for your help." He turned toward Jeff. "Better if you tell it now."

The kid was about to speak when Gerber stepped quickly toward his friend, the big right hand cocking itself to backhand Jeff the way the Pope had rousted Rex outside Alpha's cave. Only Murizzi was a little quicker, better anticipating the tacky floor.

Catching Gerber's hand in both of his, the Pope sank his thumbs into the big kid's palms and his fingers into the spaces between the small bones on the backs. Then Murizzi wrenched with his shoulders, and Mitch Gerber cried out as he toppled over, his face bouncing off the leg of a bar stool.

"My toof," said the big guy, free hand to his mouth now. "You knocked ow my fucka toof."

The bartender, who must have been hovering close to the taps, said, "I'm calling the cops."

The Pope looked at him. "I'd wait awhile."

The guy just froze.

"You," Murizzi turning back to Jeff, whose eyes had gone kind of milky. "The rest of it."

Jeff spoke toward the big man on the floor. "We hadn't been down to the river for a while, with all the police shit over Old Man River getting killed. But after you saw us yesterday, Mitch was afraid you'd use Rex to fuck us up with the dean of students."

"What, get you expelled or something?"

"Hey, we didn't know. The bum files a complaint, it goes to a hearing board and everything. So Mitch got Rick and me to go with him, kind of lean on this Rex guy. But somebody already had."

"Meaning . . . ?"

Jeff shook his head. "Meaning the dude already had one of those metal braces on his finger, like somebody'd broken it for him. And his mouth was kind of messed up, too."

"Go on," said the Pope, his voice level, as Gerber made snuffling sounds on the floor.

"So, we start ragging this Rex, telling him he'd better not be talking to anybody about us. And he spooked."

"He went crazy?"

"No. He took off running. Mitch started after him, but we quit, figuring this Rex had, like, gotten the message."

Murizzi stared at Jeff. It felt right. He moved his gaze to Rick. "You agree with him?"

Rick's eyes closed. "Yeah, that's what happened."

"When you two quit, Mitch here kept after Rex?"

Now they both looked at Gerber, then both also nodded.

The Pope dropped down to his haunches. "Mitch, I'm thinking we have a significant inconsistency here."

"Get me a fucka amboolunce."

"In a minute, Mitch. We don't know yet just how badly hurt you're gonna be when they arrive."

That got Gerber's attention.

Murizzi said, "You told me five minutes ago that you hadn't seen Rex since Old Man River got killed. Now I find out that you chased Rex last night." The beat, dah-*dum*. "That's what the prosecutor calls an inconsistency, Mitch. And inconsistencies lead to juries believing what they see in front of them. A big lout of a college kid with too many advantages snuffing out a poor homeless guy, maybe just for the hell of it."

Gerber said, "My das's a dentiss. If I don't get this toof back in soon, I—"

"The truth, Mitch. Now."

The eyes gave him up. "Aw righ, aw righ. I chase the asshole, buh I nevuh lay a hand on him. He ran ow on the ice."

"To get away from you."

"Or he waf jus crazy."

"And then what?"

"I hear crack-crack, and he's in the waffer."

"You help him?"

"Shit, due, wha am I suffosed to do? The asshole's haffway to Cambridge when he gosh under."

"You didn't yell for help?"

A shake of the head, which the Pope could tell hurt Gerber. "I didn't do nuffin."

Suddenly, Murizzi felt old and stiff and tired. Very tired. Rising to his full height, he said to the big college boy, "Mitch, you didn't do anything at all."

The Pope glanced to the bartender, who still hadn't so much as picked up a phone himself. Turning, Pontifico Murizzi walked toward the door, the crowd of kids parting before him like the Red Sea in that old Charlton Heston flick.

"MOMMA," said Billie's youngest, William.

"Dinner be ready in two minutes."

"That's not what I want to ask you."

She stopped coordinating the things on top of her stove long enough to look down at him, the other two boys watching television in the living room.

"What is it, William?"

"Did you have a good day?"

Billie found herself getting lost in those big brown eyes. The boy who asked because he cared, about both the answers and the person giving them. "Matter of fact, child, I helped somebody."

William nodded gravely. "Was it that new one?"

"New one?"

"That new lawyer at your job. Was she the one you helped?"

Thinking back over what went down at the john's apartment—and outside afterward—Billie ran her hand over her son's perfectly shaped head and short hair. "In a way, child. In a way."

"I wonder if you can help me?"

It was still mild enough that Mairead didn't have her gloves on, but she kept her hands in her coat pockets anyway, give the construction worker one less thing to stare at.

Seeming to be one of the last people on the site, he came over with that stride people who work with their bodies seem to have. *A touch of swagger, young lady.*

"What do you need?"

It sounded to Mairead like just one long word. "I'm looking for Mr. Pratt or Mr. Wyckoff."

The worker laughed. "Afraid the suits are long gone. But they might still be at the corporate office." He arced his hand around the corner. "Turn there, walk ten, twelve blocks."

She didn't have Wyckoff's business card with her. "Address?"

"I'm not too good at those. But I remember there's a coffee shop just across the street. Even has some parking spaces, you're driving."

"I'm not," said Mairead, turning to go, "but thanks."

"Hey, you can't find the suits, feel free to come back."

Mairead almost waved over her shoulder, then dug her hands deeper in her pockets.

In the middle of the twelfth block, she found a coffee bar with room for three cars in the small lot beside it. Opposite was the main entrance to an office building, and the directory inside the lobby listed Cornerstone Construction on the seventh floor. Because it was after five, Mairead had to sign in at the downstairs security desk, but the emaciated guard didn't give her any kind of visitor's badge to wear.

On the seventh floor, the arrow for Cornerstone pointed to the right. Mairead knocked on the plaqued door, got no answer, and banged a little harder, with a single "Hello?" When there was no reply still, she tried the knob, and it turned.

The suite was a more modern version of Shel Gold's. The offices whose doors were open were smaller, with just single windows looking out at another building's bricks. The furnishings had that plastic feel of rented rather than purchased.

Nobody at the reception desk, or even in sight. "Hello?" with a little more juice behind it.

"I'm gone," said a familiar, if not friendly voice.

Mairead turned toward it as Severn Pratt blew through the reception area from the office corridor behind it. Purposeful stride and dress code the same, his android blond hair a little fluffier without a hard hat to mash it down.

Mairead got as far as, "Mr. Pratt—"

"I've got another appointment, and Cornerstone's already given you as much time as we can."

Over his shoulder with "Al, be sure you lock up with her on the other side of this door," and the president was gone.

"Just a second," came Alvin Wyckoff's voice. The chief of security appeared around the corner in dress slacks and shirt and tie, but with cuffs rolled up to his elbows and tie tugged down from his throat.

"Mr. Wyckoff?"

His face wrinkled into a smile, the thinning brown hair doing a sit-up on his forehead. "Hey, the first lawyer I haven't had reason to hate. What brings you back to us?"

"Same case, different aspect." She looked toward the door. "I'd like to have talked with Mr. Pratt, too."

A nice smile. "Sorry, but he's off to warm food and strong drink, not necessarily in that order." Wyckoff motioned toward the two parallel love seats eight feet apart in the reception area. "Probably more comfortable out here. Take your coat?"

"Thanks."

Mairead watched for his reaction as he saw her hands. He looked at them, but not for long or even oddly, as he hung her coat in a small closet.

She sat on the love seat against the wall, Wyckoff the one under the window.

Wyckoff said, "I'm afraid I can't offer you any coffee. The pot's all cleaned out and put away for the night."

"You're not usually here this late?"

"Not if I can help it. Construction, you're up with the rooster, even if you're not building the project yourself. But the boss likes me to be the last one out, which means the only one after him."

Mairead said, "Remember the advice you gave me before?"

"About maybe not pressing on Tomlinson?"

"Yes."

"What about it?"

"Something's happened. Rex is dead."

"Rex who?"

Mairead decided to change the phrasing she'd used with Alpha. "Another homeless man. Drowned in the Charles. I have information that Mr. Tomlinson was giving him stuff, too."

Wyckoff shrugged. "Wouldn't surprise me. I told you, this foreman of ours was bent like a pretzel." Then Wyckoff grew more serious. "But you're telling me another bum—"

"Homeless—"

"Whatever, is dead?"

"Yes, but we don't know how."

A frown. "I thought you said a minute ago that he drowned?"

"Yes, but is it drowned or was drowned."

Wyckoff blinked several times, and Mairead sensed he'd genuinely not thought of the second possibility. He said, "There's some . . . wacko out there, targeting homeless people?"

"We don't know. But it's obviously important to us—to our case—to find out."

"Because . . . ?"

"Because if a second man was killed while our client's confined to jail, then—"

"Maybe your guy didn't kill the first one, either."

Mairead nodded.

Wyckoff seemed to weigh something. "Doesn't work."

"What do you mean?"

"Look," Wyckoff coming forward in his seat. "You've got three bums—"

"Homeless people."

"You call them homeless, I'll call them both. Anyway, two of them are dead. One of the dead ones and the only live one supposedly got stuff off our company's job site. Maybe the stuff was given to them, probably it was stolen."

"For the sake of argument, I'll give you that much."

"Now one's in jail, and the other's dead. And our foreman's flown the coop."

I don't see it, young lady. "Meaning?"

Wyckoff separated his hands, then brought them back together. "Where's the connection?"

"Maybe your foreman's a killer as well as a crook."

Wyckoff seemed to weigh that, too. "Wouldn't surprise me. But even if Tomlinson killed the first guy, why would he hang around for—what, a good month?—waiting to kill this Rex?"

"Maybe it took Mr. Tomlinson a while to find him."

"How long did it take your side to know about the guy?"

The man has a point, young lady. "Not very long."

"Plus, it doesn't make sense for Tomlinson to kill even the first bum. If Tomlinson's been ripping our company off, it's bad enough he's going to

have people like Pratt and me on his tail. Why would he want a murder rap and real cops chasing him, too?"

"Maybe Mr. Draskovic could incriminate Mr. Tomlinson."

"Only if our bent pretzel was going to hang around, though. Then it'd make sense for Tomlinson to kill your first guy. Which is why I don't think he killed either one of them."

"Then who did?"

"Your client on the first, and somebody else, unrelated, on the second."

Mairead thought about it. "Mind telling me where you were last night?"

Wyckoff grinned. Kind of a nice one, like the Pope's. "Celtics game, with three friends of mine."

"Which lets out around what, nine-thirty?"

"Past ten. Went to double overtime against the Pistons."

"And after that?"

"Drinks with the same guys till midnight. Want their names?"

Mairead said, "Was Severn Pratt one of them?"

Al Wyckoff's grin disappeared as he looked down at his watch. "I'm afraid it's time for you to leave and me to lock up."

14

PONTIFICO MURIZZI WAS LOST in thought as he moved down the catwalk toward his boat. The crime scene with Rex's body, the visit with Winston Hayes on the rich sailor's roof deck, and the rousting of the college boys in the bar combined to produce a dark frustration. He was no closer to helping Mairead O'Clare with her case, and he may even have triggered Rex's death. In fact, the Pope couldn't see how anything would—

"What's the matter, mate? You don't even look up here when you pass?"

Murizzi turned, Jocko standing on the schooner's deck, his arm around the main mast, the boy himself beautiful and buoyant.

"Sorry, Jocko. Just daydreaming."

"Well, try nightdreaming instead." He hopped down lightly from surface to surface until reaching the cockpit near the helm, almost touching distance from the Pope. "Specifically, dreaming about tonight's spectacular menu of fresh spinach salad with homemade dressing, veal chops broiled in capers and mushrooms, and baby peas with minced onions. All to be washed down by a Pinot Noir from your Oregon, of all places."

"Sounds terrific."

Jocko lifted his face toward the sea. "I'd even say this incredible January weather's mild enough to risk dinner outside on your fantail, if you'd help me carry over the goodies?"

"Sounds like just what I need, but I want to shower first."

Softer voice. "I hope you'll be wanting more than that, luv, but only after you've told me what's got you so down."

Christ, he does press the right buttons on me. "Give me twenty minutes."

"I'll be over with bells on," said Jocko.

LEAVING Cornerstone Construction's office building, Mairead O'Clare was deflated. Before going in there, she'd felt that even if Alpha was manipulating her, he might know more than she did about who really killed Zoran Draskovic. Only the more she thought through Al Wyckoff's arguments, the more Mairead agreed with him.

And I can't blame you, young lady. It's hard to see how the deaths of Old Man River and Rex and the disappearance of Donn Tomlinson could be related.

But hearing inside her head the mention of Rex's name reminded Mairead that she still hadn't confronted the Pope about his "avenging" her by breaking the homeless man's finger. And if it was possible that Murizzi could have gone over the top and actually killed him, she wanted to know about it before her feelings grew any deeper for the man.

Orienting herself, Mairead headed for the waterfront.

PONTIFICO Murizzi was just toweling dry when he felt that telltale shifting of his houseboat that told him somebody had come aboard.

Hopefully, with bells on.

The hot, needle-point spray from the shower had eased his tightness over the day, and an evening-into-night with Jocko would erase the rest. But first, a little surprise present for the boy.

The Pope wrapped the towel around his waist without doing a sarong tuck. Moving toward the closed drapes on the cabin side of his sliding glass door to the fantail, Murizzi could feel himself growing hard as he brushed against the terry cloth with each step. At the drapes, he grabbed and bunched some fabric in the same hand that he'd use to open the door.

Like gripping the handle of a stove with a pot holder.

Then, the Pope yanked the sliding glass door open with that hand while whipping off his towel with the other.

AT the sound of the cabin door, Mairead spun around.

Young lady, this is the part where you close our eyes.

But Mairead stood transfixed, not quite sure she could believe what she saw.

"Christ, I'm sorry!" said the Pope, doing a better job of closing the drapes than replacing the towel, Mairead thought.

From behind the still-open door, Murizzi's voice carried nervously through the fabric. "I'm sorry," he repeated. "Let me just get something on."

Mairead felt a laugh—equally nervous—welling inside her as she realized that's what she'd hoped for eventually: that the two of them would "get something on."

There were still chairs around the back deck of the houseboat—talk about your global warming—so Mairead sat in one, trying to make sense of what had just happened.

He couldn't have known you were coming, young lady.

No question. Which meant the Pope was expecting somebody else. And, given his . . . greeting, he was intimate—or *awesome* good friends—with a woman already.

The drapes parted then, and Murizzi came through them, now wearing a pair of jeans, a white cotton turtleneck, and a black rugby shirt with a horizontal stripe of red through it.

He would have to look great, too, even with his clothes on.

"Mairead, let me explain—"

"No." She held up her hand. "No explanations necessary."

"But I—

"Look, Pope, I came down here without calling first, and it's obvious I've caught you at a bad time."

"No. I . . . I do have other plans. But after . . ." He waved back toward the drapes without looking at them. ". . . that, Jeez, I owe you something."

Well, the evening's possibilities are shot, might as well get the bad stuff over with. "I saw Rex."

Murizzi flinched. "I wish you hadn't. The morgue's not—"

"I didn't see him dead."

The Pope squinted at her.

Mairead said, "After yesterday morning, when you picked me up in your car along the river, I went back to Alpha's cave for the books I'd promised to bring him."

"You went back? Alone?"

"Yeah, but not for long. Rex was already there. And I saw what you did to him before you picked me up in your car."

The man looked down at his deck. "The finger."

"The finger." Mairead came forward in her chair, elbows on her knees. "Pope, I want this to come out the right way. I appreciate your trying to help me. Really. But I don't want you living out some macho fantasy by avenging me whenever—"

"That low-life derelict tried to rape you."

"And I handled him."

"You got away."

"That's right."

"Leaving him hot and bothered—"

"Not from anything I did—"

"—which he might have taken out on somebody else. Or on you, next chance he got."

Mairead was about to say, "We're not in the vigilante business," but then remembered her scene with Billie and Talina at Joshua Brewer's apartment.

Then she realized the Pope was looking at her differently.

He said, "I'm not trying to scare you."

"If you are, you'll have to try harder."

"Okay." Murizzi letting out a breath. "Message received."

"If you have the time, I'd like to talk about Rex's death."

Mairead watched the Pope relax, and she knew—to the depth of her soul—that he hadn't killed the man.

But he feels guilty about it somehow, young lady. "Pope?"

"Yeah?"

"You have time to talk now?"

"A little. Here's what I found out."

Mairead heard about his first visit to Hayes and the two college boys, then his session with Mitch Gerber, then his follow-ups with Hayes on the roof deck and the three rowdies in Buzzy's.

After Murizzi finished with Gerber's "confession," Mairead thought she understood. "Pope, you're afraid that you somehow set in motion this Gerber chasing after Rex."

Murizzi looked at her differently, but a *different* differently.

He's reappraising you, young lady.

"Yeah," said the Pope. "I suppose I am."

It took a moment for Mairead to realize he was responding to what she, and not Sister Bernadette, had said. "Well, if you set that college kid in motion, then I set you in motion, right?"

"You could take that approach, yeah."

"Hey, I was raised by nuns. They practically invented guilt."

A grin, that disarming, charming one he'd trotted out the first time she'd met him, and Mairead felt a similar flutter low in her chest. Well, maybe there'll be a rebound of this puck, and I can pounce on it.

Young lady?

Mairead said, "But, bottom line, Pope, you think Rex's death came from the college kids chasing him."

"Unless something else comes up, that's my take."

Which actually made Mairead a little more confident in her earlier feeling about the case. "So, it's unrelated to Zoran Draskovic and Alpha."

"Not necessarily."

Well, that good feeling didn't last long. "What do you mean?"

"If my college boys killed this Old Man River, they might have had a reason for doing Rex, too."

"A campaign against the homeless?"

"Or the rowdies crush Old Man River's skull simply because he pisses them off. They frame Alpha—or just get lucky on him being blamed—and they have to ice Rex because he knows something."

Mairead worked it through. "Holds up, but what about a connection to Tomlinson?"

"Who?"

She filled Murizzi in on what she'd learned at the construction site and company office from Pratt and Wyckoff.

The Pope said, "You been working this case pretty hard, too."

"I don't have many others competing for my attention."

A nod, then a frown. "If Tomlinson's stealing from his boss on the project, and maybe Alpha's helping him, any chance Old Man River knew about it and was going to blow the whistle?"

Mairead thought that through. "Alpha and Rex both told me outright they got stuff from Tomlinson, so it was no secret."

"The scrap lumber and small stuff, but what about the high-end materiel? Maybe that was the secret part."

"Possibly."

Murizzi frowned again. "Doesn't feel right, though, does it?"

Jesus Mary, talk about same wavelength. "No, it doesn't."

"So, let's go back to basics. The Commonwealth's view: Alpha kills Old Man River over the coat the victim's wearing that night, an item that's been stolen back and forth a few times."

"Right," said Mairead.

"Rex involved in that at all?"

"Stealing the coat, you mean?"

"In ever wearing it himself."

Mairead went over what she'd found out. "No, I don't think so. Why?"

"A lot of these derelicts—"

"Homeless—"

"Homeless look alike to outsiders. You know, unkempt hair, scraggly beards, grungy clothes."

Mairead tried to see it. "So you're thinking that maybe somebody was trying to kill Rex and mistook Draskovic for him?"

"Could happen."

Mairead's turn to frown. "No, it doesn't wash. Draskovic and Rex didn't look at all alike. One had dark hair, the other light."

"Any color hair looks pretty dark when it's dirty."

"No. Shel's file had photos and vital statistics of the dead man. His hair was much longer than Rex's. And besides, there's the age and height

difference. Rex was maybe thirty, younger and way taller than Draskovic, who was more like . . ."

"Like who?"

"Like Alpha," said Mairead. "About the same height, a little older than our client, but in an overcoat—"

"Especially the overcoat your Alpha had been wearing, and maybe viewed from behind, where the killer's coming from . . ."

"Yeah, I suppose—no. No, that doesn't wash, either."

"Why not?"

"Draskovic had hair past his shoulders; Alpha looks almost like a Marine in boot camp."

Murizzi's head moved subtly up and down. "I'll take your word for it, but it's kind of odd for a homeless guy to have his hair cut short going into winter. Most want the extra bulk for warmth."

"Wait a minute." Mairead searched inside her brain. "There was a photo—or a bad copy of a photo—in Shel's file. It showed Alpha with longer hair. And in jail, he told me that when they brought him in, they shaved his head because of lice."

"Who's they?"

"What do you mean?"

"If it was the sheriff's people at Nashua Street, maybe what you saw in Shel's file was a copy of the mug shot the police would have taken at the booking station."

Looking out into the harbor, Mairead said, "Had to be. Alpha told me he'd never been arrested before." She came back to Murizzi. "You thinking the same thing I am?"

"The killer mistook Old Man River for Alpha."

"So, if you can get a better print of that mug shot . . ."

"Then we compare it to Old Man River's, see if maybe—"

"Ready for the first course . . . , mate?"

Mairead looked over her shoulder, seeing the punker from next door, apparently about to hop aboard the Pope's boat as she had.

Murizzi cleared his throat. "Once in a while, we cook each other dinner."

Mairead looked at the Pope now.

He said, "Jocko, this is Mairead, a lawyer I'm working with."

The punker nodded. "We met before. Pleasure, though."

"Same here."

Murizzi said, "I'm sure there's plenty, you want to stay?"

Up, young lady. "Uh, no, thanks," Mairead rising from her seat. "I have to get back to my place."

The Pope nodded neutrally. "I'll call you when I get the mug shot."

"Thanks."

She vaulted over the side of the boat and onto the floating dock. As Mairead moved toward the stairs that led to the harborside restaurant, she was pretty sure neither of the men she'd just left was talking or laughing, the way they usually did when "the girl" was gone.

Which probably means, thought Mairead, that I've gone from "Perry Mason" past "Ally McBeal" and all the way to "Will & Grace."

Young lady, you're not so old you won't get over it.

Shaking her head, Mairead O'Clare climbed the steps back up to street level and pointed herself toward Beacon Hill.

15

SHELDON GOLD SAT BEHIND his desk as he watched the three of them file into his office. Billie, carrying a pad for taking notes. Mairead, carrying what looked like notes she'd already taken. The Pope, holding a big manila envelope and now standing with his back against the old bank vault.

Admit it: This office feels like your real home, and, for one reason or another, you've come to think of these people, even the newest one, as your real family.

"Okay," said Shel when the two women were seated. "Where are we on this Alpha case?"

Mairead related the debate she'd had with Al Wyckoff over whether the deaths of Zoran Draskovic and Rex could be related to the disappearance of Cornerstone's black foreman, Donn Tomlinson. Murizzi then detailed all his "interviews" with Hayes and the college boys, concluding that while the autopsy on Rex showed he "drowned under conditions of hypothermia," the Pope was pretty sure Mitch Gerber had hazed Rex into the water.

"So," said Shel, "we have to figure this Rex—or at least his dying—isn't really connected with the Commmonwealth's case against Alpha."

Mairead nodded, then went over the conversation on Murizzi's houseboat the night before, and the possibility that the killer of Draskovic might have mistaken Old Man River for Alpha.

The Pope opened his envelope. "This morning, I got some shots from Artie Chin over at Homicide." The Pope removed several photos. Holding

up the first one, he said, "The decedent, Draskovic, Zoran, mug shot from a disorderly charge last year."

Shel noticed the audience—Billie, Mairead, and himself—staring intently at a photo taken live of someone they'd all known only in death. It showed full-front and profile views of a middle-aged man, with a weathered face, scraggly beard, and shoulder-length, clumpy hair.

Murizzi held up an autopsy shot now, eight-by-ten. "Draskovic again, on the slab. He measured out an inch shorter than Alpha, and twenty pounds lighter, but the coat would probably hide the weight factor from somebody who didn't know the two of them well. And notice, Draskovic still has the same long hair, though by now, the ME had washed it."

The Pope now held up another mug shot. "An original print of Alpha, taken just after the arresting officers pulled him out of his bed in the cave under the bridge."

Shel studied a version of Alpha he'd never clearly viewed before. "Similar features and scraggly beards, but Alpha's hair is lighter than Draskovic's."

Billie said, "At night, though, might be you wouldn't see that."

Mairead now held the mug shot of Draskovic next to Alpha's. "See how the profile shots are pretty close? Both have hair the same length and kind of . . . matted?"

Shel said, "Clumpy."

The other three looked at him.

He shrugged. "I'd call it clumpy."

Murizzi said, "Whatever. It's nighttime, and I'm after Alpha, I could mistake Draskovic for him."

Shel thought about it. "Especially if you never got a good look at the one you're after."

The Pope nodded. "Dark, and maybe some distance."

Billie said, "Don't be forgetting the coat."

Murizzi glanced to her. "Like I said before, the coat'd cover the twenty-pound difference."

"Not what I meant." Billie pointed at Shel. "Didn't you tell me the police think the reason our crazy killed the other poor man was over the coat?"

"Yes."

"Well," Billie now going back to her notes. "Seems to me a man kills another over his coat on a cold winter night, that man's gonna take that coat back with him."

Murizzi grinned. "I made the same point to Artie Chin."

Shel said, "Give me a minute here."

He closed his eyes to run this new scenario back and forth a few times, despite knowing that his face usually moved funny—lips twitching and lids quivering, as though he were deep in dreamland.

Then Shel opened his eyes. "One problem: How does our killer know where Alpha keeps his walking stick?"

The Pope raised his hand, like the kid in a classroom who thinks he's got the right answer. "Rex would have known."

Mairead shook her head. "I don't like it. I'll give you he was prone to violence, but Rex would have been the last person to mistake one man he knew for another. And what motive did he have for killing Mr. Draskovic?"

Murizzi said, "How about Old Man River just being a pain in the ass?"

Shel stretched in his chair. "I don't like it, either, Pope. Seems to me that Rex kills Draskovic, he'd take off rather than hang around for over a month."

Billie nodded. "And with that man's coat, too, if this Rex didn't have a good one himself."

Mairead said, "Of course, we don't have to prove Rex *was* the killer, right? We can just keep him in reserve, trot him out for reasonable doubt."

Shel looked at her. Admit it: She's a natural. "Brutal crime like this, though, I'd like to give the jury a live alternative." Shel took a breath. "So, let's assume we've been following the wrong road here from the beginning. Instead of focusing on who had a motive to kill Draskovic, we should think about who had a motive to kill Alpha."

Shel went from face to face in his office. "Any candidates?"

Murizzi spoke first. "This rich guy, Hayes the sailor, seems awfully interested in homeless people getting killed."

Mairead said, "The executives at Cornerstone Construction—Pratt and

Wyckoff—really wanted me to believe there was no connection between Mr. Draskovic getting killed and their foreman disappearing."

Shel nodded. "Pope, do a full background on Hayes, prep school forward."

"Shel?" said Mairead.

"Yes?"

"Maybe I can find what you need about Hayes on-line."

"By computer, you mean?"

"At my old firm. Take somebody twenty minutes."

Shel glanced to Murizzi, making sure that was okay with him. The Pope nodded.

"Mairead," said her new boss, "anybody at your old firm who could check out Cornerstone's finances the same way?"

"Shouldn't be too hard."

"Okay. I've got a friend I can call, too, see if anything's in the wind about Cornerstone and shady dealings. Which leaves this foreman who didn't show up for work the day after Draskovic was killed, right?"

Mairead went to her notes. "Let's see . . . Tomlinson, Donn . . . African-American . . . hired out of prison . . ."

"The man have any family?" asked Shel.

"Wife, but I didn't get her name."

Murizzi said, "Guy's been gone over a month now. I'll check with this desk jockey I know in Missing Persons, see if anybody's filed a report."

"Good." Shel glanced from his investigator to his secretary and back again. "Get the wife's name and address, but I think Billie might be the best one to go see her."

"Why?" said Billie, looking up sharply from her notepad. "Because she's black?"

Shel looked at her. "Yes, but mostly because—given the month that's passed—she might be a widow, too."

"JOHN Ramirez, please. . . . I'd rather not say. . . . John, Mairead O'Clare. . . . Only because I didn't tell the switchboard who I was. . . . Listen, I need a favor . . ."

"JUST tell him it's the Pope. . . . Rudy, how you doing?. . . . Yeah, same-old, same-old here, too. Listen, I need the next-of from a Missing Persons. . . . Wait? You bet I can."

"AH, Tiffany, right? . . . Shel Gold. . . . From the old neighborhood, yes. Good memory. I wonder if I can speak with Ben? . . . Thanks, I'll hold."

"ROBERT? Listen, I might have to go out tonight, so . . . No, I don't know where. . . . Yes, I would 'grill' you about it if you were calling me. . . . Now listen, can you pick up William at his straddle care and stay with him till I get home? . . . Good. . . . *Owe* you one? Let's just say this'll be one *you* won't owe *me* anymore."

"MAIREAD, if Burgess ever finds out . . ."

"Then lunch is on me for the rest of your life."

"What life?" said John Ramirez.

Mairead watched him slip into the booth opposite her at the Black Rose, an Irish pub near Quincy Market. He had his notebook computer case in his right hand, but there was no clunking sound as he put it on the table next to her pint of lager.

When the waitress came, Ramirez asked Mairead what she was having—a Harp draft—and he ordered the same.

Once they were alone again, Mairead said, "So?"

"So I did what you asked me to." Ramirez opened the computer case, slipping out a diskette. "I copied all the stuff I thought you'd need onto this. You figure our computers and software are compatible with your new ones?"

Very evenly, Mairead said, "Probably not."

"I was afraid of that." He slid a batch of papers from the case now. "So I printed these out for you."

"John, you're a prince."

The waitress came with Ramirez's beer and left again, Mairead wading through the documents.

Ramirez said, "You want a down-and-dirty summary?"

She looked up at him. "Especially if it's dirty."

A smile. "First, Cornerstone's incorporated in Delaware."

No surprise there, young lady. A state that "understands" corporate needs.

Ramirez went on. "Principle place of business, though, is Boston, and, basically, they're in over their heads."

"Incompetent?"

"*Too* competent. Keep winning all these bids—a dozen projects—but with barely enough capital to obtain performance bonds on their last three. Apparently this Severn Pratt's a Tasmanian devil when it comes to what he wants to build."

Mairead thought about Cornerstone's president and decided John's characterization fit like a glove. "So there's borrowing in the company's future?"

"I don't know much about corporate finance, but it seems to me they're the functional equivalent of being maxed out on their credit cards."

"Go on."

"I ran the three names you gave me as separate search commands. Alvin C. Wyckoff comes up lean and clean. High-school and small-college football, big security agency, then went with Cornerstone three years ago. Donn Tomlinson, on the other hand, did most of a ten-year sentence for armed robbery."

"Any details?"

"He nearly beat somebody to death."

"With his bare hands?"

"No," said Ramirez. "A tire iron."

Graduating to a shillelagh? "What else?"

"That's it for the melodramatics, at least on Tomlinson. But guess what came up for Severn Pratt?"

"What?"

"He used to work in D.C., for this company that did a lot of renovation work on federal buildings."

"And?" said Mairead.

"And Pratt was investigated for fraud."

"What kind?"

"Hard to tell from the newspaper accounts I was able to find, but basically, he and another guy supposedly diverted stuff for Project A over to Project B, where their contract with B let them goose the price for the same stuff."

Another guy. "Name of his supposed helper?"

"Julius Stein."

"Any photos?"

"Just of Pratt, coming out of a courthouse, smiling."

"Smiling? He got off?"

"Charges dropped."

"Why?"

"This Stein, who'd agreed to testify against Pratt, disappeared."

Jesus Mary. Like Tomlinson? "And so . . . ?"

"And so Pratt took the Fifth Amendment, and I guess there wasn't enough other evidence to convict."

"Any allegation of involvement in Stein's disappearance?"

"Innuendoes galore, but no proof."

Mairead tried to use what Ramirez had told her, overlay it on her fact pattern.

"Uh," he said, "there's more."

She looked at him again. "More?"

"Afraid so. This other guy you wanted—Winston Hayes?—turned out to be a real pain."

"How so?"

"Well, I ran the search command for his name, and got hundreds of hits, going back as many years."

"He's a time traveler?"

Ramirez grunted out a laugh. "No, he's Winston M. Hayes the Fourth, usually written as Eye-Vee, like the Roman numerals. Only that means there was a Third and a Second—not junior, always just Eye-Eye. But it still means I got a shitload of junk about his father, grandfather, and—"

"That all in here?" Mairead tapping on the sheaf of papers.

"Yeah. Once I realized what was happening, I plugged in a separate search delimited by his 'Fourth' and by 'years.' Also, fortunately for my time constraints, the guy's father died young."

"How young?"

"Less than forty. When your Winston was only fourteen."

"What'd the father die from?"

"Fractured skull. Seems this 'hobo,' as the old newspapers called him, broke into the Hayes family's summer home and beat Winston the Third to death with a baseball bat."

Young lady, you should find the nearest church and light a candle.

"OKAY, Golden Boy, I made some calls for you."

"Thanks, Ben," said Shel, shifting his telephone receiver to the other ear so he could pull a pad and pencil toward him. "Oh, and thanks for all the help with Little Benji, too."

"Been a hell of a week for favors. But that reminds me, I haven't heard anything on the news about him killing that beast."

"It'll work out between them, I think, once we can get the property split."

"May his divorce be happier than his marriage. No, Tiffany, that's good, good."

"Ben, if this is a bad time for you, I can—"

"Hey, Golden Boy, I'm the one's calling you, remember? Okay, let's see here . . . Yeah, Cornerstone Construction. First off, a little birdie tells me they're not connected."

Shel breathed a silent sigh of relief. He wanted no part of a Mafia business.

"Second," said Friedman, "that might not be true next week."

Shel now held his breath. "Why, Ben?"

"Seems they're running around like crazy, trying to juggle all the jobs they're doing. Moving money around, too. Kind of robbing Peter to pay Paul, you know?"

Big Ben was always into Christian expressions. Probably learned them from all the young women he—

"Golden Boy, you want to make some noises now and then, let me know you're still there?"

"Sorry, Ben. Still with you."

"Okay. This same little birdie says that Cornerstone's going to have to do some borrowing at steep rates."

"Loan sharks?"

"Let's call them lenders of last resort. Seems the head guy in the company—Pratt?"

"Severn Pratt, right."

"He got caught with his hand in the federal till, but the Feebs couldn't make it stick. Something about a witness dropping down a— No, super, babe. Just super."

"Ben?"

"So, how's that for two-hour service? Nowadays, you can't get a shirt cleaned that fast."

"I really appreciate it." Shel paused. "Anything on this Tomlinson visiting fences with construction materiel?"

"Kind of a specialized field. I've got a call in to this other guy might— No, no, that's a little toothy, Tiff."

Shel cleared his throat. "Uh, Ben—"

"You see why I wanted to call now, Golden Boy? This could be you, enjoying a little afternoon delight. But you got to stop thinking of the undercard as your spot on the marquee. Admit your old life's over, and your new one can— Oh, yes, baby, yes, yes, yes!"

"Thanks again, Ben," said Sheldon Gold, carefully replacing the telephone receiver in its cradle.

WHEN Mairead reached the front door of the office building on Beacon Street after her lunch with John Ramirez, Pontifico Murizzi was just coming out, carrying what looked like a medium-sized overnight bag.

"Mairead, Shel wants to see you upstairs."

"That's where I'm going." She gestured toward his bag. "How about you?"

"Washington."

"D.C.?"

A nod as the Pope flagged a cab. "To check up on Pratt."

"But my friend just got a lot of information about him off the computer."

"Want to hand it to me?"

"Well, it's in here someplace." She began to rummage through the packet Ramirez had given her.

The taxi pulled over by Murizzi. "Do you have anything more than Pratt being up on federal charges for fraud, and an unavailable witness resulting in a walk?"

Mairead looked up at him. "No, but how did you—"

"Hey, buddy, we going somewhere or not?"

The Pope said, "Logan Airport, shuttle to D.C." Then to her, "Shel's friends don't work off computers."

Mairead O'Clare watched Pontifico Murizzi get in the cab, his hand waving to her out a rear-seat window.

"MRS. Tomlinson, thank you so much for seeing me."

The slim, fortyish woman opening the front door from the inside looked to Billie Sunday like she was about ready to collapse. Not in the body so much as the face, especially the eyes saying, "One more straw, and this camel's sinking into the sand."

Billie had been in those kind of shoes before, and she decided that Shel probably was right to send her here after all.

As Tomlinson led her into the living room, Billie saw around her a house kept the way a neat woman can if there are no children—or a man—around to mess things up. Small, religious pictures on the walls. Big TV set on a rolling cart, VCR underneath it, cable box on top. Coffee table polished, sofa and chairs and carpet plush and colored so they set each other off beautifully,

"Can I get you something, Ms. Sunday? Coffee, tea?"

"Tea would be nice. And please, call me Billie."

"I'll be just a moment. And please, I'm Danette."

Which Billie already knew from the Missing Persons report that spooky Pope got from his police friends.

She sat on the sofa, but a "moment" was about all it took for Danette Tomlinson to be back, with a tray of cups and saucers, miniature sugar bowl and cream pitcher, and slices of cake.

A Church Lady. Which Billie knew was jumping to conclusions, but everything about this poor soul just screamed it, including having the hot water already boiled so the tea could be served as soon as the guest was seated.

"Danette, you don't sound like you're from Boston."

"No, I grew up in North Carolina. Ever been there?"

"Never, but my late husband was stationed at Fort Bragg."

"Oh, I *am* sorry. How long ago did he pass?"

"Eight years, but time heals."

"Yes," said Tomlinson, and Billie was pretty sure the Church Lady was trying to figure how long it was going to take her.

After tasting the tea and cake, Billie felt like it would be cruel to prolong things for the woman. "Danette, you know my Mr. Gold represents the man accused of killing another homeless soul along the Charles River."

"I know. In fact, Donn used to talk about him."

"Talk about . . . ?"

"Alpha was his name—is his name, right?"

Woman's thinking of her husband in the past, having to break out of it to talk about people she knows for sure are still alive.

"That's right, Danette. What did Donn say about him?"

"That he was . . . strange. But a hard worker. Donn said he wished he could hire him on for Cornerstone, but I guess the man's from Ireland and doesn't have his papers."

Honey, thought Billie, you can say that three times over.

"Danette, do you know if your husband gave Alpha things from the job site?"

"Oh, yes. But just little stuff, like scraps of lumber, some bent nails, one of Donn's old hammers. What my husband thought Alpha could better himself by having."

Donn "thought," past tense again. Maybe her faith has allowed the lady to already accept that he's gone.

Billie took another sip of tea. "So, they got along."

"Yes." A darkening, like that last straw was hanging over her right then. "But someone *was* stealing things from the site. Expensive 'materiel,' as Donn would call it."

Billie recalled Robert Senior using the same word, with an "e" where you'd think an "a" should go. "Did your husband know who?"

A shaking of the head before Tomlinson took some tea as well. "But he thought it almost had to be someone on the job, on account of how no break-ins seemed to be happening."

"Did the higher-ups suspect anybody?"

"Yes," that straw seeming to weigh heavier on Tomlinson's back as she worried the unusual wedding band on her left hand. "Donn."

"What did he do about it?"

"He had to be real careful. You see, my husband did some time in prison—where we met, actually. I used to do volunteer work for our church there."

What did I tell you? "So, he thought the company was blaming him because of that?"

"Some. And they were just under a lot of pressure, too, so maybe they felt like they needed somebody to blame pretty quick."

Billie realized that Tomlinson hadn't answered one of her questions. "But did your husband do anything about it?"

"About the materiel being taken, you mean?"

"Or about the company's suspicions."

"Donn figured that if somebody was sneaking the stuff out, maybe he could find out who it was."

"How?" said Billie.

"By punching out on the clock, then sneaking back in and hiding."

"Hiding?"

"On the site. Watch to see who might be carrying things off."

Oh, Lord. "Is that where he was the night he . . . disappeared?"

"I don't know. I help out at my church here now a couple nights each week. That was one of them, so I didn't ask Donn what he was going to be doing after work."

Tomlinson sniffed once. At first Billie wasn't sure it had happened, because the woman's face stayed the same. Like she's wearing a mask, and she's having trouble breathing behind it.

"Danette, was that the last time you saw your husband?"

"Yes. When I came home from the church that night, he wasn't here. We always had this rule."

"Rule?"

"Yes. If one of us wasn't going to be home by eleven, we'd call, leave a message on our answering machine."

"But he didn't call."

"No, so at midnight, I tried the police. They said Donn was probably just out having a good time and to call in the morning."

Billie could almost hear it. White officer picks up that the caller's a black woman, and the problem gets tossed on the you-know-how-they-are pile. "Did you try the police again?"

"Yes. Different person, same . . . attitude."

Billie nodded. "What else did you do?"

"Called Donn's company. They weren't real polite, maybe because of the way they suspected him on the materiel. Anyway, they told me he punched out on time."

"But that was what he did the nights he stayed on the site to watch for the real thief, right?"

"Right. But I didn't tell his company that, for fear they'd think Donn really *was* the one stealing, by sneaking back in."

"What happened after that, Danette?"

"I waited the time the police said, and I filed a Missing Persons report. Went down myself to the station." Two sniffs, but the mask stayed on. "I got the impression that once they found out Donn had been in prison, they . . . lost interest in me."

Billie could identify with that, too. Just one more poor black Church Lady, married an ex-con she knew was no good, just because she had to see him prove it again. Which he did, by stealing from his white boss and taking off on his dumb wife.

Billie said, "And no word about him?"

"No. And Donn wouldn't have done that. I don't mean the stealing, now. He would never take off without telling me, without letting me know he was healthy and safe." Three sniffs, and the poor soul's face began to squinch up. "He's dead. Oh, Lord in Heaven. My Donn's dead. Somebody's killed my husband."

Billie got to her feet, but couldn't prevent Tomlinson from swinging her arm and sweeping the coffee table clean of all the things she'd lovingly placed on it. Some of the china smashed when piece met piece, tea and cream spilling down onto the carpet. Tomlinson began howling, just syllables you wouldn't understand if you hadn't been listening the last fifteen minutes.

Billie wanted to take the poor woman into her arms, hug her and rock her until this spell passed. But Billie also knew what the tea and the cream would do to a carpet she expected Danette Tomlinson had spent many hours priding herself on.

So Billie first ran to the kitchen, get some paper towels and soda water. Because she didn't want the poor child to be seeing stains on her carpet and be reminded by them to start crying again over her lost husband.

Pulling at the dispenser with one hand and opening the refrigerator door with the other, Billie Sunday thought, No, Danette, over the next few years, you'll be finding yourself crying often enough as it is.

16

PONTIFICO MURIZZI NEVER CARED that much for Washington, D.C. He figured it probably stemmed from the fact that his father got lost there on a family vacation. Both parents, as immigrants from Italy after World War II, felt it important for their American-born son to appreciate what a great country they now lived in. Only thing was, they spent most of the vacation with his father cursing the street patterns—and especially the circles—Thomas Jefferson had laid out almost two centuries earlier.

And, in the Pope's opinion, things hadn't improved much since his first visit.

He had trouble finding addresses on foot, and he couldn't begin to understand the taxis that seemed to charge him different magnitudes of fares depending not on the mileage between his destinations but rather on whether the cab crossed into another "zone." Add in some really shitty weather—variable showers, temperatures in the high forties—and it wasn't a day to remember.

On the other hand, Murizzi figured he didn't do so bad, result-wise.

His first stop had been a federal agency, where Severn Pratt's predecessor company had tried to fiddle the books on a renovation project. After being shunted around, the Pope got a referral to a retired employee who really had the scoop, being the chief witness against Pratt at the abortive trial.

"Yeah," said the wiry black guy living alone in his little house tucked between two huge developments in Alexandria, Virginia. "Pratt was a

smoothy. Wined and dined us back in the first Clinton administration, when the Arkansas boys knew how to look the other way." The guy scratched himself on the right bicep under a cardigan sweater with elbow patches on it. "Always had an answer for every question my boss at the time—political hack from a cactus-and-snakes state—would ask him. But old smoothy Pratt didn't figure on me."

"I'll bet he didn't," said Murizzi, kind of liking the guy for trying to do his job despite his superiors, something the Pope remembered well from his time in the department.

"Nossir. I kept going over the numbers Severn Pratt fed us, and they just didn't add up. I kept visiting the site itself, even counted the laborers actually on the job, and they didn't add up, either. I made telephone calls, I wrote memos, even lodged a couple of formal complaints when my boss was back in his Southwest Sahara and wouldn't see them before he got back. But Pratt kept skating over the thin ice, at least till this auditor from GSA got interested in him. Then the doo-doo hit the ceiling fan."

"G-S-A?" said Murizzi.

"Stands for General Services Administration. Can't survive in Washington without you know the acronyms for everything."

The Pope wondered if that might be part of the reason he had trouble with the city himself.

"Yessir. This GSA auditor got other people interested, and pretty soon there is just an avalanche headed Pratt's way. Only thing is, despite me and a bunch of others testifying, the case against him hinged on this partner of his, Julius something-or-other. I kept thinking Julius Caesar at the time, and my poor old brain can't seem to bring back his last name now."

"You're doing fine."

Murizzi saw the guy's expression turn a little, and for a second, the Pope was afraid he'd lost him.

"Young man, I *know* I'm doing fine. I enjoy a government check every month and a bowel movement every day."

Murizzi liked the guy even more.

"Well, anyways, this Julius had the straight skinny on stuff Pratt knew or did, stuff that I could only guess about. But come a few days before trial, and Julius meets his Brutus."

"You know who killed him?"

"Nossir. Don't even know for sure that Julius *was* killed. But I was in the courtroom when the prosecutor had to admit that the man couldn't be found, and I know the look that passed between old smoothy and one of his henchmen."

"Henchmen?"

"Brutus. Now, just a minute, his real name'll come back to— No, no, it won't. Don't remember either first or last, if I ever knew them. But he was on the site from time to time, because I saw him there on some of my visits." The guy scratched his other bicep under the sweater. "Guess I should be glad I *didn't* know more, otherwise maybe old Brutus would have come after me."

"Can you describe this henchman?"

"About thirty then—so around your age now. Some size to him, but no giant."

"Hair color, eyes?"

"Didn't pay much attention."

"White?"

"Of course he was white," said the little, wiry guy. "I told you I didn't pay much attention, didn't I?"

BILLIE Sunday called out, "It's Jake over at Suffolk Superior."

"Got it." Picturing the skinny, dour court clerk in the criminal jury session, Shel Gold picked up the telephone in his office. "Jake, how are you?"

"Still taking nourishment. Listen, we just had three pleas in a row here, and Judge Cordoba craves fresh meat."

Cordoba. A stone-cold technician, could have written the book on Evidence law, but left a lot to be desired in the "have a heart" category. "What are you telling me, Jake?"

"I'm telling you that Her Honor's looking over the same docket and trial list that I am, and pretty soon she's gonna see you sitting on a slam-dunk murder."

"You speak to the other side?"

"Of course I did. Pereira says he's ready."

Shel pictured the assistant DA. Portuguese-American, from an established East Cambridge restaurant family and kind of pudgy and bumbling. Juries felt sorry for him, thought they *had* to find the defendant guilty to protect the system themselves while wondering how Pereira had ever been hired in the first place.

Which, of course, was exactly *why* the guy had *been* hired in the first place, and why he continued to play the role long after his intelligence and experience would have permitted him to grow out of it.

"Hey, Earth to Astronaut?"

"Sorry, Jake. When would you say?"

"If the judge doesn't have me phone you within two hours, I've wasted seventeen years in this chair. She'll want tomorrow morning, here in the Third Session, but if it'd make a difference to you, I can probably push for an afternoon start instead."

"My investigator's in Washington, D.C."

"Yeah, well, since the Pope isn't likely to be the first witness Pereira's gonna call for the Commonwealth, I don't see Her Honor taking that into account."

Shel did a quick assessment. "We'll be ready tomorrow at two. And Jake?"

"What?"

"Thanks for the heads-up."

"What I know about your case," said the dour voice, "it won't be enough."

"I can give you only a few moments, Mr. . . . Murizzi?"

The Pope sat down in front of the former Assistant United States Attorney/current power broker. Between them was a desk that Murizzi thought

had maybe twenty pounds on the *Lusitania*. "Yes, and thanks for seeing me at all."

"Frankly," said the guy, "I wouldn't have, if you hadn't mentioned the magic word."

"Pratt."

"I'm surprised he never changed his name, that son of a bitch." The attorney leaned forward, the way he probably did before a jury when he held a decent job. "It took me two months to crack his partner Julius Stein, and when I did, Severn Pratt had him hit."

"You know this?"

A grunt, and the guy leaned back in his chair. "Mr. Murizzi, if I *knew* that Pratt had my witness killed, do you think I wouldn't have nailed him on that?"

"So the only thing's certain is that this Stein didn't show up for trial."

"Yes." The man behind the desk suddenly seemed to change tones, personalities even, and Murizzi started to feel a little sorry for him, wondering if something like a sick wife or kids in college forced him to go from the side of the good guys to the side of the "whatever" guys. "I'd put in four years with a big law firm before I went over to the U.S. Attorney's. I'd been there only six, seven months before I drew Pratt's case." A pleading look in his eyes. "It was just a garden-variety contract-fraud case. No nuclear weaponry or state secrets. How the hell was I supposed to know the son of a bitch would whack a witness?"

"The wrong people die," said Murizzi quietly, "it's not always your fault."

"I know." The attorney seemed to change back. "Or, if I didn't then, I do now. In any event, I haven't seen Pratt since."

"Do you think Pratt did the killing himself?"

"I don't know. I mean, everybody was out on bail—Stein, Pratt himself—and I certainly didn't order any surveillance on or protection for either of them."

"Any other names from the situation pop into your head?"

The attorney gazed out his window, some monuments partially visible, even from where the Pope sat. "Regarding Pratt, you mean?"

Murizzi said, "Yes."

Finally, a shake of the head. "No."

Standing to leave, the Pope thought about the wiry black guy he'd seen earlier and decided that maybe it was a good thing after all that this power broker left law enforcement when he did.

"TOMORROW?" said Mairead O'Clare, standing at the threshold to Shel's office but not believing her ears.

"Afternoon," he replied, nodding behind his desk while riffling through a file on it.

"But at Jaynes and Ward, we'd have months' advance notice, and even then there'd be continuances for another—"

"Few months, because those were civil cases, and criminal ones take precedence, thanks to constitutional speedy-trial decisions, judges' predilections, and media pressure."

"There can't be that much media pressure on Alpha's case."

"But we do have a judge's predilection."

Mairead had no response for that.

Shel seemed to find the paper he was looking for. "I'm going to have Billie try to reach the Pope in D.C., get him back here."

"He's going to testify?"

"Probably not, but I want him serving subpoenas on the people we'll call. Meanwhile, I think you should go over to Nashua Street, let Alpha know what's happening."

"About the trial date."

"And what we've found out about the construction company, Winston Hayes, and so on."

"You want Alpha to be optimistic," said Mairead.

"I want him to be realistic. If he thinks we have a shot at winning this thing, maybe you can persuade him to be a little more cooperative in his own defense."

Mairead O'Clare hoped Shel Gold was right about that.

ENTERING the travel agency, Pontifico Murizzi thought about the call he'd gotten from Billie Sunday on his cell phone an hour before. He'd

been in a library, cranking a microfiche machine for back issues of the *Washington Post*. It didn't matter that Shel Gold wanted him to return to Boston, as the Pope hadn't found a photo caption of anybody but Julius Stein and Severn Pratt in the news coverage of the fraud trial.

However, it *did* matter that the travel agent was now telling him that her computer screen showed no flights.

"How come?" said Murizzi.

"This weather we've been having today? Well, it's pea soup at both Dulles and National—or Reagan, new name."

"Look, I've got to be in Boston tomorrow as early as I can."

"Well," she said, "I can't guarantee anything'll be flying even in the morning. But"—she tapped some buttons on her keyboard—"there is another way."

"I'll take it."

"I'∨E my blessed books now. Thank you so much."

"You're welcome."

"However, let me guess, lass," said Alpha, with that gap-toothed smile of his. "You've come not because of them but instead to tell me we're going before a kindly jury tomorrow."

Mairead stared at him in surprise as he took his seat across the table in the little conference room at Nashua Street. She waited until the guard had closed the door behind him before replying. "How did you know that?"

"Jail's like a little village, so word that a murder-one defendant is climbing into the dock spreads fast."

Mairead waited a moment. "You're okay with this?"

A shrug. "I don't see that I've much say in it. And besides, it's probably about time the truth came out, anyway."

"The truth?"

"About my not killing poor Old Man River."

Mairead tried to see where Alpha was heading. "Well, I think we've come up with some pretty good evidence of reasonable doubt."

"Have you now?"

She summarized what Billie Sunday had found out from Mrs. Tomlinson. Then what Ramirez had told her about the way Winston Hayes's father had died and about Cornerstone Construction and its president, Severn Pratt. Mairead closed with the Pope going to Washington to pursue that last.

Alpha frowned. "But how will the jury know about all this?"

"We'll subpoena them—Hayes, Pratt, everybody—and put them on the witness stand."

Alpha nodded. "I'm impressed. Truly. You've done a fine job of preparing my defense, Mairead O'Clare."

"A lot of people helped."

"But only because you believed. In me."

"I do. There's something that we've thought of, though, kind of an alternative theory of the case."

Another frown. "And what would that be, lass?"

"Maybe the killer mistook Mr. Draskovic for you."

Alpha's green eyes grew wide. "That the . . . ?"

Mairead explained, using the factors of the river scene, the long hair, and the same coat. "So, Alpha, can you think of anyone who'd want you dead?"

He didn't reply right away. Then, "For that, lass, I'll be having to take your witness stand my ownself."

If Mairead was surprised at his knowing about the trial date, she was stunned by that prospect. "What?"

"For the whole truth to come out, you'll have to ask me some questions in the courtroom."

Mairead had no real experience in criminal cases, but despite Shel's banter about calling Alpha as a witness, she knew from law school that defense attorneys virtually never put their clients on the stand if there was any possible chance of selling the jurors on reasonable doubt with other evidence. "What questions?"

"Actually, just one should do the trick. I don't know the lawyer words for it, but something like, 'Now, Alpha, would you be so kind as to tell us what happened that night?'"

Mairead felt her mouth opening, so she decided to send some words into the air. "Have you gone crazy in here?"

"I don't believe so." He closed his eyes and rolled his shoulders. "No, I think I'm still fairly sane, despite the abstinence from both grape and grain that your fine jail—"

"They'll rip you to pieces on cross! Like *Jurassic Park,* when they lowered that terrified cow into the Velociraptors' cage."

"Well now, I'd hardly be calling me 'terrified,' lass."

Steady, young lady. The man's still manipulating you.

Mairead tried to calm herself, the way she'd learned from hockey before an important face-off. Then she said, "What I mean is, the prosecutor is going to show the jury all the . . . nonsense of you being a hermit, and—"

"Mairead!"

She stared at him—he was genuinely angry, and Mairead had to resist glancing toward the panic button on the wall to her right.

In a kinder voice, Alpha said, "I'll not have you insulting my vocation on the eve of trial."

Young lady, he's playing you. Try to understand why.

"Alpha," Mairead drawing a breath before continuing, "I can't agree with how you want to live your life, but it's our job to keep the rest of it from being spent in prison. And I don't think Mr. Gold is going to put you on the stand."

"Yes, well, I've actually asked around some in here. Three other prisoners, and even a few kindly guards, have all told me the same thing about my testifying."

"That it would be stupid to take—"

"That if a defendant wants to take the stand on his own behalf, he has an absolute right to, whether he's a citizen of your fine country or not."

Mairead closed her eyes for just a moment, seeing clearly that all her efforts to help the man had been wasted. "Why, Alpha? Why do you want to do this?"

"So the truth will come out, lass." The gap-toothed smile. "Why else?"

I'd say that's the real *question, young lady.*

Mairead O'Clare stared at her client.

Why else, indeed?

T⊢E ticket read, Train 66, Car 6600, Room 6.

Pontifico Murizzi, remembering what his mother always told him about 666 being the sign of the devil, decided he was glad not to be superstitious.

Carrying his overnight bag, the Pope climbed aboard the Amtrak car. He immediately saw what he expected: one of those great big compartments, like in the James Bond movies. Only the door was marked "A," not "6."

"Help you, sir?"

Murizzi turned to the man in the conductor's uniform, one of those French Foreign Legion hats on his head but without the little hankie at the back of his neck. "You the conductor?"

"Steward, sir."

"Well, I'm looking for number six."

"Your ticket?"

The Pope handed it to him.

"Ah, this way, please."

They sort of sidled together down the narrow corridor until the steward stopped and slid open a little pocket door.

"Here you are, sir."

Murizzi stuck his head in the opening.

What he saw: A space maybe eight feet long and three feet deep, with a very low ceiling. Two seats—recliners from their design—were against the window and upholstered in some awful purple and blue pattern, with matching mini-drapes above them.

The steward said, "You can close those drapes if you want. There's a little magnet catch that clicks them shut."

The Pope looked at him. "I think you've made a mistake here."

"I don't believe so, sir." A frown as the guy examined Murizzi's ticket again. "No, this is roomette number six."

"*Room*-ette? Try *clos*-ette. I was supposed to get a compartment like that first one."

"I'm sorry, sir, but with the airports fogged in, we're pretty well booked up."

"But this isn't a sleeper."

"Actually, it is." The steward grinned, the Pope wanting to clock him. Then the guy reached up to the ceiling and yanked on what looked like a hatch handle, which made a bunk bed descend like a dumbwaiter to around eye-level.

Murizzi still couldn't believe this, but he was coming to accept it. "Where's the john?"

"Over here."

The steward tapped a tin toilet lid in the corner of the roomette, before pulling a tiny sink out from the wall. "And over there is your thermostat, reading lamp, and television/radio."

The Pope pointed at the bunk bed. "It looks like a six-foot drop to the floor. The train hits a curve, I'll roll out."

"Cargo netting goes over hooks near the ceiling. Once you're in bed, just button up and sleep soundly."

Yeah, thought Pontifico Murizzi, setting his bag on one of the lounge seats. Like riding to the graveyard in my own coffin but with an optional view through the mini-drapes.

"MAIREAD, it's his constitutional right."

"It's his path to life in prison," piercing blue eyes ablaze.

Shel Gold watched her pace left-right-left in front of his desk. He remembered back to the first criminal defendant he had insisted take the stand—a pickpocket, with arthritis yet—and Shel empathized with Mairead.

But admit it: You're also glad she *is* feeling frustrated, because that shows the passion side of her as a lawyer.

Mairead said, "So what are we going to do about it?"

"Try to talk Alpha out of testifying."

"Between now and tomorrow?"

"No." Shel shook his head, having forgotten for a moment how inexperienced she really was. "No, we'll have at least a couple of days, while the

prosecution puts in its case against him. And while we call our own witnesses to the stand, especially if the Pope comes back from Washington with something that helps us."

"And what if he doesn't?"

"Then we'll play the hand we're dealt as best we can, and hope the opposition makes some mistakes."

Shel watched Mairead struggle with something. "It just all seems so . . . iffy."

Shel felt himself shrug in his chair the way he knew juries saw him on his feet at trial. Like his whole body showed visibly what his mind was thinking silently. "That's trial work. Each side tells its best version of the case to the jurors, and then we see where in between they come down."

"In between?"

"The two versions. Twelve people don't usually buy everything either side offers."

Mairead blew a wisp of auburn hair away from her face. "Anything I can do?"

"Yeah. Try to get a good night's sleep, because tomorrow afternoon, after we finish for the day, I'm going to want you preparing your examination of Severn Pratt."

Bingo. That combination of shock and excitement you hoped would appear on her face.

Mairead said, "My what?"

"Your questions for the president of this Cornerstone company. Of course, it's possible Pereira may—"

"The prosecutor?"

"Right, Phil Pereira. It's possible he'll call Pratt as part of the Commonwealth's case-in-chief against Alpha, in which case you'll have Pratt on cross. But even if the man doesn't take the stand until we're into our defense case, you can ask the judge to declare him hostile, and you'll get to ask leading questions, anyway."

"You're going to have *me* do the actual . . ." She shook her head. "I mean, in the courtroom?"

"That's where the jury generally sits."

"You . . ." Another shake, but this time more to stop herself, Shel thought. And then Mairead said, "How are we going to get Pratt declared hostile?"

"I don't know," said Sheldon Gold, smiling in what he hoped would seem honest ignorance. "But you've met him, so you'll probably figure it out."

17

"SIX A.M., SIR," WITH a knock on the little pocket door. "Boston's South Station in thirty minutes."

Pontifico Murizzi was amazed to find he'd slept through the night. In fact, the swaying of the train and the clacking sound of the wheels on the tracks turned out to be kind of a cradle-rocking lullaby. The Pope even thought Jocko might have enjoyed it, too. Then Murizzi remembered he was riding six feet off the floor, cargo netting around him like a tuna on a dock.

At which point, the Pope began unhooking the net so he could get free.

THE *genuine article, young lady*.

Shel Gold said, "I know you were in Boston Municipal for Talina's case, but is this your first time in Superior Court?"

Mairead O'Clare looked around the large, cavernous room the way she remembered walking down Fifth Avenue in New York City on her one and only visit there. While Talina's arraignment in the BMC was like reciting poetry in a madhouse, the Superior Court room was quiet and nearly empty. The walls were wainscoted halfway to the ceiling, the tall windows majestic, like a church's without the stained glass. All the fixed furniture—the judge's bench, the witness stand, the jury box—seemed made from the same wood.

Maybe even the same tree.

"Mairead?"

"Yes," she replied. "This is my first time."

Gold frowned. "That big firm never even took you to see a motion argued or anything?"

"I was only there four months, Shel. I never saw the inside of anything but Jaynes and Ward's library."

"Okay, then. A little orientation. This is the old Federal Courthouse, which the Commonwealth kind of inherited when Uncle Sam built his new place over on Fan Pier. We're in the Third Session, or the number three room to be assigned a trial judge each day." Shel pointed to the jury box. "The witness stand is on the jurors' side of the judge's bench, so they can hear testimony the best. The party with the ultimate burden of proof gets to sit closest to the jury, so that table there is the prosecutor's. We'll sit at the table farthest from the box."

"Which I'm guessing would be an advantage in some cases and a disadvantage in others."

"Right." Shel swept his hand in a square. "This is the bar enclosure. Alpha will be sitting with us and maybe one of the Homicide detectives with Pereira. Everybody else stays in the gallery behind us once the jury's selected. Until then, the prospective jurors themselves will be sitting back there waiting as individual ones are called to the box by the clerk, working from a list of panel and seat numbers." Shel looked toward the kangaroo pouch before the empty bench. "Let me introduce you to some people."

Mairead followed him, thinking, I'm moving around a courtroom, and I feel like a lawyer.

You're getting a guided tour, young lady. There's a difference.

Shel said, "Nina, Jake, I'd like you to meet my new associate, Mairead O'Clare." The woman in the bailiff's uniform extended her hand to Mairead. Middle-aged and stolid, she'd be strong on her skates if trouble started, Mairead thought.

"Muh-*raid*?" said Jake, a skinny, expressionless man from his clerk's seat. "How do you spell that?" After she did, he started rummaging through a stack of papers in front of him. "Her Highness is in rare form today, Shel."

"A burr under her saddle?" said Shel, sympathetically.

"More like a sea urchin. Tread lightly, my advice."

"Sheldon Gold," said another voice from behind them.

Mairead turned to see a man in a suit that was better pressed than Shel's but straining at the seams to contain its occupant. Puffy cheeks, thick black

hair, sweat shining from the lines in his forehead. He stood only about five-eight, and Mairead wondered how much more weight he could afford before it'd be elevators over stairs for the rest of his life.

"Phil, how are you?" said Shel.

"Fat, tired, and stupid."

Shel smiled, but Mairead sensed that he didn't take this guy lightly. "Mairead O'Clare, Phil Pereira."

"Muh-*raid*?" The prosecutor huffed out a breath. "How do you spell that?"

"YOU look awful."

Pontifico Murizzi closed the door to Sheldon Gold's office suite. "Made the mistake of trying to shave on the train."

"Shave?" said Billie Sunday, sitting behind her reception desk like photos the Pope remembered seeing of mastiff dogs guarding the gates to villas in Italy. "On a *train*?"

"Long story. Shel in?"

"Court."

"Mairead?"

"Same."

"In court, too, or the same court?"

Murizzi loved that look of utter disapproval in Sunday's eyes, like she was hoping against hope that none of her boys turned out to be such a wiseass.

"Same court. Alpha's trial starts today."

"That why Shel wanted me back so soon?"

"Yeah, but not to join him." Sunday picked up a handful of documents. "Subpoenas. I think you'll know some of them."

Murizzi skimmed the names, noticed something. "Didn't you go talk to the missing foreman's wife?"

"I did."

"She isn't in here."

"I talked with her about it, and with Shel about it. We both decided she'd be there on her own."

"Just don't blame me if she's not."

Billie Sunday gave him another disapproving look. "What I think's going to happen in this one actually does, there'll be plenty of blame for everybody to share."

JAKE proved right: It was more like a sea urchin.

In her lobby—even after the move to the Federal Courthouse, the state judges preferred that expression over "chambers"—the Honorable Lydia Cordoba eyed Sheldon Gold sternly over her half-glasses. "The defendant's name is Alpha?"

"That's what he told us, judge."

Shel watched Cordoba shift her gaze to Phil Pereira. "Surely the police have identified him by now?"

"Uh, no, judge," said the ADA.

"Why not?"

Shel, happy to be off Cordoba's hot seat, half-listened to Pereira relate how fingerprint checks and the federal NCIC computer system all came up empty. Shel was glad to see Mairead, sitting next to him, paying rapt attention to every word from Pereira's mouth. What interested Shel the most, however, was how Cordoba was approaching the case. The lobby conference immediately pretrial was often the best barometer of how a given black robe was going to preside over a trial.

Admit it, though: Lydia Cordoba is still the same as she was trying cases for the Attorney General's Office: cold and technical, her bony shoulders, prominent cheekbones, and she-wolf's eyes commanding respect and demanding compliance.

"Mr. Pereira," she said, "I am *not* impressed by the Commonwealth's inability even to identify the defendant. It does not speak favorably of your ability to prove this homeless man guilty of murder."

"For that, judge, we do have evidence."

"Let's hear it."

As Pereira gave a jargon-filled summary, Shel continued to study Cordoba. He sensed a change come over her as his opponent ticked off witnesses and incidents.

She's heard enough to know this shouldn't be a trial.

Cordoba cut Pereira off in mid-sentence. "Mr. Gold, what will your client accept here?"

"I'm afraid he won't, judge."

"Won't consider a plea?"

"He's told both my associate, Ms. O'Clare, and me that he's innocent."

The judge squeezed her lips white. "You've explained to him the consequences of going to verdict over this?"

The veiled threat: I'll impose a lesser sentence in exchange for a plea, but I'll throw away the key if he forces the Commonwealth to the expense of an unnecessary trial.

Shel said, "I'm afraid my hands are tied here, judge. My client insists he didn't do the crime."

"Very well." Cordoba let her tone convey her displeasure. "Any unresolved motions?"

Figuring it a waste of time to ask that Pereira not be allowed to refer to the decedent as "the victim," Shel shook his head.

Lydia Cordoba turned to her court officer. "Nina, have them send us five panels."

"WHAT the *hell* are these?" said Severn Pratt, looking like a mannequin twisted into an awkward pose.

"Subpoenas." Pontifico Murizzi had stepped right up to him in Cornerstone Construction's reception area on the seventh floor of the office building something like half a mile from the construction site. "One for you, and one for you."

The Pope watched Pratt steam as he began to read his document, but Al Wyckoff, sitting kind of resignedly, Murizzi thought, didn't even open his.

The chief security guy said, "The prosecution already served one of these on me."

"Nice piece of luck. You get paid twice for the same work."

Pratt looked up from his subpoena. "What the hell does this mean, 'from day to day until concluded'?"

Murizzi turned to the president, thinking, What an asshole.

"Ask your lawyer, but I'd bet it means you two are stuck in a courtroom for the duration, unless you cut a deal with Sheldon Gold to be on telephone-call notice."

"Telephone-call notice?" Pratt's steaming boiled over its lid. "This is outrageous!"

"This is the law," said the Pope.

"I'll get a court order."

"Not my department," Pontifico Murizzi throwing that last over his shoulder as he cop-walked out Cornerstone's door.

"THE Commonwealth's content, Your Honor," said Phil Pereira, pushing himself up from his chair by his palms against its arms.

Mairead didn't know much about selecting juries, but thanks to the orphanage, she knew a lot about conducting oneself in front of authoritarian women, and in chambers, Judge Lydia Cordoba had quickly established herself in the mold of Sister Angelica of the "stigmata" comment. In fact, now that they were in the courtroom itself, two jurors had tried to weasel their way out of serving—one a young mother, the other a busy executive with an international trip in the works. Cordoba gave both of them a civics lesson before denying their requests to be excused. Pereira had not asked any individual questions of the jurors, challenging for cause only one who was a full-time employee at a soup kitchen for the homeless.

Mairead was conscious of Shel poring over the juror questionnaires they'd received, making various marks in some kind of shorthand next to the names of the ones called to the box. But he never rose to challenge any, and the sixteen people—twelve plus four alternates—were seated within an hour and a half.

Mairead herself sat between Shel and Alpha, making their client the one at their table farthest from the jury box. He didn't look half-bad: shaved and a part in his hair, but the individual strands stood up in a cowlick, giving him kind of a farm-boy look. Shel had brought Alpha a dress shirt and gray slacks so the jury wouldn't see any inmate jumpsuit, but no tie or jacket. Mairead said a silent prayer of thanks that their client sat straight up in his chair, hands folded in front of him on a notepad occupying his third of

the table. After glancing around, Mairead included in her prayer the two burly court officers who had brought Alpha in from a side door, taken off his handcuffs and ankle irons before the jury entered the courtroom, and then stood flanking Nina ever since.

Please, God, let Alpha stay calm, so these reinforcements aren't needed.

In a whisper next to her left ear, she heard "Pity we don't seem to have drawn much of a crowd, eh, lass?"

During their pretrial meeting with a then-shackled Alpha in a small, secure detention-*cum*-conference room off the Third Session, Mairead had stressed to him how important it was not to appear anything but calm—and innocent—as he sat before the jury. Swiveling her head, though, she agreed with him on the audience in the gallery. Mairead guessed that the middle-aged black woman would be Danette Tomlinson, and that the female state trooper must be the one the Pope had called Pamela Wilkins. But other than a few casually dressed couples Mairead thought might be retirees attending a different form of theater and a few shabbily dressed men obviously staying out of the suddenly wintery January air, she didn't see anyone else she could identify.

"Mr. Pereira?" said Judge Cordoba.

The prosecutor seemed to rise from his chair with a little more difficulty each time, and Mairead began to think he might be playing his appearance as a card with the jury.

In court or in life, you play the cards you're dealt.

Mairead wasn't sure that Sister Bernadette and Shel agreeing on the same gambling metaphor for trial was very reassuring.

Now on his feet, Pereira said, "Yes, Your Honor?"

"You may address the jury."

"Thank you, Your Honor." He bumbled with some papers, even fumbling a few onto the carpet. Hand on the edge of his desk, he genuflected on one knee to gather together the rest, grunting as he came back up.

Mairead leaned into Shel. "Showtime, right?"

A nod. "When we used to have a given jury pool for a month, he couldn't get away with it more than once. Now that there's a different venire each day, it's fresh every time."

Pereira stood before the jurors, rearranging in his hand the scattered notes. Mairead watched the sixteen faces in the box. Nine women, seven men. Ten whites, three blacks, two Latinos, one Asian. Their wide range of expressions and body language on Pereira went from "you poor, poor boy," to "fucking jerk, I could do a better job without going through law school."

But notice one thing, young lady: Love him or loathe him, they're all watching him.

Then the prosecutor suddenly walked back to his table and tossed the papers onto it. "Members of the jury," coming back to them, "I worked on those notes for two hours last night, but it was only when I dropped them that I realized I didn't need them. And I don't need them because this is really a pretty simple case. Tragic, but simple."

Pereira pointed toward the defense table. "You will hear evidence that the man on the far end, already identified to you as Alpha by Her Honor during your selection process, fancied himself a hermit. The first of a 'new world order.'"

A shake of the head, to let that sink in and perhaps rekindle memories of other "new world orders."

"And so he fashioned himself a 'cave,' as he called it, but not sharing it with anyone else. No, our Alpha lived among the other homeless along the Charles River, but not really *with* them. And you will hear testimony that he particularly didn't get along with a poor man named Zoran Draskovic, an environmentalist who, despite his limited resources, tried hard to protect the quality of the resource running by his meager shelter. To protect the waters of the Charles for all of us. But as the weather began to turn cold last fall, Mr. Draskovic lost his own form of protection. Or, rather, it was taken from him. By the man you see sitting at the defense table today."

Another point by Pereira, past Mairead to her client. She didn't want the jury seeing her looking at Alpha, so Mairead fought the impulse, but she hoped his expression was helpful.

Now Pereira backed up. "Mr. Draskovic worked so hard for the Charles, he was known as Old Man River, but despite the nickname, he had only one prized possession. When you have so little, a single item of material good, of warmth, can matter so much. And you will hear testimony that, for Mr.

Draskovic, such an item was his Army coat. Not a particularly desirable garment by your standards and mine, I'd guess, but to Old Man River, it allowed him to pursue his dream of cleaning up the Charles, even in the coldest of weather. Until it was stolen from him."

Pereira stopped, five feet from Alpha. "By the defendant, Alpha. A man who often didn't even bother to *wear* Mr. Draskovic's cherished coat, but just to keep it, for the sake of depriving Old Man River of his ability to pursue his dream. Until Mr. Draskovic couldn't stand the deprivation any longer, until he finally did what any reasonable citizen would have."

Mairead watched Pereira engage each juror individually. Then he began walking back toward them.

"You will hear evidence that Mr. Draskovic reclaimed his own coat from Alpha many times. That they fought over it often. That even the state police tried to mediate the dispute. And you will hear testimony that the last time Old Man River reclaimed his coat from its thief, poor Zoran Draskovic paid dearly. Paid with his life, a life snuffed out by repeated blows from a heavy club Alpha kept inside his cave. Savage blows, members of the jury. Crushing, killing blows."

Now Pereira was back at his own table, knees almost touching his chair. "Blows delivered by the man who neither lived with his colleagues nor let them live their own lives around him. Alpha, who sits to be judged by you today. Thank you."

And, with a grace Mairead had not seen Pereira display before, the portly prosecutor lowered himself into his chair, bringing his palms up to his face, as though to shield his own eyes from the scene he'd just painted.

"Not bad," whispered Shel into Mairead's ear.

"Thank you, Mr. Pereira," intoned Judge Cordoba from on high. With just a slight change in tone, a subtle shift from gratitude to attitude, she then said, "Mr. Gold, will you be opening now?"

Mairead watched him rise. "Thank you, Your Honor, but not at this time, no."

As he sat back down and the judge began speaking to Pereira again, Mairead glanced at Alpha's face and saw the same confusion there she felt inside herself. Turning back to Shel, she scribbled on a page of her

notepad, "Why didn't you take the sting out of Pereira's opening with *something?*"

Shel looked down, smiled and nodded. Leaning into her ear, he said, "We don't have many bullets, and I need to save them for bigger battles."

Mairead understood his words, if not the meaning of which "battles" he was talking about, but she nevertheless shut up and began to take notes almost as soon as Pamela Wilkins, state trooper, was sworn in as a witness.

"PONTIFICO! Today you really must join me in a brandy."

Why not?

There was a fire crackling in the hearth of the large stone fireplace in what the Pope took to be the den of the town house on Beacon Hill. It reminded him that he'd never lived in a place where you could safely build a fire indoors.

The butler, wearing a third, different sports jacket, poured from a crystal decanter on a sideboard into a pair of bell-shaped snifters. Then he brought the glasses to Winston Hayes and Murizzi before disappearing again.

The Pope watched Hayes not so much swirl the brandy around his snifter as slowly move his wrist and hand—like a Hawaiian girl doing a hula dance—so the booze coated the inside of the glass. Then the rich fuck stuck his nose all the way down, inhaling like he was a sick kid and the brandy was Vicks VapoRub.

"Ah, I think you'll like this, Pontifico."

Murizzi swished his around, then took a sniff, feeling the sinuses clear halfway through his skull. "Great stuff."

"Yes," said Hayes. "Well, a toast. To one less homeless wretch along the water."

It bothered the Pope that if another cop had said that over beers, he would have raised his glass. "Any particular wretch we're talking about here?"

Hayes sipped with his eyes closed, a blissful expression on his face. "I suppose we can take our pick, eh?"

"Our pick."

"Well, yes." Hayes opened his eyes. "There's Old Man River, and that Hobosaurus Rex you were here about last time, and now—his name is Alpha?"

"Right."

"Alpha, who according to a very back-page paragraph in this morning's *Globe* went on trial for murder today."

Murizzi sipped from his brandy. Wine you love, but the rich fuck's stuff tastes like varnish.

Hayes said, "It *is* today, isn't it?"

"The trial? Yeah. While we're on the subject, I'm kind of surprised you aren't there watching."

"Yes, well, it's one thing to be ensconced conveniently on one's own roof deck, taking the air while watching the circus perform. Quite another to be stuck in a musty courtroom, bored to tears by the droning of grasping lawyers."

"Winston?" said the Pope, reaching into his pocket.

"Yes, Pontifico?"

Murizzi took out the subpoena. "Looks like 'quite another' time's just around the corner."

"COUNSELOR, you may inquire," said Judge Lydia Cordoba.

Sheldon Gold rose to his feet. "Thank you, Your Honor."

He moved in front of the defense table, keeping his eye on Trooper Wilkins, who seemed like a good person to have police powers. Appearing on the stand in uniform, light brown hair pulled back behind her neck, she seemed comfortably alert during Pereira's direct examination. And while Wilkins also had been balanced in giving testimony, she'd nevertheless painted a picture of Alpha as a royal pain in the ass, establishing also that on a number of occasions when she'd entered his cave, the shillelagh—now known as Commonwealth's Exhibit #1 in evidence—stood inside the doorway.

"Trooper Wilkins, was the door to my client's cave locked on any of those occasions?"

Shel watched her look down for a moment, as though picturing something other than the scene in front of her just then. "No."

"Does the door even have a lock on it?"

"I don't believe so."

"So anyone could have gone inside the cave, the night of the killing or even before it, and taken the shillelagh."

"Objection," said Phil Pereira, halfway out of his seat.

The judge waited a moment, staring—Shel thought even *glaring*—when the prosecutor didn't continue. "Ground?"

"Defense counsel is asking the witness for—"

"I didn't ask you to *argue* your objection, Mr. Pereira. Simply state the ground for it."

The Guru of Evidence strikes again.

Pereira stood straighter. "Calls for speculation."

"I agree," said Cordoba. "Sustained."

A technical loss, but a functional gain, as Shel noticed one of the white jurors nodding toward him. Alpha wasn't the only person with access to the weapon that killed the decedent.

Shel took a single step toward the witness stand. "Trooper, you also recounted for us three occasions on which you personally witnessed the defendant 'fight' with Mr. Draskovic."

"That's correct."

"Each time over the coat, marked into evidence as Commonwealth's Exhibit Number Two."

"Also correct."

"On any of those occasions, did you see my client hit the decedent with a weapon?"

"No."

"Punch the decedent?"

"No."

"Not even slap him?"

"No."

"In fact, if anything, when Mr. Draskovic threw punches at the defendant, my client just held him off, laughing."

"Your client had twenty or more pounds on the victim."

Shel never liked to cut off a well-behaved witness in front of a jury, but he winced inwardly at her referring to Draskovic as the victim.

"A twenty-pound advantage, Trooper, which the defendant used only defensively when attacked."

Wilkins's voice seemed to grow a little edge to it. "When attacked by the victim trying to regain possession of his coat."

Shel turned ninety degrees toward the jury. "Beyond Mr. Draskovic and my client, have any other homeless people been living along the Charles River?"

"Yes."

"How many?"

"I don't know of any accurate census or count of them."

"Trooper, would you say, a dozen?"

"Certainly."

"Two dozen?"

"Easily."

Shel turned back to the stand. "Trooper Wilkins, have any of these other homeless people . . . died recently?"

"Yes."

"A man named Roderick Thorne, but known as Rex?"

"Yes."

"Who'd recently had his finger broken, I believe."

"Yes."

"How?"

"I don't know."

"But you do know how Mr. Thorne—Rex—died, do you not?"

"Objection, Your Honor," said Pereira. "Materiality?"

"Mr. Gold?" from Judge Cordoba.

"Your Honor, the question is material to showing my client is not the killer of Mr. Draskovic. The fact that, after my client was jailed, a second homeless person, who had previously been injured, was found dead under suspicious circum—"

"Your Honor," said Pereira. "Defense counsel is testifying."

"Agreed."

Shel felt Cordoba's withering gaze as she turned to the jury. "You will disregard Mr. Gold's characterization of the death of Mr. Thorne as being suspicious."

Shel may have been chastized, but he thought at least two jurors—a black and the Asian—got his message: Alpha couldn't kill a second homeless man from a jail cell, so maybe he didn't kill the first one, either.

Cordoba said, "Mr. Gold, do you have any further questions for this witness?"

"Yes, Your Honor. I do."

Shel took Pamela Wilkins through her observations of disputes between Zoran Draskovic and others. Laying the foundation for calling the three college students and Winston Hayes later on.

Then Shel said, "Trooper, did Mr. Draskovic resemble any of these other combatants in any way?"

"Objection to 'combatants,' Your Honor. Not supported by the record."

Shel glanced at Pereira as Cordoba said, "Sustained."

"Trooper, did Mr. Draskovic resemble any of these other people he argued with and threw stones at?"

Wilkins paused, perhaps to give the prosecutor a chance to object again. When Pereira didn't, she said, "Not that I noticed."

"How would you characterize Mr. Draskovic's dress code."

Wilkins seemed a little thrown. "Shabby, at best."

"His hair?"

"Long, dark. Kind of matted."

"Clumpy, even?" said Shel.

"I guess you could call it that."

"Not at all the way Alpha looks today."

"No. But, you see . . ."

Wilkins stopped herself, though Shel, and he hoped the jury, sensed that she had more information.

"Go on, Trooper," said Shel, like coaxing a child onto a carousel.

"Well, before Alpha was arrested, he had long hair, too."

"So, he's been altered to look good for trial?"

"No, Alpha . . . When he was brought into the station, his hair had . . . lice in it, so they shaved his head at the jail."

"Ah, so when he was arrested along the river the night of Mr. Draskovic's death, Alpha had long hair."

"Yes."

"And shabby clothes?"

"Yes."

"Alpha was homeless, too, correct?"

"Correct."

"And Mr. Draskovic was only an inch shorter than Alpha?"

"Objection," said Pereira. "Your Honor, materialty again."

"No," from the judge. "I'll allow it. Trooper Wilkins?"

"Yes, they were only an inch apart in height."

"And as to the twenty-pound difference in weight you mentioned before, if the lighter Mr. Draskovic were wearing the heavy overcoat marked as Commonwealth's Number Two, might the bulk of the coat hide that difference?"

"Objection. Calls for speculation."

"Overruled," said Cordoba.

Wilkins shifted a little before saying, "With that coat on, Mr. Draskovic would have looked pretty similar to Alpha, yes."

Shel moved toward the defense table. "And what was the air temperature the night Mr. Draskovic's body was found?"

"I didn't have a thermometer."

"Below freezing?"

"I'd say it was."

"Wind blowing?"

"Yes," said Wilkins.

"So, some wind-chill effect as well?"

"Yes."

"Were you wearing an outer coat?"

"Yes."

Shel turned toward the jury. "A hat?"

"Yes."

"With side flaps?"

"Yes."

"That act as earmuffs?"

"Yes."

Shel wanted to ask if Wilkins had those flaps down against the cold, but not knowing what her answer would be, he didn't want a negative reply to dilute what he'd gained so far. "And Mr. Draskovic, what was he wearing?"

"There's an inventory that would tell you in detail."

Shel nodded, sagely he hoped, showing the jury he was a professional who naturally already knew that. "Trooper Wilkins, without resorting to the inventory, was the decedent wearing Commonwealth's Exhibit Number Two?"

"Yes."

Shel held it up, struggling a little with its heft. "This green overcoat?"

"Yes."

Close the first day on a high note. "The very coat the defendant supposedly was trying to keep away from Mr. Draskovic so that my client could wear it himself on cold winter nights like the one when Mr. Draskovic was killed?"

"Objection," said Pereira. "Asked and answered."

Shel Gold didn't mind Judge Cordoba's sustaining the prosecutor that time, because he could see four jurors—different ones than before—nodding before Pereira had even spoken.

"I'M very impressed by your courtroom manner, Mr. Gold."

Mairead O'Clare watched Shel accept the compliment from Alpha with a whole-body shrug. It was just after the end of the day's testimony, and the three of them were sitting again in the secure conference room off the Third Session. Alpha, reshackled, rattled whenever he moved hands or feet. Mairead wondered if the two burly bailiffs just outside the closed door could hear the sound.

Shel pointed to the restraints. "I'm sorry those have to keep going back on, but it's a regulation."

Alpha smiled, the gaps in his teeth giving him an almost cartoon-character quality. "Don't trouble yourself about it, Mr. Gold. I'm used to them by

now." Then he looked to Mairead. "Lass, you've not forgotten to summon those others to my trial, now?"

She said, "Our investigator was supposed to serve the subpoenas today, so the people should all be there tomorrow."

"And where exactly is 'there'?"

Shel answered for her. "Sitting in the gallery—the audience part of the courtroom." Now he seemed to study Alpha. "Why?"

A grin without showing teeth or gaps. "Probably just an aspect of being in jail for too long, but I like to know everybody's whereabouts. At least," said Alpha, rattling his cuffs, "everybody who's not wearing these blessed bracelets."

Pay attention, young lady. There's something afoot in that man's mind.

18

PONTIFICO MURIZZI AWOKE TO the smell of coffee and the sudden sensation that he was alone in bed. As he swung his legs over the side to get up, Jocko poked his head around the corner from the galley.

"Looked like yesterday'd been a long one, so I thought you might enjoy a bit of breakfast in bed."

Christ, this guy's a treasure. "Sounds good."

Jocko ducked back into the galley, his voice trailing around the corner. "So, what was it you were doing?"

The Pope sank back into the pillows. "Serving subpoenas for a trial."

"This the case of the Homeless Harp?"

Murizzi didn't like that, any more than he would "wop" or "guinea," but he decided to let it pass. "Yeah."

"Are you going to attend yourself?"

The Pope thought of Severn Pratt blowing up at Cornerstone when he received his subpoena. "I'm thinking about it."

"Well, I guess we'll have to skip the British breakfast sausage, then."

For a second, Murizzi didn't get it. This guy, he thought, chuckling to himself.

WHILE Mairead waited with Shel Gold at the defense table for the bailiffs to bring Alpha into the courtroom, she looked out at the gallery. A smattering of people stood near or sat on the pewlike benches. She didn't recognize many, but there were several familiar faces. Severn Pratt, scowling as he played with an electronic pencil on what she assumed was a PalmPilot.

Al Wyckoff, sitting next to his boss, occasionally being spoken to tersely and dialing on a cell phone, handing it to Pratt from time to time for equally terse conversations, during which the president of Cornerstone would glare at Mairead, who always tried to smile back.

Best not to bait the man, young lady.

Mairead switched her attention to the black woman from the day before, dressed as though for church and seated about halfway back on the aisle. Now fairly certain she must be Danette Tomlinson, Mairead watched a hankie dab at her eyes.

Across the aisle was an older man in what Mairead always thought of as pretty-in-preppy clothes: khaki slacks, blue blazer, striped tie. His rectangular head seemed large, even on his tall body. She guessed him to be the rich sailor, Winston Hayes. He seemed to focus on her and smile whenever their eyes met.

But there's something else about him, Mairead thought. A hollow . . . coldness?

She decided not to make eye contact with the guy anymore, engaging instead the three college-age boys sitting, almost lounging, on the rearmost bench until Nina the bailiff went over and said something that made them sit upright. They looked sullen, but whether specifically from being dragged into court or generally from being hungover, Mairead couldn't judge.

Then she heard the shuffling steps and rattling of Alpha's shackles. When he drew even with her, the two court officers sat him down and removed the irons so Nina could bring in the jury.

From his chair, Alpha swiveled his head toward the gallery. "Ah, lass, quite the party today, isn't it?"

"The more the merrier," said Mairead.

Alpha looked at her. "You're doing a fine job, Mairead O'Clare. And justice may yet come of it."

Which made her decide to turn around to the gallery again, her heart nearly stopping.

Steady, young lady.

Waddling down the center aisle was Hadley Burgess, head of Litigation at Jaynes & Ward. After glaring at her, he stopped at the row where

Winston Hayes sat, the distinguished sailor shaking hands with the fat senior partner in a perfunctory way. Then Hayes made room for the lawyer to join him on his gallery bench.

"HEY, Billie, what do you say?"

Lord forgive me, but this spooky man does make me jump.

Looking down at the form she was typing, Billie Sunday reached for the little bottle of Wite-Out to use on the last two letters she'd hit by fright when the Pope popped through the suite door. Wite-Out itself was getting harder to find, which alone was going to make the new child Mairead right about the office having to go over to computers.

"Billie?"

She looked up at Murizzi now. "You made me make a mistake."

"Sorry," with no conviction behind it.

"What do you want?" with no warmth behind it.

"Thought I'd check to see if Shel needed anything brought over to him."

"At the court, you mean?"

"If that's where he is."

"Uh-huh." Billie capped the little bottle. "Third Session, but he didn't say or phone me about anything."

"Guess I'll just stroll over then, broaden my horizons."

"Pope?"

"Yeah?"

"Anybody ever call you glib but shallow?"

"Anybody ever call you a woman of great dimensions?"

Murizzi was through the door before the bottle of Wite-Out hit it.

Damn wiseass spooky man. Like to white *him* out sometime.

"NOW, Mr. Wyckoff," said Pereira. "Can you tell us how you came to meet the defendant, Alpha?"

"Never did."

Shel wondered who had taught Pereira the trick of examining a witness from the gallery side of the jury box farthest from the stand, to be sure each juror heard every question to a witness and every answer from one.

It took you months of trials before you realized how smart that was. Maybe now they have courses teaching it in law school.

Mairead passed a note to Shel, reading, "Why does Pereira always stand there on his direct?"

Shel nodded to himself. Well, they can't have courses on everything. But at least she noticed.

And admit it: A lot sooner than you ever did.

Pereira now began covering how Cornerstone came to be aware of Alpha getting lumber from the construction site. It was all hearsay, but Shel believed in not objecting when the other side wasn't hurting you. Also, even if Judge Cordoba sustained an objection, Pereira would just recall Trooper Wilkins to the stand, who could establish the wood scraps given by Donn Tomlinson based on what Alpha, the defendant, had told her himself.

But then Pereira asked, "Mr. Wyckoff, who was this employee of yours who supposedly helped the accused?"

"Tomlinson, Donn Tomlinson."

"His job?"

"He was a foreman on the site."

"You say *was* a foreman?"

"Yes."

"Cornerstone fired him?"

"No," replied Wyckoff, looking straight at Alpha. "No, he just never showed up for work one day."

Mairead scribbled furiously and slid the pad to Shel. It read, "Shouldn't we be objecting?"

He shook his head.

The prosecutor said, "What day was that, Mr. Wyckoff?"

He gave a date in December, and Pereira repeated it. "The day after Zoran Draskovic was murdered."

Even Judge Cordoba now reacted. "Mr. Gold?"

"No objection, Your Honor," said Shel, half-rising to show respect for the court if not concern over the testimony.

Pereira appeared uncertain, then said, "Mr. Wyckoff, was anything else missing from the site besides these scraps of wood?"

"Yes. Some very expensive materiel, actually."

"Can you give the jury some examples?"

A laundry list of copper tubing, temperature-control devices, etc. Shel jotted down a few buzzwords.

When Wyckoff finished, Pereira moved away from the end of the jury box and back toward his table. "Did you suspect theft, then?"

"We did."

"Did you have anyone particular in mind?"

"Yes."

"And who was that?"

"Donn Tomlinson."

Shel could hear someone in the gallery crying softly, guessed who it would be, and squeezed his eyes shut for a moment.

You have to do this, but she didn't have to come and hear it.

Pereira said, "And why him?"

Wyckoff seemed to speak to the gallery now. "Because he was an ex-convict we hired, trying to help him out."

Shel could hear the crying grow louder, Judge Cordoba and several jurors glancing out there, too.

"Thank you." Pereira looked up at the bench. "Pass the witness."

Before Shel could rise, Cordoba said, "I think now would be a good time for a short recess. Counsel in my lobby, please."

"HERE to gloat, Pontifico?"

"No. Just like to admire the results of my work."

Winston Hayes went off down the corridor outside the Third Session with an obese guy in a corporate suit. Probably headed for the newstand. Murizzi decided not to tell them the court officers wouldn't let anybody read a paper or magazine once the judge was back on the bench.

The Pope swung his head over to a corner of the corridor. Pratt and Wyckoff were sitting together on an old love seat–style bench built in the last century, when people were a lot smaller. Squeeze two normal-sized guys into it now, and they're like Siamese twins joined at the hip, both babbling into cell phones.

Murizzi went to hit the men's room, smelling beer piss as soon as he walked through the door. Looking under the stalls, he saw three pairs of shoes at different angles around one toilet base, but no sounds of peeing or dumping.

Just chugging.

The Pope rapped once on the door to the stall with his knuckles. "I don't hear you peabrains pouring out that beer and flushing it away, I'll ram the bottle up somebody's ass."

"Fuck."

"Oh, shit, just do it, okay?"

"We got most of it, anyway, Mitch."

Pontifico Murizzi listened carefully, smiling and feeling pretty good about himself, truth be told.

"ALL right," said Lydia Cordoba from behind her chambers desk, Mairead wondering if she always stayed in her robe, not like on TV when all the judges seemed to take theirs off whenever they could. "Just what is going on out there?"

Mairead thought both Shel and Pereira were the souls of innocence as she herself tried to figure out what Hadley Burgess was doing in the courtroom, period, much less with Winston Hayes.

Cordoba looked over her half-glasses at the prosecutor. "Is there a connection between our murder and this foreman Tomlinson disappearing?"

"I can't say for sure, judge," a little trickle of sweat rolling down from the fat man's hairline.

Now Cordoba looked to Shel. "And you're not objecting to a string of speculation and hearsay a mile long?"

"I thought it was interesting information, judge."

Cordoba looked from one to the other, said what Mairead suddenly thought. "Counselors, have you got some kind of side game going in my courtroom?"

"No, judge," said Pereira.

"Never, judge," said Shel.

Cordoba clearly wasn't buying either denial. "I want the jury to hear what

happened, but I'm not going to stand still for a slipshod trial." Then she surprised Mairead. "Last question: Who was the woman crying in the gallery?"

Pereira shook his head, palms upturned.

Shel said, "Mrs. Tomlinson, judge."

Cordoba looked from one lawyer to the other. "Is one of you planning to call her as a witness?"

Pereira shook his head again. "Not me, judge."

Shel said, "I doubt it, too."

Cordoba's nostrils flared a little, and Mairead was pretty sure she wouldn't want this woman mad at her in open court. "Then why is Mrs. Tomlinson out there?"

Very quietly, Shel Gold said, "Maybe she believes Mr. Draskovic's death and her husband's disappearance *are* related."

Cordoba stayed silent for a good ten seconds. "All right, let's get back at it."

SHEL Gold heard Murizzi's voice before he saw him, leaning over the bar enclosure. "In case you need me for anything."

"Thanks, Pope." Shel stayed turned. No sign of Danette Tomlinson.

Admit it: You'd rather not have her here for this next part.

He noticed Mairead looking back into the gallery, too. She whispered, "Shel, there's something I've got to tell you."

Before he could reply, Nina the bailiff intoned, "Courrrrt!"

Everyone stood as Lydia Cordoba ascended the bench.

"Be seated," she said, looking to Shel.

"I have some questions for Mr. Wyckoff, Your Honor."

Jake the clerk said, "Alvin Wyckoff, please retake the witness stand."

As Wyckoff moved through the swinging gate of the bar enclosure, he looked straight ahead, turning to face Shel only from the stand.

Cordoba said, "Sir, you are still under oath."

"Yes, Your Honor."

"Mr. Wyckoff," Shel moving toward the jury box. "You testified before the recess about suspecting Donn Tomlinson, a foreman on the project, of stealing materiel from the site."

"Yes."

"Because he'd served time in prison."

"Yes."

"Then why hire him in the first place?"

Wyckoff shifted a little. "I don't . . . That's not my end of the business."

"It's not?"

"No."

"You're the chief security officer for Cornerstone Construction, correct?"

"Correct."

"You therefore handle security matters for the company?"

"Yes."

"Such as checking out prospective employees?"

"Yes."

"And you found Donn Tomlinson had a criminal record."

"Like I testified already."

"Found it out before you hired him."

"I didn't hire him."

"Who did?"

"Severn Pratt, our president."

"And did Mr. Pratt tell you why he hired Mr. Tomlinson?"

Wyckoff paused, and Pereira pushed himself up to say, "Objection, Your Honor. Hearsay."

"Sustained," from the judge.

Try a different door. "Did the company have a policy on hiring people with criminal records?"

"You mean, like in writing now?"

"Yes."

"No."

"How about an oral policy?"

"Objection," Pereira barely a quarter out of his seat. "Hearsay again."

Cordoba looked at the prosecutor. "Counsel, the company policy, whether written or oral, would be hearsay. However, I'll overrule the objection if Mr. Gold can explain why he is pursuing this line of questioning."

"Your Honor," said Shel, "if I may ask more questions, I think we'll know all we need to."

Cordoba said, "Very well, but I'll be counting them."

Shel faced the stand again. "Mr. Wyckoff, did you notice a woman in the audience crying while you were offering your suspicions about Mr. Tomlinson—an African-American woman?"

"Yes."

"Do you know who she was?"

"Tomlinson's wife."

Shel turned toward the jury, most of them looking into the gallery, hopefully for someone they could empathize with. "Now, Mr. Wyckoff, this materiel missing from the job site. Sounded pretty heavy to me."

"Some of it. The tubing, for example. But other stuff, while valuable, could fit in a pocket."

"Or a briefcase?"

"I guess."

"How could someone remove the heavier items, though?"

"We have a security guard on duty, but he can't be everywhere all night long."

"So," said Shel, "all someone would need to do is hide on the site till after dark, then sneak the materiel out when the guard wasn't looking."

"Basically, yes."

"And how many workers are on that site during a given day?"

"It varies."

"As chief security officer, can you give me an estimate?"

"Not too accurate a one."

"Over a hundred people?"

"I'd say probably that, most days."

"More than a hundred, and yet you suspected Mr. Tomlinson."

"He was an ex-con, like I said."

"And black."

Shel could feel the whole courtroom stop for a beat.

Don't gild the lily. "No further questions, Your Honor."

PONTIFICO Murizzi watched Phil Pereira take Artie Chin through the drill, catching the look on the jurors' faces at the mention of Artie's rank, most of them probably thinking Sergeant Detective should be said the other way around.

On the whole, though, while Phil might not be pretty, when it came to the job, he got it done.

And Artie was good, too, in his quiet, kind of military way, as he identified photos showing the gruesome damage to the vic. The Pope scoped the jury again then. While some averted their eyes, most looked angry, and so far, Alpha was the only flesh-and-blood person their anger could target.

Artie was followed to the stand by some lab techs. The first of them, whom Murizzi knew well, established the defendant's shillelagh as the murder weapon through hair and tissue analyses, stuff the Pope always found fascinating, if a little ghoulish.

After she finished testifying, a lab fingerprint expert, whom Murizzi never met, took the stand. This guy matched a thumb and and two index finger impressions by twenty to thirty points of comparison to the booking station prints of Alpha.

When Pereira passed the witness, Shel Gold stood. "Now, sir, you found three of my client's fingerprints on the murder weapon, is that correct?"

"Yes."

"Only three?"

"Three very clear ones."

"But no other 'clear' ones?"

"Well, some smudges."

"Smudges. Of other fingerprints, you mean?"

"Yes, but that's always going to happen."

"I don't follow you," said Shel, the Pope thinking he did, and perfectly.

"You see," said the expert, "whenever someone picks up an object a number of times, his palm or the edge of his hand will smudge the earlier-applied prints."

"Now I get you. While some of the earlier prints were Alpha's, this later-

application principle means that other prints could have been smudged or blurred."

"Right."

"Smudged or blurred, say, when someone other than my client picked up the shillelagh."

"Objection," said Pereira. "Relies on facts not in evidence."

"Sustained," from Lydia Cordoba.

Murizzi watched Shel nod, as though he'd just been helped by what happened. "Tell us, do you wear gloves at crime scenes?"

"Yes. Latex ones, like you see on nurses."

"And could later-applied gloves smudge earlier prints, too?"

The expert got a little prickly. "Not the kind we wear."

"How about the kind someone might have been wearing on a cold winter's night?"

"Your Honor," said Pereira in a tired voice.

"No," Cordoba leaning a little toward the witness. "I'll allow that."

The expert glanced at the judge, then came back to Shel. "Yes, winter gloves could smudge earlier prints."

"Thank you." Shel Gold returned to the defense table. "No further questions, Your Honor."

"MR. Burgess."

"I was wondering if you'd observe the amenities, Ms. O'Clare."

Mairead didn't extend a hand to shake in the corridor outside the Third Session, and her old boss didn't, either. She could see Winston Hayes, perching on a bench near the staircase, flipping through a magazine.

She came back to Burgess. "Is there a reason you're attending this trial?"

He made a noise that actually sounded to Mairead like "harrumph," then said, "Ms. O'Clare, if you learned only one thing in your four months at Jaynes and Ward, it should have been that I never do anything without a reason."

Mairead felt her antagonism toward the man revive itself with a vengeance. "And what is that reason, Mr. Burgess?"

"Quite simple, really." He inclined his horsy face toward the bench near the staircase. "You've inconvenienced one of the firm's most valued individual clients."

Mairead tried to stem the tide of issues flooding into her head, from protecting John Ramirez to professional conflict of interest on her part, being adverse to a client of her former firm. "Winston Hayes?"

"For his entire life, thanks to a trust created by his father. Which conflict of interest I shall raise with relish before Judge Gordova—"

"Cordoba—"

"—at the first inkling that your Mr. Gold is calling Mr. Hayes to the stand."

"Mr. Burgess, I had no idea that he was—"

"I doubt the Board of Bar Overseers will care, once I raise the issue regarding your license to practice law as well."

Mairead couldn't believe this. "The Board of—"

"You've made your bed, Ms. O'Clare. Now . . . *die* in it."

Wearing a smug smile, Hadley Burgess turned and waddled toward one of Jaynes & Ward's most valued individual clients.

"AND how would you rate this second day, Mr. Gold?"

"Pretty good, all things considered."

They were back sitting around the table in the conference room off the Third Session. Shel figured apologizing to Alpha on behalf of the system for the shackles wasn't something he had to repeat. And he liked the way Mairead was absorbing the drama of trying a serious case. But Shel also wanted to know just what was going on in his client's mind.

Alpha said, "How many more days of trial would you say we'll be having?"

Shel looked at him, the defendant talking in a tone like a non-farmer kibitzing on the possibility of rain. "The prosecutor doesn't need much more to survive a motion."

"Survive a . . ."

"Motion for a Required Finding of Not Guilty. It's a request I'll make to the court at the end of the prosecution's presentation. If the judge grants my

motion, she's ruling that no rational jury could find you guilty, and you'd then be set free."

To Shel's surprise, Alpha frowned. "I wouldn't get to testify?"

Mairead said, "None of our witnesses would."

"But I *want* to, lass. I told you that, back in the jail version of this very room we're sitting in."

"Whoa." Shel held up both hands, one palm facing each of the other two people at the table. "First, the judge isn't likely to allow my motion. I'll still make it, for appeal points, but I'd say Pereira's put in enough evidence to establish all the elements of murder, including malice from the various squabbles you and Mr. Draskovic had over that coat and extreme atrocity and cruelty from the way the decedent was killed. Not to mention motive, means, and opportunity."

Alpha seemed to absorb Shel's explanation. "Then why wouldn't I get to testify?"

Mairead said, "If we can bring up enough reasonable doubt through Shel's questioning of the prosecution's witnesses—and maybe one or two of our own—we won't need to call you."

Alpha shook his head. "No, lass. No, I'm sorry if it somehow offends your lawyerly sense of aesthetics, but I'm taking the stand in my own behalf."

Mairead's voice grew louder. "That's a decision—"

"We don't have to make yet," said Shel Gold, wondering just what game their client was really playing.

"THE heavyset guy who was sitting next to Hayes today?"

"I'm afraid so, Shel. And I'm sorry."

Mairead watched her new boss weigh the news about her old boss. After the bailiffs had taken Alpha away for the night, she'd stayed with Shel in the conference room to brief him on what Burgess had told her.

Then Shel said, "Well, I can't blame you for not knowing your old firm represented one of our witnesses."

"I should have had my friend there run Hayes through the client/conflict index."

"No sense worrying about that now, especially since I don't see it bothering Judge Cordoba, or the Board of Bar Overseers, that much."

Mairead tried to believe her ears. "You don't?"

Shel spread his hands. "All the lawyers switching jobs in this town, the issue comes up, but there's no direct problem here. While you were at Jaynes and Ward, you never worked on anything for this Hayes, right?"

"Never even heard the name. In fact, it sounded to me like he was more a client of the Trusts and Estates department than Litigation, and, from the way Hayes and Burgess greeted each other in the courtroom, I'm not sure they'd even met before."

"Hmmmm," said Shel Gold, and then, to Mairead's surprise—and, to some extent, her relief—he changed the subject over to why she thought Alpha was so hell-bent on taking the stand.

19

"THAT'S THE COMMONWEALTH'S CASE, Your Honor."

"Thank you, Mr. Pereira."

Mairead watched the prosecutor sit back down and Lydia Cordoba turn to Shel.

"Mr. Gold?"

"The defense has a motion," he said.

The judge turned to the jury box. "You'll be excused for a while so I can hear arguments on a matter that doesn't involve you. Please, as always, do *not* discuss the case—not testimony, not issues, not personalities—in any way until the entire trial is over and I've given you instructions on the law."

Cordoba nodded at Nina, who escorted the jurors out through the side door. Mairead could hear several people in the gallery behind her getting up and walking away down the center aisle.

When the jury door closed again, Shel moved to Jake the clerk, handing him two pieces of paper, Jake standing and passing one—Mairead assumed the original—up to the judge. Shel gave Pereira another copy, the prosecutor barely glancing down at it.

Without looking up from her copy, Cordoba said, "Mr. Gold, I'll hear you, but only briefly, please."

Mairead thought, This one's dead before it hits the water.

She watched and listened as Shel, from counsel table, argued the defense's Motion for a Required Finding of Not Guilty on the elements of

first-degree murder. When Shel finished, the judge nodded at Pereira, who stood and ticked off pieces of evidence and passages of testimony. When he finished, too, Cordoba began writing on Shel's paper while speaking, as though dictating to herself.

"Motion denied. Mr. Gold, you'll be opening to the jury?"

"Yes, Your Honor."

Cordoba said, "Nina?"

The bailiff brought the jurors back into the courtroom, Mairead wondering if they had any idea what occurred in the halls of justice when they weren't there to see and hear it.

"YOUR boss doesn't seem to be prevailing, Pontifico."

The Pope crushed his empty paper cup and foul-shot it into a wastebasket outside the Third Session. "He's not my boss, Winston. I just work for him once in a while."

"Ah, an independent contractor, eh?"

"I suppose. You enjoying yourself in there?"

"Surprisingly, yes," said the man, dressed in what Murizzi could see was a different blazer than he had worn the day before. The Pope wondered if the man and his butler coordinated their wardrobes so they'd have contrasting outfits each day. Murizzi didn't see the obese corporate guy from the prior afternoon.

Of course, you got to figure that anybody as fat as that probably has to take pretty frequent leaks, ease the bladder.

Now Hayes gestured with his coffee cup toward the courtroom's double doors. "I must say, Pontifico, the seating is rather harsh, the way I've always imagined a Catholic Church must be in terms of—well, shall we just say, saddle sores? And the quality of the coffee from the stand downstairs won't have Starbucks lying awake nights in fear of competition. But it *is* rather fascinating to see played out a matter in which one knows—even just casually—the players involved."

The Pope wished he could disagree with the rich fuck, but in fact, he felt kind of the same way himself.

"I don't suppose," said Hayes, the bushy black eyebrows going up a notch, "that you'd know when—or even whether—I'll be asked to take the stand?"

"No idea. But didn't somebody or other write a poem about how anticipation makes the eventual experience even better?"

"Why, Pontifico, I am truly impressed. You've got that nearly right."

"Means a lot to me," said Murizzi. "I mean, coming from you and all."

SHEL Gold knew that Lydia Cordoba was a stickler for courtroom protocol, so he waited until she nodded to him before standing and moving toward the jury box. As he reached his favorite spot, Shel could see the carpet was worn unevenly there, as many other litigators liked the same place. Not close enough to touch the jurors, but close enough to reach out and touch.

Shel always wondered if the ad exec who worked for the phone company had been a trial lawyer beforehand.

"Members of the jury, as Her Honor informed you, my name is Sheldon Gold." He stuck a hand into his pants pocket, motioning politely with the other. "My associate, Mairead O'Clare, and I represent the defendant in this case, a man who chooses to be called Alpha." Shel began to stroll, parallel to the jury box, so as to spend equal time in front of each person. "Now, I don't know about you, but as somebody who's had to bear 'Sheldon' as a burden all my life, I kind of envy anyone who's comfortable enough *with* himself to pick a new name *for* himself."

Several jurors smiled, one even putting her hand to her mouth to cover a giggle. Good: They might not think of the defendant as the guy causing those crime-scene and autopsy photos of Draskovic if you can humanize Alpha for them.

Shel reversed his stroll. "You've already listened to a lot of information, so let me speak only briefly to you now. What my client decided to do is become a hermit, the first of a new group of them here in this country, and so he named himself Alpha, after the first letter in the Greek alphabet. He eked out a modest life in a little shelter under some bridge stanchions, a place you've heard called his 'cave,' which he built with the help of Mr.

Donn Tomlinson, a foreman on the Cornerstone company's construction project. There were other homeless men—and some not at all homeless—who interacted with Alpha near and around his cave, much the same way that you have neighbors or customers or just plain folks walking around near your home." Shel reversed his stroll a final time. "We're going to be hearing from some of them, especially those who had reason to wish the decedent in this case harm. In the end, it will be for you to decide whether the prosecution has proved beyond a reasonable doubt that my client, Alpha, killed Mr. Draskovic. For now, though, please sit back, relax if you can, and try to focus on what you're about to hear so you'll recall it when you retire to deliberate. Thank you."

"MR. Gold," said Lydia Cordoba, "your first witness, please."

"Thank you, Your Honor, but my associate, Ms. O'Clare, will be conducting the examination."

Mairead rose as Shel sat, her legs feeling a little rubbery. Thanks to the kindness of Jake and Nina, Mairead had been allowed to go back into the empty Third Session before going home the night before. She remembered the trial advice of her Evidence professor at New England School of Law: Rehearse in the real theater before appearing on stage in front of a live audience.

And so the prior evening, Mairead had moved around the Third Session by herself, like a lonely little girl imagining guests at a tea party. She got a sense of the friction of the carpeting on her shoes, the relative distances in strides between the defense table and the clerk's pouch. And the witness stand, and the jury box. She tried out her voice, thought it sounded a little loud, then realized it also would be muffled in an occupied courtroom by bodies absorbing the sound. She practiced taking documents from her file folders, finding it especially useful to have her questions written out in a shorthand way, so she could glance down at the words without having to read aloud a sentence.

After an hour of that, Mairead had felt ready. Now, on the verge of the actual moment, she wasn't so sure.

The judge said, "Ms. O'Clare?"

"Your Honor, the defense calls Severn Pratt to the stand."

And suddenly, as some people began shuffling positions in the gallery behind her and Jake the clerk rose in front of her toward administering Pratt's oath, Mairead realized she was utterly, perfectly calm, not even self-conscious about how her hands would look to the jury. It was like the anxiety—the "jitters," she used to call it—before a hockey game, when the stomach would be churning and the legs unsteady and the focus gone. After the first shift on the ice, though, the first body contact or touching of the puck, those jitters would vanish, replaced by an irresistible, undebatable conviction that she was doing exactly what she wanted. And hearing her own words resound clearly in a real courtroom had done the same for her in this new endeavor.

Pratt took the stand, Mairead noticing that some nervousness had woven itself into the android's typical anger.

Make the one feed the other, young lady.

Mairead said, "Could you please state your name?"

"Pratt—that's P-r-a-t-t. First name Severn, S-e-v-e-r-n."

As often as she'd had to spell out her name for people, Mairead nevertheless thought that Pratt sounded like a pompous ass doing it. "And your position at Cornerstone Construction?"

"President."

"Now, Mr. Pratt, are you here today of your own free will?"

"Of course not. I have a business to run."

Mairead thought at least a few of the jurors might be thinking, Hey, so do I, buddy.

"And how did you come to be in this courtroom?"

"I *came* to be here because one of your people handed me a subpoena."

"As president of Cornerstone Construction, are you familiar with its various projects?"

"Of course I am."

"How many sites is your company now building?"

"Ten."

"Can you name them?"

"Objection, Your Honor," from Pereira. "Materiality?"

"Counsel?" said the judge, not unkindly.

"Your Honor," said Mairead, "I'm seeking to establish that the loss of expensive materiel on Cornerstone's Boston site was particularly difficult for the company given how many projects it was trying to build."

Cordoba nodded. "I think 'ten projects' already makes that point without a roll call of them."

"Thank you, Your Honor," said Mairead, figuring the judge's comment had made her own point with the jury. "Now, Mr. Pratt, ten projects is quite ambitious for a company your size, is it not?"

"I'm an ambitious person, and we can handle it."

"What's the most projects Cornerstone has had during any prior period?"

"I don't know."

"I thought a moment ago you said that as president you 'of course' were familiar with the company's projects?"

"Objection," Pereira barely rising. "Impeaching her own witness."

Cordoba looked down. "Counsel?"

A pattern, young lady. When he objects, she's going to give you a chance to argue on it.

"Your Honor," said Mairead, measuring her words, "while we called Mr. Pratt to the stand, he had to be subpoenaed, and his attitude suggests he's a hostile to the defense."

Another nod. "So ruled. Would the reporter read back the question for the witness?"

Mairead heard her own words of "familiar with the company's projects" end in a questioning lilt from the court stenographer.

"And I meant what I said," Pratt bristling visibly. "But I can't keep track of when all of them over history were going on at the same time."

Mairead bored in, allowing a piece of paper she was holding appear to him by its masthead, BANKER & TRADESMAN. "An estimate then. As many as ten?"

Pratt looked uncomfortably at the masthead. "Probably not quite ten."

"More like seven, then?"

"Five, I'd say." A little squirming. "Four or five."

"So, you have twice as many projects going now as at any other time since you've been president of Cornerstone."

"Yes."

"And how long have you been president?"

"Four years next month."

"And before that?"

"I was . . . at another similar firm."

"Which did a renovation project on a federal building in Washington, D.C.?"

"Your Honor," said Pereira. "Materiality here?"

The judge looked down. "Ms. O'Clare, I don't see it, either."

Mairead tried to focus her thrust. "Your Honor, I have reason to believe there were problems on this other site as well."

Pratt began to say, "Honey, there're problems on every—"

Cordoba snapped at him. "Sir, you are *not* being spoken to."

Pratt turned to the judge, his lips clamped tight, but he shut up and turned back toward Mairead.

"Objection overruled," said Cordoba. "The witness will answer the question."

"There were problems, as I *tried* to say before."

If a man in a hole wants to keep digging, young lady, hand him a shovel.

Mairead said, "Problems of theft from the work site?"

"Yes," with a coat of frost on it.

"And of billing to the federal government on the project?"

"Allegations of it only."

"Which went to trial against you, correct?"

"Objection, Your Honor," said Pereira. "Impeaching by prior bad act without—"

"Sustained."

Mairead plowed on. "A trial which ended because the main witness against you disappeared."

Before the prosecutor could rise again, Cordoba said, "Ms. O'Clare. Not another word along that line."

"Yes, Your Honor." Mairead took a moment composing herself for the next—and last—questions, finding herself reluctant to leave the stage, to come off the ice because she was enjoying playing the game too much. "Mr. Pratt, was Donn Tomlinson employed on that project in Washington, D.C.?"

"No, he was not."

"Do you have any reason to believe my client, Alpha, was in Washington, D.C., back then?"

"He's a bum, right? He could be anywhere."

End it now, young lady.

"Your Honor," said Mairead O'Clare, "I have no further questions at this time.

AS Severn Pratt fumed through the double doors into the crowded and noisy corridor outside the Third Session, Pontifico Murizzi gave him a pantomimed round of applause. The Pope noticed the security guy, Wyckoff, edge over, almost between them.

In a low voice, Pratt said, "You fucking asshole."

"Hey," replied Murizzi, "Washington was beautiful this time of year. Don't know why you ever left. Oh, wait. Yeah, I do know."

"I'll kick your teeth in, then I'll go back in there and—"

The Pope stepped into his face, aware of Wyckoff putting a strong hand on both his and Pratt's forearms. "You don't touch me, pal, or anybody with me. Understand?"

"Severn," said Wyckoff, tugging now on Pratt's forearm while fending off Murizzi's. "Come on. We've got work to do."

As they turned and walked away, the Pope said, "Wouldn't leave the building, you guys."

Pratt broke free of Wyckoff's grip, but didn't start walking back. "What's that supposed to mean?"

"Subpoenas control through the end of trial. You're stuck here till testimony closes."

"Asshole," yelled Pratt, loudly enough for everyone else in the corridor to stop talking and stare.

Pontifico Murizzi, in a conversational voice that now filled the silent hall, said, "Pal, you're doing a lot better out here than you did in that courtroom."

"MAIREAD O'Clare, you and Mr. Gold make quite the team."

Shel thought she almost blushed in saying, "Thanks, Alpha."

They were in the secure conference room, trying to make use of the recess. But suddenly, Alpha had became a chatterbox.

"Reminds me of my time playing Irish football. As a tinker, I moved around too much to play with any local club for long, but I was a fair middy."

"A 'middy'?" said Mairead.

"Mid-fielder, lass. Of fifteen players—not counting the goalie—there'd be eight forwards and five backs, but only two middies. Which means that the other lad and I would have to coordinate what we did. Just like you and Mr. Gold. Yes, they're strange and wonderful games, football and litigation."

Shel said, "There a reason you're so . . . forthcoming?"

"Well, 'tis like I said before. You two are a fine team, and so you reminded me of my own. But I also have to get in practice, don't you think?"

"Practice," said Mairead.

"Practice on my speaking, lass. Toward taking the stand."

Shel shot a glance at Mairead, then said, "We still haven't called the college rowdies or this rich sailor, Hayes."

"So, I've a bit more time to prepare myself, then?"

"What I mean, Alpha, is that their testimony might deflect the jury from Pereira's view of what happened that night."

"All well and good, Mr. Gold. And I don't deny you'll continue to do a fine job there. But all that means is the jury might not be convinced I did the killing, while they instead should be informed of who did."

"Not our job," put in Mairead before Shel could react to what Alpha had just said.

"Maybe not, lass, though I don't pretend to understand entirely the lawyer's role in this fine system of justice you have. But I do know my role, both as a hermit and as an innocent party caught up in that system."

"And what role is that, Alpha?" said Shel.

"Why, to be the truth-teller, naturally."

Shel came forward in his chair. "Are you telling us you know who killed Mr. Draskovic?"

"And with certainty."

Mairead said, "Then who is it?"

"No, lass, for that to come out, I'll have to be taking your blessed witness stand."

Shel Gold watched the guy's goofy smile for what felt like an eternity.

STILL a little in shock from what Alpha had told them—and refused to tell them—in the conference room, Mairead took notes as Shel did a fine job of making the three college boys, called in succession, look like the sworn enemies of Zoran Draskovic and the nervously evasive persecutors of Rex, the homeless man who "drowned." When Pereira finished his cross of the last one, Mitch Gerber, the judge said, "Mr. Gold?"

"Your Honor, Ms. O'Clare will examine our next witness, Mr. Winston Hayes."

Mairead had no trouble standing now, but she'd barely reached her full height when Hadley Burgess's voice boomed behind her.

"Objection, Your Honor. Counsel for the proposed witness has a motion to quash the subpoena served on—"

Mairead saw Lydia Cordoba blink a few times, as though someone had just played the tuba during a violin concerto.

"That's enough, sir," said the judge. "A brief recess, with all counsel *and* the proposed witness in my lobby."

CORDOBA glared over the half-glasses, not even sitting behind her desk. "And just who are you?"

Shel Gold watched Hadley Burgess hunch forward in his chair to hand

the judge a business card. They were short a seat on this side of Cordoba's desk, Winston Hayes insisting that Mairead have the last, which she declined, resulting in the two of them standing at opposite ends of the semi-circle formed by Burgess, Pereira, and Shel.

Cordoba didn't even glance down at the card. "Counsel, when I ask a question, I expect an audible response."

"Uh, sorry, Your Honor. I rarely appear in state court, as my practice is principally federal corporate, and therefore I'm unfamiliar with—"

"Sir, I am trying a case, and you are trying my patience. Who . . . are . . . you?"

"Hadley Burgess, of Jaynes and Ward."

"Thank you."

"Representing Mr. Winston Hayes on this motion to quash the subpoena so cavalierly served on—"

"Mr. Burgess," said Cordoba, now sinking into her chair. "It seems that once you begin answering, you don't stop."

Shel was thinking, As long as you get to talk first, Hadley, I shouldn't have much to worry about.

Cordoba sighed. "Very well, sir, give me and other counsel this motion of yours."

Burgess distributed the copies.

Shel read his. Cutting to the car chase, it was essentially requesting that Shel and Mairead be disqualified as counsel for the defendant or, in the alternative, that Winston Hayes not be called by either of them as a witness, both prongs based on Mairead's having been an associate at Jaynes & Ward, longtime counsel to the prospective witness.

Cordoba looked up from her copy as Shel finished reading his. "Ms. O'Clare, is the factual basis of the motion accurate?"

"I was at Jaynes and Ward for four months, judge."

"Ending?"

"A week ago."

Cordoba frowned. "Ever do any work there for Mr. Hayes?"

"None. I didn't even know he was a client of the firm."

"Your Honor," said Burgess, pulling a half-inch, bound document from

his briefcase. "I have a brief on the relevant authorities, both state and federal, addressing the many issues of professional responsibility raised by—"

Shel braced himself for the firestorm.

"Counsel," Cordoba riding over Burgess's words, "we are conducting a murder trial out there. I do not have the time to read your brief prior to resuming this proceeding. When did you know Ms. O'Clare was summoning Mr. Hayes to testify?"

"Why, only two days ago, when my client was served by—"

Cordoba held up her hand. "Stop. If you knew two days ago, you could have brought your motion then."

"But I didn't see it as *ripe* until—"

"And you began attending the trial yourself yesterday. Either way, though, I could have considered your brief overnight and ruled on your motion the following morning, giving all concerned the benefit of knowing which ground rule might have changed so they could adjust their strategies accordingly. Now, it seems to me, you've waited too long."

"But, Your Honor," said Burgess, "at least ask Ms. O'Clare if she used her former position at Jaynes and Ward to enhance her proposed examination of Mr. Hayes."

Shel held his breath, wanting to look at Mairead, let her know by eye contact that it was all right to reveal that.

But Cordoba was already fixing her. "Ms. O'Clare, did you take advantage of your situation at the firm in any way toward preparing for Mr. Hayes?"

Shel could feel the silence in the room, the "dilemma gap" as he thought of it. Do you admit something embarrassing that the other side may not be able to prove, or do you functionally lie to the court by telling a narrow, misleading truth? Shel thought he was about to learn a lot about Mairead's—

"Judge," she said, "I can't answer that question yes or no."

Shel now felt his advocacy quotient drop and his admiration quotient rise.

Cordoba's expression changed, even . . . softened? "Then answer my question in your own words, counsel."

Mairead said, "Judge, after our investigator, Mr. Murizzi, interviewed

Mr. Hayes, I asked a former colleague at Jaynes and Ward to run a simple computer research check, both on this witness—"

"You what?" the words bursting from Burgess. "Who? I demand that you—"

"Sir," said Cordoba, steel in her eyes. "I am conducting this discussion, and you do not 'demand' anything. Ms. O'Clare?"

"The former colleague found me newspaper articles on Mr. Hayes. There was no confidential information conveyed to me, except by Mr. Burgess himself, in telling me yesterday that Jaynes and Ward had done a trust for the Hayes family. And I have no reason to believe the former colleague knew that Mr. Hayes was a client of the firm in any way."

"Your Honor," said Burgess the instant Mairead finished. "Obviously we must know the identity of this former colleague so we can ask whether he or she knew of Mr. Hayes's being a client of Jaynes and Ward."

"Give me a moment."

Cordoba reread the motion. Or at least, Shel thought, pretended to as she mulled things over. Then the judge looked up.

"Ms. O'Clare, I've no reason to disbelieve you, but I am troubled by the appearance of impropriety this 'coincidence' could create. And, with Mr. Hayes here, I assume he would not waive any objection he might have to the defense using information gathered and provided by his longtime law firm, however discoverable by a simple newspaper search."

"Madame?"

Shel craned his neck. The unfamiliar voice belonged to Hayes himself.

"Yes?" from Cordoba.

"Based on what you've just said, I think there's something you should know. When the defense's very pleasant Pontifico Murizzi served that subpoena on me, I naturally consulted my attorney on the Trusts and Estates side of Jaynes and Ward. That good fellow referred me to Hadley here, who by telephone told—"

"Objection," said Burgess. "Don't say another word."

Hayes stared down at his lawyer. "I beg your pardon?"

Cordoba sent the steely look at Burgess again. "Counsel, you may state

your objection, I assume based on attorney-client privilege, but I will not have you telling anyone in my lobby what he or she can or cannot say."

"I'm sorry, Your Honor, it's just that—"

"Enough." Now to Hayes. "Sir, as the holder of the privilege, you can decide to tell us, or not tell us, a confidential communication between you and your lawyer. And, if you'd like, I'll give you time to discuss with Mr. Burgess whether or not to reveal what was said between you."

"Well, madame, that's what I was trying to get at, as it were. When I spoke with Hadley here, I told him about the subpoena and the names of the lawyers on it. He became quite miffed and told me the subpoena was improper, and we should oppose it. Since I believe in doing that which *is* proper, I of course agreed with him. But do I now understand from what you've said, that the law somehow allows *me* to decide whether or not Ms. O'Clare can ask me questions in your courtroom?"

In what Shel would have called a low, edgy voice, Cordoba said, "Mr. Burgess, you never explained that to your client?"

"It seemed premature, Your Honor. I mean, you hadn't even seen, much less ruled, on my motion to—"

She held up her hand again, and Burgess stopped short.

Then the judge looked at Hayes. "You can waive any objection to Ms. O'Clare's examining you in this context."

"Well then, by all means. After sitting on that rude bench for so long, I'd hate *not* to have a crack at the witness stand."

Shel Gold shook his head. Everybody's dying to testify in this one, and you can't figure out why.

MOVING to the far end of the jury box, Mairead said, "Your name, sir?"

"Winston Hayes," said the self-satisfied voice, a beaming smile on his blocky face.

"And do you use any suffix to that?"

He lost a glimmer of his smile. "Well, I was born Winston Hayes the Fourth, but all my forebearers with the same name have passed on, so I'd think myself rather haughty to use it today."

Two jurors laughed. While Hayes glanced over at the box, Mairead doubted he got the joke.

"Sir, how did you meet the decedent, Zoran Draskovic?"

"Well, 'meet' is rather a polite word for our encounters. I would sail my dinghy—a Fatty Knees design, by the way, excellent little craft—into what he felt were spawning grounds for various fishies."

Mairead thought even Judge Cordoba had to clench her jaw shut on that one. "And what would Mr. Draskovic do as a result?"

"Pelt me with stones. There's still a devilishly bad bruise on a gunwale from one of his rocks."

"So, he treated you rather poorly."

"Rather violently, I'd say."

"And on how many occasions?"

"Oh, a dozen, perhaps, and rather more closely than I would have preferred," Hayes putting his index finger and thumb on either side of his nose, pressing the nostrils closed.

Most of the jury laughed this time. Cordoba said, "Mr. Hayes, please just answer the questions."

Mairead waited. "Could you describe Mr. Draskovic?"

"A rather typical homeless person, actually. Disheveled, smelly clothing, too much of it worn in summer, and probably not enough in winter. Long hair, dirty face . . ."

A shrug, as though Hayes had exhausted the subject.

Remembering her Evidence class again, Mairead moved to her table and picked up a photograph. Shielding it from the jury, she said, "Your Honor, permission to approach the bench?"

"Granted," from Cordoba.

Mairead walked to the clerk. "May this be marked as Defense Exhibit Number One for Identification?"

Jake held it up so only the judge could see it.

"It may be so marked," said Cordoba, her eyebrow arching.

Mairead carried the photo to the court reporter, who entered the identifying information on it. Mairead then moved to Pereira, showing him the photo. He frowned but handed it back to her.

"Your Honor," said Mairead now. "Permission to approach the witness?"

"Granted."

Mairead walked to the stand and held up the photo about three feet from Hayes. It was a cropped mug shot showing just the profile of a long-haired man.

"Ah, I'm not surprised," said Hayes.

"You can identify Defendant's Exhibit Number One for Identification?"

"Of course. And I'm not surprised to find Old Man River had been photographed by the police."

"Objection!" Pereira slapping his palm on his table. "Your Honor, that's not a photo of the decedent."

"Counsel," said Cordoba to the prosecutor. "You're an advocate here, not a witness." She turned to Hayes. "Would you take a closer look at the photo, please."

Mairead brought it two feet, then one foot away.

Hayes blinked, glanced over to the defense table, then repeated the process before saying, "Good Lord, it's not Old Man River at all." Hayes pointed. "It's the defendant over there, though when he must have had much longer hair."

"Yes, Mr. Hayes," Mairead moving back to her table. "It would have been easy to confuse the two of them."

"Objection," said Pereira. "Counsel's commenting on the—"

"Sustained," ruled Cordoba, rather sternly.

"Mr. Hayes," said Mairead, "one final point. You mentioned earlier that you are Winston Hayes the Fourth, correct?"

"Correct."

"So your late father was the Third?"

A little crack in the facade. "Yes, indeed."

Mairead moved back toward the defense table, picking up the copy of a newspaper article John Ramirez had given her. "And how did your father die?"

"Objection," boomed Hadley Burgess's voice from the gallery. "She has no right to—"

"You are out of order, sir," said Cordoba. "Sit down, and not . . .

another . . . word." Now the judge turned toward the witness stand. "Answer the question, please."

Hayes fixed Mairead, but not with a smile. *No, young lady, this is that cold, hollow look of his.*

"My father was killed by a hobo who attacked him in a cottage at our family's summer compound."

"And how was your father killed?"

"I just told you. A hobo—"

"I'm sorry, Mr. Hayes. By what means or weapon?"

The man on the witness stand lowered his voice an octave, suddenly seeming almost menacing. "My father was bludgeoned to death. With a fireplace poker that split his skull."

"No further questions." Setting down the newspaper article she hadn't needed, Mairead O'Clare felt pretty confident in her own competence. At least until Shel whispered that she hadn't offered Alpha's mug shot into evidence so the jury could see it, too.

"WELL, Mr. Gold?" said Lydia Cordoba in her lobby.

Shel resettled uneasily in his chair. He looked past Mairead and Pereira to Alpha, sitting shackled, the two burly court officers looming behind him.

"Judge," Shel began, "our client insists on testifying."

Cordoba blinked twice, then looked over at Alpha with what Shel took to be a mixture of wonder and pity. "Sir, do you realize the consequences of taking the witness stand?"

"And those of not, Your Honor."

"Your counsel has explained to you that Mr. Pereira will be able to cross-examine you, not only on your testimony, but also your past, including any criminal record you might have?"

"Fortunately, I'm without any such, Your Honor, as I'm sure your kindly police have established with my fingerprints. And I completely absolve my fine lawyers from any responsibility in warning me, which they've labored mightily to do. But regardless, I want to be having my say, so long as it's my case after all, and my right under your blessed Constitution."

Cordoba looked back to Shel now.

Admit it: She pities you, too.

"Very well," said the judge. "Let's wrap this one up."

"Your Honor," Alpha speaking softly now. "Just one more thing, if you please?"

"What . . . is . . . it?" said Cordoba, that sea urchin definitely under her saddle again, thought Shel.

"I'll be wanting Ms. O'Clare to ask me my questions."

"That, sir," Cordoba now standing and gathering the folds of her robe, "is between you and your attorneys."

"ALPHA," whispered Mairead, "this is crazy!"

"As you yourself once implied, that might just be consistent with my mental state."

Control your anger, young lady. Keep your head.

Mairead, now sitting with Shel Gold and their client at the defense table, knew she didn't have much time before the jury would be brought back into the courtroom, so she struggled to follow Sister Bernadette's good advice. "I've never done a trial before, much less examined the defendant in a murder case."

"You did fine with the others you questioned, and you deserve this chance."

"To do what? I don't even know what you're going to say."

"Ah, but trust that I do, lass. Trust that I do."

The judge must have nodded to Nina the bailiff, because the door already was opening near the box, and the jurors were filing in. Mairead looked down at her notes, knew immediately they'd be no help to her, and turned toward the gallery behind her.

Well, young lady, at least you have a full house.

Mairead looked from Hadley Burgess to Winston Hayes, from Severn Pratt to Al Wyckoff. The Pope sat on the bench behind the college boys. Even Danette Tomlinson was on the aisle again, a hankie clutched in her lap.

Jesus Mary, what have I gotten myself into?

"Counsel?" said Cordoba.

Mairead turned back, then stood. "The defense calls Alpha."

She watched her client rise, and with an easy, athletic stride, move to the witness stand.

Mairead suddenly realized she'd never seen him walk before. At the jail, he'd just come through the door opened by the guard, and in the courtroom, he'd been shackled except while sitting in the chair next to her. On the way to the stand, though, and even as Alpha took the oath, Mairead could easily imagine him as the Gaelic football player he claimed to have been.

Among his many other claims.

"Would you state your name for the record, please?"

"Alpha."

"And that is the only name you go by."

"Correct."

"And why is that?"

Mairead paid only partial attention to what Alpha told the jury about his hermit philosophy, watching the jurors themselves and buying time for herself to think of what to ask next.

One good thing, young lady. The faces in the box are paying attention and aren't seeming to think he's a lunatic.

Alpha finished his answer, and looked back to Mairead.

"Do you recall the night Zoran Draskovic was killed?"

"I do indeed."

Here goes. "Can you tell us what happened?"

She watched her client turn halfway to the jury, as though positioning himself for a long siege. "Early that evening, I went to the construction site where Mr. Tomlinson was foreman. He'd kindly given me—and other homeless persons, like the man Rex you heard those college fellers talk about—scraps of wood and bent nails so we might improve ourselves, or at least keep out some of the cold of your approaching winter. It was a cold night itself, that one, and so I was wearing the coat I'd acquired from Mr. Draskovic, the poor soul some called Old Man River. When I was at the site, I met Tommy—Mr. Tomlinson—and he had some more old lumber for me.

Yes, he was a kindly man." Alpha dropped his voice. "And a terrible shame he had to die."

Mairead heard a female wail in the gallery. Turning, she saw Mrs. Tomlinson, her head down, and the Pope—bless him—moving over to her bench to comfort the woman. Mairead herself felt as though someone had speared her in the solar plexus with a hockey stick, because she didn't believe there was enough air inside her lungs to form a question for Alpha beyond, "What?"

Her client glanced at her, then refocused on the jury. "While I was loading the wood on my shoulders—taking care to avoid my longish hair then—I heard a guy come up to Tommy, and they started arguing about goods being—"

"Objection, Your Honor," said Pereira, "Hearsay."

"Counsel?" from Cordoba.

"If the two . . ." Mairead hadn't completely recovered from her client's bombshell about Donn Tomlinson being dead, so she started over. "The witness has testified that the two men were arguing spontaneously, Your Honor. That would make their out-of-court statements 'excited utterances,' and therefore admissible despite being hearsay."

"Agreed," said Cordoba. "The objection is overruled."

Mairead looked to Alpha, who seemed not to miss a beat. "As I was saying, they were arguing over goods being missing—'materiel,' they both called it—and about concrete to be poured the next day. Well, I didn't want to get Tommy in any trouble, so I hefted my lumber and began walking away. That's when this other guy yelled, 'Who the—' a swear word here, Your Honor."

The judge looked down on him from the bench. "Tell us what was said to the extent you remember it."

"Yes, ma'am." Alpha turned back toward the jury. "This other guy yelled at Tommy, 'Who the fook was that?' And Tommy said, 'Just some poor homeless guy, lives in a cave under a bridge on the Charles.' Well, when Tommy's looking to me, I see this other guy pick up a piece of pipe and hit Tommy just a terrible blow, and from behind, too, the coward. So I drop my load and run."

That didn't feel right to Mairead. "You ran away?"

"Indeed, and fast as I could. We homeless get blamed for everything, so I ran back to my cave. And, being upset, I got myself a bit drunk in the bargain. But once I was nicely warmed by the booze, I took off that heavy coat."

"Your Honor," said Pereira. "Materiality? The indictment is for the murder of Zoran Draskovic, not—"

"Overruled. Proceed, Ms. O'Clare."

Mairead said, "What happened next?"

Alpha shook his head, ruefully. "I'm guessing that poor Mr. Draskovic came over to my cave, in the hope of reclaiming his blessed coat."

"Objection," Pereira sounding to Mairead a little strident now. "Sheer speculation by the witness."

"I'm going to give defense counsel a little leeway. Objection overruled, but renewable."

Mairead figured that meant not much more time. "And?"

"And," said Alpha, his head now down. "I'm guessing that Mr. Draskovic came into my cave while I was dead asleep, moved my holy shillelagh from where I kept it near my bed to the outside of my door, and retook his coat. I'm also guessing that the guy who struck poor Tommy down at the construction site found my place and mistook Mr. Draskovic for me, the eyewitness to his crime earlier that night. And then that guy must have used my shillelagh to clobber—"

"Your Honor," said Pereira, now sounding to Mairead beyond even exasperation, "move to strike all of defendant's testimony. From 'I'm guessing this' to 'then he must have,' it's speculation on speculation on—"

"I take your point, counsel." Now Cordoba looked at nothing but the ceiling, Mairead and everyone else waiting silently in the courtroom. Then the judge seemed to focus on some commotion in the center aisle. Mairead turned to see Nina and the Pope helping Danette Tomlinson, who seemed conscious but barely able to walk, down the aisle and out through the double doors.

Cordoba's voice snapped Mairead's head back toward the judge's bench.

"I'm going to reserve my ruling on the Commonwealth's Motion to Strike until the conclusion of Mr. Pereira's cross-examination of this witness. Ms. O'Clare, any further questions on direct?"

Mairead thought about it, thought about forgetting to offer the mug shot into evidence, and felt her brain clear enough to see what she hadn't done yet. "Alpha, did you recognize the man you saw strike down Donn Tomlinson at the construction site?"

"Not until he testified in this very courtroom."

Jesus Mary, I *am* Perry Mason. "And who is that?"

Her client pointed, and every face in the courtroom followed his outstretched finger.

Alpha said, "Mr. Severn Pratt, the president of Cornerstone."

Mairead wasn't sure she could account exactly for what happened next. A ballistic Pratt leaped from his seat, shouting obscenities at Alpha, Wyckoff trying to restrain his boss. The two burly court officers moved toward the witness stand, but Alpha just crossed his arms, no expression revealing his feelings. Mairead caught maybe two frames of Winston Hayes clapping, Hadley Burgess tugging on his sleeve while shaking his head. The college boys actually were the best behaved of the lot, just standing and watching like awed kids at a magic show.

The judge began rapping her gavel, ordering that the gallery be cleared of spectators immediately. Nina, now back in the courtroom, took one of Pratt's arms, and Wyckoff the other, shuffling the president into the corridor. Everyone else filed out on their own, possibly hoping, thought Mairead, that the action might continue outside the Third Session.

Cordoba's voice said, "Ms. O'Clare?"

Mairead turned back toward her. "Your Honor, I had no idea—"

"Stop." The judge inhaled. "Do you have any more questions?"

"No," she said, trying to walk steadily back to a nodding Shel Gold. "Not at this time."

Cordoba spoke her next words slowly. "Mr. Pereira, I'm calling lunch recess now, and we'll have any cross-examination afterward." Turning to the jurors, the judge hammered home the same "Don't discuss, don't

decide" instruction she'd given them earlier. Then, once the jury was led out of the courtroom by the again-returned Nina, Cordoba directed that Alpha be shackled once more.

As they stood for the judge to leave her bench, Shel Gold said to Mairead, "Well, that was easy enough, huh?"

20

"BUT IF YOU KNEW all that," said Mairead, pacing in the little conference room off the Third Session, "why didn't you tell us *before* you went on the stand?"

Alpha, the image of innocence in Shel's mind, looked back up at her. "Lass, I didn't see anybody believing me."

"Could be you're right," said Shel, testing him.

Their client's eyes came over. "What do you mean?"

Shel shrugged in his chair. "I was watching the jury. Any group of sixteen people is hard to read, but I didn't see a lot of them nodding in agreement with what you were saying."

Alpha's face went down toward his clasped, manacled hands on the tabletop. "Well then, they don't really want the truth."

Shel could see Mairead's face flush to nearly the shade of the fists on her hips. "Well, *I* wanted the truth. I believed in you from the beginning. Instead of manipulating me when I saw you in jail, why didn't you tell me what you saw Pratt do to Tomlinson and what you think Pratt did to Draskovic?"

Alpha looked back up at her. "I was afraid, lass."

"Afraid of what?"

"Given that Pratt killed Tommy and Old Man River, I sorely feared he'd do the same to you."

Shel thought it was time for another test. "As if that wouldn't still be possible."

Both Mairead and Alpha turned toward him, their client saying, "How's that again?"

Shel shrugged once more, feeling his chair creak from it this time. "A corporate big wheel like Severn Pratt? He could probably get bail set and post the bond, especially since the hot-blood/sudden-argument you described at the construction site might reduce the murder charge from first degree to second."

Mairead said, "But what about the killing of Draskovic? That was certainly premeditated."

Her boss looked up at her. "What Alpha *thinks* happened to Draskovic works a lot better as evidence of reasonable doubt for our client than as evidence of Pratt's guilt."

Shel watched Alpha bow his head. "'Tis as I'd feared then."

Mairead seemed about to reply when Shel shook his head.

Alpha spoke to his clasped hands. "If you could leave me now, I'd like to be thinking about what that fine prosecutor feller will be asking me."

"One last thing?" said Shel.

"Yes," without lifting his head.

"Pereira's probably going to ask whether you consulted with your lawyers after you testified. Answer yes. Thanks to attorney-client privilege, you don't have to give him any information about what we talked about. Otherwise, though, I want you to tell nothing but the whole truth to that jury. Understand?"

"I understand, Mr. Gold."

Shel considered asking for a promise as well, then decided this client's word would probably be as suspect as everything else that came from his mouth.

MAIREAD looked around the courtroom, thinking the audience seemed larger now, despite the continuing absence of the Pope and Mrs. Tomlinson. Counting heads, Mairead saw the three college kids (*genuinely interested in* something *educational, young lady*), Pratt (*fuming*) and Wyckoff (*wary*), Hayes (*bemused*) and Burgess (*impatient*). The rest of the crowd was unfamiliar. *Maybe word of a bombshell in one courtroom draws regulars from the others.*

Judge Lydia Cordoba's voice came from the bench. "Mr. Pereira, you may inquire."

The prosecutor heaved himself from his chair. "Thank you, Your Honor." He moved to the midpoint of the jury box. "You call yourself Alpha, correct?"

"Correct, sir."

"And what name were you born with?"

"That no longer matters."

Mairead scribbled a note to Shel.

Pereira said, "Your Honor?"

"Answer the question, sir."

Shel glanced at Mairead's "Can't we do something?" and shook his head.

Alpha looked to the bench. "A hermit has no past, no—"

"Answer the question," from Cordoba in a voice that could etch glass.

Alpha turned back to Pereira. "James Joyce, Esquire."

"James . . . ? Are you telling the truth now?"

"No, sir, I am not."

Mairead expected Pereira to appeal to the judge again. Instead the prosecutor took a step toward the witness stand.

"But before, when your lawyer asked you to describe what you saw at that construction site, you were telling the truth then?"

"I was."

"Let me get this straight, sir. Sometimes you tell the truth under oath, and other times, you don't?"

"Just that last one there."

"Ah." Pereira turned now toward the jury. "You were given materiel of various kinds by Donn Tomlinson, a foreman on the Cornerstone project?"

"Bits of wood and nails, yes."

"He was kind to you."

"Most definitely. Tommy—"

"But you saw this kind man be struck down by Severn Pratt."

Alpha seemed to scan the audience, perhaps for Tomlinson's wife, Mairead thought, before answering, "I did, yes."

"Yet you ran away as the man who'd helped you was being brutally attacked."

"I was scared."

"Because Mr. Tomlinson had identified you to the killer?"

"By where my cave was, yes."

"But you ran to that same cave."

"It's my home."

"Where the 'killer' would know to find you."

"If he'd paid attention to what—"

"And you got drunk."

"I did, sir."

"Drunk enough not to hear this terrible *second* killing committed almost on your doorstep."

"Correct."

"Mr. Draskovic's skull being crushed."

"If you say—"

"By your own club."

"As I understand it, yes."

"And when is the first time you mentioned any of this to anyone else?"

Mairead sensed Shel getting ready to rise from his chair, but Alpha merely said, "Earlier today, from this very witness stand."

Pereira wheeled on Alpha. "And after you testified, did you speak with either of your attorneys during the recess?"

"With both of them, yes."

The prosecutor looked to the defense table, then to the jury, then up to the judge. "Nothing further, Your Honor."

"Ms. O'Clare?" said Cordoba.

Shel laid a hand on Mairead's forearm lightly and briefly before she could rise, him standing instead. "Your Honor, may I conduct the redirect of this witness?"

Mairead felt herself getting chilly as the judge said, "No, Mr. Gold. It was the defense's decision to have Ms. O'Clare examine on direct, and I think it would be confusing for the jury for her not to do any redirect as well."

Shel sat back down, whispering to Mairead, "Remember what I said in that conference room, then walk back over here."

"Ms. O'Clare?" Cordoba's voice sharper now.

Mairead stood, feeling that shakiness of having to go back out on the ice for an unexpected overtime when the opponents tied the score in the last minute of regulation. Then she remembered the early bird game the morning of her first visit to Alpha's cave, and the way she juked the center man on the other—

"Ms. O'Clare, today, please?"

Mairead glanced up at the bench. "Sorry, Your Honor." Approaching the gallery end of the jury box in what she hoped was a steady walk, she began speaking. "Alpha, you just testified on cross that you hadn't told anyone about what you saw at the construction site that night until this morning, in this courtroom."

"Correct."

Mairead braced herself. "Why not?"

Alpha looked at her, then toward the defense table. Mairead kept her eyes on him.

He came back to her. "I was afraid that Pratt, having killed poor Tommy, would do the same for you or anyone else who tried to help me."

"And when did you tell us—Mr. Gold and me—that?"

"Right after I testified, in the conference room."

"Alpha, do you remember what Mr. Gold told you there?"

"I do."

"And what was that?"

"Objection, Your Honor," Pereira rising. "Hearsay."

"Ms. O'Clare?"

"The prosecution opened the door to this topic by a question on cross that implied we'd somehow coached the witness. For the sake of completeness, Your Honor, I think the jury ought to know what we told him."

"Agreed. Objection is overruled."

"Alpha?" said Mairead.

"Mr. Gold told me to tell the truth, the whole truth, and nothing but the truth."

"And have you?"

"Except for that bit about my birth name, I have indeed."

Mairead nearly said, "No further questions," but fortunately she had the good sense to glance over to the "coach" first. Shel was pointing to a piece of paper on her side of the table.

"Your Honor," said Mairead. "A moment?"

"A brief moment," replied Cordoba.

Walking to the table, Mairead tried to guess what the note would say. When she read it, her guess proved wrong.

Mairead turned back toward the witness stand, but didn't move toward it. "Alpha, what happened to Mr. Tomlinson's body?"

Quickly, the man said, "I'd have to think Pratt buried him under the very concrete they were to pour that next day."

"Objection and move to strike, Your Honor!" Pereira literally pounding the table in front of him. "Rank speculation."

Mairead expected Cordoba to reply immediately. When she didn't, the young lawyer looked up at the stern judge.

Cordoba's eyes were fixed on the ceiling again. "Mr. Gold, I expect you'll be presenting a motion?"

"Yes, Your Honor," said Shel, rising beside Mairead as though he knew exactly what the judge was talking about.

"Then I'll reserve judgment on Mr. Pereira's Motion to Strike—and his earlier one as well—until after I've heard argument on yours." Cordoba turned to the jury and told them she hoped this interruption wouldn't be a long one.

As the jury filed out, Mairead O'Clare sat back down, wondering what was going to happen next.

"MY motion, Your Honor," said Sheldon Gold, "is that you order an excavation of the construction site in order to find—"

"What the hell!" came a loud voice from the gallery.

Shel turned, though he was pretty sure who'd spoken. Any doubt vanished when he saw Severn Pratt, standing, his knuckles white as his hands gripped the back of the bench in front of him.

Cordoba said, "Sir, sit down and be quiet. One more out—"

"Do you have any idea of the *cost*, the delay to—"

"Sir, sit down and shut up or I'll have you removed."

"This is my money you're throwing away, and I have a right—"

"Court officers?"

Shel watched Nina and one of the bouncer guys move toward Pratt. Wyckoff stood as a buffer, tugging on his boss to get him out into the aisle, both uniforms following the two men into the corridor.

Shel addressed the bench. "Should I continue, your Honor?"

"Yes," said Cordoba, in what seemed to Shel a tired tone. "But not now. However rudely he may have raised the issue, Mr. Pratt does have a point. I think your motion should be argued only with counsel for the construction company here as well. I'll release the jury for the day, and hear arguments tomorrow morning from all parties. Mr. Gold, can I ask you to inform Mr. Pratt to have his attorney here at nine A.M.?"

"Certainly, Your Honor."

As the two bailiffs returned to the courtroom, Cordoba said, "We're in recess, then."

When the judge closed the lobby door behind her, Jake the clerk looked up. "I'll give you this, Shel: You're never boring."

MAIREAD O'Clare followed Shel down the aisle, carrying her briefcase in her left hand as he shifted his to the right. "The judge knew you were going to make that motion, and you knew she knew."

Over the shoulder with, "Yes."

"How?" as they hit the double doors.

A full-body shrug as he turned to her. "You get a feeling, like when you knew exactly the right questions to ask Alpha just now without any prepping."

In the corridor, Mairead saw Pratt and Wyckoff near a bench. Pratt was still ballistic, Wyckoff trying to calm him down.

Shel said, "I guess I'd better give them their notice, huh?"

As they walked toward the two men, Mairead noticed the bailiffs were gone. She thought about keeping herself within checking distance of Pratt, just in case he made a run at the cause of his current distress.

When Pratt saw the two lawyers coming, though, he moved faster than

she—or apparently Wyckoff—anticipated. In fact, they were face-to-face in half the time Mairead thought possible.

"You fucking kike bastard!"

"Mr. Pratt, the judge wants—"

"Fuck that spic, too," he said, swinging a roundhouse left at Shel's head.

Mairead had to replay the next few seconds in her mind several times before they made sense. Shel, hampered by the briefcase in his right hand, ducking under Pratt's punch. Shel, incredibly quick, driving his left fist no more than a foot, but directly into Pratt's midsection. The president of Cornerstone Construction, woofing out a breath and dropping to his knees.

"Wow," said Mairead, feeling like a kid in a schoolyard seeing the class bully get his from the class nerd.

"As I started to say," Shel shaking out his shoulders while Pratt dry-heaved. "Judge Cordoba wants your company's attorney before her tomorrow at nine A.M. to argue my motion."

Pratt tried to speak. "My lawyer's . . . sue your ass . . ."

"See you tomorrow at nine."

As Shel moved off down the wide corridor, Mairead fell in beside him. "Mind telling me where you learned to do that?"

He looked at her, none of that gloating macho sheen on his features. If anything, his eyes held that cocker-spaniel sadness. "A place that taught me courtrooms made more sense."

Mairead O'Clare began nodding without quite knowing why.

"SO," said Billie Sunday from the reception desk as her two lawyers came through the suite door. "How did it go today?"

Shel picked up his phone messages. "Pretty well."

Billie searched Shel's face for any shadings on his answer.

Waste of time. Aggravating man never lets on a thing through his expressions. No, with Shel, it's all in the body language.

The new child, on the other hand, was aglow. Like the best-looking boy in the high school just asked her to the prom.

Billie said to Mairead, "You like being in the courtroom?"

"Yes, especially when you get to do stuff there."

Do *not* follow up on that. Child wants to brag about something that probably Shel did, anyway.

Billie said, "The Pope called a couple minutes ago."

Shel looked up from his messages. "Oh?"

"Said he took Danette Tomlinson home, account of she was in pretty bad shape."

"That was good of him."

"Pope also wanted to know if you need him for anything else."

"Yes." Shel moved toward his office, making Billie swivel in her seat. "I'd like him to drive Mrs. Tomlinson tomorrow morning, have her in the Third Session by quarter to nine."

Billie shook her head. "Let me guess. You'd like me to call her about it first."

"I'd consider it a genuine favor," said the aggravating man, closing his door behind him.

21

INSIDE THE THIRD SESSION, Pontifico Murizzi checked to be sure the judge wasn't yet on the bench. Then he guided Danette Tomlinson to a seat near the center aisle, which was what the woman seemed to like, anyway. After that, the Pope walked to the bar enclosure, waving to the court officers hanging near Alpha. Shel was talking with the defendant, Mairead reading something.

Murizzi spoke her name, watched her turn, smile, and stand up to come over to him.

Jeez, if you were hetero, this'd be a good one.

"How are you, Pope?"

"Not bad. Mrs. T told me Billie called her last night, but didn't say why Shel wanted her here."

Mairead dropped her voice to a whisper. "We're arguing a motion that might tell us where her husband is."

"Her husband, or his corpse?"

"That's what we're hoping to find out."

Murizzi nodded. "I'll sit with her, then."

"And maybe keep an eye on Severn Pratt when he shows up."

"The president guy?"

"Right," said Mairead. "He threw a punch at Shel yesterday."

Christ. "Tell me about it."

When she finished, the Pope said, "And that surprised you?"

"What?"

"Shel putting the guy down with one punch."

"Yeah, it surprised me."

"Shel surprises a lot of people. But I'll make sure Pratt doesn't try anything else."

"Thanks," she said, touching Pontifico Murizzi lightly on the forearm in a way that somehow he didn't mind so much.

"MR. Gold," said Cordoba from the bench, "I'll hear you."

Shel stood up, walked around the defense table toward Jake's clerk pouch in a way that let him look into the gallery. Before court had started, he sat with Mrs. Tomlinson to explain why he wanted her in the room for the motion, the woman twisting the distinctive wedding band on her ring finger all the while. But now Shel could spot the college rowdies, Winston Hayes and Hadley Burgess, and Al Wyckoff. Severn Pratt sat inside the bar enclosure, next to his lawyer, at a third table brought in by the court officers and positioned near Pereira's.

Pratt, however, burned his gaze into Shel from his chair.

Good. The madder he looks when the jury comes back in, the better off Alpha is.

And now for something that should make Pratt even madder.

"Your Honor," Shel began, "the defense motion is for an order from this court, requiring Cornerstone Construction to allow us onto their site for the purpose of excavating toward finding the body of Donn Tomlinson."

Shel half-expected to hear Mrs. Tomlinson begin to cry.

Admit it: A cruel way to bring her closure, but the only one you can think of, and it can help your client, too.

"The motion is based upon the testimony of the defendant, Alpha, to the effect that he witnessed Mr. Tomlinson being killed, and that no body has been found."

"Enough for now, Mr. Gold," said Cordoba. "Mr. Pereira?"

Shel moved back toward the defense table as he watched the prosecutor hoist himself from his chair but stay at his own table.

"Your Honor, we're trying a case against the defendant for the murder of Zoran Draskovic, not Donn Tomlinson. And, if Your Honor allows my

motions to strike the testimony Mr. Gold just referred to, there is no evidentiary basis for this excavation motion you're entertaining right now."

"Thank you, Mr. Pereira. Mr. Sandersen?"

Shel now watched Gerhard Sandersen—a stocky, sour man—rise ponderously from his seat. "Your Honor, first of all, Cornerstone Construction strenuously objects to the unconscionably short notice it was given of this hearing."

Cordoba tilted forward in her chair. "And I consider it unconscionable to hold a jury any longer than I have to, particularly in a murder case."

Shel thought, Great start, Gerhard.

"Secondly," said Sandersen, "Cornerstone is not even a party to this litigation. Only the Commonwealth and the—"

"I'm well aware of the parties to a criminal case, counsel."

Strike two, thought Shel.

"Third, I have before me a brief arguing conclusively that this court is without jurisdiction to order a non-party such as Cornerstone to permit—"

"A brief?" said Cordoba.

Sandersen seemed confused. He reached down to his table and lifted a document bound by some intricate metal fasteners. "A written legal argument of some forty-three pages addressing—"

Shel seriously wondered if maybe Gerhard Sandersen and Hadley Burgess had been law school classmates.

"Counsel," said the judge. "Spare me, all right? I know what a brief is, too. I'm just wondering how many excavation motions your firm has handled."

"How many? Believe me, Your Honor, this affront by the defendant's attorney is the very first time that—"

"In other words, your shop turned out a hefty brief in what you considered a minute ago to be 'unconscionably short notice'?"

Strike three, thought Shel.

Sandersen seemed chastened instead of ruffled. "Your Honor, please appreciate our situation. It has been over a month since the defendant claims to have seen Mr. Tomlinson attacked by someone."

"Not 'someone,' counsel," said Cordoba. "He was pretty specific that it was your client, Mr. Pratt."

"The *president* of my client, then. But nevertheless, the project itself has progressed now to the point where a wholesale *archaeological* intrusion would result in over two million dollars of construction costs wasted and countless millions more in delay damages that Cornerstone would owe to the owner of the property."

Uh-oh, thought Shel.

The judge paused before saying, "Mr. Gold?"

"A moment, Your Honor?"

"Half a moment."

Shel turned to Alpha, holding a legal pad up to the conjunction of their faces to muffle any whispers. "Can you pinpoint the spot on the site where Tomlinson was struck?"

"I can."

Shel rose to his feet. "Your Honor, my client can identify the precise spot he saw Mr. Tomlinson attacked."

Pereira got up now. "Your Honor, the Commonwealth would object to any murder-in-the-first defendant being allowed to wander about a construction site, given the proximity of tools as weapons, the risk of escape, etcetera."

Sandersen had remained standing. "And, Your Honor, even if the defendant saw *some*one attack Mr. Tomlinson at Point A, how could the defendant or anyone else know whether the body was buried at Point A, Point B, Point C . . ."

Now Shel did hear Mrs. Tomlinson, crying softly in the gallery behind him.

Lydia Cordoba heard her, too, and closed her eyes for just a moment on the bench. "Mr. Gold, I'm sympathetic to your desire to corroborate the defendant's testimony and to perhaps resolve the disappearance of Mr. Tomlinson. But Mr. Sandersen is right. To allow you to go chopping through concrete in a half-completed building without knowing exactly where to look for a body is beyond what I'm prepared to order."

Shel didn't have a card left to play when Mairead suddenly stood up beside him. "Your Honor," she said, glancing back into the audience, Shel thought at Hadley Burgess of all people, "there may be a way we *can* know where to look."

JOHN Ramirez said, "I sure hope this works."

"*You* hope?" replied Mairead O'Clare.

Standing next to Sheldon Gold, she was shivering a little, despite the layers she'd put on toward standing around the construction site in the cold. Back in the courtroom, Hadley Burgess had fussed and fretted about *another* Jaynes & Ward client being dragged into a murder trial, but Judge Lydia Cordoba had been intrigued by Mairead's summary of technology that could see through rock for bodies and John Ramirez's later elaboration of surface penetrating radar. Mairead's other concern at that moment had been that Burgess would tumble to which associate at the firm probably helped her on the Winston Hayes information.

Now, however, inside the gate of the Cornerstone project, she watched Ramirez approach his expert, who was fiddling with the machine, which reminded Mairead of a golf bag on wheels, but with one yellow box on the handle and another hugging the ground. Burgess hovered around the expert, too, occasionally glaring at Mairead. Cordoba stood near Gerhard Sandersen and Severn Pratt, nearly defying the company president, Mairead thought, to try something, even with the two big bailiffs by her side. The Pope stood off in a corner, talking to Sergeant Detective Arthur Chin. Phil Pereira did the same with a technician from the Crime Scene Unit carrying what looked like a big toolbox. A bunch of construction workers milled around at a distance.

But no Alpha. The judge had refused to permit him to join them, so he'd drawn and described the point at the site where he'd seen Tomlinson be attacked

"This is ridiculous," said Pratt in a loud voice.

Cordoba glanced over. "I'm beginning to agree with you."

"Judge," said Shel, Mairead thought kind of quietly, even for him, "it's still our best chance."

And even though he didn't mention Danette Tomlinson's name, Mairead had the impression that both Shel and the judge were picturing the woman crying in the courtroom.

Ten minutes later, as the expert trundled his machine around the site and everyone migrated with him, Pratt said, "This is still ridiculous."

Cordoba didn't comment now, but she did hunch her shoulders and pull her coat closer to her throat.

Five more minutes, then five more. Mairead believed Alpha, though she began to wonder if maybe Pratt, despite his protestations, had been smart enought to move the—

"Got something," said the expert, peering closely at his box on the handle. "Definite anomaly."

Nobody spoke as the man worked his way around the cement floor, as though his lower box were vacuuming.

"Well?" said the judge.

"Can't tell what it is for sure, ma'am. But it's about two meters long and one wide."

"The size of a man," offered Shel.

The judge looked at him, then said to the expert, "How deep?"

He shaded the right side of the upper yellow box with his hand. "One point three meters." He shuffled a little, "One point five here." A little more, "One point six now."

Cordoba nodded. "What do your blueprints show down there?"

Pratt sighed melodramatically, then walked over to a slanted table with a construction lantern clipped to its edge. After a moment, he said, "Should just be clean, solid fill."

"As in dirt?" asked the judge.

"Gravel, sand, dirt."

The expert shook his head. "I'm getting something that's different from everything else around it."

Cordoba said, "How long to scan the rest of the place?"

He looked around. "Hour, maybe two."

Cordoba turned to the blueprint table. "Mr. Pratt?"

"Now what?"

"Can my court officers borrow a jackhammer?"

ADMIT it: From the time you tried your first murder case, you've always wanted to witness a crime scene.

Shel Gold watched the technician who'd been talking to Sergeant

Detective Chin use some chalk from her toolbox to draw a rough outline around the perimeter where the machine expert tapped his toes. It took two Cornerstone laborers about three minutes to crack through the cement and clear it away in big chunks, like shoveling packed snow with their gloved hands. When they got down to bare earth, Chin said, "How's about we take over from here?"

Cordoba said, "Fine with me."

Chin turned to Pratt. "What do you have for shovels?"

The Pope once mentioned to Shel that he'd trained Chin on the niceties of crime-scene preservation, but out here in the cold over a certainly month-old and only-possible corpse, you couldn't blame the homicide detective for plowing through. However, every shovel of dirt from the surface to thirty inches down went into big bags. For eventual sifting, Shel figured, assuming that would prove necessary. At the two-and-a-half-foot depth, Chin and the technician switched from Cornerstone spades to gardening trowels that she took from her toolbox, painstakingly digging now in a process Shel might have called "nibbling away at the ground."

Three minutes into that, the technician said, "I've got a left hand, upturned."

Shel noticed Mairead moving toward the hole as most everybody else backed away. She hasn't disappointed you so far.

The technician exchanged her trowel for a brush and began whisking away the dirt from ghostly pale fingers.

Mairead said, "But this . . . this person's white."

Chin didn't look up. "You're seeing the palm side, which is lighter on African-Americans. Also, it's been cold awhile."

But Shel knew. As soon as the technician had gotten below the third joint on the ring finger, he knew.

Because, when Shel had sat down that morning before the hearing with Danette Tomlinson in the gallery, the distinctive wedding band she'd been twisting was a perfect match for the one he could see on the hand sticking out of the ground.

And Sheldon A. Gold said a silent little prayer for a good husband he'd never met.

A S the crime-scene tech called for reinforcements, Pontifico Murizzi left his former colleagues and sidled over to Al Wyckoff. "Talk to you a minute?"

Wyckoff glanced at Severn Pratt, who the Pope had noticed was deep in discussion with Sandersen, the company lawyer. "Sure."

Murizzi walked Wyckoff to an empty alcove on the site. When they got there, the Pope said, "Your boss is a hothead."

Wyckoff glanced over to Pratt and Sandersen again. "Sometimes he scares even me."

"I heard about the boxing match outside the courtroom."

"Wasn't much of a match."

"Shel Gold can take care of himself," said Murizzi. "It's his associate I'm talking about."

"Mairead?"

"That's right. I don't want to see your boss near her, no matter how this thing finally turns out."

"I can tell him," Wyckoff glancing over a third time, "but I can't control him."

"What's that they say, 'Forewarned is forearmed'?"

Al Wyckoff stared at the Pope. "I'll tell Pratt that, too, for all the good it'll do."

22

"THE QUESTION BEFORE US becomes," said Lydia Cordoba from the bench, "what evidence should be presented to the jury?"

Mairead watched Pereira rise to his feet, waving to the now-empty box along the wall beyond the table where Severn Pratt and his lawyer, Gerhard Sandersen, were seated. "Your Honor, I don't see that *any* evidence from the excavation is admissible in the case before you. As I argued already, the defendant, Alpha, is being tried for the murder of Zoran Draskovic, not Donn Tomlinson. All the finding of the body at the construction site means is that Mr. Tomlinson was killed also, perhaps even by Alpha himself that night in a dispute over scrap lumber that might have paralleled the defendant's disputes with Mr. Draskovic over the green coat."

"Mr. Gold?"

Shel stood next to Mairead, Alpha leaning forward on the other side of her and following the argument intently. Which went for everyone in the gallery, too, though Mrs. Tomlinson was absent again. And, as far as Mairead knew, the woman hadn't been told as yet about what the excavation had found.

"Your Honor," Shel himself gesturing toward the empty box. "The jurors have heard my client give his version of what happened that night. We now have physical evidence which corroborates that version. And while someone certainly killed Mr. Tomlinson—and at least apparently by bludgeoning him—I concede that it's possible my client could have done it. On the other hand, I don't see a rational plan in which my client would first

have killed Mr. Tomlinson at the construction site and then returned to his cave area along the river to kill Mr. Draskovic. It seems to me far more likely that whoever killed Mr. Tomlinson, with my client as happenstance witness, then went bridge to bridge until finding the man he *thought* was that witness—Mr. Draskovic in the green coat—and silencing him by another bludgeoning. Therefore, I would argue that the evidence of finding Mr. Tomlinson's body, and the manner of his death, be offered by me to the jury through Sergeant Detective Chin and the assistant medical examiner."

"Thank you. Mr. Pereira?"

"I don't think 'rational plan' is the issue here, Your Honor. Alpha is charged with killing Mr. Draskovic, and the fact that the defendant may have killed someone else like Mr. Tomlinson for another reason doesn't make the finding of the body—"

Cordoba shook her head. "You're going in circles, Mr. Pereira. Mr. Sandersen, while Cornerstone technically has no standing on this issue, do you have anything helpful to add?"

Sandersen leaned into his client just long enough, Mairead thought, to receive a one-word answer. Then the lawyer stood and said, "Thank you, Your Honor, but nothing to add at this time."

As Sandersen sat, Cordoba said, "All right, then here's my ruling. If the ME's report on Mr. Tomlinson's autopsy comes back consistent with Alpha's version of the killing, the evidence on excavating the site, the finding of the body, *and* the manner of death come in. We should have the report by tonight, so let's schedule a pretrial hearing tomorrow at nine here, jury to come in at nine-thirty. Any problems with that?"

After the judge left the bench, Severn Pratt came toward the defense table. One of the burly bailiffs left Alpha as his mate shackled the defendant.

Pratt said, "Sandersen's going to sue over your assaulting me yesterday."

Shel Gold dug into a side pocket of his suit jacket. "I'm in the book, but give him my card, you think it would save time."

Nice touch, thought Mairead.

Pratt stared down at the little piece of white cardboard, his cheeks glowing. "I don't play messenger, I pay them."

Shel waited until Pratt looked back up. "Or kill them when they bring news you don't like?"

"Gentlemen," said the bailiff.

"I have to go, anyway," said Shel.

"Running off?" from Pratt.

Mairead watched Shel's shoulders slump a little, and somehow she didn't think he was going to crack wise again. "I thought I should tell Mrs. Tomlinson her husband won't be coming home."

Severn Pratt grinned. "Give the thief's widow my regards," before turning and walking back to his attorney.

AT 8:20 A.M. the next morning, the new child came bounding into the suite. Billie Sunday barely needed to look up at her.

Mairead said, "We were supposed to get a fax from the medical examiner's office."

"We did." Billie pointed at the paper near her left hand on the reception desk.

As the new child skimmed it, Billie said, "Mrs. Tomlinson's taking it pretty well, thanks for asking."

Mairead looked up from the document. "I thought Shel was going to tell her?"

"We both did. In person."

A little whine in, "I would have gone, too."

"You wouldn't have helped things any."

"You mad at me for something, Billie?"

Set the child straight. "I'm mad at the law, for imposing on that poor Church Lady to give our client an edge."

"Without the law—and Shel's argument and some pretty sophisticated techology—Mrs. Tomlinson would still be hanging fire over what happened to her husband."

"Bad news is better than no news?"

Mairead went back to the report. "I've always thought so. Wait one . . . 'Cause of death: fractured skull from multiple blows delivered by a heavy, blunt instrument.' Bingo!"

Though Billie knew the child was just imitating Shel, she nevertheless said, "Bugle."

"I'm sorry?" Mairead looking away from the paper.

"Some funerals, they play a bugle."

"I didn't mean—"

"Shel wanted to see you soon as you read that thing," said Billie Sunday, trying hard to go back to what she was doing and trying harder not to go back to the day she buried Robert Senior.

SHEL Gold had felt his insides settle down nicely after going over the autopsy report on Donn Tomlinson, but he still allowed himself a deep breath before pushing through the double doors into the Third Session. Shel was pleased to see both Sergeant Detective Chin and the assistant ME present in the gallery. While Winston Hayes was there, too, his lawyer, Hadley Burgess, was not. And the two executives from Cornerstone also were sans attorney, even though the Pope seemed to be sitting closer to them in their row than the crowding of the courtroom otherwise required. Shel was a little surprised to see the three college rowdies still hanging around, then decided they probably didn't know when they could *stop* coming under their subpoenas.

Judge Lydia Cordoba held a rubber-stamp hearing, holding her copy of the medical examiner's findings. After Nina led the jury back into the box, Shel put Chin on the stand and guided him through as nongory a recounting of the prior day at the construction site as possible.

Admit it: One thing you learned from Alfred Hitchcock movies was to go easy on the blood and guts. Less was more, and the jurors' imaginations could fill in the rest.

The assistant ME was fine, too, backing Alpha's version of the attack almost to a T, differing only to say that, in his expert opinion, the blows had been struck horizontally from the side rather than vertically from the back. On cross, Pereira tried to make some hay using that discrepancy, but watching the jurors, Shel didn't think the distinction mattered to them.

"Redirect, Mr. Gold?" said Cordoba when Pereira passed the witness.

"No, Your Honor. And that's the defendant's case."

"Thank you. Mr. Pereira?"

"Nothing on rebuttal, Your Honor."

"Are we then prepared for closing arguments?"

Shel and his opponent almost chanted yes.

Cordoba checked the time. "Morning recess, then closings and instructions, even if it means a slightly late lunch."

"SO," said Mairead, balancing her awful coffee in one hand while reaching for a pencil with the other, "what are you going to hit in your closing?"

"I don't plan it out in too much detail," said Shel, eyes not coming up from the yellow sheet he wrote on in the conference room off the Third Session.

"How come you didn't want Alpha here?"

Shel still didn't look up. "The closing's based on the evidence, not anything he suddenly remembers now."

Mairead toyed with a question she'd wanted to ask Shel throughout the trial. "You think our client's really innocent?"

Now the eyes came up from the sheet. "Do you?"

"I asked first."

Shel said, "Speaking of asking, remember me saying to you after you first met Alpha, 'Do you trust him?'"

"I think it was do I 'believe' him, and I said, 'Yes, but I don't trust him.'"

"Well, with me, it's kind of the opposite."

Mairead stopped in mid-sip. "You trust him, but you don't believe him?"

"That's right."

"Wait a minute." She put down her plastic cup. "He was right about Tomlinson being killed and even where he was buried."

"Like Pereira argued, maybe that's because Alpha killed and buried him."

"Shel, you can't think that."

"It's possible. I said back in the courtroom that it wasn't a rational plan, but maybe it doesn't have to be. Rational, that is. Or maybe Alpha's being rational, and I just don't see it yet."

"See what?"

"Why he'd risk taking the stand when even a layman had to feel we'd established reasonable doubt without it."

"Shel, Alpha's weird, but, in a way, he's an upstanding guy."

Mairead watched her boss's eyes turn kindly. "And that's why I trust him. I just don't know that he's told us the truth, which is something we'll probably never know anyway."

Mairead O'Clare wanted to continue, but when those kind eyes went back to his scratch sheet, she decided Shel Gold might need the remaining time to focus on his job and not on his qualms.

ADMIT it: You've got a bad feeling about this.

Shel Gold stood as soon as the judge nodded toward him, trying to push his own doubts aside in favor of creating doubt in the jurors' minds.

Though Shel never really agreed that a jury did that "reasonable doubt" balancing. Debating it in law school had been interesting, but once he'd begun trying cases in the real world, he pretty quickly came to the conclusion that jurors thought one of two things: The defendant did it, or he didn't. If they thought he did it, they didn't tax themselves by running the intellectual gauntlet of measuring how much doubt equated to "reasonable." If they thought he didn't do it, same thing, but from the opposite starting point. So Shel had always felt that in a case where the death couldn't have been an accident, he had to hand the jury a credible alternative to the defendant-as-killer.

Shel began at the end of the box farthest from the witness stand, since that's where they'd last heard him, on direct of the assistant ME. "First, thanks for your patience. Because of Judge Cordoba, this has been an exceptionally efficient and fair trial, but nevertheless I know how hard it can be to serve on a jury, especially in a capital case. One of murder in the first degree."

Shel turned sideways, took a single step. "As Her Honor will instruct you, your decision must be that the defendant, Alpha, is guilty 'beyond a reasonable doubt.' You've heard evidence from Pamela Wilkins, the state trooper who mediated squabbles among the homeless community along the

Charles River. You heard Trooper Wilkins say she never saw Alpha be violent with Mr. Draskovic, the decedent. You heard evidence from Mr. Hayes, the sailor, and Mr. Gerber, the college student, about how Mr. Draskovic angered many other people himself. And you heard testimony from the executives at Cornerstone Construction, who suspected one of their own employees, foreman Donn Tomlinson, of stealing from them."

Now Shel turned toward the gallery, finding Pratt easily, because Cornerstone's president was shooting daggers at him. "The same Mr. Tomlinson that Alpha says he saw killed by one of those executives, Mr. Severn Pratt, who complained of thefts from his building site here in Boston. The same Mr. Pratt who had crime problems in Washington, D.C."

Shel couldn't be more specific because the judge had excluded as evidence Mairead's attempts to get into the fraud case, but he did turn back toward the jury. "Given the thefts from the Boston site, I'd ask you to think what motive someone like Mr. Pratt might have had for wanting a current employee of his disappear. I'd ask you to think how long it could have been before Mr. Tomlinson's disappearance was resolved if the excavation at the construction site hadn't occurred and found his body. And then I'd ask you to think of why Alpha, who was *given* scraps of lumber and bent nails by Mr. Tomlinson, would have any motive for killing him. Doesn't it seem far more likely that the murder at the construction site was the trigger for the same killer pursuing my client, Alpha? To pursue him but also to mistake poor Mr. Draskovic for the eyewitness to the murder? And to fall upon Mr. Draskovic, and kill him with Alpha's readily available walking stick? Surely this is far more credible than to think my client would have killed Mr. Draskovic over the coat, only to leave that very coat on the body rather than retake and wear it himself on a cold winter's night."

Shel moved toward the witness stand. "You heard that testimony—and more—from here. Now you're listening to me, and soon you will hear Mr. Pereira's arguments, too. I told you a few minutes ago that I know it's hard to be a juror in a capital case. Well, it's also hard to be the defense attorney, because under the laws of Massachusetts, the prosecution, which has the burden of persuading you of the defendant's guilt beyond a reasonable

doubt, therefore gets to speak to you last. Accordingly, I would ask only one final thing of you. Should Mr. Pereira raise any point I haven't covered, please think to yourselves, 'What would Shel Gold have said back to that?' Please use your memories, and your patience, and your good common sense to deliberate under the instructions Her Honor will give you, and I have no worry about the decision you will reach. Thank you."

As Shel moved back toward the defense table, he was aware that Mairead was staring at him. He was a little surprised to see Alpha doing the same. When Shel sat down, he was most surprised when Mairead gave the elbow closest to her a squeeze.

Admit it: You're glad professionally, if sorry personally, that she didn't pat you on the rump.

MAIREAD was mesmerized by Shel's closing. Not because he shot off fireworks or provoked tears, but rather because he simply had a conversation with the jury. A reasonable, if one-sided, chat on an important issue that involved everyone in the room but could be discussed without resorting to thunder or emotion.

And she wondered whether having to close first really *was* a disadvantage, if Shel performed like that every time out.

"Members of the jury," said Pereira, rising only after Shel was seated. "This is really a very simple case. The defendant, who prefers the name Alpha, admits from the stand that, as a hermit, he sometimes lies, even under oath."

Mairead watched Pereira pace nervously more than walk, his body shape turning a waddle into almost a scramble.

"Alpha asks us to believe that a highly placed executive like Severn Pratt would kill an employee on his own construction site. According to the medical examiner's report, Alpha is wrong about seeing the employee hit vertically—from above—rather than horizontally—from the side. Oh, but never mind that. Alpha then 'supposes' that Mr. Pratt would take the time to bury the body, and then *stalk* a homeless man along the river in the cold of a December night. Only to kill that homeless man, too, but with the defendant's

own walking stick. What a piece of luck for Mr. Pratt, according to the defendant Alpha's version of what 'must have happened.' An incredible stroke of good fortune, don't you think, to find Alpha's very own walking stick as a handy weapon? And also to mistake Mr. Draskovic among all the other homeless along the river for the eyewitness to his other crime? And all this while Alpha, who supposedly had just seen his kindly friend, the foreman, killed, and who supposedly ran terrified back to his cave instead of going to the police, lies drunk and unconscious in his bed.' "

Pereira finally came to a stop. "I began my closing by saying that this is a very simple case. Let me end the same way. The defendant, Alpha, wanted Mr. Draskovic's coat. Alpha took it, and Alpha resisted all Mr. Draskovic's efforts—even through the police—to reclaim it. And when Mr. Draskovic engaged in a little 'self-help,' Alpha killed him for it."

The prosecutor began moving back toward his table, but slowly, one step at a time. "For a coat." Step. "For an old, dirty coat." Step. "The price of a man's life . . . ," Pereira reached his seat, ". . . at least in Alpha's view of the world."

Mairead scribbled a note that said, "He hit 'Alpha' a little too hard in those last few sentences." She passed it to Shel, who seemed to read it, nod, and write something under her words.

Taking back the note, Mairead O'Clare saw, "I wish he'd made some other mistakes."

"I thought the kindly judge seemed fair enough in her statements to the jury, but, Mr. Gold, you were positively grand."

"Thank you, but it's what the jury thinks that matters."

The three of them sat in the conference room off the Third Session, Alpha beaming, Mairead decompressing, Shel observing.

Admit it: You'd love to know what this guy's really thinking.

"So," said Alpha to Mairead, "and what happens now, lass?"

"Don't ask me. This is my first trip around the block."

"Basically," Shel rubbing his shoulders a little against the back of his chair, "we wait."

"For how long?"

"Depends. I've known juries to come back in half an hour or five days."

"Five days?" Alpha seemed truly astonished. "And what could they be talking about all that time? They heard my story. Won't they either be believing it or sending me to the hole?"

Shel said, "The jury decides guilt, not sentence."

"Even so."

"We'll give it an hour, then I'll let the court clerk know that Mairead and I are leaving for the day."

"But what if my jury comes back after you've gone?"

My jury, thought Shel. "Then the clerk will call me, and we'll hustle back over here."

Alpha seemed to be gauging something. "Ah, I think I've tumbled to it, now. Waiting around is dead time, isn't it? You'd rather be in your office, getting some real work done."

"Yes," Shel seeing if it would goad Alpha into something.

The something turned out to be a deep laugh. "You're a treasure, Mr. Gold. And I'm damned lucky to have had you on my side in this." He stuck out his manacled hands, and shook Shel's right one with both of his. Then Alpha turned to Mairead. "And you as well, lass. If you've learned from all this, then at least my jail time won't have been wasted."

Shel watched the way Alpha took her hand, the redness of it so alien, yet so . . . authentically a part of her.

Admit it: For this moment alone, you're envying him.

"IS Shel on the phone?" said the new child from her office.

"No," answered Billie Sunday, searching through the latest bank statement on Shel's clients' funds account, trying to figure out whether the forgetful man did or did not deposit the check from that divorce case he was fretting about.

Billie could hear Mairead getting up with a huff. Bet the next car payment she hasn't gotten a lick of work done since they came back from the courthouse.

"What are you doing?" said the child from behind her.

"Nothing you can help with, so you might as well talk to Shel, waste his time instead of mine."

"Thanks for being so understanding."

"Comes from being a mother," said Billie Sunday, who then bit her tongue, remembering about Mairead being an orphan on top of the atomic hands.

PONTIFICO Murizzi sipped on his hot chocolate from the coffee bar. Funny, all the units he ever served in, all the weird-ass shifts he ever pulled, and the Pope never developed a taste for coffee. But he found out early that it wasn't the coffee, it was the caffeine, and chocolate had plenty. Usually, he'd just pop a candy bar, get the sugar hit as well. But outdoors on a cold day, it was better to have your caffeine hot.

And it was cold, even parked in the small lot across from the building where Cornerstone Construction had its corporate offices, twelve blocks from the job site itself.

Murizzi didn't like the version of the incident outside the Third Session that Mairead had described for him, and he especially didn't like that Wyckoff couldn't keep his boss in line. Hard to blame the guy for that: Everybody needs a job. But while Shel boxed professionally, and Mairead played hockey, either of them might underestimate a guy like Pratt. The Pope sure as shit couldn't watch both possible victims—Shel lived in Brookline, and Mairead on Beacon Hill.

And if you stuck just to Mairead, and she spotted you, she'd be royally pissed, at least based on how she reacted to your "talk" with that derelict Rex. So, do the next best thing: Target the suspect instead.

Not call Pratt on the phone or send him letters or get in his face, even in public. The Commonwealth now had an antistalking statute with some teeth in it. No, best to just camp on the guy's doorstep, shadow him for a while. Without letting the arrogant fuck know it.

The Pope smiled then, but stopped when he realized he'd somehow already sucked down all of his hot chocolate.

"IT'S been almost three hours," said Mairead.

She stood her ground at the threshold to Shel's office while he glanced at his wrist over the open book on his desk.

Tapping the face of the watch, he said, "Two hours, twenty-seven minutes, thirty-... five seconds."

"Is that a good sign or a bad one?"

"What, me knowing exactly how long the jury's been out?"

Mairead folded her arms. "No, that they've been out so long."

The whole body shrug, not even looking up from the book. "It's not that long yet."

"But is it better for them to be deliberating for this kind of time?"

Another body shrug. "Hard to say. The courthouse touts'll tell you the longer a jury's out in a criminal case, the better it looks for the defendant. They're arguing, they can't make up their minds on whether he did it, and so on. But I've seen juries come back not guilty in thirty minutes and come back guilty after three days, so I gave up handicapping them years ago."

Mairead inclined her head toward the book on his desk. "How can you get work done on anything else?"

Now Shel looked up at her for the first time, his suit jacket on the clothes tree, his shirtsleeves rolled up. "I can't."

Yeah, right. "Then what's that you're reading?"

"An appellate case, but I'm just kind of browsing."

"Browsing," in that deadpan tone Mairead liked to use when she thought people were treating her like a child.

Shel frowned, though. "At that big firm, you did most of your research with a computer, am I right?"

"Through a computer, accessing on-line databases."

Shel waved a hand. "Whatever. You typed in 'find me X,' and then the screen shows the information."

"Essentially."

"But if you didn't ask the right question, you wouldn't get the right answer."

"Well, no. Of course not."

"So, okay. When I don't know what I'm supposed to even be *asking*, I pick up a book with answers in it, and I browse. And sometimes, just sometimes, I find an answer that tells me what question I should have been asking. Understand?"

Mairead turned to go. "I'll get back to you on that."

"Hey?" she heard from him, and turned back.

Shel Gold said, "Waiting is waiting. You can waste it, or you can do the best with it you can. I browse. Find what works for you, only be ready here if that phone rings."

Which, Mairead jumping at the sound, it did right then.

From the reception area, Billie Sunday said, "It's Jake over at Suffolk Superior. Your jury's coming back in."

LIKE children who just heard the circus parade's going by.

Billie watched the two lawyers nearly knock each other over, trying to get their coats on and out the suite door. Mairead, now, Billie could understand. First real bit of lawyering, you don't count the posse thing for that working-girl Talina over at her john's place. But Shel, that little boy of a man, he still gets so excited by those clerk calls.

Billie, suddenly alone in the office, just shook her head.

Suppose if you really loved football, the way Robert Junior does, you'd know what it feels like. And Shel, from having been in the ring, he probably knows what it's like to wait for the judges to say who won when neither fighter knocked the other one out. Or Mairead, waiting to see if she scores a goal when she whacks at that puck.

But to Billie, it was just another day at the office. And a body was supposed to work there, not sit around fidgeting for hours on end, waiting to hear that twelve other people finally made up their minds about your client.

MAIREAD could feel the tension in the courtroom. Now it wasn't like the moments before the beginning of a hockey game, the jitters. It was more like a curtain hung heavily over your face, the material thick, clogging your nostrils and making it hard to take a deep breath.

Maybe this is what it'd feel like if I tried to climb a tall mountain, the air getting thin, the fatigue dragging—

"Courrrrrt!" said Nina, moving from the chambers door ahead of Lydia Cordoba. As the judge took the bench, Nina opened the jury door, and Alpha squeezed Mairead's hand, just once.

It's all right to feel close to the man, young lady.

As the jurors filed into the box, Mairead studied faces and body language, none of them looking toward the defense table. She wanted to ask Shel if this was a bad sign, but then figured she'd know soon enough for herself.

The foreman of the jury handed a folded slip of paper to Nina, who brought it directly to the judge. Cordoba opened it and silently read with a poker face. She then handed the paper to a standing Jake. He read it to himself as well, then said to the foreman, "On the single count of the indictment, murder in the first degree, how do you find?"

The foreman looked at Alpha now. "We find the defendant . . . *not* guilty."

People in the gallery began talking loudly, and Mairead turned to hug Shel, realizing as she did that maybe she should have started with their client, if she was to hug anyone at all in a courtroom. But when she did turn to Alpha, he didn't have his hands out, wasn't even smiling. He just looked . . .

"Indifferent" is the word I'd use, young lady.

"Are you okay?" said Mairead.

"I'm fine, lass. Why?"

"You just don't seem very . . . happy."

"Happy? With what, now? I knew I was innocent of killing Old Man River. You 'believed' me, but you still needed to have that belief vindicated by your own legal system, didn't you?"

Mairead was stumped there.

The judge gaveled for order, and the courtroom noise dwindled to silence. "Members of the jury, thank you. Mr. Pereira, in light of the testimony and result at this trial, does your office intend to seek a new indictment against a different defendant?"

"That'll be up to my superiors, Your Honor."

"Very well," said Lydia Cordoba, and Mairead thought for sure the judge looked out into the gallery toward where Severn Pratt was sitting. "Please confer with them soon, then. As for now, the jury is excused, the defendant is released from custody, and this court stands adjourned."

Alpha reached past Mairead at that point and shook Shel's hand. "Mr. Gold, what did the prosecutor mean just then about a 'new indictment' being 'up to his superiors'?"

Shel glanced toward the gallery. "If the district attorney indicts Pratt for Tomlinson's and/or Draskovic's murder, Pereira's worried that Pratt's lawyer would just recycle the testimony from this trial to create reasonable doubt at his own."

"You mean," said Alpha, kind of resignedly, Mairead thought, "that the real killer could use me the way we used him."

Shel took a moment before saying, "Basically."

Resignation turned into something else. It wasn't until the court officers led Alpha away—not in shackles this time, but just to get back his books and other personal items from the jail—that Mairead O'Clare thought she could put a name to the expression on her first major client's face.

"Determination" is the word I'd choose, too, young lady.

23

PONTIFICO MURIZZI SWUNG HIS Ford Explorer slowly into the line of traffic, three cars behind Severn Pratt's Jaguar.

With a vanity plate, yet. CORCON, for Cornerstone Construction, probably.

The Pope didn't have a lot of confidence doing vehicular tails. In fact, he could count "on the fingers of one elbow" (his mother's favorite expression) the times he'd had any in the Homicide Unit. But Murizzi had also been relieved to find that nobody else—even the FBI, with all their training and "superiority complex"—was very good at it, either.

Following Severn Pratt, though, was a walk in the park.

One, the guy never speeded or ran a light. Two, he never looked around him. And three, you know where he's going.

It was pretty clear, as soon as they left Storrow Drive at the wrong exit for Cornerstone's corporate offices or construction project. The Pope lagged behind just enough to keep the Jaguar in sight as Pratt drove around the Public Garden and onto Beacon Street. Then up the Hill past the State House, stopping only once for a nontraffic reason.

Right in front of Shel Gold's office building.

Murizzi couldn't see clearly what Pratt was doing, other than maybe staring out the driver's-side window at the entrance. Then slowly—the Pope thought almost reluctantly—the Jag slid back into the flow and east toward Cornerstone's own offices.

"WELL, lass, I expect this is good-bye, isn't it?"

Mairead stood with Alpha on the steps of the Nashua Street jail. Cold air

whipped around the corner of the reddish-brick building, but while she felt awkward, the wind wasn't the reason.

More as though it is the end of a blind date, young lady.

Mairead brushed the hair away from her eyes as Alpha shielded his with a hand, like an Indian scout in the old Westerns.

He said, "After so much time in there, I'll have to be getting used to the wondrous light of the sun again."

Alpha was dressed in the sort of clothes you'd expect on a homeless person, his philosophy books under his arm, and for Mairead, it somehow accented the end of their relationship.

"Lass?" he said, concern veiling the gap-toothed smile.

"Sorry. I just . . ." Mairead decided not to go lite on the guy. "I just want you to know that in your case, the system *did* work, and representing you is the first time I've felt like a real lawyer. And felt pride in being a part of the profession."

Sensing her voice was about to crack, she shut up.

Alpha stuck out his hand. Mairead took it.

Squeezing only a little, he said, "Then I'm glad for you, Mairead O'Clare. And with luck, your tenure'll be long and happy."

And Alpha skipped down the steps, his whole body seeming to bounce with each stride once he hit the street. Mairead followed his bobbing head with her eyes, her vision a little blurry, until he disappeared around the corner and into the wind.

BILLIE Sunday said, ". . . and you should return these three first, in the order I'm handing them to you, and then your dentist called—why haven't you been in for nine months?"

She watched the sneaky man, trying his hardest to change the subject. Shel motioned toward her desk. "Champagne?"

Billie nodded. "Thought maybe we should celebrate. You don't win that many cases anymore, and it's the new child's first."

"Mairead did well. A lot better than . . ."

Billie watched the man change, that worn old face going sad on her as he looked at the office the new child now had.

Shel said, "Poor Vincent."

Billie shushed him. "Wasn't your fault, and you know it. That poor boy didn't have the fortitude for this type of practice, and it's better all around that he found it out early."

Shel just shook his head. Billie had heard Jake, the clerk from Suffolk Superior, tell Shel the whole thing. That poor Vincent just froze in the courtroom. "Like a stone statue, Shel," Jake had said. The judge tried to help him—"Like talking a jumper down from the ledge"—but Vincent just started shaking, then crying, then collapsed into his lawyer chair. Billie remembered making the long-distance call to his parents, giving them directions to the mental hospital Shel took him to.

Then she snapped back. "But the new child does."

Shel looked from the office door to Billie. "What?"

"This Mairead. Not my cup of tea, maybe, but she'll take it and she'll make it. You mark my words, Sheldon A. Gold."

And Billie Sunday actually thought the aggravating, sneaky, sad man just might.

PONTIFICO Murizzi parked again in the lot of the coffee bar across from the building where Cornerstone Construction had its corporate offices. The entrance and exit to the skyscraper's underground garage were side by side, and Pratt's Jaguar had gone in but not out. The Pope passed the time watching people use the building's front doors, making sure none of them was Severn Pratt while appreciating a couple of the better-bunned men climb curbs or steps.

Truth to tell, for a minute Murizzi thought he wasn't the only one surveilling the building. A guy wearing sunglasses and a ball cap stood on an opposite corner, seeming to focus on the main entrance, too. The dying sun was slanting wrong for a good look, but—

A car started up and out of the garage, and Murizzi brought his attention back to the exit. It was just a four-door domestic sedan, though, Al Wyckoff at the wheel and the only occupant. The security chief didn't seem aware of the Pope, which was fine by Murizzi, though how the guy could hold his fancy corporate job without noticing those kinds of things was beyond him.

Pontifico Murizzi watched the sedan continue down the street. When he turned his head back to the other corner, the guy in the shades and cap was gone.

"SO," said Mairead, a glass of champagne in her hand and a solid, if bittersweet, tingling in her heart. "Where's the Pope?"

Billie Sunday motioned toward the console on her desk. "I tried him on his cellular, but he must have it switched off."

Shel Gold raised his own drink. "Well, in his absence, thanks to him, and to both of you."

"If I'd known we were going to celebrate, I'd have invited Alpha," said Mairead.

She caught Shel and Billie exchanging glances. "What?"

The secretary/receptionist said, "We kind of let the clients celebrate on their own."

Mairead thought about it.

Probably makes sense, young lady. It's one thing for the team to celebrate, another for the fans to join in.

Yeah, only after hockey games in college, the neat thing about the women's varsity was that the parents of the players—of those who *had* parents—joined in celebrating with cookies and cider and—

Mairead interrupted herself. "How come we don't invite them?"

Shel said, "The clients, you mean?"

"Yes."

He set down his glass. "A lot of our clients won't tend to be people you want to have a long-term social relationship with."

Mairead couldn't believe she was hearing this from her *new* boss. "That's kind of elitist, isn't it?"

Billie put her own glass on the desk. "It's kind of realistic. You keep everything with clients strictly business, they don't get other ideas in their heads."

"What kind of ideas?"

Shel said, "Stalking ideas."

"Oh," said Mairead, finishing her champagne with a little chill that didn't come from its temperature.

EVEN inside his Explorer, Pontifico Murizzi was getting cold.

It'd been three hours since Pratt's Jag had gone into the garage, and neither he nor his car had come back out. The Pope had gone through three hot chocolates, but they weren't enough.

And if you have any more caffeine, you're not going to sleep no matter how much Jocko tires you out.

Crumpling the third, now-empty cup, Murizzi left his vehicle, tossed the cup into a trash barrel, and walked four doors down the street to a Federal Express office.

"CALL for you," said Billie Sunday around 7:30 P.M.

Mairead raised her head from an armed-robbery case file Shel had given her. First we celebrate, he'd said, then we "cerebrate." Well into the evening.

"Who is it?"

"Man won't tell me."

Mairead picked up her telephone. "Hello?"

"Without saying my name out loud, do you recognize my voice?"

No question, having heard it a number of times before. "Yes."

"All right, then. I've got the goods on Pratt, though more for Tomlinson than the homeless guy. But I'm scared."

Mairead said, "Then go to the police."

"Not a chance. Either they'll hold me as a material witness, or they won't protect me at all. And you know what a maniac Pratt can be."

Mairead pictured the punch-up outside the Third Session. "So why call me?"

"I watched you in the courtroom. You know what you're doing, and I think you want to see Pratt pay for what he did. So here's the deal. I'll give you the documentation I've got on Pratt and Tomlinson, but then I'm bolting."

Mairead didn't want to lose him, but she also wasn't sure she wanted to get in any deeper. "What if this documentation is no good without you to testify about it?"

"Then that's your problem. Or the DA's. Or maybe it'll go like O.J. The criminal case tanks, but the civil case for Mrs. Tomlinson brings her millions. All I'm saying is, I'm willing to stick my neck out far enough to give the stuff to you, but no police, and no bodyguards on your side to try and hold me."

Mairead thought of Danette Tomlinson crying softly at the trial. Then of her dead husband's hand sticking up out of the dirt, close enough to Mairead for . . . touching. Finally of not being invited to break the news to the widow because, in Billie's words, "you wouldn't have helped any."

Mairead said, "Where and when?"

"Tonight. Eight o'clock at the job site."

Alarm bells, young lady. "Why there?"

"Because I buried the documentation under the construction trailer so Pratt couldn't find it."

Mairead weighed things one last time. "Eight o'clock."

"I'll be at the front gate," said Al Wyckoff's voice before he hung up on her.

PONTIFICO Murizzi walked through the big glass door and into the lobby. Just as he remembered from serving Shel's subpoenas, there was a security desk in a half-moon shape before the banks of elevators. A skinny old guy in a red blazer with some kind of crest on it sat behind the desk now, watching black-and-white television monitors.

The Pope said, "Got a package here for a Severn Pratt at Cornerstone Construction."

The scarecrow looked up from his screen and said, "You don't look much like a FedEx-er."

"My outfit just use their boxes. Makes it easier."

The scarecrow said, "You don't recognize me, do you, Pope?"

Murizzi took a closer look. "Dan? Dan Clooney?"

"In the flesh," the scarecrow standing up unsteadily. "What's left of it, anyway."

The Pope stared at him. Clooney looked like he'd been shrink-wrapped, the skin hanging off a frame that used to be six-three and two-twenty.

Shaking hands, Clooney said, "My liver. Too much bad hooch."

Murizzi released the man's hand. "Christ, Dan, I'm sorry."

"Hey, self-inflicted wound." Clooney sat back down. "And, it gets too bad, I just eat my gun for breakfast, right?"

The Pope didn't want to answer that. "So, can you let me up to see this Pratt?"

"I could, but it wouldn't do you any good. He left."

"He left?"

"Yeah. With Al Wyckoff, their security guy."

Murizzi closed his eyes once, like a violent blink. "You saw them go?"

"I saw them get into the garage elevator."

"Notice anything odd about them?"

"Not if you know them like I do. Pratt was ranting, as usual. Wyckoff was trying to calm him down, as usual."

"Who was in the lead?"

The Pope saw Clooney's expression change, from scarecrow back to cop. "Wyckoff, with Pratt kind of prodding him from behind."

Pontifico Murizzi checked his watch. 8:05 P.M.

MAIREAD O'Clare checked her watch: 8:05 P.M.

On a freezing cold night now, the January thaw seeming a distant memory. *Could be worse, young lady.*

Yeah, it could be snowing.

Mairead stamped her feet outside the padlocked, chain-link gate of the construction site, nobody in the little sentry box. As she pulled back the cuff of her coat to look at her watch again, a powdery flake fell onto the crystal and melted immediately.

Five more minutes. For Danette Tomlinson.

Then Mairead heard the crunch of a footstep on frozen earth, and she wheeled around.

Al Wyckoff, a sheepish smile on his face, approached from inside the fence. "Sorry, I got delayed."

"Where's Pratt?"

"I don't know, and right now, I don't care. Come on."

He opened the padlock by key instead of combination, swinging the person-sized part of the gate only wide enough to let her pass before closing it and reengaging the hasp. Turning back to Mairead, he said, "This way."

"Where are the documents?"

"I dug them up. The reason I was delayed."

"But where are they now?"

"In the trailer. Come on."

As the snow began to fall more heavily, Mairead followed Wyckoff through the site, him guiding them around the now-tattered yellow police tape left from Donn Tomlinson's shallow grave.

Jesus Mary, like when I first visited Alpha's cave.

Just past a junk pile of lumber in all shapes and sizes—Alpha again leaped to mind—the construction trailer came back into view, partially hidden from Mairead's angle by one wall of the building. She thought the site looked eerie now, much of it still gray concrete and steel I beams, almost as if the steady snow were magically completing the superstructure.

There were a couple of concrete blocks forming a rough stoop for the trailer. As Wyckoff stepped onto the first of them, his face suddenly whipped to the left. "Oh God, Pratt! Get down!"

Mairead turned the same way, seeing in the half-shadow of an unfinished alcove ten feet away the face of Severn Pratt, a gun glinting in his hand. She dropped to the ground, feeling her chin scrape on a jutting piece of frosty earth. As she began to roll toward the trailer, to gain some cover if Pratt started shooting, her head slammed into something she hadn't seen, and the night suddenly became very clear and starry.

"SHEL, it's the Pope."

"Where are you calling from?"

"My cellular. Listen, is Mairead with you?"

Watching the falling snow melt on his windshield, Pontifico Murizzi could sense the pause as well as measure it.

Finally, Shel said, "But this is my home phone."

Murizzi swallowed his impatience. "I know that, but I tried your office and got the tape, and then Mairead's home number and got no answer."

"Well, it's only a little after eight. She could be almost—"

"Look, Shel. I lost Pratt."

"You lost . . . ?"

"I was staking him out, making sure he didn't come after either of you guys on the sly, and I think he made me."

Shel said, "We worked late tonight, and Mairead got a call."

"From who?"

"I don't know, but when I went to go home, Billie said Mairead'd already left, something about having to meet somebody."

Christ. "Who?"

"Pope, I didn't ask."

"All right." Crisis-management mode. "Call Billie at home, see if Mairead told her anything more. Then call me back."

"Where will you be?" asked Shel.

"I think Pratt forced Wyckoff to drive him somewhere."

"Meaning?"

"The arrogant fuck needed a car, and he seems to like doing things by the Charles."

At which point, Pontifico Murizzi cut the connection to punch in the number for Trooper Pamela Wilkins, have her dispatch a couple of state cruisers along the river.

GROGGY . . . woozy, too . . . Hands and legs numb, unattached.

Fight the gag reflex, young lady.

Got my bell rung, blind-side check by some ass—

"Good to have you back with us, Mairead."

She looked up . . . double vision . . . snowy.

Clear your head, young lady. And fast.

Mairead shook her shoulders, immediately regretted the pain that streaked across her head and neck.

"Of course, I'm using 'us' just in the technical sense."

Focus, young lady. Now!

Mairead squeezed her eyes shut and opened them. No hockey gloves on her hands, no helmet on her head. And broken, white ground in front of her instead of scored ice.

"Over here."

Mairead willed her burning chin to turn, her eyes taking in the middle distance now, the falling snow softening everything.

"That's better," said Al Wyckoff.

He's standing in front of that shadowy alcove, where Pratt . . .

"Look out," Mairead said, barely recognizing her own voice.

Then Wyckoff stepped to the side, and even through the flakes, she could see Pratt again. Still where he'd been.

Exactly where.

Mairead watched Wyckoff move toward his boss. When the security chief laughed and gently pried the gun from Pratt's hand, the light began to dawn.

Then Wyckoff grabbed the lapel of Pratt's coat and hurled him from the shadowed alcove toward Mairead, the sound of some wood clattering together before the president of Cornerstone crumpled to the ground like a rag doll.

"Funny," said Wyckoff. "I thought with it being so cold, he'd be stiffer. But I had to use these scraps from the pile over there to prop him up."

Pratt's head was no more than three feet from Mairead's. She could see his now-broken front teeth, some blood oozing rather than flowing from his gums onto the snow. His eyes were open, but rolled halfway up, and there was a red puncture on the right side of his head, some ghostly yellow showing through the charcoal ring around the wound.

"Shot himself," said Wyckoff, checking the gun he'd taken from the dead man's hand. "Couldn't face the humiliation."

Buy time, young lady. For your arms and legs to come back.

"What . . . humiliation?" asked Mairead, trying to clench her fists, wiggle her feet.

"Of being ruined a second time. Pratt really did defraud the feds on that project in D.C. Afterward, he 'resolved' to be squeaky clean. And got his chance, thanks to me."

"Thanks to . . . ?"

"Who do you think did the dirty work down there on his partner Stein? Once I 'disappeared' the major witness against him, Pratt had to tolerate me, or go to jail for sure, this time as a conspirator to murder."

Mairead felt pins and needles in her right foot, the same sensation in her right hand. She forced them to move a little, bring back circulation. "You killed Stein, and Tomlinson, too?"

Wyckoff spat. "That fucking meddling spade. He was like Pratt, a reformed thief. And, like a reformed smoker, he couldn't stand to think somebody else was 'sinning' around him."

"The . . . materiel."

"It wasn't that hard for me. Just make sure some lame, deaf guard was on when I wanted to move stuff off-site. Or, like tonight, give the guy a break, tell him I had to be here anyway."

"But then the police will know." Mairead took advantage of the excuse of pointing at Pratt's body to shift her own, to a position like one of those stupid nymphs by a reflecting pool in the old paintings. Her shifting brought the agony of sensation, the thundering in her head worse than all the rest of the pain combined. "They'll know you killed him."

"No, Mairead, they'll have just my version. That Pratt made me drive him at gunpoint from the garage under our field office downtown. And I'll even have your friend Mr. Murizzi to corroborate that part."

THE Pope had just switched his wipers onto high, knock the snow off a little faster, when his cell phone bleated.

Murizzi picked it up and clicked receive. "Talk to me, Shel."

"I caught Billie just as she got in her door. Mairead's caller was male, but wouldn't give Billie his name."

Terrific. "Any ideas on who he was?"

"Billie just said he sounded white and middle-aged."

The Pope thought, So do we. "Shel, I'm on Storrow Drive, heading west toward Alpha's cave. I'll call you if—"

Just then, Murizzi cleared a curve in the road and saw blue strobing

lights along the river. He clicked the end button and watched for a curb-cut through the guardrail.

"T H E Pope?" said Mairead.

"Yes." Wyckoff laughed, the falling snow making it louder. "The perfect nickname for Pontifico. He was outside our office building, probably because he was afraid old Severn here would pull another stunt like the one on your boss at the courthouse."

Now some real feeling flowed back into Mairead's lower legs and forearms, the pins and needles inching upward toward her quadriceps and triceps.

Just a bit longer, young lady.

Mairead said, "Alpha had it right, didn't he?"

"All but the punch line. Tomlinson figured it was me, and he hung around one night for a confrontation. Your client saw that, but left before Tomlinson got rough and before I had to kill him."

"Before?"

"Appreciate my position, Mairead: I couldn't very well plead self-defense to killing Tomlinson when I was stealing from our joint employer. But this Alpha seeing us argue was the only thing connecting me to Tomlinson's death. So, after I buried the body as best I could, I set out after this long-haired bum in a green coat 'who lived under a bridge by the river.'"

Mairead could flex most of her arms and legs now. "And, outside Alpha's cave, you mistook Zoran Draskovic for him."

Wyckoff frowned and sighed. "Can you imagine how frustrating that was for me? I mean, I spot the 'same' bum in the 'same' coat coming out of this hovel under a bridge, and there's even a handy club, right outside the door. I finish him off, and I'm home free. But, even though I made that mistake, at least my luck held."

"The police arrested the wrong man."

"Who, when he finally got the chance to testify, himself identified the wrong man, old Severn, as the one who killed Tomlinson. Kind of a neat circle, huh?"

Mairead shoved with all her strength, all four limbs, getting herself up off the ground. She wanted to run toward the pile of scrap lumber, but realized she was at best lurching, zigzagging rather than heading straight toward it, the pain in her skull like staring at fireworks without being able to blink.

"No, no," said Wyckoff, almost kindly, his free hand closing on the crook of Mairead's left arm. "We can't have old guilt-ridden Severn shooting you in the back, now can we?"

You knew he was going to kill you, young lady, but that doesn't make it any easier to hear.

SHEL Gold pounced on his telephone before the first ring ended, Moshe jumping down off his lap. "Pope?"

"Yeah," his voice scarred with static, some parrotlike squawking of a radio in the background. "I'm at Alpha's cave with a couple of staties. They've been up and down the Boston side of the river with no sign of Pratt, Wyckoff's sedan, or Mairead."

Damnit. Damnit to hell.

"Shel, you still with me?"

"Yes, Pope."

"Any ideas?"

"What about the construction site?"

Shel Gold could barely hear Pontifico Murizzi say, "Shit," followed by, "I'm halfway there."

MAIREAD shook Wyckoff off her arm, but she stumbled and fell at the edge of the scrap pile doing it.

"Toned, aren't you?" said Wyckoff. "Too bad about DNA testing, or we could show each other a good time here first." Wyckoff looked around, like a demanding guest approving a hotel room. "Ever done it in the snow, Mairead?"

She made herself focus on the scrap pile.

Not this one, young lady, or that, either. But maybe . . .

Mairead said, "Then why lure me out here? You could have had Pratt just 'commit suicide' anywhere to get you off the hook."

"But I'm only 'on the hook' because of you! The bitch lawyer who wouldn't stop trying her best for that bum Alpha. You had to keep digging—oh, that's ironic, isn't it?"

"What is?"

"My using the word 'digging.' First Tomlinson got buried, and now," Wyckoff glancing over his shoulder at Pratt's body, "even our poor departed president will be—"

In one sweeping gesture, Mairead used the man's backward glance to wrench a piece of lumber the size of a hockey stick from the pile of scraps. Churning her legs like she was driving another player into the boards, Mairead gripped the lumber with both hands and cross-checked Wyckoff in the face.

He yelled, the gun was knocked from his hand and bounced five feet away on the frozen ground. Blood started pouring from his nose and split lips, both hands coming up to protect his face as he retreated.

Mairead lunged toward him, turning the lumber to spear him in the ribs or solar plexus.

And hit a patch of ice with her right foot.

She struggled to maintain her balance, but the inner ear still wasn't right, and from her experience skating, Mairead knew she was going down. Hard.

The impact with the ground caused one of her hands to let go of the lumber. As Mairead tried to clutch the stick in her other, Wyckoff came forward and kicked it out of her grasp.

"You fucking bitch!" The blood nearly cascading down his face and coat. Backing toward the gun, he scooped it up.

Mairead struggled to get to her feet, but the ankle she'd hurt with Rex buckled under the weight she tried to put on it.

Wyckoff moved toward her, swiping at his face with his free forearm, nearly bellowing words through the pain Mairead felt certain he'd caused himself by the gesture. "You wrecked my fucking plans, and now Severn Pratt is going to take out the lawyer of the bum who identified him."

As Wyckoff aimed his gun, Mairead closed her eyes and braced herself for the unknown horror of a bullet impacting her flesh. Then she heard, "And why not that 'bum' himself?"

She opened her eyes to see Alpha, wearing a baseball cap, charging at Wyckoff from the shadows of the unfinished building. He covered the ground like a punt returner, dodging and weaving.

Gaelic football, young lady.

Wyckoff fired. Once, twice, three times.

Mairead could see puffs of snow and a mist of red come off Alpha as he spun around, keeping his feet but losing his stride. The man kept coming as Wyckoff fired again, and again, and—

Up, young lady, as best you can. Up!

Mairead got onto her good leg, hopping while dragging the bad one behind. Making noise on the dusting of snow, but with the piece of lumber back in her hands.

Alpha, badly slowed, was almost on Wyckoff when the security chief turned toward Mairead, muzzle raised.

Alpha roared something in a language she didn't understand.

But Wyckoff reacted by turning back halfway, and Mairead's client, arms outstretched, slammed into him, the gun flying from Wyckoff's hand upon collision.

In the wink of a moment, Mairead thought, Jesus Mary, we're saved. In the next, But Alpha's been shot. And, in a third, she watched, nearly dazed, as Alpha straddled Wyckoff's torso, her client's strong hands on the security chief's throat. Wyckoff's cheeks turned a dull red, his own hands flailing at Alpha's face.

Mairead said, "Alpha, stop."

"No, lass," his features contorting monstrously. "The murderous bastard killed Tomlinson. And poor Old Man River."

Wyckoff's complexion shaded toward blue, his eyes bulging.

Mairead said, "That's over. Let him *go!*"

"This was the one I saw that night here, but I said in the courtroom it was Pratt to throw Wyckoff off." Alpha's shoulders hunched forward. "And to get to him my ownself, to avenge poor Tommy."

Mairead tried to move forward, nearly falling on the bad ankle. "You can't bring Tomlinson back."

"Then think of yourself. I got here in time to hear Wyckoff say he was going to kill you for ruining his plans. Just for the aesthetic of it, lass."

Mairead saw the security chief's tongue push out between his teeth, arms just flopping now. "The court will try him!"

"He's a corporate bigwig. Your own Mr. Gold said they always find a way to get off." Alpha's face was nearly the color of Wyckoff's now. "But even if a jury convicted, there's no death penalty in your fine state. So think of this as . . . uncommon justice."

Mairead stumbled toward them, Wyckoff making horrible hacking sounds from the death mask of his mouth.

"Alpha, no!"

And she swung the piece of lumber at his head.

Connecting, a sickening sound.

But Alpha only sagged, his hands still around Wyckoff's throat, the legs and arms under her client not flailing anymore.

"No!" yelled Mairead, hitting Alpha again.

This time he slumped off the man on the ground, Mairead for the first time getting a clear look at her savior's chest.

Mortal wounds, young lady.

Mairead hardly felt the piece of lumber drop from her hands. She staggered to Alpha's side, falling to her knees.

His green eyes were open, blinking rapidly, snowflakes in the lashes. His breathing came very ragged, pink froth burbling through the front of his clothes.

As she took Alpha's right hand in both of hers, he said, "You're true to yourself . . . Mairead O'Clare, but I fear you can't save . . . either of the murderous bastards before you."

"I hope to hell I never have to come back to this building once it's finished."

Pontifico Murizzi turned away from the three bodies at the construction site and toward Artie Chin, finding himself agreeing with his old friend.

Now Chin inclined his head, a watch cap over the crew cut. "She gonna be all right?"

The Pope looked toward Mairead, sitting with two blankets wrapped around her, part of one over her head. An EMT wearing latex gloves—even in the fucking cold and snow, the guy had taken off his woolies to do the job right—daubed something on her chin.

Murizzi said, "Not for a while, Artie, but after that? Yeah, I think so."

THE next morning, Mairead limped to the same bench in the Commons. The one she sat on when she met Shel Gold—could it be less than two weeks ago?

Driving her home to the Beacon Hill apartment the night before, after she'd refused a trip to the hospital, the Pope had stopped at a drugstore, buying some over-the-counter sleeping pills. Mairead had swallowed three of them, finally dropping off, only to awaken at 9 A.M., feeling a desperate need to be outside, unconfined. To think, to decide if she'd taken a terribly wrong turn in her life.

And hopefully to forgive yourself, young lady, from any blame in what happened.

Mairead closed her eyes, gnawing on her chapped lower lip.

A now-familiar voice said, "You don't mind my saying, it's a shame to see somebody so pretty seem so sad."

It made Mairead smile, in spite of herself. "Thanks."

This time Shel Gold sat next to her on the same bench. She couldn't see much under his overcoat, but Mairead was sure that his suit jacket would be as rumpled as his trousers.

"Thanks for what?" he said.

"When the Pope was taking me home last night, he went over everything you guys did, trying to find me."

"Sorry we guessed wrong about the where."

"I don't think it would have made a difference, Shel." Mairead found herself looking out over the frozen park. Enough snow had fallen that kids were sledding down the hummock of a hill in the center, but not so much

snow that the Frog Pond rink wasn't open, people skating round in circles to canned music. "Three people dead because of me."

Shel shook his head. "Wyckoff killed Pratt because of his own agenda, and Alpha got shot trying to protect you."

Mairead turned her face toward him. "Not what I meant. Alpha intended to kill Wyckoff all along. Our client was just using us to spring him so he could avenge Tomlinson's murder."

"I can see how you're troubled, but—you don't mind some advice—it's not your fault."

"I was the cause."

"Mairead, at most you were the condition. Because of your vigorous advocacy for an innocent man, other people did what was on their agendas. That's not something you caused, just something that came about because you did your job."

"But I helped Alpha kill somebody, Shel. I sensed he was manipulating me in our jail talks, but I didn't get the why until it was too late."

Her boss's eyes went sad. "Mairead, what's bothering you is that you wanted to be in control of your situation. And thought you were in control of at least part of it, only to find out the situation itself wasn't yours, but Alpha's. That's not helping one person to kill another. That's just . . . life."

"Or death."

"You get older, you're going to find the two come together a lot. You want to remain a lawyer, and stay sane . . ."

Mairead suddenly sensed something was throwing Shel off.

He went on, though. "Staying a lawyer *and* sane means you plant your feet on the ground and try to give the world a little better spin than it would have without you. Reaching for something more than that is fine, but you can't expect it every time."

Mairead looked at him then, really into the man's eyes, and saw more hurt and pain roiling than she'd ever known herself. "Shel, could I impose on you?"

"Impose?" with genuine confusion.

He's truly one of the good ones, young lady.

Mairead said, "I'd consider it a real favor if you'd give me a hug."

And the man in the rumpled suit edged awkwardly closer to her on the bench as Mairead buried her face in the hollow of his shoulder. She first sniffled, then cried, then racked her strong body with shuddery sobs.

It was only after a while that Mairead O'Clare became aware that Sheldon Gold's strong, lumpy fingers were stroking her long hair gently, the way she imagined he might a kitten.